VIRAL

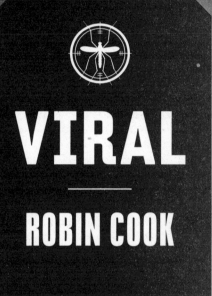

VIRAL

ROBIN COOK

G. P. PUTNAM'S SONS
New York

PUTNAM
— EST. 1838 —

G. P. Putnam's Sons
Publishers Since 1838
An imprint of Penguin Random House LLC
penguinrandomhouse.com

Library of Congress Cataloging-in-Publication Data

Names: Cook, Robin, author.
Title: Viral / Robin Cook.
Description: New York : G. P. Putnam's Sons, 2021.
Identifiers: LCCN 2021021034 (print) | LCCN 2021021035 (ebook) |
ISBN 9780593328293 (hardcover) | ISBN 9780593328309 (ebook) |
Subjects: GSAFD: Suspense fiction.
Classification: LCC PS3553.O5545 V57 2021 (print) |
LCC PS3553.O5545 (ebook) | DDC 813/.54—dc23
LC record available at https://lccn.loc.gov/2021021034
LC ebook record available at https://lccn.loc.gov/2021021035
p.   cm.

Printed in the United States of America
1st Printing

BOOK DESIGN BY KATY RIEGEL

*This book is dedicated to the fervent hope
that members of the US Congress will comprehend
the need to enact, at the very minimum,
a viable public healthcare option.*

PREFACE

The Covid-19 pandemic has thrust the virus center stage as a dangerous and dreaded foe similar to the way the influenza pandemic did a century ago. The causative viruses, SARS-CoV-2 and influenza A(H1N1), produce respiratory illnesses that are easily transmittable person to person and thereby quickly swept around the globe. Within months, both scourges sickened millions of people, and many died.

Although these two biologic entities currently dominate the spotlight, there are other viruses that deserve equal fear, concern, and attention, since some of the resultant diseases have a higher lethality as well as the capacity to cause more serious complications. Although these diseases are not transmitted by aerosol and are thereby less communicative, they, too, are spreading around the world at a slower—yet ever-quickening—pace thanks to climate change and human encroachment into previously isolated environments. In particular, a number of viruses have cleverly hijacked the mosquito to ensure their survival. These viruses are responsible for illnesses such as yellow fever, dengue, West Nile fever, and an array of diseases that cause dangerous inflammation of the brain called encephalitis. This includes eastern equine encephalitis virus, or EEE, which is known to have a death rate as high as thirty percent. As climate change advances, aggressive mosquitoes like the Aedes Asian tiger mosquito, which carry these dangerous viruses and which had heretofore been restricted to tropical climes, are progressively and relentlessly spreading northward into temperate regions, currently reaching as far north as the state of Maine in the USA and the Netherlands in Europe.

These other, fearful viruses couldn't have picked a better vector. As obligate bloodsuckers to enable breeding, mosquitoes are high on everyone's nuisance list. Most people can recall a disrupted summer slumber, or evening stroll, or hike in the woods, or barbecue on the beach, heralded by the characteristic whine of the female mosquito. As a creature superbly designed after almost one hundred million years of adaptive evolution (even dinosaurs were plagued by mosquitoes), the female mosquito invariably gets her blood meal or dies trying. For some reason that has yet to be explained, the female Asian tiger mosquito is particularly attracted to human females with blood type O, although other blood types or even human males will do in a pinch.

As a testament to the effectiveness of the mosquito–pathogen partnership, almost a million people die each year from a mosquito-spread illness. Some naturalists even posit that mosquito-transmitted illnesses have killed nearly half of all the humans who have ever lived.

—*Robin Cook, MD*

VIRAL

PROLOGUE

Although mosquitoes cause more than two thousand human deaths every day, their pernicious impact doesn't necessarily stop there. The deaths they cause can result in further serious societal complications. Such a story of a sad serial tragedy started in the summer of 2020 as the result of a cascading series of events that began in the idyllic town of Wellfleet, Massachusetts, nestled on the bay side of Cape Cod. It all started within the confines of a discarded automobile tire leaning up against a dilapidated, freestanding garage. Inside the tire was a bit of stagnant rainwater where a pregnant female Asian tiger mosquito had deposited her raft of eggs.

On the twentieth of July this clutch of eggs hatched, starting the mind-boggling ten-day metamorphosis from larvae to pupae to adults. The moment the mosquitoes emerged as adults, they could fly, and within three days they followed the irresistible urge to reproduce, requiring the females to obtain a blood meal. By using their highly evolved sense organs, they detected a victim and zeroed in on an unsuspecting blue jay. Unknown to the mosquitoes and to the blue jay, the bird had been infected earlier in July by the eastern equine encephalitis virus. Neither bird nor the mosquitoes cared since birds

such as blue jays are a normal host for EEE, meaning they live together in a kind of passive parasitism, and in a similar fashion, the
mosquito's immune system keeps the virus at bay. After getting their
fill of blue jay blood, the mosquitoes flew off to find an appropriate
place to deposit their eggs.

Several weeks later the infected band of mosquitoes had moved
eastward toward the Atlantic Ocean. They were now considerably
reduced in number from having been prey to numerous predators.
At the same time, they were now more experienced. They had learned
to favor human victims as easier targets than feathered birds or furred
mammals. They also learned the beach was a promising destination
in the late-afternoon/early-evening because there were always relatively immobile humans with lots of exposed skin.

At three-thirty on the afternoon of August fifteenth, this cluster
of EEE-carrying female Asian tiger mosquitoes awakened from their
daytime slumber. They had found refuge from the midday summer
sun beneath the porch planking of a building on Gull Pond. A few
moments later, ravenous for a blood meal, the swarm became airborne
en masse with their characteristic whine. Save for several unlucky
individuals, they avoided the many sticky and dangerous spiderwebs
and emerged into the sunlight. Regrouping, they set off like a minia-
ture fighter squadron. Instinctively they knew the beach was six hundred yards to the east beyond a forest composed mostly of black oak
and pitch pine. Barring being eaten on the way or having to navigate a stronger than usual headwind, it would take the swarm around
three-quarters of an hour to reach a crowd of potential targets.

BOOK 1

CHAPTER 1

August 15

O kay, you guys! It's four-thirty and time to get this barbecue show on the road," Brian Yves Murphy ordered, clapping his hands to get his family's attention. His wife, Emma, and his daughter, Juliette, were draped over the living room furniture in the modest two-bedroom cottage they had rented for two weeks across from a hardscrabble beach in Wellfleet, Massachusetts, just beyond the town's harbor. All of them were appropriately exhausted after an active, fun-filled midsummer day that marked the beginning of their final week of vacation. Because of the SARS-CoV-2 pandemic, they'd opted for a road trip vacation rather than flying down to Florida to use Emma's parents' empty condo, as was their usual summer getaway.

"Can't we just recover for ten to fifteen minutes?" Emma pleaded jokingly despite knowing full well that Brian wouldn't hear of it. In truth, she was as compulsive as he in terms of getting the most out of every minute of their vacation while the weather held. On top of that, she was also as compulsively fit and active as he. That morning she had awakened just after dawn and had soundlessly slipped out of the house for a bike ride and to be first in line at PB Boulangerie for their one-of-a-kind, freshly baked almond croissants. It had been a welcome surprise when they discovered the French bakery so far from what they called civilization. As lifelong residents of Inwood, Manhattan, they considered themselves quintessential New Yorkers and assumed anything outside of the city was hinterland.

"Sorry, but no rest for the weary," he said. "I'd like to get to the Newcomb Hollow Beach parking lot before the evening rush to make sure we get a spot." They had found over their first few days that Newcomb Hollow was their favorite Atlantic-side beach, with fewer people and high dunes that acted as partial windbreaks from the onshore breeze.

"But why the rush?" questioned Emma. "We already got a beach parking permit when we got the fire permit."

"The parking permit lets us park, but it doesn't guarantee a spot. Plus, Newcomb Hollow Beach is a popular spot for obvious reasons."

"Okay," she said agreeably. She got up and stretched her shoulders, which were mildly sore from the kayaking on Long Pond they had done that morning, an unusual workout for both of them. Then in the early afternoon she and Brian had done their daily mini-triathlon that involved biking ten miles to Truro and back, swimming for one mile in the bay, and running for five more into the Cape Cod National Seashore. Meanwhile, four-year-old Juliette had spent time with a local high school girl named Becky whom they had luckily found to serve as a daily sitter on day one. The lucky part was that Becky, despite being a teenager, was surprisingly acceptive and attentive to the required testing, mask wearing, and social distancing mandated by the Covid-19 pandemic.

"I'll get towels, the grill, briquettes, beach chairs, and toys and load it all in the car," he rattled off, heading into the kitchen. He'd been looking forward to the barbecue for several days. Although they wouldn't have the sunset like they did every evening over Cape Cod Bay, the Atlantic side was glorious, especially compared to the narrow, seashell-littered beach in front of their cottage.

"Ten four," Emma said. She glanced down at Juliette. The child seemed to already be asleep, although Emma was aware she could be pretending, as she often did when she didn't want to be bothered. With her eyes closed and lips slightly parted, she was clutching her favorite toy and constant companion named Bunny: a foot-long, very floppy, light brown, worse-for-wear stuffed rabbit with one missing eye. Emma couldn't help but stare at her with loving eyes, thinking as a mother that Juliette might very well be the world's most beautiful child, with her slightly upturned sculpted nose, Cupid's bow lips, and thick blond hair.

Initially both she and Brian had been taken aback by their daughter's hair as it grew in. The expectation had been that it would either be Emma's flaming red or Brian's blue-black. Instead it had come in as blond as golden corn, establishing from the outset that Juliette was her own person. The same thing happened with her eye coloration. She ended up green-eyed in contrast to Emma's hazel and Brian's blue. But there were some definite commonalities. All three Murphys had pale, almost translucent, Irish skin that required constant application of sunscreen to keep from getting burned. Also similar were their well-muscled and long-limbed figures. Even at age four, Juliette promised to be as athletic and tall as both her father and mother, who stood at six-one and five-eight, respectively.

"Hey! What are you doing?" he questioned as he wheeled a small portable kettle charcoal grill through the living room. He'd caught her hovering over Juliette. "Chop chop! What's holding up the show?"

"I was just momentarily overwhelmed by our daughter," Emma

confessed. "We are so lucky she's healthy and so damn cute. In fact, I think she might be the most beautiful child in the world."

Brian nodded but rolled his eyes playfully. "Sounds like a serious case of parental bias. There's no doubt we're lucky, but let's please hold up on our appreciation until we've parked and are on the beach."

She threw the Speedo swim cap she was holding at Brian, who laughed and easily ducked away before pushing out into the front yard, letting the screen door bang behind him. The characteristic noise reminded Emma of the summers she'd spent as a child out on Long Island. Her father, Ryan O'Brien, had done very well for himself and his family after starting a successful plumbing company in Inwood. Emma and Brian had both grown up among Inwood's sizable Irish community and had actually been aware of each other as grammar school–aged children while attending PS 98 even though he was two grades ahead of her.

For her part in preparation for the barbecue, she went into the kitchen, got out the cooler, and after putting in the cold packs from the freezer, filled it with the hamburger patties she'd made the previous day, the fresh de-gritted clams they had gotten earlier that morning at the harbor, a bottle of prosecco, and some fruit juice for Juliette. The unhusked summer corn was in a separate shopping bag, as were the mille-feuille from the bakery.

A half hour later the family was in their Outback Subaru, heading east toward the Cape Cod National Seashore preserve. Juliette was buckled into her car seat next to the cooler, an inflatable boogie board, and three folded beach chairs. As per usual Juliette was holding on to Bunny while watching a cartoon on a screen built into the driver's-side headrest. At Juliette's feet were the rest of the beach toys, including pails, sand molds, shovels, and a pair of Kadima paddles.

After crossing Route 6, both Brian and Emma eyed the Wellfleet Police Department as it came into view. The building was a quaint, gable-roofed white clapboard structure with dormers that looked more like a country inn than a police department.

"I can't help but wonder what it would be like being a police officer way out here in the middle of nowhere," she observed. She turned to get a final glimpse of the picturesque building with a split log fence defining a visitor's parking area. There was not a squad car in sight.

"It is hard to imagine," he said with an agreeing nod. He'd had the same thought simultaneous with Emma verbalizing it. This was a frequent occurrence, and they attributed it to how closely their lives had coincided. Not only had they grown up several blocks apart in the same neighborhood in Manhattan and gone to the same grammar school, but they had both ended up majoring in criminal justice in college, with Brian attending Adelphi on Long Island and Emma going to Fordham in the Bronx. Although they also had gone to different high schools, their transcripts were remarkably similar. Both had done well academically, and had been very active in athletics in high school and college. For Brian it was soccer, wrestling, and baseball, and for Emma it was field hockey, basketball, and softball.

"Compared to our law enforcement experiences, it must be incredibly boring," she said as she faced around to look out the windshield. Both she and Brian had matriculated directly into the New York Police Department Academy after college, serving as patrol officers at very busy NYC precincts. After five years of exemplary service, they had been accepted into the elite and prestigious NYPD Emergency Service Unit. It had been when Emma was a cadet at the ESU Academy that their remarkably parallel lives temporally aligned. Brian, who was a member of the ESU A team, volunteered on his days off to help the ESU Academy instructors. It was his way of staying up to date and in shape, and his reward was meeting one of the few female ESU cadets, falling in love, and gaining a wife.

"Especially off season," he said. "To tell you the truth, I wouldn't be able to do it. No way."

They were now passing through mostly pitch pine and black oak forests. They also passed Gull Pond, which was north but near Long Pond, where they had kayaked that morning. As it was their first trip to Cape Cod, they had been pleasantly surprised by the many freshwater ponds with crystal-clear water so close to the ocean on one side and the bay on the other. They'd asked a local about them and had been told it had something to do with glaciers back in the Ice Age.

Gross Hill Road dead-ended into Newcomb Hollow Beach, and as they pulled into the parking lot, they were encouraged. A lot of bedraggled people were heading from the beach to their cars, carrying an enormous quantity of gear, including beach chairs, sun umbrellas, and impressive coolers that made the Murphys' Styrofoam model seem embarrassingly chintzy. Some were tanned regulars, but most were clearly burned visitors.

"Ouch," said Emma, looking at one adolescent girl who appeared as pale as the Murphys. "She's going to be sorry tonight."

"We're in luck," he exclaimed, pulling into a vacant slot remarkably close to the pathway that led from the parking lot to the beach up over an impressive fifty-foot grass-covered dune. As usual, Juliette was excited at the prospect of being on the beach, so she was first out of the car and impatient as Emma and Brian unloaded. Despite her agitation, she was willing to accept carrying the bag of corn and most of her toys in addition to Bunny. While Emma carried the cooler and towels, Brian handled the grill, the briquettes, and the aluminum beach chairs.

It was late afternoon and the sun streaming over their shoulders painted the entire scene in a rich, golden glow. Everyone they passed leaving the beach was wearing their pandemic mask, as were the Murphys. When they crested the dune, Emma and Brian paused to take in the dramatic sight of the wide, sandy beach and the large expanse of the Atlantic. The breeze was onshore, and it carried the sound of the two-to-three-feet-high waves as they broke. Since the tide was going out, there were numerous tide pools, which Juliette loved, since she was a bit intimidated by the ocean. Capping the impressive scene were large cumulus clouds that hung over the vista like dollops of whipped cream.

"Which way?" Juliette called over her shoulder.

"What do you think?" Brian asked Emma.

"I'd say north," she responded after glancing in both directions. "There's less people. And there's a good-sized tide pool directly in front."

"To your left," he shouted to Juliette, who had already run down toward the water's edge.

They set up their camp about a hundred feet north of the path and up against the steep dune embankment. While Brian struggled with the grill, Emma put sunscreen on Juliette before handing the spray can to him. After tossing Bunny onto one of the towels, Juliette immediately bounded off for the tide pool.

"Don't go in the waves until I'm down there with you," he yelled to her, and she waved back to signal that she had heard.

"When do you think we should eat?" she asked.

Brian shrugged. "It's up to you. Just give me fifteen to twenty minutes' notice to get the briquettes fired up." He poured them into the grill and closed the lid. "Meanwhile, let's join Juliette."

For the next forty-five minutes they ran in the wash from the surf, either chasing or being chased by Juliette. At one point he managed to get Juliette to venture out into the breakers with him holding her hand, but he could tell she really didn't like it, so they quickly went back to the tide pool. Shortly after, Brian could see that Emma was already back preparing the corn at their campsite, which was now in shadow. Taking the hint, he told Juliette it was time to start the barbecue and that he would race her with him running backward. Delighted at the prospect of beating her father, Juliette took off with a squeal and, mostly thanks to Brian getting a late start, gained a commanding lead.

"I'm afraid we have some unwelcome visitors," Emma announced the moment they came running back.

"What do you mean?" he asked. He glanced around, mostly skyward. On their previous visit to Newcomb Hollow Beach they'd had a run-in with a few very persistent seagulls and had been amazed at the birds' boldness.

"No seagulls," she said, reading his mind. "Mosquitoes."

"Really?" he questioned. He was surprised, considering the significant onshore breeze.

"Yes, really," Emma said. "Look!" She raised her left arm and pointed to the base of her deltoid muscle. Poised and obviously preparing to bite was a black mosquito with white markings, but before the insect could do its worst, she slapped it with an open palm. When she pulled her hand away, she could see that the creature was reduced to a tiny bloody corpse, indicating it had already bitten someone else but still wasn't satiated.

"I don't think I've seen a mosquito like that," Brian said. "Rather distinctive coloring."

"I have," Emma said. "It was an Asian tiger mosquito."

"How the hell do you know about Asian tiger mosquitoes?"

"During one of my ESU Academy medical lectures, we learned about arboviral disease and climate change. The lecturer specifically talked about Asian tiger mosquitoes, which used to be restricted to the tropics, but now have spread widely northward all the way up to Maine."

"I never got that lecture," he complained.

"Times have changed, old man," she said with a laugh. "Remember, you were two years ahead of me."

"What's arboviral disease, anyway?"

"Remember reading about yellow fever and building the Panama Canal? Well, yellow fever is an arboviral disease."

"Yikes," Brian said. "Has there ever been yellow fever in the USA?"

"Not since 1905 in New Orleans, if I'm remembering correctly," Emma said. She abruptly ran her fingers through her hair and then waved her hand above her head. "Uh-oh, I can hear more of the bastards. Aren't they bothering you?"

"Not yet. Juliette, do you hear any mosquitoes?"

Juliette didn't answer, but like her mother, she suddenly waved her hands around her head, suggesting she was hearing them.

"Did you bring the bug spray?" Emma asked with urgency.

"It's in the car. I'll run and get it."

"Please," Emma said. "The sooner the better. Otherwise we are going to be miserable."

With no further urging, Brian grabbed his mask, jogged down the beach, and then went up over the dune. As he expected, he found the can of OFF in the glove compartment. When he got back to the beach less than ten minutes later, Juliette was again in the tide pool.

"I tell you," Emma said as she began to apply the repellent, "these winged bastards were aggressive while you were gone. I had to send Juliette down to the water."

"I tried to be quick." He took the spray and applied it as Emma had done and then called Juliette back from the water's edge to protect her as well.

Once the Murphys had the mosquitoes at bay, they were able to get back to their barbecue. The corn cobs went on the grill first, followed by the hamburger patties, and finally the clams. By the time the food was cooked and served, the entire beach was in the shadow of the dunes even though the ocean and the clouds were still in full sun.

After they had eaten their fill and partially cleaned up, Brian and Emma relaxed back into their respective beach chairs to finish the prosecco, have dessert, and savor the view. The setting sun, which was out of sight behind them, was tinting the puffy clouds pink. Juliette had retreated back down to the edge of the tide pool to make sandcastles in the damp sand.

For a while neither spoke. It was Emma who finally did. "I hate to break the spell," she said, turning to Brian, "but I've been thinking. Maybe we should consider heading back to New York a little early."

"Really? Why? We've got almost another week with the cottage." He was surprised by her suggestion since coming to Cape Cod for vacation had initially been her idea, and they all seemed to be enjoying it immensely. Even the weather was cooperating.

"I'm thinking that maybe if we were back home we could do something to possibly drum up some business."

"Do you have some new idea of how?" he asked. "What little work we had in the late spring totally dried up in July."

Eight months earlier, Brian and Emma had retired from the NYPD to start their own personal protection security agency, which they appropriately called Personal Protection LLC. They had begun the firm with high hopes of success, considering the level of training and experience they had after being NYPD ESU officers—Brian for six years and Emma for four years, on top of each having been a regular police officer for five years. At the time of their retirement from the NYPD, both were sergeants and Brian had already passed the exam for lieutenant with flying colors. A consulting firm that they had hired at the end of the previous summer to advise them had projected rapid success and expansion for Personal Protection after supposedly taking all potential factors into account. Yet no one could have predicted the Covid-19 pandemic, which had reduced the demand for their services to almost nothing. In fact, during the last month they'd had no work whatsoever.

"No, I haven't had any sudden brainstorms," Emma admitted. "But I'm starting to feel uneasy and guilty about us up here lazing around, enjoying ourselves, not knowing what the hell the fall is going to bring. I know we needed a break after being cooped up all spring with the pandemic, especially Juliette, but we've had our fun. I'm ready to go back."

"The fall is clearly not going to be pretty," he said. "As soon as the United Nations Week got canceled, I knew all our projections went out the window. That week alone was going to put our company on the map." With their professional connections with the NYPD, they had had hundreds of referrals, seeing as United Nations Week was an enormous strain on NYPD resources. Back in December they

were concerned about having enough manpower to cover even half
of the requests.

"Aren't you worried about how we are going to weather this pandemic with all the talk about a fall surge?" she asked. "I mean, we're
already behind on our mortgage."

Both Brian and Emma had been thrifty and fiscally conservative
even as children. When they started working for the NYPD, they'd
saved more than their friends and colleagues, and also invested wisely.
When they had married following Emma's graduation from the ESU
Academy and just before Juliette's birth, they'd been able to splurge
on one of the few freestanding, Tudor-revival, single-family homes
in Inwood, on West 217th Street. It was a mere block away from her
parents' home on Park Terrace West. The house was their only major
asset besides the Subaru.

"A lot of people are behind on their mortgage payments," Brian
countered. "And we spoke with our loan officer. Plus, we do have
some cash receivables. The mortgage is not going to cause a problem.
I think we've made the right choice to keep our cash to cover our
other major business-related expenses, like Camila's salary."

Camila Perez was Personal Protection LLC's only employee. When
the pandemic exploded in the New York area, she'd moved in with
the Murphys and had been living with them ever since. It was one
of the benefits of having a house with adequate living space. Over the
course of the spring she'd become more like family than an employee. The Murphys had even encouraged her to come with them to
Cape Cod, but she had responsibly declined in order to handle anything that came up in relation to the company. During the previous
week, there had been a couple of inquiries about Personal Protection
providing security for some high-end fall weddings in the Hamptons.

"You are obviously handling this all better than I am," Emma confessed. "I'm impressed that you're able to compartmentalize so well."

"Truthfully, I'm not doing that great. I'm worried, too," he admitted. "But my worry comes mostly in the middle of the night when my mind can't shut down. Out here on the beach with the sun and surf, thankfully it all seems so far away."

"Do you mind if we continue talking about this now, while we're enjoying this glorious scene? Or do you want me to shut up?"

"Of course I don't mind," Brian said. "Talk as much as you want!"

"Well, what's bugging me at the moment is whether it was a good idea for both of us to leave the NYPD together," she said. "Maybe one of us should have remained on salary."

"In hindsight that might have been prudent," Brian agreed. "But that's not what we wanted. We both felt an entrepreneurial tug to do something creative and outside the box. How could we have decided who would have the fun challenge and who would have had to continue slogging with the same old, same old? Draw straws or flip a coin? Besides, I'm still confident it is all going to be just fine as soon as this damn coronavirus disaster works itself out. And we're certainly not alone. Millions are caught in this pandemic squeeze."

"I hope you are right," Emma said with a sigh, before quickly slapping the side of her head. "Damn! Those mosquitoes are back. Why aren't they biting you?"

"No clue." He reached behind her chair for the can of OFF and handed it to her. "I guess I'm just not as sweet as you," he said with one of his typical mischievous smiles.

CHAPTER 2

August 19

It was the raucous sound of a flock of seagulls loudly arguing with one another out in Wellfleet Harbor that awoke Brian after yet another pleasant night's sleep. Rolling onto his back, he looked out the window through the white sheer curtain fabric, wondering what time it was. He looked at his phone and saw that it was 6:25. Glancing over to Emma's side of the bed, he saw that she was already up, like almost every morning lately, and he smiled in anticipation of the pastries that would be waiting for him once he got out of bed.

With the birds still squawking in the distance, Brian got up to use the cottage's single bathroom, but just before entering from the common hall, a glance into the living room surprised him. He could see Emma fast asleep on the couch. Being that she was an early riser, he guessed she'd possibly had a poor night's sleep, perhaps from worrying about their precarious financial situation, a subject she'd been raising every day since the night of their barbecue. Fearing he was correct, he made it a point to be as quiet as possible. Coming back out of the bathroom, he had another idea that would make it even less likely he'd disturb her. He'd be the one to head out and get the pastries. Whatever the reason was that had her sleeping outside of their bed, he thought she deserved as much time to rest as she wanted.

After silently pulling on some bike shorts and a shirt, Brian checked to see if Juliette was stirring. She wasn't, which he expected. With the amount of exercise she'd been getting combined with being allowed to stay up later than usual in the evening to play board games, she must have been exhausted. Satisfied, he carried his bike shoes while tiptoeing through the living room. As carefully as he could, he closed the otherwise noisy screen door without a sound, pleased he'd managed to leave without waking his wife.

Cycling past the Wellfleet Harbor, he could see the source of the seagulls' frenzy, which was still ongoing. Fishermen were cleaning their catches. Beyond the harbor, Brian passed through the attractive downtown of Wellfleet with its well-maintained period buildings, some of which were hundreds of years old, and he was particularly enamored of those with neo-Grecian Doric columns.

Unfortunately, most of the rest of the trip was on the main highway, which lacked the scenery of the smaller roads. But it wasn't far and there was almost no traffic. To get maximum benefit from the exercise, he cranked up his speed, arriving at the bakery in less than fifteen minutes. Although the shop had yet to open, there were already several people waiting as a testament to its popularity.

Twenty minutes later, Brian was back on his bike, now heading north. When he arrived at the cottage, he returned his bike to the garage and then entered as quietly as possible. To his surprise, Emma was no longer on the couch. Instead, she was now back in their room curled up in a fetal position on the bed, and though her eyes were open, she didn't stir upon his arrival.

"I feel terrible. I had a very bad night."

"I'm so sorry, my sweet," Brian said as he sat on the edge of the bed. "What's wrong?" He was surprised to see her sick, because she was the most resistant of the three of them when it came to winter colds and other ailments. The usual progression was Juliette first, probably picking up something at preschool or at one of her play-dates, and then she'd give it to him. More often than not, Emma wouldn't succumb, despite being the major caregiver.

"I just feel awful all around," Emma managed.

"Do you feel feverish?"

"Yes. I've had chills and I've been sweating."

Gently Brian reached out and placed his palm on her forehead. There was no doubt in his mind that she was burning up.

"I've also been vomiting," Emma continued. "I'm surprised I didn't wake you."

"I wish you had," he responded worriedly.

"Why?" she said with seeming irritation. "What would you have been able to do?"

"I don't know," Brian said. "Just be with you."

"There's nothing you could have done," Emma countered. "I also ache all over, and I have a bad headache and a stiff neck. I've never felt this terrible."

"Can I at least get you an ibuprofen?" He reached out and tried to rub Emma's back, wanting to help somehow, but she moved away from his touch.

"I suppose an ibuprofen can't hurt," she said, resettling herself in the center of the bed.

"Have you had a sore throat, cough, or any difficulty breathing?"

"No," she said with force. "I know what you're thinking, but this isn't coronavirus. I can't imagine it could be, from what I've heard about Covid-19. I also haven't lost my sense of smell. Nothing like that."

"Nonetheless, we will have to get you tested for coronavirus," Brian said calmly. "We have to rule it out."

"Whatever," Emma said irritably.

"Are you hungry at all?" he asked. "I've brought back almond croissants."

"I told you I feel sick to my stomach. Do you really think I'd want an almond croissant?"

"Okay, okay," Brian soothed. "I'll get you an ibuprofen. Maybe two." He stood up and went into the bathroom to get the pills, and then into the kitchen for a glass of water. He was a little surprised at Emma's apparent anger. It wasn't like her in the slightest. Whenever she felt under the weather in the past, she never acted irritated. If anything, she tended to downplay her symptoms.

After he gave her the pills, she took the medication and then flopped back onto the bed.

"I'm going to find out where the hospital is out here," Brian said. "Is there anything I can get for you at the moment?" She merely shook her head and closed her eyes.

Out in the living room, Brian opened up his laptop to search for the nearest hospital, thinking that would be the easiest way to get Emma tested for coronavirus. Knowing the variability of the Covid-19 symptoms, he wondered why she was so sure she didn't have it. One way or the other, they needed to know. He also briefly thought about trying to find a local MD but doubted a country doctor could add much to what he already knew. The medical courses he'd taken at the ESU Academy had been extensive, certainly qualifying both him and Emma to be full-fledged EMTs. If he had to guess, he thought that Emma had most likely contracted a case of food poisoning, possibly from the clams they had had for dinner even though he didn't seem to have any symptoms. What he hoped was that within twenty-four hours or so, she would be on the mend.

It didn't take long for him to find out what he needed, and after he had, he returned to the bedroom. She was lying on her back in the center of the bed with her eyes closed.

"Emma?" Brian whispered. If she had fallen asleep, he didn't want to wake her.

"What?" she said without opening her eyes.

"The closest hospital is Cape Cod Hospital," Brian said. "It's in Hyannis, which is forty-five minutes away. I suggest we drive to the hospital as soon as you feel up to it. The sooner you have a coronavirus test, the sooner we'll get the results."

"I don't want to go to some fly-by-night hospital out here in the sticks." She looked up at him with her hazel eyes on fire.

"I don't think you're being fair," Brian argued. "From what I've read online, it seems it's held in reasonably high esteem. Besides, at the moment all we're looking for is a coronavirus test."

"No way! I want to go back to New York. If I need a hospital, I want a real hospital."

"You really want to go home today?" he asked.

"Yes," Emma snapped. "I don't like how I feel and I'm worried I might get worse. This isn't just some cold."

"Okay, okay," Brian said reassuringly. "We'll head back today. I'll pack our stuff, load the car, and strap on the bikes and the kayak. Try to take it easy in the meantime."

CHAPTER 3

August 19

Packing all their belongings and loading the car took a lot longer than Brian had anticipated. Part of the problem was having to deal with Juliette. Emma's irritability particularly disturbed Juliette, who didn't seem to understand why she was being ignored by her mother. As a consequence, he had to spend a lot of time trying to console her and keep her occupied. What worked the best was getting Juliette intimately involved with the packing and loading, but the problem was that it then took far longer than if Brian had been able to do it all on his own.

It was just after eleven when they were finally able to pull out of the driveway and start the five-hour drive back to the Big Apple. Since Juliette's car seat was behind the driver's side, Brian was able to lower Emma's seat back to a reclined position. He'd made some sandwiches and stocked the cooler with water and fruit juice for their ride. He wanted to get Emma home as soon as possible.

For most of the way Brian was on his own, as Juliette was watching cartoons and Emma was sleeping, with her head on the pillow pressed up against the side of the car. A bit of perspiration dotted her forehead, indicating her fever was persisting.

The quiet gave Brian more time to worry anew about the condition of Personal Protection LLC. As he had confessed to Emma, being on vacation in a totally new location had made it possible for him to put work completely out of his mind. But now that they were heading home, all his concerns came flooding back. The reality was that very few wealthy businesspeople who needed security were traveling into the city because of the pandemic, and with the expected fall surge that probably wasn't going to change. All he could hope for was that one of the rare inquiries they'd gotten about the high-profile fall weddings would pan out to be an actual gig. For that reason, he was looking forward to finding out from Camila if there had been any movement whatsoever toward a possible commitment.

Although traffic had only been moderate without any significant delays, he felt definite relief when they reached the Henry Hudson Bridge. It meant they were almost home, and he was anxious to get Emma into bed and take her temperature. A small amount of sweat had continued to dot her forehead for the entire trip, and he also knew that Juliette was nearing the absolute end of her patience while strapped into her car seat.

So when disaster struck, Brian's mind was completely absorbed by the details of how he would manage getting both Emma and Juliette out of the car and into the house efficiently. The first hint of a calamity was a peculiar rhythmic thumping coming from someplace under the car's dash. Within seconds he was aware of movement to his right that coincided with the noise. As his eyes darted in that direction, he realized to his horror that Emma was caught in the agonal throes of what could only be a seizure. Her feet and legs alternately pounded against both the underside of the dashboard and the floorboards of the car. At the same time, she was grotesquely arching her back, straining against her seat belt with her arms wildly flailing and her head slamming again and again against the car's window.

Practically losing control of the car as he ducked away from Emma's pummeling left hand, Brian fought with the steering wheel as the vehicle heaved from side to side, tires screeching. The instant he regained control, he slammed on the brakes and with difficulty managed to pull to the side of the road despite angry honking and rude gestures from other drivers. By now, Juliette was screaming.

From his EMT lectures, he knew he had to keep her from injuring herself until her seizure abated, and thankfully the car's seat belt helped. His biggest concern was her head, which he was able to keep away from the car's metal frame, letting it hit up against the pillow during her violent contractions. With his other hand he tried to keep her powerful legs from injuring themselves against the dash. The fact that she was in such good physical shape made it that much more difficult. Brian had to use all the strength he had.

Although at the time it seemed interminable, finally her contractions lessened and then abated altogether, and Brian could let her sag back against the seat and the car's door with her head against the window. Instinctively he knew it had only been a couple of minutes. A bit of blood trickled from her mouth, suggesting she had bitten her tongue, but he could see that she was breathing normally again.

He straightened up in his seat and quickly unbuckled his seat belt. Juliette was crying uncontrollably in the back, so after leaping out of the car, Brian opened the back door, leaned in, and enveloped his daughter in his arms. He told her over and over that all was okay, that Mommy was fine, and that they would take her to the hospital.

"Now Daddy has to keep driving, okay, sweetheart?" Brian soothed at length when Juliette's tears lessened. Gently he removed her arms from around his head.

Somewhat reluctantly, Juliette let him straighten up. After he gave her shoulder another reassuring squeeze, he got back into the front seat and checked Emma again. She was awake, but seemed disoriented. He told her that they were almost home but that he was going to take her to the hospital, the same hospital where Juliette had been born. He also told her that she had just had a seizure, to which she nodded but didn't respond audibly.

After exiting the Henry Hudson Parkway at the Dyckman Street exit, it was only a short drive to the Inwood campus of the Manhattan Memorial Hospital. Like all New York City boroughs, Inwood had several hospitals. The Murphys had chosen the MMH, as it was known in the neighborhood, for Juliette's birth because it was where Emma had had her tonsils removed when she was a child. It was also familiar to Brian. During his second year as an NYPD patrolman, he'd been assigned to the 34th Precinct for a number of months to fill in for someone on sick leave and in that capacity had spent quite a bit of time at the hospital, particularly getting some work on many of his days and evenings off. It had been a way for him to make extra money, as the hospital liked having a uniformed officer on-site. He had spent enough time there that he'd even gotten to know a few of the doctors and nurses on a first-name basis.

"Is Mommy going to stay at the hospital?" Juliette asked as Brian turned off Broadway onto the hospital grounds.

"I doubt it," he said. "But we have to see what the doctors say. We just want to make sure she's okay."

Brian drove up to the Emergency Department entrance and pulled to a stop at the ambulance dock.

"Emma, how are you doing now?" he asked. "Are you okay walking into the hospital or do you want me to get a gurney for you?"

"I'm okay," she said in a monotone, speaking up for the first time since the seizure.

"Are you sure?" To Brian she still seemed somewhat disoriented, certainly not herself. Even though she didn't answer, he got out of the car, got Juliette out, and walked around to the passenger side. When he opened the door, Emma made no effort to move, so he reached in and undid her seat belt. He then made sure they all had their face masks on.

"All right," he said. "Let's get you inside." Gently he encouraged her to climb out of the car and with somewhat unsteady legs she walked into the ED holding Brian's hand for support.

CHAPTER 4

August 19

As it was 4:30 and getting close to dinnertime, the Emergency Department was only moderately busy. The Murphys had to stand for a short time at the information counter, but when Brian explained why they were there, a pleasant triage nurse immediately ushered them into a treatment cubicle and encouraged Emma to lie down. As she took Emma's vital signs and got more of a history, a clerk who had accompanied them got their name and health insurance information. The clerk also got Brian to sign a permission-for-treatment form. Once the paperwork was done, Brian and Juliette hurried back outside to deal with the car.

At the car Juliette started crying inconsolably, demanding that she wanted her mommy through near hysterical tears. Although normally quite patient with his daughter, Brian felt unnerved himself, and when she refused to get into her car seat, he had to forcibly control himself. Doing so made him realize that he needed some backup. Although he could have called his mother, Aimée, he chose to call Camila, who'd become almost a surrogate mother for Juliette over the previous five months. As he expected, Camila was horrified

when she learned what had happened to Emma and immediately offered to come over to MMH to take charge of Juliette.

"Okay, sweetie pie," he said to Juliette as he disconnected the call.
With help on the way, he felt he had a better hold on his emotions.
"Camila is coming to take you home."

Juliette greeted this news with even more forceful tears, but Brian
took it in stride. He knew she would feel better as soon as she was
back in familiar surroundings. He picked up Juliette and held her
close to comfort her, and though she continued to cry with less intensity, she still pressed her face into the crook of his neck and
hugged him forcibly.

In just a little more than ten minutes, Camila arrived. A moment
later she was reaching out for Juliette, who was happy to transfer from
Brian's arms to Camila's. "Oh, my poor baby," she said while hugging
the child. It was obvious she had a strong maternal instinct, and he
greatly appreciated her presence in his life in moments like this.

Camila was a thirty-two-year-old first-generation Cuban American with an engaging, upbeat personality, a ready smile, and frequent
laughter. She looked more like a teenager than an adult, especially
with her preferred dress being fashionably ripped jeans. She was of
medium height and build with long dark hair parted in the middle
and an olive complexion that both Brian and Emma coveted, as she
never had to bother with sunblock. Like Brian and Emma, she had
spent most of her life in Inwood, and they shared some common
friends. The difference was that she had grown up on the predomi-
nantly Latino east side of Broadway whereas Brian and Emma had
been on the largely Irish west side.

Like Brian, Camila had gone to Adelphi University but had ma-
jored in business, which was the reason she'd responded to Brian

and Emma's employment search. They had specified that they were looking for someone to help with a startup security business. Luckily for both parties, from day one it had seemed a match made in heaven since Camila's business know-how complemented Brian and Emma's law enforcement experience. When the pandemic exploded in the New York area in March, asking Camila to move in was an easy decision, as was her decision to accept. She had several aging grandparents living at home with serious health issues whom she wanted to avoid putting at risk.

"I'll be home with Emma as soon as possible," Brian told her as he gave Juliette Bunny, which she grabbed and enveloped with a bear hug.

"No worries," she said. "I'll grab dinner and make sure Juliette is occupied."

"I can't thank you enough. You're a lifesaver."

After watching Camila drive away and knowing Juliette was being taken care of, he felt significantly more at ease and capable of dealing with the situation. The first thing he did was go back to the check-in counter to ask if there was any information available on his wife, but all he was told was that the doctor would be out to talk to him shortly.

Brian took a seat as far away from other people as he could, which required moving to the end of the room since the ED was already busier than it had been only fifteen minutes earlier. From his previous experience at the hospital as a uniformed patrolman, he remembered there was always a buildup of activity just before and then another after dinner.

The time passed slowly. To entertain himself he took out his phone, and with some reluctance he called his mother, Aimée. He knew that, as the family matriarch, she would be very upset and insist on helping, possibly by offering to come directly to the hospital, even though it would probably cause more stress than good. But he felt an obligation to let her know what was happening. She answered with her lilting and charming French accent, which she had never lost.

Aimée had grown up in the northern part of France—Normandy, to be exact—and had come to the United States forty-one years ago to attend prestigious Barnard College. It was there that she had met Brian's father, who happened at the time to be attending Columbia University on a sports scholarship. Aimée's maiden name was Juliette, a somewhat rare family name even in France, and in her honor Emma and Brian had named their daughter Juliette.

Brian evaded any small talk with Aimée, immediately telling her that he was calling from the MMH ED because Emma had suffered a seizure in the car as they drove into Manhattan following her sudden flu-like symptoms from the morning.

"Oh, my goodness. I'm so sorry to hear," Aimée said with concern. "Is she all right now?"

"There's been no word yet from the doctors," he informed her. "She is being seen as we speak. She walked in under her own power but seemed somewhat disoriented."

"Do you think she has coronavirus?" Aimée asked.

"I hope not," Brian said. "Actually, I don't think so because she didn't have any of the big three symptoms, like cough, difficulty breathing, or loss of sense of smell. But who knows? She did have a fever. We'll have to see."

"And where's Juliette?"

"Camila came to pick her up just a few minutes ago. We've only been here an hour or so."

"How about you? Are you okay?"

"I'm hanging in there," he said. "Though I'll admit it's been a bit unnerving. This is the first time I've ever really seen Emma sick."

"I can well imagine you'd feel out of sorts. Do you want me to come and keep you company?"

"It's not necessary," Brian said. "I'm doing okay now that Juliette is being taken care of. Besides, the hospital is discouraging family visitors with the pandemic going on for obvious reasons. I promise I'll let you know as soon as I know anything."

"D'accord," Aimée said. She had a habit of sprinkling French expressions into her conversations. "I'll call Emma's mother and let her know. Of course, she may want to come to the ED. You know Hannah has a mind of her own."

"Please try to discourage her. I'll let you know the moment I learn anything, and you can let her know."

After speaking with his mother, he debated whether to call his two older brothers or his younger sister, more as a way of keeping his mind occupied than anything else. While he was still debating, he heard his name called out by a tall, slim, relatively young doctor who'd stepped into the waiting room from the depths of the ED. Dressed in rumpled scrubs, a surgical hat, and face mask, he looked the part of a harried emergency physician with a raft of pens jammed into his breast pocket and a stethoscope slung around his neck.

Brian stood up and waved to get the doctor's attention.

"Mr. Brian Murphy?" the doctor questioned yet again as he neared. He had lowered his voice considerably. "You are Emma Murphy's husband?" He had a lilting accent Brian associated with people from the Indian subcontinent.

"I am," Brian responded. He felt himself stiffen, sensing from the doctor's tone that all was not well.

"My name is Dr. Darsh Kumar. I have important news about your wife."

"Okay," Brian said slowly, bracing himself for what he was about to hear.

"She's going to be admitted to the hospital. In fact, she has to be taken to the Intensive Care Unit."

"Okay," he repeated, feeling increasingly panicked but trying to calm himself. "Why the ICU?"

"She had another seizure while she was being examined," Dr. Kumar explained. "However, we were able to control it rapidly since we already had an IV running. She's resting comfortably now, but is disoriented. We want her to be closely monitored."

Brian nodded. His mind was racing around at warp speed. "More disoriented than when she arrived?"

"Probably, but not necessarily. I can't say for sure."

"Is there a diagnosis? Could this be coronavirus?"

"It's possible, but not probable with these symptoms," Dr. Kumar said. "What we are certain of is that she has some sort of encephalitis, meaning an inflammation of the brain."

"I've heard of encephalitis. I've had EMT training," Brian explained.

"What we don't yet know is the specific etiology," Dr. Kumar continued. "We suspect viral. We did a spinal tap and have sent the specimens to the lab. They will soon let us know what we are dealing with. If I had to guess, I'd say possibly something like West Nile virus or possibly even Lyme disease. Did you have much contact with mosquitoes or ticks while you were on Cape Cod?"

"No ticks, but we did have some mosquitoes during a beach barbecue four or five days ago."

"That could be it, which would favor a viral disease. But there is no reason to speculate at this point. It won't change our treatment."

"What's the treatment?"

"Essentially just supportive. She's on supplemental oxygen. Even though we were able to stop her seizure quickly, her oxygen level fell considerably."

"Can I see her?" Brian asked desperately.

"Not at the moment," Dr. Kumar said. "She's getting an MRI and a CT scan."

"Both? Why both?"

"I leave that up to our radiology colleagues. Meanwhile the business office needs to speak to you about your wife's admission." He pointed across the room to a door that had ADMITTING stenciled on it, and then turned and started to leave.

"Excuse me," Brian called after him. "I would like to see my wife when I can."

"I'll let the nurses know," Dr. Kumar said over his shoulder before quickly disappearing whence he came.

After taking a deep breath to fortify himself, Brian picked up the few things he had brought in with him and walked over to the Admitting office. He had no idea what they wanted from him since he'd already given their information to the ED clerk.

It was a reasonably sized room with several rows of chairs facing two desks. On the cream-colored walls were multiple framed photographs of mostly serious-looking men in business suits although there were several women. He assumed they were hospital administrators. Only one of the desks was occupied, by a middle-aged woman with dark hair and eyes. She was wearing a colorful flower-print dress under a white lab coat.

"Mr. Murphy?" the woman called out as soon as Brian entered. She and Brian were the only people in the room.

"Yes," he said. "Brian Murphy." He could see her name was Maria Hernandez. He approached her desk, where a large plexiglass shield had been added in recent months. Like a cashier's window at a bank, there was a slot for passing papers to and fro along its base.

"Brian Murphy," Maria repeated while tilting her head to the side to give him a good once-over. "Were you related to Deputy Inspector Conor Murphy, the commanding officer of the 34th Precinct, by any chance?"

"He was my father," Brian said, surprised that she recognized him with his face mask. Luckily the short time Brian had been assigned to the 34th Precinct was before his father had become the CO.

"I knew it the moment you walked in here," Maria said, as if proud of herself. "You're certainly your father's son. My husband, Adolpho, who was the sanitation supervisor for Inwood, knew your father very well. In fact, they shared many an after-hour beer."

"Unfortunately, my father shared far too many beers," he responded. He didn't want to be reminded of that aspect of his father, who ultimately fell victim to the Irish curse of alcoholism and had died a year and a half earlier. At the same time, Maria's comment reminded him of the benefit as well as the disadvantage of living within one of the many tight-knit New York neighborhoods. Lives were inextricably intertwined.

"Isn't that the truth," Maria said grimly. "Same can be said about my Adolpho, bless his soul. Aren't you a policeman, too?"

"I was. In December I left the force to start my own business. One of my brothers is a cop and so was my uncle, grandfather, and great-grandfather." Brian had loved being a policeman and had longed to become one for as long as he could remember. But part of the reason he left the force was to avoid the trap that had ensnared his father, grandfather, and great-grandfather. The security business had been a way to use his law enforcement background and experience in a new and creative way, without it becoming too routine or depressing.

"And who is this Emma Murphy?" Maria said, holding up the admission papers.

"That's my wife," Brian said. "Emma O'Brien. You probably know her father and mother. Her father started Inwood Plumbing and Heating."

"Yes, I know of her. I'm sorry she's being admitted, especially to the ICU."

"I am, too. What do I need to do here?"

"Just sign these admission forms for me," Maria said. She slid the stack of papers through the slot in the plexiglass.

He leafed through the stack, and he could see it was the usual legalese that he detested and for which he had little patience. It reminded him of income tax forms. "What is all this?" he asked.

"The customary material. It's mostly to give the hospital and our fine doctors and nurses the right to take care of your wife. It also means you are agreeing to pay for the necessary services."

"Does it have our health insurance information?" Brian asked.

"Whatever you gave to the ED clerk, I put in there," Maria said. "Slip it back to me and I'll make sure."

Brian did as he was told. Using her index finger, Maria rapidly flipped through the pages. In a moment she'd found the correct one. "Yes, here it is. Peerless Health Insurance with the policy number. You're fine."

"Okay, good," he said with relief. "Let me sign it."

Maria shoved the pages back through the hole in the plexiglass. While Brian was signing, she asked: "Why do you have Peerless insurance? Why don't you have your official NYC insurance? I mean, you were a policeman for years, right? I still have my Adolpho's plan. It's really terrific."

"When Emma and I left the force to start our company, which was far more expensive an undertaking than we thought, we had to pinch pennies. We couldn't afford the premiums to keep our NYPD insurance, so we turned to the short-term market. Peerless offered what we needed. We felt obligated to be covered because of our daughter. She'd been a preemie." He slid the signed document back through the plexiglass.

"It does seem to be a quite popular company," Maria agreed. "I've seen a lot of it lately. Okay, you are good to go, and I hope Emma gets better quickly."

"Thanks, Maria. Nice chatting with you."

Brian returned to the main waiting area. As someone who was a committed "doer," he found this kind of inactivity a strain. Yet he couldn't leave without having more information and reassurance about Emma's condition. To make certain that the powers that be knew he was still there, he went back to the information desk and essentially rechecked in. He told the clerk that Dr. Kumar had informed the nurses that he wanted to see his wife as soon as her MRI and CT scans were done. The clerk assured him that the nurses would surely let him know the moment they could. With a strong suspicion the woman was merely placating him, he nonetheless took a seat as far away from everyone as possible and committed himself to waiting.

Another hour crept by. Brian watched as an endless cast of characters either walked into the ED or were carried in. Some came with extended family, most of whom were denied entry by the security people because of the coronavirus situation. Under less stressful circumstances he might have found the scene mildly entertaining as a reflection of life in Inwood. He even recognized some of the patients or the accompanying family members, but he didn't talk to anyone, preferring to hide behind his mask and just observe.

"Mr. Murphy?" a voice asked.

Brian turned away from the scene of another ambulance arriving to find himself looking up into the masked and shielded face of Ms. Claire Baxter, RN, as evidenced by her name tag.

"Yes, I'm Brian Murphy."

"Dr. Kumar said you'd like to see your wife before she is transferred upstairs. Come with me."

He quickly got to his feet and followed the nurse back into the Emergency Department's busy hinterland. He was shown into one of the larger treatment rooms, where Emma was seemingly asleep on a gurney with its rails raised. To his great relief she looked entirely normal save for a nasal cannula providing oxygen and a stocking cap covering her red hair. She even had a very slight but healthy-looking tan on her normally porcelain cheeks, which made the IV and an oximeter on one of her index fingers look totally out of place. Dr. Kumar was busy studying MRI images on a flat-screen monitor.

Brian approached the gurney and closed his fingers around Emma's forearm, hoping that she'd wake up. She didn't budge.

"She's sleeping off the considerable medication we gave her to control her seizure," Dr. Kumar explained, speaking rapidly. He quickly moved around to the other side of the bed. "She is still quite disoriented, but I'm happy to say that her oxygen saturation now is entirely normal. That means her lung function is steady, which we feel lessens the chance we are dealing with coronavirus or will be in need of a ventilator. She tested negative for SARS-CoV-2, by the way."

"That's encouraging," he said. "What did the MRI and the CT scans show?"

"Both are consistent with viral encephalitis," Dr. Kumar said. "More importantly I spoke with an infectious disease specialist. She told me that considering the history of you and your wife having just been on Cape Cod and that beach incident you recounted, she'd favor a diagnosis of eastern equine encephalitis rather than West Nile, which we'll be testing for. She reminded me that Massachusetts has seen an uptick in EEE over the last couple of years."

"I've never heard of EEE."

"You and a lot of other people," Dr. Kumar said. "But that's going to alter with climate change. Mark my words."

"Is EEE serious?" Brian asked hesitantly, not sure he wanted to hear the answer.

"Yes, it can be. Particularly when there are neurological symptoms."

"Like my wife is experiencing."

"Like your wife is experiencing," Dr. Kumar agreed. "It's why I want her in the ICU. I want her to be closely observed, particularly for more seizure activity and changes in her orientation and oxygenation level."

"How long do you think she will be in the ICU?" Brian asked. "I think it might stress her out even more."

"With luck, just a few days," Dr. Kumar said. "One of the ICU hospitalists will call you in the morning and let you know how she is doing."

"I appreciate that," he said. "Tell me, is EEE contagious?"

"Not from person to person," Dr. Kumar assured him.

"At least there's that," Brian said.

"It's a mosquito-borne illness, which, simply enough, means it's becoming more and more important to avoid mosquitoes. Especially during evening barbecues like you mentioned. That's when those Asian tiger mosquitoes are out in force."

At that moment several orderlies appeared. Without a word one went to the head of Emma's gurney, where he disengaged the brake, while the other went to the foot and began guiding it out of the treatment room. Brian was able to follow and quickly give her arm one more squeeze before watching her disappear from the room. He couldn't help but wonder when he would be seeing her again, especially since he assumed that ICU visitation was most likely limited these days.

"I can show you back to the waiting room," Ms. Baxter offered.

Brian merely nodded and followed the nurse, passing out through the same door as Emma had just been pushed, but turning in the opposite direction once out in the hallway. He'd hoped to feel more encouraged after seeing Emma for himself, but he didn't. He also didn't respond to the nurse's small talk, too distracted by a wave of anger directed at fate. First it had been the coronavirus that had derailed all their carefully laid plans for their new security business. And now it was this illness he'd never heard of threatening his wife. And to make matters worse, it happened while they were trying to make the best of a difficult situation by having a bit of family fun in the face of the pandemic.

Five minutes later Brian started the short walk from MMH to his home on West 217th Street. Just getting out of the hospital helped his mindset to a degree. Yet he still felt as if he'd run an emotional marathon. Transitioning from yesterday to today boggled him. He couldn't imagine two days being so different. Yesterday he'd been capable of feeling relatively happy despite the obstacles they faced, and today he was overwhelmed with worry about Emma.

When he walked into the house, he was relieved that Juliette was already fast asleep in bed. He'd been concerned about how he would find the patience to deal with her needs. Camila said she hadn't eaten much dinner but had been eager to go to bed after having a long bath.

"You are more than a lifesaver, you're a godsend," Brian told her after looking in at his peacefully sleeping daughter clutching her beloved Bunny. "You certainly have a way with her that I'm so thankful for. As hard as she was crying at the hospital, I was worried she'd be up all night."

He closed Juliette's door silently to avoid waking her.

"She's a joy," Camila said. "Emma's seizure and then the hospital frightened her, and she just needed to get home to calm down. How is Emma?"

"I only got to see her for a few seconds," Brian said. "She was sleeping off some medication, so I wasn't able to speak with her."

"I'm sure she is going to be just fine. Did they give you any idea when she might be coming home?"

"No, they didn't. I guess we'll just have to see how it goes and keep our fingers crossed." He didn't mention that Emma had had a second seizure. He wasn't sure why, although he guessed it was because he was trying to forget it.

"How about we have some dinner?" Camila suggested. "On the

way home from MMH I picked up enough take-out from Floridita for the three of us: pulled pork, black beans, and yellow rice. Juliette didn't do it justice."

"That was thoughtful," Brian said. "The idea of dealing with food hadn't even occurred to me. What did we do to deserve you?"

"I think the feeling's pretty mutual," she said with one of her characteristic laughs. "It's been a real win-win situation."

Over dinner Camila shared some good news. She said that she'd gotten a serious inquiry that afternoon about security needs for a weekend-long wedding planned for the middle of October out in Southampton. "Apparently it's going to be a sizable affair with people flying in on their private jets from all over the country. The man's name is Calvin Foster of Priority Capital. He made the call himself, which impressed me. He asked to speak to you directly and gave me his number. I told him that you would call him back tomorrow."

"Wow," Brian said. "Did he say anything at all about Covid-19 restrictions?"

"He did," Camila said. "Everyone will be required to be tested before arrival, and he's going to have an on-site testing setup."

"Whoa! That is good news," he said. "A big wedding like that will be a significant financial shot in the arm, especially if we will be tasked to take care of some of the guests as well."

"The number to call is on your desk in the office," she said. When Emma and Brian had started Personal Protection LLC, they'd turned the home's formal dining room into a dedicated office with desks for all three of them.

"Did he happen to mention how he got word about us?" Brian asked. The conundrum of publicity from day one had only been made worse by the lockdown. Lately they had only been doing online advertising and not even much of that. With people staying at home, there was simply no real need for security.

"He did. He said he'd gotten the number from Deputy Chief Michael Comstock."

"Really? Terrific! That's encouraging," he exclaimed. Deputy Chief Michael Comstock was the commanding officer of the Emergency Service Unit of the NYPD. Brian had served under him for the six years he'd been with the unit and Emma for four. When Brian and Emma had resigned from the NYPD, they had been mildly concerned the CO was resentful, since he skipped their departure party without any explanation. The fact that he was now recommending Personal Protection was a very good sign.

After dinner, while Brian cleaned up the kitchen, Camila went back to the office to work on their accounts receivable in hopes of scaring up some receipts. A bit later he joined her to do some research on eastern equine encephalitis. After he spent some time reading about it, he wished he hadn't, especially given the paranoia about viruses engendered by the Covid-19 pandemic. EEE was a very alarming illness with a variety of possible consequences, and now that his beloved wife had possibly contracted it, he had a nagging fear that they would be facing a long road to recovery.

CHAPTER 5

August 20

It was one of the worst night's sleep Brian could remember having. He kept waking up, tossing and turning, wondering how Emma was faring in the ICU. He hoped that the heavy medication they had given her to stop her second seizure kept her asleep, so she wouldn't be tormented by the stressful environment. At just after four A.M. he was wandering around the house for the second time, arguing with himself about whether to call the hospital and check on Emma's status. Ultimately, he didn't call, not because he didn't want to but because he doubted he'd get through, and the effort might make him feel even more frustrated and nervous than he already was.

By eight o'clock both Juliette and Camila were up, and while Juliette watched cartoons, Brian and Camila had coffee in the breakfast nook. He told her what a bad night he had had, and she wasn't surprised.

"I think it would be best if you try to keep yourself as occupied today as possible," Camila said in response. "Make that call to Calvin Foster. It would be terrific for multiple reasons if you could secure us a major security engagement. It would keep Personal Protection moving in the right direction."

"That's the understatement of the year," Brian said. "Good suggestion. I'll make the call for sure. How about you?"

"I think I'll concentrate on keeping Juliette happy and calm," Camila said. "She is going to miss Emma terribly. I know because my mother was hospitalized with pneumonia when I was about Juliette's age, and I still remember how devastated and abandoned I felt."

"She is suffering," he agreed, glancing over at Juliette. "I can tell. I didn't know four-year-olds could get depressed, but she's acting that way. Usually she wakes up a ball of energy. This morning I found her in her bed awake, just lying there and staring into the distance. Let's be more lenient than usual with the cartoons." Under normal circumstances Juliette's screen time was sharply limited, but they needed something to keep her distracted.

"I agree," Camila said. "Since there's nothing for me to do in the office and since it's a nice summer day, I'll take her out to Isham Park this morning to let her get some exercise. She loves climbing on the rocks."

"Great idea to get her out and active," Brian agreed. "I'll make an effort to take her to the Emerson Playground after lunch, which she also likes, particularly the swings."

By nine o'clock, with Camila and Juliette out of the house, he parked himself at his desk in the home office. The first thing he did was google Calvin Foster and Priority Capital. He was duly impressed. It was one of the larger New York private equity firms and had a stellar record, and Calvin Foster was considered a particularly sharp financier and shrewd investor. Just when he was about to try to call him, Brian's phone rang. It was Dr. Gail Garner, one of the MMH intensivist physicians.

"Mrs. Murphy is doing well. Although she has a low-grade fever, her other vital signs are normal and stable. The problem is that she is still not entirely oriented to time, place, or person, although that seems to be slowly improving. We are pleased that her respiratory status is entirely normal without the need for ventilatory support and, as I believe you already know, her coronavirus test was negative."

"Has a diagnosis been confirmed?" he prodded.

"Yes, it has. As predicted, she's positive for eastern equine encephalitis, or EEE."

Brian swallowed as his throat had suddenly gone dry. After what he'd read on Wikipedia the night before, he'd hoped for a different diagnosis, and the terrifying feeling of serious impending consequences came back in a rush. The fact that she was having neurological symptoms was not a good sign. It seemed unbelievable to him that apparently due to climate change his wife had come down with a serious viral illness he'd never even heard of.

"As required, we have reported this case to the New York State Health Department," Dr. Garner continued. "You might hear from them for more information, although we were able to tell them that the patient had recently been on Cape Cod, Massachusetts, and had reportedly been exposed to mosquitoes. Do you have any questions for me?"

"Can I visit her?"

"I'm afraid that with the Covid-19 situation, visitation in the ICU has been restricted."

"I assumed as much," Brian said. "How long do you think she will be kept in the ICU?"

"Perhaps another twenty-four hours. If she stays stable, we will send her to a normal hospital room. She'll be having a neurology consult today, which might influence timing depending on what they find."

"Will I be kept up to date on her progress?"

"If there are any changes, absolutely," Dr. Garner said. "And I can call again in the morning if you would like."

"I'd appreciate it," Brian said.

After hanging up, he found himself literally shaking at what he'd just found out. He didn't even want to contemplate what could be in store for Emma.

Feeling obligated and with trembling fingers, Brian put in calls to his mother, Aimée, and Emma's mother, Hannah, to tell them what the hospitalist had told him. Both had more questions than he could answer, and he promised he'd let them know as soon as he heard any updates.

After taking a deep breath to try to calm himself, he placed a call to Calvin Foster, desperate to think about something else besides Emma's situation. Luckily it turned out that not only was Calvin Foster seemingly a first-class financier, he was also personable, easy to talk to, and informed. What was particularly helpful was that Brian didn't have to sell himself. After only a few minutes of conversation it was apparent that Calvin knew a great deal about Brian's NYPD background, including his time in the Emergency Service Unit's elite A team.

"How do you know Deputy Chief Comstock?" Brian asked. As the conversation progressed, it became apparent he and Calvin were more than acquaintances.

"I've known Michael since high school," Calvin said jovially. "He's the one who recommended your security firm. I must say, he was full of praise. He said you'd gotten a few awards for exemplary service as a policeman."

"A lot of officers get awards," Brian replied. He was never one to brag or boast, mainly because he always thought he could do better no matter what others thought of him.

"I even heard you won a sniper award when you were an ESU cadet," Calvin commented.

"Luckily that's a skill that doesn't have a high demand."

Calvin laughed. "No, I suppose that's true. Nonetheless, I'm impressed."

"So, how can I help you?" Brian asked, eager to get down to business.

"I'd like to know if your company could cover my daughter's wedding that we've scheduled for the middle of October despite the pandemic. It's kind of a 'hurry-up' affair that we're throwing together but still trying to keep safe. It's going to be outside under an open tent. Kids today live in a different universe than you and I occupied, if you know what I'm saying."

"And it's only getting more different every day. I understand the affair will be at your Southampton summer home?"

"That's the plan. I've been told there will be about fifty guests with about half flying in private, some with their own security. Do you have adequate personnel to handle a job like this?"

"Our business plan is to utilize off-duty NYPD Emergency Service Unit officers, of which there are always a sizable and eager number. I'm certain we could provide the required security."

"Wonderful. What I would like beforehand is a security evaluation and an estimated budget. How soon might you be able to provide that?"

"First, I'd need a guest list with contact information, and I'd have to make a site visit to your Southampton home to view the venue. I can do that in the next few days." Brian welcomed the idea of the diversion, yet he wasn't entirely sure he'd feel comfortable leaving town with Emma in the hospital, even though Southampton was only two hours from the city.

"I'll have one of my secretaries email the Southampton address and guest list to you today, and I'll let my wife know to expect you. She's been living out there along with one college-aged daughter full-time since March, and I've been going back and forth."

After setting up plans to reconnect after Brian submitted his security evaluation and budget, they disconnected the call. The second he put the phone down, concern about Emma flooded back.

"Good God," he murmured, wondering if he could handle this potentially complicated engagement requiring interfacing with other security people while dealing with the stress of worrying about what Emma's status might be in mid-October and without her business input. Personal Protection LLC had always been something they were to do together, but Brian would have to find a way to fare on his own.

CHAPTER 6

August 20

It was after one o'clock in the afternoon when Brian and Juliette started walking home from the Emerson Playground. It wasn't far, only five or six blocks. Try as he might, he had been unable to get Juliette to do anything at the playground. Instead, she sat with Brian on a park bench holding Bunny, content to watch the other children play. To Brian she seemed completely out of character, acting listless and disinterested. Eventually he ran out of things to talk to her about, especially since he had admitted early on that he didn't know when Emma would be coming home from the hospital.

"We're home," he called out the moment they entered the front door. In response, Camila quickly emerged from the dining-room-cum-office to welcome them as they took off their shoes.

"How was your time at the playground?" Camila asked Juliette with forced positivity. "Did you have fun?"

"I want to watch cartoons," Juliette declared, ignoring the question and heading for the kitchen.

Brian and Camila exchanged a concerned glance. "She's not happy," he mouthed. "She didn't want to play with the other kids."

"It was the same this morning at Isham Park," Camila said with resignation. "I'll see if I can interest her in a bite of lunch."

"Any communication from Calvin Foster's people while I was out?"

"Yes, there's an email with the venue address and a preliminary guest list. There was also a call from the hospital."

"Really? Was it one of the doctors?" Brian asked nervously.

"No," Camila said. "It was a Roger Dalton from the hospital business office. He requested a call back as soon as you can. I left his direct-dial number on your desk."

"The business office?" he questioned. He felt relieved but curious. "What do they want?"

"He didn't say. He just said for you to call. Apparently, it is something important."

Brian nodded. He couldn't imagine what it was about since he'd already spoken with Maria Hernandez and had signed the admission papers. Sitting at his desk and with the number in hand, he took out his cell phone and dialed. The line was answered quickly by a commanding, whiskey-baritone voice with a strong New York accent. Brian identified himself and mentioned that he'd gotten the message to call.

"Yes, thank you for getting back to me," Roger said. "I've been assigned as the case manager for Emma Murphy. A problem has developed. I think it is best if you come into the hospital, so that we can discuss it in person."

"What kind of a problem? Is Emma okay?" Brian asked urgently.

"It's a problem with your health insurance coverage."

"I gave all the appropriate information to Mrs. Hernandez and signed the admission papers. Have you spoken with her?"

"This is not about Emma Murphy's admission to the hospital,"

Roger said. "It's about her visit yesterday to our Emergency Department, and I need to speak to you directly to set up a payment plan."

"What are you talking about? What kind of 'payment plan'?"

"I can explain it far better in person. I see that you live here in Inwood, so it shouldn't be too much of an imposition for you to come in? I will be here all afternoon."

Suddenly Brian realized the line had been disconnected and that the man had hung up. With a sense of impatience, he put the phone down. He didn't know whether to feel irritated or concerned, and what tipped the balance was a mild worry about the possible impact on Emma's treatment if he didn't comply. He didn't think that would really happen, but the mere thought of it made him decide not to make an issue of the situation. Instead, he got up, told Camila that he had to return to the hospital to visit the business office, and set off.

As Brian entered through the main entrance, he could see multiple ambulances pulled up to the ED dock. The main lobby was moderately full, and he had to wait for his turn at the information desk. From his time at the hospital when he'd done off-duty patrolman work, he knew where the hospital administration offices were, but he didn't know if Roger Dalton's business office would be there as well. He found out quickly enough that it was.

Moving from the impressively renovated but cold marbled lobby into the admin section of the hospital was a stark transition. Now footsteps were muffled with carpet and the forest-green walls were hung with real art. To him the area looked more like a prosperous international corporation rather than the nerve center of a city hospital. There was even a glass-fronted conference room with a large mahogany library table and captain's chairs that looked to Brian more like it belonged in a bank. Next to the conference room was what he assumed was the hospital's CEO's office, outfitted as impressively as the conference room. As a police officer, he'd met the hospital president at the time, a doctor who had transitioned to administrative work, but Brian knew that had changed when the Inwood Community Hospital was purchased by the Manhattan Memorial Hospital corporation eight years earlier and became MMH Inwood. Under new management, it had undergone a major makeover before officially joining the ranks of the hospital chain.

Asking directions from one of the many secretaries, he quickly found Roger Dalton's office, but then he had to wait for a time while Roger finished with someone else. Finally, after nearly twenty minutes, Dalton appeared in his office's doorway and beckoned for Brian to enter.

Brian's first impression was that Roger Dalton didn't look anything like his imposing baritone voice implied. Instead of a commanding figure, he was a tall, thin man whose sports jacket looked more like it was draped over a metal hanger than over a pair of shoulders. His face behind his mask looked haggard, and he had deeply set eyes behind heavy-rimmed glasses. With slicked-back hair streaked with gray, he looked like a man who was either a heavy smoker and drinker or battling a serious illness.

"Thanks for coming," Roger began while taking his seat behind his desk and directing Brian to a chair front and center. "You're probably wondering why I insisted you come in. I'm afraid I have some bad news for you."

Although Brian knew from his call that Roger wasn't talking about Emma, for a second his heart stopped until Roger added: ". . . your insurance carrier, Peerless Health Insurance, has declined to cover your wife's $27,432.88 Emergency Department bill."

"You have already heard from Peerless?" Brian asked. He was astounded by Roger's comment on many levels, but for the moment the speed with which it had been discovered that Peerless wasn't paying took precedence. Emma had only been admitted yesterday, and he assumed the insurance matters took weeks, if not months.

"Yes, we have," Roger said. "As you might be aware, hospitals are being financially stressed through this pandemic. Our usual major sources of operating income such as elective surgery have been curtailed, forcing us to be strict in other areas, particularly the ED, whose operating costs are enormous. I was distressed when I saw that your carrier was Peerless. Our experience with them has been difficult at best, so I wanted to file the claim as soon as possible. True to form, they let us know immediately they were declining the claim, which I'm afraid to say is their normal modus operandi. It seems Peerless often finds creative ways of avoiding paying claims."

"Why would they decline my wife's ED visit?" Brian asked, still perplexed. "That doesn't make any sense."

"As I said, Peerless is particularly creative," Roger said. "But my guess in this particular instance is that the rationale is pretty straightforward. Even some of the big insurers like Anthem and United are getting involved. Here's the deal. There is a lot of talk of the cost of healthcare needing to be curtailed, and that insurance companies have an obligation to put on the brakes or at least appear to be doing so. One area that stands out is the 'emergency' overuse situation. Running emergency departments, particularly Trauma 1 centers like ours, is very, very expensive, and far too many people are abusing them for non-emergency ambulatory care rather than for true emergencies, like heart attacks, strokes, massive trauma and bleeding, and the like. Many insurance carriers feel that they have to put a stop to such abuse by denying claims, especially during normal business hours when patients can see their general practitioners or visit small, independent urgent-care centers."

"You mean that Peerless is saying my wife, who had suffered a grand mal seizure, shouldn't have come to the MMH Inwood ED?"

"That's exactly what I believe they are saying by denying the claim," Roger affirmed.

"Well, that's preposterous," Brian sputtered. "A grand mal seizure is surely a medical emergency."

Roger shrugged his narrow shoulders and spread his hands, palms up. "I'm afraid that is going to be between you and your insurance carrier. Meanwhile, there is this sizable bill that needs to be addressed. That is why we need to set up some sort of payment plan going forward, especially now that your wife is an inpatient and using significant resources like an intensive care bed."

Brian's thoughts were churning a mile a minute in every conceivable direction. How could this be happening to him? Was his wife's care now in the balance because of their irresponsible insurance carrier? The whole situation was ridiculous, and mind-boggling.

"Well, what has Peerless said about my wife's hospitalization?" Brian managed to ask while trying to rein in his thoughts.

"They have said nothing because they have yet to be billed for that," Roger said. "Here's what I propose. If you were to, say, pay five thousand a month, we would be willing to accept that without adding interest. We realize that this is an imposition to anyone's budget."

"Imposition?" Brian exclaimed. "You don't understand. I don't have that kind of money, and certainly not under these circumstances."

"Well, you tell me what kind of time frame you have in mind," Roger offered, tenting his fingers, elbows on his desk.

"Well, first, let's talk about this bill," Brian snapped. "Twenty-seven-something thousand dollars! How in heaven's name did the bill come to that? I could buy a new car for that kind of money."

"That's easy," Roger said. "It's par for the course and certainly not out of line. As I mentioned, Emergency Department care is very expensive. Your wife had multiple radiographic studies, a spinal tap, various consults, expensive pharmacological agents, many sophisticated laboratory tests, and her care tied up a number of highly paid nurses and doctors. She also had a seizure while being attended, which had to be treated. It adds up quickly."

"I want to see a copy of the bill," Brian demanded.

"You can request a copy from the billing department. That's certainly your right."

"I want to see a copy right here and now," Brian said. "It's all computerized, so it can be printed out in minutes."

"The way it will immediately print out won't be understandable to you."

"I don't care," Brian countered. "I want to see it."

"Suit yourself," Roger said. He picked up the phone and made a quick call. It was obvious that he was now finding the meeting almost as vexing as Brian.

While Roger was on the phone, Brian tried to calm himself. He realized he needed to talk directly to Peerless. It was absurd to think that a health insurance company wouldn't cover an obviously necessary ED visit even if some other people abused the situation. It had to be some kind of misunderstanding. Maybe they didn't know there had been several seizures involved, as well as a serious diagnosis thereafter.

"Okay," Roger told him, hanging up the phone. "I'll have a copy of the bill in short order."

"Can the ED bill be added on to the bill that will be generated by my wife's admission?"

"No, it can't," Roger said. "The ED bill must be taken care of separately. Can you give me an idea of what kind of time frame you would be able to propose?"

"I'm even behind on my mortgage," Brian blurted. "With the pandemic tying the economy in knots, how the hell do you think I can come up with twenty-seven thousand dollars within any conceivable time frame without being a goddamn fortune-teller?"

"Please, calm down," Roger snapped. "Let's try to have a civil conversation."

"You're right," Brian said. He had to get himself under control. "You'll have to excuse me. I'm just blown over by this whole situation. I never thought about any of this. I've always had good health insurance. I guess I've just taken it for granted. What I need to do is talk directly with Peerless and get them to step up to the plate and take care of this."

"That is a good plan, but you have to do it right away," Roger insisted. "You can't put this off. Talk to your carrier and then get right back to me. As I'm sure you understand, MMH has its own financial responsibilities it has to meet on a daily basis."

After a knock on Roger's door, a secretary came in with a small stack of papers and handed them over to him before retreating. Roger briefly glanced at them and then handed them over to Brian. "Good luck," he said as he did so.

Brian took the papers and glanced through them. It was immediately clear that Roger had been correct. The bill was entirely unintelligible, with every page mostly composed of long lists of alphanumeric entries followed by dollar amounts. Disgusted, Brian tossed the stack onto the desk. "It's not in English. It's all in goddamn code!"

"I warned you that it would be incomprehensible."

"Why is it in code? Why isn't each procedure or product just listed with a price? This format doesn't make any sense."

"Prices are proprietary information," Roger explained. "We have to keep that information confidential for our negotiations with insurance companies."

"I don't follow," Brian said. "Isn't there one specific price for every product and procedure?"

Roger scoffed at Brian's naivete. "There are different prices for different insurance companies. It's all a matter of bargaining. Surely you must know this."

"That's crazy," Brian said. "I've never heard of such a thing. Do I get a chance to bargain?"

Roger genuinely laughed, although he was obviously losing patience. "No, you don't get a chance to bargain. As an individual, you have to pay full freight."

"Why is that? Why do I have to pay more than health insurance companies for the same service?"

"This is how American hospital-based medicine works," Roger snapped. "I don't have time to explain it to you, nor is it my job. It's complicated. But, look, I can have a slightly more comprehensible bill drawn up, which I can email to you if you give me your email address."

"I never had any idea of any of this," Brian said as he dashed off his email address and handed it over. "I'll call Peerless as soon as I get home, and I'll let you know what they say. There has to be a misunderstanding."

"Fair enough," Roger said. "And you'll hear from me as soon as I can get the billing department to expand the bill however much is possible. But I warn you: It still isn't going to be much more understandable than this one. As I told you, hospital prices are proprietary information."

"I'll take my chances." He then added with mild sarcasm: "Thanks for your time."

Leaving the administration area, Brian briefly debated whether to try to visit the ICU because he knew where it was on the second floor. He decided against it for two reasons. One was that it might upset the powers that be, and two, if Emma was still disoriented, she wouldn't even remember he'd visited if he was able to pull it off. Instead, he used one of the courtesy phones in the main lobby and called to see if any of the ICU hospitalists were available, but had no luck.

Brian walked out of the hospital into a warm late summer day, which was beautiful weather-wise but totally lost on him. He walked out to Broadway and turned south as if he were in a trance. Not only was he terrified about the prospects of Emma's condition, he was now discombobulated and mortified about the possibility that he was facing a horrendous bill he could not pay. All he could hope was that Peerless Health had made a mistake, one that could be rectified by a phone call. Yet from Roger Dalton's comments, Brian wasn't all that optimistic. He felt as if he were caught in the outer edges of a whirlpool that had the power to suck him under and drown him.

CHAPTER 7

August 20

The twenty-minute walk from the hospital to his house on West 217th Street was just long enough for Brian to recover, calm down considerably, and think. He had always been a doer who saw adversity as a challenge. By the time he'd turned onto his street, he was back to giving Peerless Health Insurance the benefit of the doubt. He was now progressively convinced that there had to be a major misunderstanding about the nature of Emma's condition, and that a simple phone call to point it out would surely clear things up. With that issue possibly solved, he was able to think more about hospital prices and the incredible amount of money involved in healthcare. It seemed preposterous that it could cost more than twenty-seven thousand dollars for a single emergency visit, yet Roger Dalton obviously didn't think it was at all exceptional. In fact, he had actually said it wasn't out of line.

Back when Juliette had been born prematurely, Brian was vaguely aware of sky-high hospital bills, but that was for more than a month of neonatal intensive care. But even those bills hadn't caused a fuss in his personal expenses, since his and Emma's NYPD health benefits covered it in its entirety. Actually, as Brian turned onto his walkway, what bothered him the most at the moment was Dalton telling him that hospital costs varied depending on which health insurance company was involved and that he, as a nobody, had to pay "full freight." He couldn't imagine what people with no insurance at all had to do.

"What a crazy, screwed-up, unfair system," Brian pondered aloud as he mounted the front steps of his house, one of the very few houses left standing among the myriad of apartment blocks of Inwood, Manhattan.

Once inside, the first thing Brian did was go into the kitchen, where he could hear a cartoon soundtrack. He found Juliette parked in front of the TV and Camila on her laptop at the kitchen table.

"How is everyone?" Brian asked, trying to sound chipper.

"Juliette isn't hungry," Camila said. "I've tried to tempt her with eggs and bacon, which she usually adores, but she doesn't want any."

"How about Bunny?" Brian asked Juliette. Bunny as per usual was tucked in next to her on the banquette. "Is she hungry for bacon and eggs?"

"Bunny has a headache," Juliette said, without taking her eyes off the screen.

"I forgot about that," Camila chimed in. "Juliette says she has a headache."

"I'm sorry," Brian said. "Maybe Bunny shouldn't watch so much TV. Do you think that could be causing her headache?"

"I learned something interesting," Camila said when it was apparent Juliette wasn't going to respond. She took Brian aside, lowering her voice. "I researched whether young children can be depressed. Apparently, they can, but reactive anxiety is more common a problem. I think we are dealing with significant anxiety here with Miss Juliette."

"That makes a lot of sense. Witnessing her mother having a seizure and then being kept in the hospital is certainly enough to cause anxiety. Hell, I'm experiencing it myself."

"I guess we just have to be as supportive as we can," Camila said. "At the moment it means letting her watch TV."

"Agreed," Brian said.

"So, what happened at the hospital? Any word on Emma's condition?"

"No word on Emma. As for the hospital, they're demanding to be paid out of pocket for Emma's ED visit yesterday afternoon."

"Wow! They don't waste any time, do they?"

"And you won't believe the amount they're asking for," Brian said. "It's criminal. As for the speed, I got the sense that MMH Inwood is struggling financially with the coronavirus situation just like we are. Also, it seems the hospital has had a bad relationship with our particular health insurer. True to form, the company already denied the claim. But I'm hoping it's a misunderstanding. I've got to call them and straighten it all out. Are you all right here with Juliette for now?"

"I'm fine," Camila assured him. "Make your call, and good luck dealing with them. Last year I had a terrible time with my grandmother's health insurance company."

Back in the office, Brian searched in the upright file for the Peerless policy to get the policy number and the company's phone number. When he found it, he noticed it was a Manhattan exchange and a Midtown Manhattan address. Sitting at his desk with the information in front of him, he placed the call. As it went through, he vaguely wondered how many of the Peerless employees were working from home and how many were actually going into the office, as it varied from company to company.

When the line was answered automatically, Brian had to listen to a long list of possible alternatives. He chose one of the last: customer service, which resulted in another extensive list of choices. Five minutes later, when he finally got to speak to a real person and explained that he was calling to contest a denial of claim, he was told that he had to speak to the claims adjustment supervisor on duty. Frustratingly enough, that required another wait of almost thirty minutes while Brian was forced to listen to insipid elevator music. As time passed, he struggled with rising impatience.

"This is Ebony Wilson," a strong, compelling, yet mellifluous voice suddenly declared, breaking through the background music. "With whom do I have the pleasure of speaking?"

Brian gave his name and then explained why he was calling, namely to discuss the denial of a claim involving a visit to the MMH Inwood Emergency Department. He went on to say that there must have been a misunderstanding and that he wanted to clear up the situation.

"I'm sure I can help," Ebony said graciously. "Can I please have your Peerless Health Insurance policy number?"

Brian gave the number, enunciating each letter and number so there would be no mistakes and he could get this done as quickly as possible.

"Just a moment, please," Ebony said. In the next instant Brian found himself back to suffering through more background music. He knew that it was supposed to be calming, but under the circumstances it was having the opposite effect. Just when he was ready to figuratively scream, Ebony's assertive and pleasant voice returned. "Okay, Mr. Murphy," she said. "I have the claim here in front of me. It's from Manhattan Memorial Hospital Inwood concerning an Emergency Department visit for Emma Murphy. Is this correct?"

"Yes, that's it," Brian said. In contrast to the elevator music, Ebony's voice had a welcome and distinctive soothing quality. "Out of curiosity, are you in the Peerless Midtown office or are you working from home?"

"I'm in the office," Ebony said. "As a supervisor, it works better for me to be here, same with senior management. Most of the secretaries work from home. Why do you ask?"

"No real reason, just curious. It's such a crazy time, what with most people working from home if they can. I was wondering how the health insurance world was faring."

"Okay, I have read through the adjuster's report," Ebony said, ignoring Brian's comment. "Everything seems to be in order here. Why do you think there was a misunderstanding?"

"My wife had a grand mal seizure on the Henry Hudson Parkway after feeling ill all day," Brian told her. "As soon as the seizure was over, we drove directly to the MMH Inwood Emergency Department."

"Yes, that is documented here in the claim," Ebony agreed. "But it also says that Emma Murphy walked into the ED without assistance at four-thirty and waited in line to be helped."

"That may be true, but she was disoriented. I could have called for an ambulance, but that would have taken longer. When she had her seizure, we were in our car fifteen minutes away from the hospital."

"I agree perfectly with your assessment, Mr. Murphy. An ambulance surely wasn't needed and would have been an unnecessary expense. But so is the kneejerk reaction to go to a Trauma 1 Emergency Department when your wife should have been seen by her general practitioner, or perhaps an urgent-care center."

"We don't have a general practitioner," Brian interjected. "My wife and I have been in perfect health. We work out every day. For our four-year-old we have a pediatrician, but we haven't needed a GP."

"Doesn't your wife have a gynecologist?"

"Yes, of course she does, for her yearly checkup."

"GYNs frequently function as general practitioners for young women. Your wife could have gone to her GYN, who could have seen her and admitted her to the hospital if necessary."

"That's absurd," Brian practically shouted.

"Calm down, Mr. Murphy. Anger will get you nowhere. Let me explain something to you. Peerless Health Insurance and our CEO, Heather Williams, are responsible members of our community, our city, and our country. We provide health insurance coverage with the lowest-priced premiums possible, but it comes with responsibility on the part of our members. Let me ask you something, Mr. Murphy. Did you read your Peerless policy as carefully as was recommended by our agent?"

Brian glanced down at the thick stack of papers on his desk. The truth was that he had not read the policy at all and didn't know if Emma had, either. He'd never read any of the health insurance policies he'd been given, even while an NYPD officer.

"I glanced at it," he said, embarrassed to admit otherwise.

"Well, you should have read it carefully to know what you were buying," Ebony said. "I recommend you go back and do so now. You see, to make our short-term policies affordable, we have made it a point to spell out specific limitations and define responsibilities of our members. Within our policy it is very clear what will be covered in the Emergency Department, particularly during normal business hours when urgent-care clinics and doctors' offices are open. You see, we take our role seriously in trying to do something about the rise of healthcare costs in the United States."

As Ebony droned on about the overuse of emergency medical facilities and the need to cut down healthcare costs in general, Brian's mind suddenly harkened back to Roger Dalton and how right he'd been. But then Ebony got Brian's attention by saying: ". . . but if you disagree with our adjuster's decision, you have the right to request a review online."

"I'm thinking I will do more than request a Peerless review," Brian snapped. "Denying a legitimate claim like this seems criminal. I think this deserves a review by an attorney."

"Of course, consulting an attorney and even initiating a lawsuit is your right," Ebony said. "But, let me say this, attorneys are very expensive. And in my experience, which is rather extensive, as I do this day in and day out, you'll be wasting your time and money. Peerless Health knows the ins and outs of this business extremely well, which is why we are so successful. We also have in-house counsel to deal with lawsuits. My advice, for what it is worth, is for you to request a Peerless review and see if it changes the situation. Occasionally it comes to light that an adjuster has made a mistake and the claim is reversed upon review. Is there anything else I can do for you today?"

Similar to how he'd felt after his conversation with Roger Dalton, it took Brian a few minutes to calm down enough to think clearly after disconnecting with Ebony Wilson. He was in no way a litigious person: far from it. As a committed law enforcement officer, he wasn't fond of lawyers. And he recognized Ebony was probably right about the futility of hiring an attorney to try to deal with a company that undoubtedly was "lawyered up" and prepared to deal aggressively with any legal action. He was left with no other option than to request a review.

He brought up the Peerless Health Insurance website to log in, but before he did so, he decided to give the website some attention, seeing as it was basically his second time on there. After a quick glance at the section trying to sell policies to new customers, Brian clicked on the investment section. He learned that the company had had a wildly successful IPO two years ago and that the stock price had doubled since then, making it one of the fastest-growing companies on NASDAQ. It was immediately apparent that the entire success of the company was attributed exclusively to its wunderkind CEO, Heather Williams. Brian looked at the woman's picture. He was impressed with her youth as a CEO of a public company— somewhere around thirty was his guess—and the intensity and imperiousness of her gaze.

Finding himself curious, Brian opened up a new page and looked up Heather Williams. He was surprised by the amount of material available on her and clicked on a recent biographical article. Now he was confronted with a second picture of the CEO that was starkly different from the typical businesslike head-and-shoulder pic on the Peerless website. This was a picture of a painting featuring a haughty Heather Williams in a foxhunting outfit with a horse on one side and a foxhound on the other. Brian's immediate reaction was shock. In his mind foxhunting, like polo, was something reserved for English royalty or those people who aspired to be demonstratively aristocratic. His second reaction was to acknowledge that she'd probably had a very different and a much more privileged upbringing than he had. Beginning the article, he learned that she was the scion of a west Texas oil family, had gone to boarding school in England, and then graduated from Yale undergraduate and finally Harvard Business School.

"Good grief," Brian exclaimed as he read on. She'd been hired by Peerless directly out of business school. At the time Peerless was a small company founded by a group of young entrepreneurs trying to break into the health insurance market by taking advantage of the passage of the Affordable Care Act and the subsidies it offered. Heather Williams quickly and cleverly saw a different path, and instead of relying on politically susceptible subsidies, she strenuously pushed the company to embrace the short-term health insurance market. Within just a few years, thanks to her aggressive and creative marketing, she was elevated to chief financial officer, or CFO, and two years later to chief executive officer, or CEO. In recognition of her single-handedly tripling the company's stock value, she'd become a recognized and applauded darling of Wall Street.

After he finished the article, Brian returned to the picture of Williams in her foxhunting outfit. As he stared at it, he found himself wondering how much her and Peerless's financial success were dependent on Peerless quickly denying claims, as had just happened to him. After entertaining the thought for a few minutes, Brian decided to move on and return to the Peerless website. He had more immediate concerns, like requesting a review of the claim denial for Emma's ED visit, which he sincerely hoped would result in a reversal and possibly save his family's fortune.

With that unpleasantness out of the way, Brian gave Camila a break from being with Juliette by spending almost an hour reading

The House at Pooh Corner to his daughter in her bedroom. After finishing the fourth chapter, Brian looked up to discover Juliette had fallen asleep. Being as quiet as possible, he tiptoed out.

"How much information do you want on each of these guests for the potential Foster gig?" Camila asked as Brian came into the office and sat at his desk. She was at her desk on her computer.

"The more the merrier," he said as he booted up his machine. He hoped that the Foster affair would take place despite the growing concern over a second wave of Covid. With that thought in mind, he went online to look at the Personal Protection LLC bank balances to figure out if there were adequate funds to somehow at least appease the hospital while Emma was an inpatient, especially in case Peerless wasn't going to participate. As he expected, the balances weren't encouraging, and they were going to be hard put to cover basic expenses and put food on the table if some significant business didn't materialize during the next month.

"Our cash flow is a bad joke," Brian voiced out loud. It was depressing, and for many reasons he wished he and Emma had not decided to take the vacation on Cape Cod even though they had gotten the cottage for a steal. Continuing in that trend of thought, he wished they had at least avoided the beach barbecue. Things could have been so different.

"As if I didn't know," Camila said. "We're in dire need of some luck. Fingers crossed for this Foster event. One thing I'm going to insist on: Stop paying my salary until things turn around."

"Camila, we couldn't," Brian countered and meant it.

"I know that neither you nor Emma have taken any salary for months. It's only fair, especially since you're giving me room and board."

"At this point you are more like family," Brian said. "How about we defer your salary? I'm willing to consider that under the circumstances."

"That's fine, if that's what you want to call it," Camila said.

With Camila's suggestion of deferring, he looked back at the numbers. From that perspective it seemed possible that Brian could manage five to ten thousand dollars to placate the hospital, provided the bank was willing to continue deferring the mortgage payment on the house. With the mortgage question in mind, Brian decided to put in a call to their banker, Marvin Freeman. As the call went through, Brian thanked his lucky stars that he and Emma had not taken a business loan to start their security company and instead renegotiated the mortgage on their house. After the usual superficial pleasantries, Brian got right down to the reason for the call.

"Our business is suffering, as you might expect with this coronavirus situation."

"You and a thousand other businesses."

"What do you think the chances are that we could renegotiate our mortgage yet again to give us some operating cash to carry us through?"

"We just renegotiated your mortgage not even a year ago, Brian," Marvin said. His voice lost some of its friendliness, becoming significantly more businesslike.

"I was afraid you'd say that," Brian said. "What about a business line of credit? Something to get us cash if we get desperate."

"What kind of collateral are you thinking of offering for a credit line?" Marvin asked. "Do you have any stocks and bonds?"

"No, we don't have any collateral. The house is our only asset."

"Having no collateral ties my hands, my friend. There's no way I could get a line of credit for you without it. Plus, the bank is already allowing you to defer your mortgage payments for the immediate future."

"Yes, and I appreciate that, Marvin. I suppose in a way that is already a line of credit."

"You could look at it that way, but I should warn you that it is not going to last."

"I understand, but thanks, Marvin."

"Sorry I can't be of more help."

Disconnecting from the call, Brian went back to staring at the meager bank balances. After hearing the bank's position, he really didn't think he could pay MMH very much without putting himself, Emma and Juliette, and his fledgling business in jeopardy. Now more than ever, it seemed tragic to live in a wealthy country where basic emergency healthcare could put a decent, hardworking family like his at risk.

CHAPTER 8

August 27

Brian stepped out of his front door a little after eight in the morning, and as he put on his face mask, he surveyed the street in front of his house. The roadway was in the process of being re-paved but so far had only been ground down and striated. It was a mess, dangerous to walk on, and he had no idea when it was going to be put back together. In many ways it seemed symbolic of his life in the past week.

Emma was still hospitalized after a week and not doing as well as Brian hoped. During her first twenty-four to forty-eight hours in the ICU, he had been told she'd improved and had regained a reasonable degree of orientation. But then when she was transferred into a normal hospital room and he was able to see her, he found her mental state varied from day to day. Sometimes she didn't even seem to recognize him, and she spent most of her time sleeping. She had continued to run a fever, suggesting that the EEE virus was still active despite whatever antibodies her immune system was making.

But at least being in a normal hospital room made it possible for Brian to see her, and thanks to Camila, his mother, and Emma's mother, he'd been able to spend considerable time doing so while the women took turns taking care of Juliette. His poor daughter missed her mother and was sulky, irritable, and withdrawn despite a lot of effort on the part of all three extra caretakers. To everyone's concern, Juliette wasn't even eating properly. Brian was enormously thankful that taking care of her wasn't on his shoulders alone, as he wondered if he would find the patience it required. Just being with her during the night could be trying enough when she'd wake up crying.

Although he had taken one entire afternoon to run out to Southampton to check out the Fosters' palatial summer home and meet the bride-to-be so that Camila could come up with a budget for the wedding, he spent every other day with Emma. It was his feeling that the nursing staff wasn't spending the time necessary to make sure his wife was being appropriately mobilized. From his EMT training, Brian knew how important it was for a patient not to remain in bed continuously.

Multiple times every day, Brian forced her to get up and walk up and down the hallway despite her constant complaining. While walking with her two days before, he'd noticed a change in her stride. It was a kind of clumsiness that was almost imperceptible at first, but slowly progressed over the next twenty-four hours. Yesterday morning when he got her out of bed, it was definitely more apparent, and he brought it to the attention of Dr. Shirley Raymond, the hospitalist responsible for Emma's care. She in turn alerted the neurology consult who had been following Emma. This new symptom, labeled by the doctors as spasticity, had raised Brian's concerns, and as he started out toward MMH Inwood, he wondered if he would find Emma even worse today.

Feeling the need for exercise, which Brian wasn't getting, he literally ran to the hospital. The face mask made it a bit more difficult, but he was willing to put up with it. As he entered through the front entrance into the marbled lobby, one of the women behind the information desk called his name. With as much time as he'd been spending at the hospital on a daily basis, he was becoming a known commodity.

"Mr. Murphy! Harriet Berenson would like to see you," one of the pink-smocked ladies said.

"Who is Harriet Berenson?" he questioned. He was moderately out of breath, even though it had only been a little more than a week since he and Emma had done their daily mini-triathlons.

"She's one of our discharge planners. Her office is on the second floor."

Brian was taken aback. He never even knew there was such a position as a discharge planner. And why would a discharge planner want to talk with him—unless they were thinking of discharging Emma? But how could that be, particularly with her developing a new, alarming symptom? After hesitating for a moment to decide whether to go up to Emma's floor first or visit Harriet Berenson, the latter won out. He needed to know sooner rather than later if there was even talk of Emma being discharged. The idea of having to take care of her at home terrified him.

"Ah, yes," Harriet said once he had made it to her office. She picked up one of the folders on her desk and opened it. "Emma Murphy is to be discharged today. I want to arrange for post-hospital services."

"My wife cannot be discharged," Brian stated simply. As far as he was concerned, she was hardly capable of even basic functions. "That's not going to work. Our house is ill-equipped to handle her needs. I'm not even sure she can climb a flight of stairs in her condition and the bedrooms are upstairs."

"That's good to know," Harriet said. "That's what I am here for: to make sure your wife gets the care she requires. We can certainly arrange for extended care in a nursing home."

"But she's developed some difficulty walking," he argued. "And it's getting worse."

"Do you think a rehabilitation hospital would be a better solution?"

"I don't know," Brian stammered. "I hadn't given it any thought. I certainly didn't think she was ready to be discharged. She's still symptomatic from the EEE virus. In fact, she still has a fever as far as I know."

"That's not what Dr. Kathrine Graham thinks," Harriet countered. "She wrote the discharge order this morning."

"Who is Dr. Graham?" Brian asked. He'd never heard the name.

"She is our Chief Medical Officer here."

"Does Dr. Shirley Raymond know that my wife is to be discharged?" He had briefly seen Dr. Raymond around noon the day before, and she'd not mentioned anything.

"I'm sure she does," Harriet said. "As I said, Dr. Graham is our CMO. If your wife needs help regaining strength for things like walking, a rehabilitation hospital would be the proper choice, no doubt. How does the Hudson Valley Rehabilitation Hospital sound to you? It's in Hudson Heights, so it's close by, and it is an excellent facility. We send a lot of our patients there."

"I guess it sounds better than a nursing home," Brian assented. A rehabilitation hospital sounded decent, but he was hardly enthusiastic.

"Okay, then I'll get right on it," Harriet said. "I know Hudson Valley has room because I placed someone there just yesterday. Now, I was told that you must see Roger Dalton right after talking with me. Do you know where his office is located?"

"I do." He didn't like the idea of seeing Roger Dalton again. He'd not spoken to the man since their less than personable visit a week ago and, from Brian's perspective, it was better to let sleeping dogs lie in regard to the outstanding, humongous ED bill. Yet now that there was a possibility of Emma being discharged, it probably wasn't avoidable.

Leaving Harriet's office, he briefly debated whether to see Dalton first or check in on Emma. Reluctantly, he decided it best to get the Dalton meeting out of the way, as he might find it difficult to leave Emma if she became upset about being discharged. Using the stairs, Brian descended to the first floor and entered the administration area.

With Roger Dalton, Brian wasn't so lucky as he'd been with Miss Berenson. Not only was there someone in the man's office, but there was another individual waiting to see him, too. At least the wait gave him a chance to think about Emma's discharge. He still did not like the idea, but he admitted he knew nothing about the Hudson Valley Rehab Hospital other than approximately where it was. Being that it was rehab hospital, maybe Emma would get more attention, but the uncertainty bothered him, as he didn't know what to expect going forward.

When Brian finally walked into Dalton's office and sat, he thought he was prepared for whatever the man was going to say, but he wasn't, especially since the meeting started out on the wrong foot.

"I thought you were going to get back to me about the outstanding Emergency Department bill?" Roger said with a definite accusatory tone.

"I was planning on it," Brian said in his defense. "I have applied for a review of the decision to deny the claim, and I've been waiting for a response."

"You got your response," Roger spat. "You were informed the claim again had been denied by email yesterday. I know because I'd resubmitted the claim when I hadn't heard from you."

For a brief moment Brian let his eyes drift away from Roger's masked face as a minor flash of anger consumed him. He'd developed a distaste for this bureaucrat on their last meeting and his current holier-than-thou attitude was reminding him why.

"I suppose you are going to tell me you didn't see the email," Roger continued derogatorily.

After a short pause to control himself, Brian said: "You are correct. I have yet to see that particular email from Peerless. As it is, I've been busy trying to help my wife, who is not doing all that well. Is the ED bill the reason you asked to see me?"

"No, it is not," Roger snapped.

"Well, perhaps you can tell me what it is then."

"I'm afraid I have more bad news for you. When I was informed yesterday by our Chief Medical Officer that your wife was going to be discharged, I put together a preliminary hospital bill. Because we have had a history of such bad luck with Peerless Health, I wanted to get it to them ASAP. Well, my efforts were rewarded with Peerless informing us that they will not be covering any of the currently estimated $161,942.98 in-house bill, either."

For a few moments of stunned silence, Brian's mind tried to wrap itself around two incredible facts: the sheer size of the in-house hospital bill and the idea that a health insurance company would contend it wasn't going to be involved with a sick patient's required care. He didn't know which was more outrageous.

"What am I supposed to gather from your silence, Mr. Murphy?" Roger demanded. "We have a major problem here. Frankly, we as an institution are finding it very difficult dealing with these short-term insurance policy companies, especially since they have proliferated during this coronavirus pandemic with people losing their employer-based coverage."

"More than one hundred and sixty thousand dollars is a big bill," Brian managed to say, thinking out loud as he tried to conceive of such a number.

"It is not an exceptional hospital bill by any stretch of the imagination in this day and age," Roger said. "Remember, your wife spent several days in the intensive care unit, which, like the Emergency Department, is very expensive to maintain and run. And she has had many tests over the eight days, including several MRIs and a number of electroencephalograms."

"I suppose," Brian said distractedly. Once again, his mind was going a mile a minute, trying to put this cost into the perspective of his life experiences. The only time he'd dealt with such a number was when he and Emma had bought their house. But that was an investment, not a one-time expense, and his wife was still ill.

"Mr. Murphy, please," Roger said. "This is a major problem, and I need your full attention. We have to decide on a course of action."

"Did Peerless give a reason why they wouldn't be covering *any* of the hospital bill?"

"Yes, they did," Roger said. "I was told it had to do with your deductible, all of which was spelled out clearly in your policy. Did you read your policy, Mr. Murphy?"

"Not carefully," Brian admitted, fully aware that he was fibbing similar to the way he'd done during his conversation with Ebony Wilson.

"Well, it sounds like that was a big mistake," Roger said patronizingly.

With some difficulty Brian resisted the temptation to ask Roger how many novel-length, legalese-strewn health insurance policies he'd read in his lifetime.

"I know my policy had a ten-thousand-dollar deductible. Doesn't that mean the insurance company is then supposed to cover the rest?"

"All policies are different," Roger said. "It's up to you to find out. Meanwhile, what do you propose to do about the now $189,375.86 bill that is owed to MMH Inwood? We need to know, or we will have to turn this over to collections."

"I intend to resolve this situation with Peerless today," Brian insisted. "And I'm not going to try to do it over the phone. This sort of money calls for an in-person visit."

"All right, that's up to you," Roger said. "But you must get back to me soon. You can't ignore this situation."

"I'll get back to you right away, but before I go, I need to ask something. What came first: the decision to discharge my wife or the hospital getting word from Peerless that they were not going to cover the bill?"

"I don't think I understand the question." Roger sat back in his chair, wrinkled his forehead, and stared at Brian through his thick-framed glasses.

"I can't help but worry that the reason my wife is being suddenly discharged is because of the outstanding ED bill along with the new fear that her hospital bill might not get paid in a timely manner."

"That is a preposterous accusation," Roger said, taking immediate offense. He rocked forward, glaring at Brian. "The clinical people, meaning the doctors and nurses, make all the decisions about patient care. We on the business side are not involved, ever! All we do is strive to keep the institution solvent. The two do not mix on any level whatsoever."

"Really?" Brian questioned. "There had been no talk of her being discharged as far as I know, and I've made it a point to talk daily with Dr. Raymond, who's been in charge of her care. This all seems very quick and out of the blue. And my wife has recently developed a new symptom of spasticity. From my vantage point, she's no better off now than when she was admitted."

"Let me tell you something, young man," Roger said as he used a mildly crooked index finger to point repeatedly at Brian. "This hospital never allows financial concerns to affect patient care decisions. Never! I'm offended you would even suggest such a thing."

"I wonder," Brian questioned while provocatively raising his eyebrows. He was getting a smidgen of pleasure from being the cause of Roger's apparent indignation and discomfort. After a pregnant pause, he added: "Who actually is Dr. Graham, this supposed chief medical officer? I've never met her, and I have been coming here every day for more than a week to see my wife. Is she more on the clinical side or the administrative side?"

"What on earth do you mean?"

"What I'm wondering is whether she is more concerned about patient welfare or institutional welfare. It's as simple as that."

"Dr. Graham is part of the administration, but she is also a doctor," Roger sputtered. "Once you are a doctor, you are always a doctor. That should be plenty obvious."

"I hope you're right," Brian said. He stood up, knowing that the chances of getting a straight answer were slim. "Meanwhile, I expect to get a copy of the hospital bill, and I'd like it in English. Even the second ED bill you sent me seemed like it was done on an Enigma machine."

"I'll see what I can do," Roger said. "But let me warn you in advance: The hospital bill will definitely be more complicated than the ED bill, especially the part involving the ICU. And the bill from MMH Inwood is not the only bill you will be getting. You'll also get bills from individual doctors not employed by MMH who saw your wife during her stay."

"What kinds of doctors?" Brian demanded as he sat back down. This sounded like insult added to injury or, more accurately, like a kind of extortion.

"Specialists of various kinds," Roger answered vaguely. "Some of the consults are independent practitioners."

"Is this the surprise medical billing I've vaguely heard about?"

"It is," Roger admitted.

"Well, get me what you can," Brian said while regaining his feet in preparation of leaving. "Meanwhile, I'll be back to you after I have a face-to-face visit with Peerless Health, which will hopefully be today."

As he rode up in the elevator, he couldn't get the concern out of his mind that Emma was being discharged on account of economics, which was an infuriating thought. When he walked into Emma's room, he found her asleep, which was happening more frequently of late. Instead of waking her, he let her be and returned to the nurses' station. Over the preceding week he'd gotten to know many of the day-shift nurses, including the charge nurse, Maureen O'Hara, whose brother Brian knew well. They'd shared a class in grammar school and had attended the NYPD Academy together.

"So, Emma is being discharged," Brian said when he managed to get Maureen's attention. She was a no-nonsense, squat, and powerfully built woman just like her brother, and she ran the fourth floor with an iron fist. She, like most of the floor nurses, was wearing a plastic face shield as well as a mask.

"That's what I've been told," Maureen said. "To tell you the truth, it took me by surprise."

"Do you think it's appropriate?"

Maureen shrugged. "We're not doing all that much for her. In fact, you are doing more than we are, even more than physical therapy. The thing that I am most concerned about is the seizure monitoring."

"Me, too," he said. "What's the story with this Dr. Kathrine Graham?"

"What exactly do you mean?"

"I'm not sure. I was just told she was the one who wrote the discharge order."

"That's not surprising," Maureen said. "She does that a lot."

"What kind of doctor is she?" Brian asked. "I've never met her."

"She doesn't often come to the floor. She has an office in admin. My understanding is that she was an internist before becoming the Chief Medical Officer."

"What about Dr. Raymond? Where is she today?"

"She's back in the chart room. I saw her go in there not five minutes ago."

Knowing full well he was overstepping his bounds to a degree,

Brian went to the door to the chart room and pushed it open. Instead of being full of charts as he was expecting, the room was made up of countertops and computer monitors. Dr. Raymond and several other people were busy entering data. The only noise was coming from the keypads.

"Excuse me, Dr. Raymond," he called out self-consciously. "Could I please have a word?"

To Brian's relief, she immediately stood up and came to the door. Speaking in a whisper, she asked what he needed.

"I've just heard my wife is being discharged," Brian whispered back.

Dr. Raymond graciously stepped out of the chart room, allowing the door to close.

In contrast to Maureen, Dr. Shirley Raymond was rail thin and imbued with a nervous energy. "Yes," she said. "I was informed of the discharge plans this morning."

"So, this wasn't your decision?" Brian was surprised to learn that she hadn't been involved in the order.

"No, it wasn't. It's apparent to me that Emma still has an active viral infection. She also seems to be somewhat drowsier and more confused. And, as far as I know, neurology hasn't finished evaluating the spasticity that's emerged."

"The current plan is to send her to Hudson Valley Rehabilitation Hospital."

"Oh, I didn't hear that," Dr. Raymond said. She shrugged. "That will work, I guess. She should be under a seizure watch since the encephalitis is still obviously active, and they're capable of doing that at Hudson Valley. Although, if it were up to me, I'd keep her here in an acute care facility."

"I was told she was discharged by a Dr. Graham. Do you know her?"

"Of course. She's one of the kingpins around here."

"Is she a good doctor?"

Dr. Raymond laughed nervously. "That's a strange question. Yes, I guess she is a good doctor."

"To be frank, I'm a little worried. Do you think there is any chance that finances influenced the decision to discharge my wife?"

She shook her head. "No. That's not how we practice medicine. There must be a valid reason Dr. Graham gave the discharge order. Perhaps it's to free up beds for the expected Covid-19 surge."

"That's reassuring coming from you. Well, thank you for talking with me and thank you for taking care of Emma."

"You're very welcome. And good luck. I'm afraid you are in for a long haul with Emma. EEE is a persistent illness."

"Yes, I've gotten that impression," Brian muttered and turned to return to Emma's room, significantly more confused and daunted by these conversations than he was expecting.

CHAPTER 9

August 27

It was just after two in the afternoon when Brian walked out of the Hudson Valley Rehabilitation Hospital and paused on the steps to regroup. He was feeling out of sorts. It had been a stressful morning. Emma had resisted the idea of leaving MMH Inwood, but there had been little he could do, and it was true to an extent that MMH wasn't doing very much in terms of therapy. It was also true that Emma had not had another seizure since the one in the Emergency Department, so maybe the need for seizure monitoring was less important. Plus, the term "rehabilitation" had a nice ring to it as far as Brian was concerned, and he hoped that there would be more opportunity for Emma's walking difficulties to be addressed. But that was before he had seen the hospital.

During the admission process, Brian again had to sign papers giving the name of their insurance carrier and committing to being responsible for all charges. Knowing what he did about Peerless, it was obvious he was accepting even more debt despite having no possible way to come up with the money he already owed.

And if all this wasn't bad enough, Hudson Valley Rehabilitation

Hospital had been a disappointment. In sharp contrast to the renovated MMH Inwood, the building was aged and shabby, especially
Emma's room. And worse still, the number of patients per nurse was
significantly higher than at MMH, meaning Emma probably wasn't
going to be receiving a lot of seizure monitoring or monitoring in
general. Luckily she seemed oblivious to the nature of the hospital
surroundings and had fallen into a deep sleep almost immediately
after she'd been put in her bed and her vital signs were taken. The
transfer procedure had been stressful for her even though MMH had
arranged an ambulance service, and she had been moved in and out
of both institutions on a gurney. The ambulance ride itself had been
only fifteen or twenty minutes, and Brian had been able to ride
with her.

From his perspective, this whole experience of Emma contracting
a disease that he had never heard of from an innocent barbecue had
been a rude awakening. As a conscientious hard worker who followed the rules, he'd always felt reasonably in control. Now it was
the exact opposite. It was as if he and Emma had been poised on a
precipice and didn't know it, and now that Emma had slipped off,
Brian and his family were only holding on by their fingertips. To
make matters worse, he'd never had any inkling that the cost of a
week's stay in a hospital could potentially upend his life thanks
to an unscrupulous health insurance company. It seemed criminal
that he was now almost two hundred thousand dollars in debt and
counting.

Pulling his phone out of his pocket, Brian made a quick call to
Aimée to let her know that Emma had been moved and to ask her to
let Emma's mother know as well. He then passed along the current
visiting restrictions and requirements. Toward the end of the call, he

experienced a sudden and unexpected surge of emotion, bringing him almost to tears.

"Are you okay, Brian?" Aimée asked, detecting a catch in his voice.

"This is all more stressful than I could have imagined," Brian managed after a pause. He'd not shared any of the financial problems with his mother, nor his worry that Emma might have been discharged from MMH because of the bill. "I hope this Hudson Valley Rehab Hospital works out."

"I'm sure it will," Aimée assured him. "I've had a number of friends who have been hospitalized at HVR, and they did well. It's not the Ritz or even MMH, but the staff is friendly and caring."

"They better be, or there's going to be hell to pay." As quickly as his surge of emotion had appeared, it metamorphosed into anger, and he was reminded of his planned visit to the Peerless Health Insurance offices. "Mom, I'm sorry, I've got to go."

"Okay, dear," Aimée said. "I'll let Hannah know that Emma is situated at HVR, and we'll plan out a visiting schedule. You get home and take care of that darling daughter of yours. She needs your attention, too."

Brian disconnected the call, eager to make the visit to Peerless. The question was: How to get there? With his anger ramped up and wanting to get it over with quickly, he decided on the subway. From Inwood it was by far the fastest way to get to Midtown Manhattan.

Ten minutes later he was on the A train thundering south, and as he rode, he thought about the hospital bill that Roger Dalton had emailed to him and that he'd glanced at briefly on his phone while waiting for Emma to be discharged. As Roger had suggested, it was mostly incomprehensible and in code similar to the ED bill, but there were some bits of it that were perfectly understandable and that riled Brian to no end. One of those was an outlandish charge of $970 for a supposed "physical therapy evaluation session."

From the date of the service, Brian distinctly remembered the episode. A young, bouncy, and very friendly woman had appeared at Emma's bedside, gotten her out of bed, and proceeded to merely walk her up the corridor exactly as he had done fifteen minutes earlier. Another was a thirty-dollar charge for a single ibuprofen tablet that Brian had requested for Emma on that same day when she complained of a headache. From Brian's perspective, if such charges were representative of the entire bill, the whole thing bordered on being absurd, if not out-and-out fraud.

From the Columbus Circle express stop it was a relatively short walk to the building on Sixth Avenue where Peerless Health Insurance had their home office. He found it strange to be walking the streets of Midtown Manhattan and seeing so few people. Like on the subway, most of the few people he encountered were masked. Reaching the proper building, Brian thought it a coincidence that it happened to be a few doors down from where Priority Capital was located. Thinking about Priority Capital and Calvin Foster made Brian hope that his proposed budget for the fancy Southampton wedding was being well received, and that he could be on the verge of securing some income.

He had purposely not called ahead to schedule a meeting with Peerless, as he doubted that they would be willing to see him. These days, companies limited physical contact, often preferring phone or, better yet, impersonal email exchanges. Dealing with an unhappy customer like Brian was far easier at a distance, particularly online. Of course, there was still the problem about physically accessing the

Peerless Health Insurance office with the security Manhattan commercial office buildings invariably employed. But Brian still had his duplicate NYPD shield and ID. The fact that his ID card had RE-TIRED under the photo hardly limited its effectiveness in providing access to most everything in the city. Besides, he also knew that many of the NYC commercial office buildings employed retired NYPD officers as guards.

As he negotiated the revolving door, he withdrew his wallet to have it ready. Similar to the street outside, the interior of the building was almost deserted. As he approached the security desk, he was encouraged to see, seated behind a plastic shield, a well-groomed, silver-haired, mildly overweight gentleman who looked the part of a retired cop with his crew cut and mustache. With practiced nonchalance, Brian flashed his ID quickly and the two men exchanged a convivial, knowing greeting, like members of a private club.

"How are you, my friend?" Brian said.

"Fine, thank you," the security man replied with a broad smile. "Are you with Midtown North Precinct?"

"No, ESU."

"Oh, wow!" the guard said. The ESU was highly regarded by the entire NYPD, since they were the ones called in whenever the regular patrolmen confronted a major problem. "How can I help?"

"How about yourself? What was your last command?"

"I retired from Midtown North. It's how I got this job."

"Good for you, but it looks like you're not very busy these days."

The security guard laughed. "It's unbelievable," he said. "It's like a morgue around here. It makes me wonder if it's ever going to go back to normal. So, what can I do for you?"

"I need to talk to someone at the Peerless Health Insurance office," Brian said. "Are many of them here or are they all working from home?"

"A few of them come in. Mostly the brass. None of the secretaries or grunts."

"How about Ebony Wilson?" he asked. "Do you know her, by any chance?"

"Of course I know Ebony. She's one of the ones who comes in every day. Treats me like a person, and always says hello. Not like the Peerless boss lady."

"Are you talking about Heather Williams?" The eccentric and rather outlandish image of the woman in the pretentious foxhunting outfit popped into his mind.

"I don't know her name," the guard said. "I made a point of not wanting to know it."

"Why is that?"

The guard looked to both sides as if to be sure no one was listening, even though the expansive lobby was otherwise deserted. A janitor who'd been wiping down the turnstiles with disinfectant when Brian had first entered had disappeared. "She's extremely snotty and thinks she's better than everyone else. That's my personal assessment. Not only does she not say hello, but she doesn't even acknowledge that I exist. She waltzes through here with her entourage like she's the pope."

"What do you mean, 'entourage'?"

"She's always surrounded by three or four people rushing around her doing this and doing that, fawning over her. It's ridiculous. She doesn't even push her own elevator button. And several of them are armed bodyguards. I know because I had a conversation once with one of them. He's a former marine."

"Armed guards? That's rather surprising," Brian observed. "But are you sure about that? Don't you think maybe this former marine was pulling your leg?"

"I swear on a stack of Bibles," the guard promised. "I'm not exaggerating."

"But why?" It seemed excessive, to say the very least.

"The ex-marine I spoke to says she's become really wealthy. He bragged she's been making ten million a year."

"That can't be true." The idea that the CEO of a small, up-and-coming health insurance company could make that kind of salary seemed ridiculous.

"It's not out of line," the guard insisted. "As a small-time investor, I happen to know that some of the CEOs of the big health insurance companies that I've invested in make upward of twenty million a year."

"Really?" Brian questioned. He never knew that such salaries existed in healthcare, though Emma's astronomical hospital bills were beginning to make more sense. Someone had to benefit.

"It's true. Health insurance companies are good investments. Mark my words."

"I'll give that some thought," Brian replied for lack of another response. He wondered if the security guard was exaggerating. Twenty million for running a company that sold health insurance seemed preposterous.

"You learn a lot being one of the security guards in a building of this size," the guard added.

"I bet you do. How about today? Did you see Ebony Wilson?"

"Oh yeah," the guard said. "She's upstairs."

"Well, she's one of the people I need to talk to."

"Is she in trouble?"

"No, no," Brian said quickly. "I just need to chat with her about Peerless. What floor?"

"Fifty-fourth. Do you want me to call up there and let her know to expect you?"

"I'd rather you didn't. You know the trick. It's often better to catch certain people unawares, because you might learn more."

"Gotcha." The guard gave him a knowing look and a thumbs-up. "Use the turnstile farthest to the left."

"Will do," Brian said as a youthful, casually dressed man in jeans, polo shirt, and tennis sneakers entered through the revolving door. As he passed, he flashed a card at the security guard and headed for the turnstiles.

"Hello, Mr. Bennet," the guard called out. Then to Brian he whispered: "He's with Peerless."

"Now, that might be handy," Brian said, making a rapid decision. Quickly he headed for the visitors' turnstile and pushed through. Hurrying after Mr. Bennet, who had boarded one of the elevators that served floors forty through sixty, he was able to catch the elevator door before it closed.

"Sorry about that," Brian apologized as he stepped in.

"Not a problem," Mr. Bennet replied graciously.

"The guard happened to mention that you are with Peerless Health," Brian said, making it sound like a casual statement.

"I am indeed," Mr. Bennet agreed. "Director of sales. And you?"

"I run a security firm," Brian said. "I'm impressed, and I hope you don't find this offensive, but you look more like a college student than a health company executive."

"I'll take that as a compliment," Mr. Bennet replied with a laugh, tossing a bit of his blond hair out of his eyes.

"I've heard that Peerless is doing very well."

"You heard correctly."

"So, you think the stock is a good investment?"

"It's an excellent investment," Mr. Bennet said. "Especially with the coronavirus pandemic, we're selling short-term health policies like no tomorrow. I'd certainly advise you to pick up some stock if you are in the market."

"Maybe I will," Brian said, nodding his head. "Thanks for the tip."

"You're very welcome."

The elevator came to a stop on the fifty-fourth floor and Mr. Bennet got off. Brian followed right behind. With an entry card, the man unlocked the door into the Peerless suite. A moment later they were standing in front of an empty reception desk in a posh lobby furnished with high-end leather furniture and with a view to the west over Sixth Avenue that included a tiny wedge of the Hudson River. But by far the most dominant object in view was the near life-size painting of Heather Williams dressed in her foxhunting finery.

"Excuse me," Mr. Bennet said, turning to face Brian. "Who are you here to see, if I may ask?"

"Ebony Wilson," Brian answered distractedly. It was hard to take his eyes off the painting, especially remembering the security guard's impression of her personality and narcissism.

"Is she expecting you?"

"Absolutely," Brian assured him. "Can you tell me where her office is?"

"Of course. Follow me!"

After skirting a number of empty secretarial desks, Mr. Bennet stopped at an open door and leaned in. "Ebony, there's someone here to see you."

"Who is it?" Brian could hear her ask.

Mr. Bennet turned to Brian, raising his eyebrows questioningly.

"Brian Murphy," Brian declared as he advanced to the doorway and looked in. In sharp contrast to Roger Dalton, whose deep baritone voice belied his appearance, Ebony Wilson and her assertive voice were well matched. She was an athletic-looking African American woman with a smattering of freckles over her face. Her dark hair was done in a braid, and she was sitting behind a monitor.

"Nice chatting with you, Mr. Murphy," Mr. Bennet called out before continuing on to his office down the corridor.

"Likewise," Brian called after him.

Ebony leaned back in her chair and removed wireless earbuds she used for her phone conversations as a claims adjustment supervisor. She tilted her head to the side as she gave him a studied look. "Brian Murphy?" she questioned. "Do I know you?"

"Somewhat," Brian said vaguely. He stepped into the small office and sat down uninvited in one of two side chairs. "We spoke on the phone about a week ago."

"I speak to people all day every day. You'll have to be more specific. Are you an employee of Peerless?"

Brian laughed mockingly. "No, I'm not an employee of Peerless, and we certainly have never met. We spoke about Peerless denying a claim for an Emergency Department visit at MMH Inwood for my wife. You advised me to request a review, which I did, and which has again been denied. But that's not why I am here."

"How on earth did you get in?" she demanded as she straightened up in her chair.

"I walked in," he said.

"I don't mean how you physically got in. I mean how did you get past security and into our office suite?"

"Mr. Bennet was nice enough to get me in the office," Brian said. "As far as building security was concerned, all I did was show the guard my NYPD ID. Would you like to see it?" Brian leaned forward to allow him to get out his wallet.

"No, I suppose not since you are already here. Okay, so you are a Peerless customer. If you are not here about a claim denial, why exactly are you here?"

"I didn't say it wasn't about a claim denial," he corrected her. "In fact, it is. It's just not about the Emergency Department claim we spoke about. It's now the inpatient hospital bill that I'm concerned about. I've been told today that Peerless will not be covering that either, and I want to know why. This situation is the reason my wife and I made sure we had health insurance: in case one of us had to go to the hospital."

"Maybe you better show me your NYPD ID," Ebony said. "None of this makes sense."

Brian complied, flashing the ID the way he'd done for the security guard, but she wasn't to be fooled, and she demanded to see it up close.

"I see. So you are retired," she said, handing it back. "You hardly look old enough to retire."

"My wife and I started a security company," Brian explained. "She was also an NYPD officer."

"Which I assume is the reason you purchased a Peerless policy."

"That's correct. We were trying to be responsible because we couldn't afford the COBRA premiums that would have allowed us to stay covered by the NYPD health insurance."

"Do you have your Peerless policy number with you?"

"I do," he said, and he gave it to her. She used her computer to bring up the record. As she read, Brian glanced around at the surroundings. Even this small office was opulently decorated, making him wonder what kind of sumptuous, over-the-top quarters Heather Williams occupied. It also made him wonder how such extravagance could be supported by the mere two-hundred-dollars-a-month premium he and Emma had been paying. But then he remembered that when they had bought the policy in December, they'd been told such policies like theirs were selling like hotcakes because a huge number of self-employed people couldn't afford standard health policies that commercial businesses were buying for their employees. And that was before some twelve million Americans lost their jobs and their employer-based health insurance during the pandemic. Even if just a million of those people bought Peerless policies, that could mean $200 million a month revenue for the company.

"Okay, I found your case and have read through the latest adjuster's decision. It's actually pretty simple. Did you carefully read your policy like I suggested during our phone call about the Emergency Department bill? I remember you said you hadn't when you purchased it."

"No, I haven't," Brian admitted. "My wife's illness has taken precedence since we talked."

"Okay, tell me this. Are you aware your policy has a sizable deductible?"

"Of course," he said. "The sales agent let us know that it was ten thousand dollars."

"How about the amount that Peerless would pay per day for hospitalization?"

"I'm not sure I remember that."

"It clearly states in your policy on page thirteen that Peerless will pay a thousand dollars a day after the deductible is satisfied."

Brian suddenly felt embarrassed, realizing what fools he and Emma had been. Although a thousand dollars a day had sounded like a lot of money when they bought the policy, Emma's stay in MMH Inwood had been well over twenty thousand dollars a day.

"So now let's talk about the deductible," Ebony continued. "Are you aware how the Peerless deductible works?"

"I assume so," Brian said. "It means that we are responsible for the first ten thousand dollars. After that, Peerless steps in."

"No, that's not how the Peerless short-term policy deductible works. This is why you should have carefully read your policy, Mr. Murphy. With Peerless Health Insurance the deductible relates to Peerless payments, not to the policy holder's payments."

"I don't follow," he said, confused by all the semantics.

"Peerless doesn't pay the thousand dollars a day until it would have paid ten thousand if there was no deductible. Essentially that means the hospitalization has to be for more than ten days. Starting on the eleventh day, Peerless pays a thousand dollars a day. It is a permutation of the deductible concept devised by Heather Williams, our esteemed CEO, when she was our chief financial officer."

"But that's totally crazy," Brian managed. "That's the opposite of what everyone understands about a deductible."

"Excuse me, but it is very clearly explained in the policy. It's the reason you were advised to read it carefully. All our salespeople make a big point of making sure our customers understand their policies. And it is all spelled out in our extensive promotional materials, which I'm certain you were given."

"Maybe it was described," Brian admitted, yet he still felt cheated and incensed. Actually, he barely remembered how he and Emma had ended up with their Peerless Health Insurance in the first place. Was he the one who had found it or had it been Emma? He didn't know. All he could recall was talking with her about the need to have something for the rare "just-in-case" possibility and that they needed to look into the short-term policies the government was pushing. In many ways they were between a rock and a hard place thanks to a screwy healthcare system dependent on corporate or government employment.

"Is there anything else I can help you with?" Ebony asked. He could tell she was at the end of her patience with his unexpected appearance. "I really have to get back to work, and I have at least a dozen people on hold."

"I have a few more questions," Brian demanded, his rising anger causing him to flush. "I'm staring at a nearly hundred-and-ninety-thousand-dollar bill and counting, which boggles my mind. I had no idea hospitalization was so expensive. But you and your friends here certainly knew since you're in the damn healthcare business. Here's my question: Above and beyond the screwy deductible business, how the hell can you people possibly justify selling a policy that's going to bankrupt a family by only paying a thousand dollars a day? I mean, in contrast to all of us common folk with limited experience with hospitals, all of you insurance types surely know that a thousand dollars a day for hospital costs is equivalent to pissing on a forest fire."

"Just a minute, Mr. Murphy!" she stammered with obvious indignation. "I'm not going to sit here and allow you to verbally abuse me."

"Maybe I should be complaining to someone higher up," Brian said, reining in his anger by recognizing he was talking with a mere functionary. "I apologize for singling you out. But try to understand my situation. I'm facing financial ruin, and maybe the details of my insurance coverage were spelled out in the small print, but as a member of the general public, this seems to amount to a type of fraud. Maybe I should file a complaint of unfair and deceptive business practices with something like the Better Business Bureau."

"Filing a complaint or even instigating a legal action is your right, as I told you a week ago on the phone," Ebony said, partially mollified by his apology and the change of his tone. "But, as I also told you, the chances of anything like that going anywhere positive are just about zero. We here at Peerless are filling a needed niche, as the government has encouraged us to do, at the lowest possible price. Anyone can get health insurance that pays a higher portion, if not all of hospital costs, but insurance is like anything else: You get what you pay for."

"What about arranging for me to have a talk with this esteemed CEO of yours? She's the one who needs to have an idea of what she is doing to real people buying her policies."

Ebony's jaw dropped open in mock shock. "Now, that would be an interesting confrontation," she choked out. "Let me tell you something: Heather Williams is riding the crest of a wave and doesn't talk to mere mortals. I'm doing well with this job and I'm appreciated, but there is no way that even I could arrange to have a meeting with her. Even high-flying investment types often have to pay for her time."

"She sounds charming," Brian said sardonically, also remembering the security guard's description.

"She's a piece of work, no doubt about it. But she is extraordinarily good at what she does. I have to say we are all appreciative of the ride she's engineered for us, especially with the employee stock she's doled out to encourage company patriotism."

Fifteen minutes later and more irritated and strung out than he ever remembered feeling, Brian left Ebony's office. He felt as if he'd accomplished nothing. Reaching the empty Peerless lobby with its vacant reception desk, he collapsed onto one of the leather couches, wondering how much of the expensive piece of furniture his and Emma's premiums had paid for. Adding insult to injury, he found himself staring again at the haughty foxhunting portrait.

A sudden clamor of voices at the far end of the long hallway caught his attention. A few moments later a throng of five people entered the room, heading for the door out to the elevators. Leading the pack was none other than the woman in the painting herself, perhaps having aged maybe five or ten years. In Brian's estimation, she appeared to be maybe a year or two younger than Emma's thirty-four. As she swept past with a determined, rapid gait, she glanced in his direction. For a moment a look of mild disdainful bewilderment flashed across her thin-lipped, carefully made-up face, but she didn't slow down.

"Excuse me! Heather Williams?" Brian called out on a whim. "I need to talk to you. I think you're in need of some moral advice." His unplanned outburst surprised even himself, but it had the desired effect. The Peerless CEO came to a stop at the threshold of the lobby

door that had been opened for her. She turned to treat Brian to a
shocked but clearly contemptuous inspection.

"You are going to give *me* advice?" she questioned with a disbe-
lieving tone. "Who the hell are you?" Her voice was shrill. She was
obviously unaccustomed to being accosted by a stranger, especially
in her own office. "Do you know it costs a thousand dollars a minute
to talk with me?"

"That sounds like a bargain to me," he said as he leaped to his feet.
He wanted to take full advantage of this serendipitous encounter by
looking at her eye to eye. "I was guessing more like two or three
thousand at the very least."

In spite of her obvious irritation, Heather laughed. Apparently,
Brian's mocking humor appealed to her narcissism. From the vantage point of his six-foot-one stature, he guessed she was somewhere
around Emma's five-eight but of much slighter build. What he didn't
expect was that his sudden standing up alarmed two of the four men
in her entourage, including the one who had rushed ahead to open
the lobby door. Both of these men were dressed in dark, ill-fitting
suits and wearing prototypical aviator sunglasses. Instantly it occurred to Brian that the two older men were the bodyguards the
building security guard had described.

As the two men started toward him, reaching under their lapels
presumably for their firearms, Brian instinctively went for the P365
Sig Sauer nine-millimeter automatic pistol holstered in his waist-
band, which he carried religiously ever since he'd been a cop. Brian
was a firearms expert par excellence, particularly with a handgun,
which he had trained with on a regular basis and was fully licensed
to carry. Luckily, in this instance, a potentially bad situation was
averted by Heather, who snapped her hands out laterally to restrain

her overeager escorts. Brian relaxed the fingers wrapped around his gun's grip.

"I repeat: Who are you?" Heather demanded. "And what makes you possibly think you can give me advice?"

"I'm a very, very dissatisfied Peerless Health Insurance customer," Brian answered. And then while poking his index finger accusatorily toward Heather's face, he added: "You should be ashamed of yourself for designing and selling your worthless policies."

Reacting to Brian's possibly threatening hand gesture, the two bodyguards surged forward once more only to have Heather restrain them for the second time. There was little doubt that in his angered state he could more than handle these two mildly overweight, out-of-shape men who looked more like bouncers at a small-town bar than proper security personnel. In his aggravation, he would have actually enjoyed giving in to his bottled-up emotions and taking them down.

"Worthless?" Heather questioned in an overly mocking tone. "I beg your pardon, but thousands of extremely happy investors would tell you how wrong you are. How in God's name did you get in here, anyway?"

"You're the second person who has asked me that question," Brian said, imitating Heather's sarcastic tone. "I merely walked in, which means that not only are you selling morally suspect crap, it seems that you are in dire need of some professional security advice. Luckily, I happen to be an expert in that realm, and I'd be happy to give you one of my cards if you are interested."

"Get the hell out of here!" Heather snapped, pointing to the door to the elevator lobby. "And if you ever venture to come within a hundred yards of me again, I won't restrain my pit bulls."

Despite himself, Brian laughed while glancing briefly at the two supposed pit bulls. "I hope that's a promise, not a warning. But I can tell when I'm not appreciated, so I'll take your suggestion and leave. But, your threat notwithstanding, I have a sense that you are going to hear from me again very soon. You, your attitude, and your company continue to ruin my life. It's just not right, and I'm going to do something about it."

Without looking back, he walked to the door, deriving a bit of satisfaction from the shocked silence his little speech had engendered. Unfortunately, when he got there, he couldn't open it and had to wait until one of the younger men in Heather's entourage came over and used a magnetic card.

"Thank you," Brian said with forced dignity as he strolled out into the elevator lobby.

CHAPTER 10

August 31

Brian awoke Monday morning way before he intended but instantly knew he would not be going back to sleep. It was the characteristic whine of a mosquito that had rudely awakened him. Sitting bolt upright in bed, he listened intently. The sun had yet to come up, but dawn's twilight filled the room with more than enough light for him to see. A moment later he caught sight of the insect as it landed on his upper left arm just above his elbow. For a split second he watched as it prepared to bite. He noticed that it was the same species that had plagued them at their beach barbecue, an Asian tiger, with its characteristic white marks on its black body and legs.

With fear-fueled speed, Brian slapped the insect with enough force to make his arm sting. The blow reduced it to a smudge of blood, suggesting it had already feasted. After using a bedside tissue to wipe off the remains, he bounded out of bed to check the open window. Sure enough, one corner of the screen was not fully engaged in its track, providing an opening to the outside. Brian quickly pulled it in tightly and set the small spring lock in place. With his heart racing, he climbed back into bed on his side and pulled up the covers, marveling at the fact that the Asian tiger mosquito could haunt such a highly urbanized area.

When he'd gone to bed just before midnight, he'd been totally exhausted both mentally and physically. The five or so hours of sleep he'd gotten clearly weren't adequate, yet the confrontation with the pesky mosquito started him thinking. It was depressingly clear to him that there was no guarantee that things were going to improve as he faced another difficult week ahead. Rolling over onto his back, he stared up at the blank bedroom ceiling to make sure no other mosquitoes had gotten in. Although he knew more sleep was out of the question, he didn't get out of bed, preferring to wallow in self-pity and lament his life. He'd never realized how tenuous it had been. Friday had started out bad, when a call from Calvin Foster's executive secretary came in informing him that the October wedding had been canceled until further notice, meaning that even that modest potential income was off the table.

Right after that bit of disappointing news, Juliette had a melt-down while Camila tried to make her eat some breakfast. As if that wasn't bad enough, then Brian started getting a flurry of calls on both the business landline and his mobile phone as well as multiple emails from a company called Premier Collections, which was threat-ening both a lawsuit over the $189,375.86 MMH Inwood bill and a sharp decrease in his credit rating if he didn't immediately set up a payment plan. The harassing communications had shocked him af-ter having had a face-to-face meeting with Roger Dalton just the day before. When he'd tried calling him for an explanation of why it was happening so quickly, he'd had to leave a voice message.

Continuing to stare up at the ceiling with unseeing eyes, Brian wondered how his bill was so astronomical, especially when he considered that MMH Inwood hadn't really done anything besides just watch Emma go downhill. Except for handling the seizure in the ED, they hadn't really treated her, and they certainly hadn't cured her. In many ways, she was worse off when discharged than the day she walked into the Emergency Department. And then to truly add insult to injury, he had gotten three more non-hospital bills by email. The smallest invoice was from the ambulance company, Adultcare, who had had the nerve to charge nine hundred dollars to drive Emma about twenty blocks from MMH Inwood to the Hudson Valley Rehabilitation Hospital. At the time the MMH discharge people had arranged the transportation and if Brian had been given any warning about the cost, he would have driven Emma himself.

And then worse still were two other much larger bills from doctors. The biggest was from the neurologist who was not employed by MMH Inwood but had been asked to see Emma. The cost of his evaluation was $17,197.50. The second bill was for an out-of-hospital cardiologist in the amount of $13,975.13 after a nurse had possibly detected a few extra heartbeats when taking Emma's pulse. In the end, Emma's heart function was determined to be entirely normal, and all this meant was that his debt had reached a staggering $221,448.49.

The blaring of a horn accompanied by an angry shout out on West 217th Street briefly interrupted Brian's thoughts, but a moment later he was back to his musing, specifically about how financially predatory and overly expensive the healthcare industry had become, particularly the hospitals. What he realized was that most people with good insurance, like he and Emma had had when employed by the NYPD, were ultimately complicit in allowing this ridiculous situation to happen. If hospital bills got paid, and of course they did, who cared or questioned how much the costs were, especially if trying to figure them out was practically impossible? Now he saw that such an attitude over time had contributed to allowing prices to climb exponentially, making it a recipe for disaster when someone lost their insurance or had bad insurance like the short-term policies Peerless offered. From his perspective it all amounted to a type of tolerated fraud, seeing as hospitals like MMH Inwood could create their own demand and then charge whatever they pleased. On top of that, less than ethical companies like Peerless could latch on and enjoy the ride while making a fortune.

As bad as Friday had been, Saturday was even more upsetting for Brian. It had started encouragingly enough when Aimée had called early and offered to come over and help with Juliette, whose behavior was getting worse. In many respects Juliette was as attached to her paternal grandmother as she was to her mother, and with Aimée present she'd eaten a decent breakfast for the first time in several days and for a while was her old self and content watching her cartoons. The reprieve gave Aimée and Brian a few moments to talk, which he used to share the disturbing news about Emma's astounding hospital bill. Shocked at the amount, Aimée had suggested he contact a medical billing advocate.

"What the hell is a medical billing advocate?" Brian had asked. "I've never heard of such a person."

"Apparently they help people with hospital bills," Aimée had responded. "I hadn't heard of them, either, but a friend of mine had a problem with an MMH Inwood bill and told me a billing advocate had helped her. The advocate's name is Megan Doyle, and she has an office here. You should let her help you."

Following that relatively pleasant morning and with Aimée

entertaining Juliette, and Hannah expected to join them, Brian had gone to Hudson Valley Rehabilitation Hospital with the intent of spending the day with Emma. His plan was to get a true idea of how much rehabilitation she was actually receiving. But similar to what had happened at MMH Inwood on Thursday, as soon as he had entered HVR, he was told he needed to see Antonia Fluentes in the business office immediately.

With some trepidation Brian complied, but the moment he entered the woman's office, he knew from her body language that trouble was afoot, and she confirmed it immediately.

"It's been brought to our attention that your MMH Inwood bill is outstanding with no payment plan arranged," Antonia said. She stared at him expectantly with dark, piercing eyes framed with equally dark glasses.

"It's only been a few days since my wife's discharge," Brian said evasively.

"But we also have learned that your account has been turned over to collections. As you can imagine, that is not encouraging for us."

"It's not great for me, either," he responded.

"We've also not had a good experience with your insurance carrier, Peerless Health."

"That doesn't surprise me," Brian added.

"I'm sure you can see our dilemma. Due to the pandemic, Hudson Valley Rehabilitation Hospital has been struggling financially, like most healthcare facilities. To be perfectly honest, we are going to need upfront coverage for your wife if we are to continue with her rehabilitation."

"I see," Brian said, feeling like he was taking yet another low blow. "Exactly what kind of figure do you have in mind?"

"Minimally we are looking for two thousand dollars a day for the first ten days. At that point we can reassess the situation and her progress."

"I'm afraid we don't have a spare twenty thousand lying around." He could hardly keep the sarcasm out of his voice.

"I figured that might be the case, so I spoke with our chief medical officer, Dr. Harold Spenser," Antonia continued. "Medically he doesn't see any reason your wife cannot be discharged and have her rehabilitation carried out at home by local physical therapists who will be up to you to retain."

"What about somewhat of a lower advance, say, in the five-thousand-dollar range?" Brian said. "This would be a gesture of good faith to keep my wife here as an inpatient."

"I'm afraid not. Your wife's current bill is already almost five thousand dollars."

At that point the conversation went downhill as he became incensed that Emma's charges could already be at the five-thousand-dollar mark, considering she'd only been there two full days, the shabby state of the facility, what seemed like a lack of staff, and that she'd essentially received no treatment. In the end, it was decided that Emma had to be discharged, and to avoid another thousand-dollar ambulance bill, Brian had to drive her home himself.

Although getting Emma into the car had been a struggle, once they'd gotten underway, she perked up. "Being discharged was unexpected, but I'm looking forward to getting home," she'd said. She was out of breath from the effort of climbing into the car's front seat. There was no doubt her spasticity was worse.

"I can well imagine. We are all going to be thrilled to have you, especially Juliette, who's really missed you."

"I've missed her, too," Emma confessed. "And how about the business? I've been afraid to ask."

"Not good," he told her regretfully. "There was a possibility of a wedding in October out in the Hamptons, but just yesterday it was canceled. Camila is constantly trying to scare up some business with social media."

"How are our finances?" Emma asked.

"Also not good, I'm afraid," Brian said with a wince. He'd not mentioned anything to Emma about the problems with Peerless or the hospital bill and didn't intend to until she was fully recovered, seeing no reason to stress her out.

At first Emma's homecoming had been well received, especially since both Aimée and Hannah were there to greet her with Juliette and Camila. Juliette was obviously thrilled, at least initially. But the bonhomie didn't last, as Emma's physical limitations and precarious emotional state put the festivities to a quick end. She quickly tired, had no patience with Juliette, who needed constant attention and reassurance, and soon just wanted to go to bed and sleep. Getting her up the stairs to the master bedroom became an exhausting ordeal for everyone; although she could walk on the flat with some difficulty, the stairs were almost impossible.

For him it had been the night that was by far the most difficult part, when he was left alone with his ailing wife. Although Emma had slept most of Saturday afternoon and evening, at night she was mostly awake, emotionally unstable, and rather restless, putting Brian's patience to a true stress test. She even managed to fall out of bed around four A.M. On top of that was the difficulty of getting her from the bed to the toilet on multiple occasions. He'd barely slept a wink, and it also made him understand why it had been far better that he'd become a policeman rather than a medic, a notion he had entertained for a short time as a teenager.

Sunday had been spent trying to make the home situation tolerable for everyone. Luckily Hannah had an acquaintance with a late husband who'd been chronically sick and had required a hospital bed with guardrails for the last years of his life. Since she no longer needed the bed, she'd graciously offered it to Brian to install in the second-floor guest room, across from Camila's room. To his great relief, Hannah had insisted she'd spend the night with her daughter to give him a break and a good night's sleep.

The sound of the front door chimes ringing shocked Brian from his recollections of the past few difficult days, and he leaped out of bed, grabbing his robe in the process. As he headed for the stairs, he wondered who in God's name could be ringing his doorbell before eight on a Monday morning.

Grabbing a mask off the console table in the front foyer and looping its strings around his ears, he pulled open the door. His wild rush had been hopefully to prevent whoever was there from impatiently ringing the doorbell yet again. About eight feet away, standing on the top step of a mini flight of stairs in the middle of Brian's front yard, was a white-haired, moderately well-dressed gentleman in a white shirt, poorly knotted tie, and sports jacket. Despite only seeing the man's forehead and his blue eyes through rimless eyeglasses above his face mask, Brian sensed that he vaguely knew the person. The man was holding an envelope in his right hand, although his arms were limp along his sides.

"Can I help you?" Brian asked, trying not to be irritated. It wasn't a convenient time to be bothered, especially with the possibility of rousing Emma and Juliette. Thanks to phones and email, house visits of all sorts were rare these days, especially with the pandemic.

"I apologize," the man said with a mild Irish accent. "Really I do."

The combination of the sound of the man's voice and the other visual cues brought some memories back. "Grady?" Brian questioned, tilting his head to the side to get a slightly different view. "Grady Quillen?"

"Yeah, it's me. Sorry to bother you like this at the crack of dawn."

"It's not a problem. It's not that early, Grady. I was awake, although the rest of the brood is still asleep. What's up?" He recognized him as one of the patrolmen of the 34th Precinct when Brian's father had been the commanding officer. He also knew Grady lived not that far away, on Payson Avenue in an apartment overlooking Inwood Hill Park.

"Believe it or not, I have to ask you if you are Brian Yves Murphy."

"Is this some kind of a joke?"

"I wish," Grady said, looking sheepish.

"How's the family?" Brian asked. "Everybody staying well in this crazy time?"

"Yeah, we're fine and healthy. Thank you for asking, but you are making this harder for me than it needs to be. Are you Brian Yves Murphy?"

"Okay, yes, I'm Brian Yves Murphy. Are you happy?"

"Hardly," Grady said as he handed him the envelope. "After I retired from the NYPD five years ago, I sat around for a few months and drove my wife batty. You know the expression: 'for better or worse but not for lunch.' Then I took a job as a process server for

Premier Collections. It's kept me married and pays for the Jameson. I'm sorry, Brian."

"So, I guess I've been served?" He looked at his name typed on the front of the envelope, and with his background in law enforcement he knew full well what it meant. The fact that Grady had become a process server didn't surprise him in the slightest. Like being a commercial building security guard, being a process server was common for retired New York City patrolmen.

"I'm afraid so," Grady said. "It's a complaint and a summons. I apologize for being the bearer of bad news, but I couldn't refuse just because I know you."

"If you have a few minutes, let's sit and chat," Brian suggested while pointing down toward the ground. "Sorry I can't invite you inside, so this will have to do." He stepped out and sat on the single step leading up to his front door. Moving more than the mandated six feet away, Grady sat on his step and turned sideways. It was pleasant enough with the morning sun and mild temperature, surrounded by Brian's shrub-and-tiger-lily-filled front yard.

After briefly leafing through the papers Grady had provided to confirm what they were, Brian replaced them in the envelope and looked up. "Please don't feel in any way responsible for this. My getting served is not unexpected except for the speed involved. If this was going to happen, I thought I'd at least have the usual thirty days."

"It's been my experience that MMH Inwood has been progressively aggressive with collections over the last few years," Grady said, "but with the pandemic throwing a monkey wrench into the hospital's finances, it's gone through the roof."

"So I've heard."

"To give you an idea, just since March they've had me running ragged, averaging ten to fifteen services a week. And I'm not the only Premier process server. There's three of us."

"Are you guys serving just people in Inwood?" he asked, taken aback by the numbers from just one community.

"The vast majority," Grady said. "There's always a few from Hudson Heights."

"How do you know it's the hospital behind the uptick and not the collections people themselves?"

"That's easy. The hospital actually owns Premier Collections. They are part and parcel of the same organization."

"You're kidding?" Brian questioned, even more shocked by this than by the numbers. Learning that MMH Inwood was in the collection business meant that the hospital was even more predatory than he thought.

"I'm not kidding in the slightest," Grady said. "It's all the brainchild of the hospital CEO, Charles Kelley."

"How do you know?"

Grady gave a short, sardonic laugh. "I know because he's a cult figure around Premier Collections and with the hospital admin people, too. They all think he's a financial genius. He's also liberal with the MMH stock with higher-up employees, meaning, of course, I've been out of luck. I tell you, if I had any extra cash, I'd buy some of the MMH stock because I hear that it's a winner, constantly going up."

In an uncomfortable way, Charles Kelley and his tactics were sounding rather similar to Heather Williams's business model.

"I'd like to meet this Charles Kelley sometime," Grady continued. "I've heard his compensation is more than five million per year. Can you imagine? I think the only hospital CEO who makes more is the guy who runs the University of Pittsburgh Medical Center. He gets over six million. It's crazy."

Knowing the ridiculous amount of money he owed from Emma's seven days of hospitalization, he could now believe it rather easily. He'd never had any idea what an impressive gold mine medical care could be.

"So, what are you going to do about this situation?" Grady asked. "As a friend, I want to make sure you know you have to respond to the summons within thirty days or there will be a summary judgment against you."

"Yeah, I know," Brian said.

"Obviously I couldn't help but see that MMH Inwood is suing you for almost one hundred and ninety thousand dollars. Who in your family needed hospitalization?"

"My wife, Emma," he told him. "She caught a bad mosquito-borne illness while we were on Cape Cod. It isn't contagious, if you are worried."

"I'm not worried," Grady said. "What a bummer. How is she doing?"

"So-so," Brian admitted, unwilling to provide any specifics. "At least she's home."

"I'm glad to hear it. What's the story with your health insurance? I heard you and your wife were with the ESU."

"We were until we retired in December to start our own security company," Brian said. He was getting tired of explaining. "When we retired, we lost our city insurance and were forced to rely on a short-term policy that's not worth the paper it's printed on. They aren't contributing a penny."

"Ouch," Grady said. "Have you talked with a lawyer?"

"Not yet. That would cost more money."

"Money well spent," Grady said. "Take my word."

"I think I'll go back and try to reason with the MMH Inwood business office and come to some understanding."

"From my vantage point the chances of that helping are piss poor. You need a lawyer, because Premier is dogged. I'm telling you: They won't give up, and they'll go after everything, including your house. By the way, this is one of the nicest houses in Inwood."

"We were lucky to get it."

"I'm serious about Premier being hard-nosed. You might know a neighbor of mine, Nolan O'Reilly."

"I know the family," Brian recalled. "What about him?"

"I had to serve him. He ended up losing everything, and his and his wife's salaries have been attached from now until hell freezes over."

"Was that a hospital bill, too?" he asked.

"It sure was, about twice yours. It involved surgery on their son, and to make matters worse, the kid died."

"That's awful."

"I know a lawyer," Grady continued. "He's down on Broadway. A local kid, and he's really good. I gave his name to my neighbor, and he fell over backward trying to help him."

"Is this the neighbor who lost everything?" Brian asked.

"Unfortunately, yes."

"That's not a very good advertisement for your lawyer acquaintance," Brian countered.

"I know it sounds that way, but my neighbor had failed to respond to the original summons, and there had been a summary judgment.

When that happens, it's almost an impossible uphill struggle, so please respond!"

"I'll definitely take care of it. What's the lawyer's name?"

"Patrick McCarthy."

At that moment, he saw Aimée turn into the walkway, carrying a white bag from CHOCnyc, an Inwood French bakery. Both Brian and Grady immediately got to their feet. She stopped when she saw Grady, and like Brian had done earlier, she tilted her head and wrinkled her forehead, obviously recognizing him on some level but struggling to place him.

"Hello, Mrs. Murphy," Grady said to help her. "It's Grady Quillen."

"Oui, Grady Quillen," Aimée repeated. "So nice to see you again."

"I'm sorry about Deputy Inspector Murphy's passing," Grady said, bowing his head.

"Thank you," Aimée responded kindly. "It was a shock to us all." Brian's father had died of a heart attack a year and a half earlier while on the job as commanding officer of the local precinct.

After a few minutes of small talk, Grady went on his way, saying he had more work he needed to do. After he was out of sight, Aimée turned to Brian. "What was he here for so early?"

He waved the envelope. "He's a process server, and he served me. I'm afraid MMH Inwood is already suing me for Emma's care."

"C'est terrible," Aimée said, worry creasing her face. "Why so soon?"

"It is terrible," Brian said, mimicking his mom's French accent. "I feel like my life is coming apart at the seams, and I don't even know where to begin to try to fix it."

CHAPTER 11

August 31

It was just after eleven o'clock in the morning when Brian slowed his running pace as he neared MMH Inwood and then jogged up the driveway. As religious as he'd been about keeping himself in superb physical shape with weight training and cardiovascular exercise since high school, he seriously missed his daily workouts and hoped that with Emma at home and Aimée and Hannah offering to help, he could get back to some semblance of a routine. His mother and Emma's mother certainly had helped that morning and had allowed him and Camila to spend a few hours in the home office brainstorming potential ways to drum up business for Personal Protection LLC. While they were strategizing, several more harassing calls came in from Premier Collections, confirming Grady's assessment of their persistence.

After having been duly served with a complaint and summons, Brian had been eager to see Roger Dalton in the hopes of stopping the collection process, so as soon as he could, with Aimée's and Hannah's blessings, he'd set out. Now as he entered, he wondered if his visit would turn out to be worthwhile. After Grady's estimate that the chances of reversing anything were "piss poor," he wasn't optimistic, but he couldn't see any harm in trying.

As he entered the hospital's swank admin area, he was reminded that he'd always thought of MMH Inwood as a positive asset to the community. Now he was thinking the opposite, especially knowing how many other Inwood residents were being pursued for collection of most likely seriously inflated hospital bills.

Brian had not called ahead, preferring just to show up and plead his case. But he soon began to think he'd made a mistake, as he was subjected to a considerable wait. When he was finally ushered into the office, Roger added to his pessimism by announcing that Brian had better make it quick, as he didn't have much time.

"I'll try to be fast," he said, struggling to control his emotions. He was beginning to hate this thin wasp of a man. "I'm shocked and disappointed that my case has already been turned over to Premier Collections and they are already hounding me. From my memory, that's legally questionable. Besides, you and I have been in continuous contact, and you know that I am taking this situation seriously enough to have made a personal visit to Peerless Health Insurance late last week."

Sighing with boredom and annoyance, Roger tented his skinny, gnarled fingers. "To be honest, I didn't have any choice, not under these trying times. Turning a case over to collections immediately has become standard policy dictated from above when it's obvious the situation is futile, which is what you have led me to believe. You refused to set up an agreeable payment plan. Case closed."

"I can't set up a payment plan in this financial environment with the pandemic going on," Brian said irritably. "My company's income these days is zero."

"That's my point precisely," Roger said. "You are not going to agree to a reasonable payment plan. So we agree."

"What exactly do you mean, 'dictated from above'?"

"Exactly as it sounds," Roger answered.

"How far above?"

"The top."

"Let me ask you this," Brian said. "Does MMH Inwood own Premier Collections?"

"Why do you ask? What difference does that make? You owe what you owe."

"I think it makes a lot of difference," Brian argued. "And your response certainly confirms my suspicion. When you say policy is dictated from the top, I assume you mean the CEO, Mr. Charles Kelley?"

"Obviously," Roger said as if progressively bored by the conversation. "He is the chief executive officer, after all."

"So he must be really hands-on if he's concerned about the nitty-gritty goings-on in the hospital, like collections and speeding up the process."

"Oh, yes," Roger said with emphasis. "Mr. Kelley is the man behind MMH's financial success and massive building campaign. Both this campus and MMH Midtown have been totally renovated, bringing everything up to twenty-first-century standards. All that takes money, so Mr. Kelley has made us, the Business Department, feel as essential to the hospital mission as any other department. Charles Kelley is a superb businessman. Mark my words!"

"I'm beginning to think 'ruthless' might be closer to the truth than 'superb,'" Brian said. "Did you know that I have already been served?"

"I did not," Roger said. "But I'm not surprised. Once an account is moved to collections, I'm no longer involved."

"I'd like to get you reinvolved and hold up the legal maneuvering. Why don't you and I go back to talking about some kind of goodwill payment to carry us through this pandemic?"

"That's not possible." Roger shook his head firmly.

"Why not?"

"Mr. Kelley, the superb businessman he is, has insisted that Premier Collections operate as a separate entity even though owned by MMH Inwood. For accounting and tax reasons, Premier has bought your debt. I'm no longer involved, so you have to deal with them from now on."

"But if Charles Kelley were to give you license to get reinvolved, would that work?"

"Obviously," Roger said with a dismissive laugh, as if that was the most ridiculous idea he'd heard all day. "But that's not going to happen."

"How often does he come here?" Brian asked. He'd noticed that on all his recent visits to the MMH Inwood admin area, Charles Kelley's office and its neighboring fancy conference room were empty.

"Not that often. Maybe once or twice a week. He's mostly at his MMH Midtown office, which is a facility four times the size of this one."

"Is he approachable?" Brian asked. "I mean, could I set up a meeting with him? As good a businessman as you think he is, maybe he should hear from someone in the community being adversely affected by his policies. Ultimately, he must be concerned about the hospital's image in the community, which I think is suffering. I've learned I'm not the only one being sued."

Roger laughed even harder than he had a moment earlier. "You would not be able to arrange a meeting with Charles Kelley," he scoffed. "No way. His time is inordinately valuable. Besides, he doesn't have the time to get involved with individual patient accounts."

"Maybe he should be," Brian insisted. "As a businessman in a service industry, I would think he'd be very interested in the hospital's image. What do you think about me approaching him on my own?"

"He wouldn't waste a minute talking with you," Roger said. "I'm telling you: He's a very, very busy man. Besides, you'd be taking a risk going up to him unannounced."

"How so?" Brian asked.

"He has an armed driver."

"Why would a hospital CEO need an armed driver?" Brian asked. As a security-minded individual, Brian was legitimately interested.

"Because he is an inordinately important man running several large institutions," Roger said impatiently. "It's to protect him from people like you, if you want to know the truth. What a ridiculous question."

"Okay," Brian said, trying to maintain his composure. "Let's move on to another issue. Did you or anyone here make it a point to contact the Hudson Valley Rehabilitation Hospital and report that my wife's hospital bill had been turned over to collections?"

"I can't imagine. It certainly wasn't me, if that is what you are implying."

"Someone did," Brian said. "Last week I was dragged into their business office and presented with an ultimatum: Either I came up with a twenty-thousand-dollar advance or my wife was going to be booted out for the second time because of nonpayment of exorbitant hospital charges."

"I resent that statement," Roger said irritably. "It seems you're implying that your wife was discharged from here because of nonpayment of her bill and that our charges are not appropriate. Both statements are patently untrue, as I've told you before." He stood up. "This meeting is over. I want you to leave, or I am going to call security, and they will throw you out."

For a brief moment of irrationality, Brian fantasized about refusing to leave in hopes of having a half-trained hospital security person or two try to throw him out. Instead, feeling chagrined at being summarily dismissed after he'd made a sincere effort to come in and resolve the hospital bill problem, Brian stormed out of Dalton's office. Cursing under his breath and feeling a searing anger at a system designed to make money more than anything else, he strode toward the door leading into the hospital lobby. But on his way out he couldn't help but stop and stare in at Charles Kelley's empty office and fancy glass-walled conference room.

Motivated by morbid curiosity, Brian walked in through the open office door. He was looking for the equivalent of Heather Williams's ostentatious foxhunting portrait, and he wasn't disappointed. Hanging above a faux fireplace was a nearly full-sized painting of a blond-haired middle-aged man in a three-piece business suit, arms folded, leaning up against an impressive desk similar to the real one in the room. Just to be certain, Brian approached to read the engraved plaque. It was indeed Charles Kelley. Although pictorially tame in contrast to Heather's outlandish portrait, Charles's painting conveyed the same sense of entitlement and privilege, with an equally haughty, superior-than-thou smile. "Two birds of a feather," Brian observed out loud as he shook his head in disgust.

"Excuse me!" a voice called. "What are you doing? You are not allowed in here!"

Brian turned to face a secretary clearly outraged at his violation of Charles Kelley's inner sanctum.

"Just enjoying the artwork," Brian said with a fake, innocent smile.

A few minutes later as he was passing out through the main entrance's revolving door, with his irritation and anger still at a boiling point, Brian thought again about the two CEOs and how they seemed to be poster children for what was wrong with American medicine and unbridled entrepreneurial capitalism. And as a doer, he knew he couldn't just passively allow their greediness to go unchallenged and dictate the unraveling of his life. He had to do something. He just didn't know what.

CHAPTER 12

August 31

As Brian turned from Park Terrace East onto West 217th Street and slowed to a walk on his torn-up street, what was becoming progressively clear to him was the need to retain a lawyer despite the added cost. The question was: Should he use the counselor Grady suggested, who had some experience dealing with MMH Inwood, or should he use a lawyer from the white-shoe firm he and Emma had employed to set up Personal Protection LLC? As he climbed the stairs in the middle of his front yard where Grady had been sitting that morning, he decided to give Patrick McCarthy a try, as the cost would undoubtedly be appropriately and remarkably less. But that wasn't the only reason. Brian also thought that Patrick's experience with MMH could be significant in addition to his being a local boy. In a community like Inwood, being part of the neighborhood made a difference.

Reaching the top step and despite his preoccupations, he paused. He couldn't help but appreciate his surroundings. He was standing with his profusion of riotously beautiful orange tiger lilies flanking both sides of the walkway, which had been planted by the house's previous owners in lieu of a minuscule lawn. After admiring the flowers, he then looked up at his home with its striking Tudor revival mixture of brick and stonework. He and Emma loved the house and had admired it during their childhoods. Brian was proud that they owned it, but now, with MMH Inwood's Premier Collections on his case, he knew that the property was potentially in jeopardy. The thought shocked him back to reality and reawakened the anger he'd felt in Roger Dalton's office, forcing him to try to think about something else.

The something else was what he would be confronting once he entered through the front door. The one positive thing that he hoped would have resulted from Emma's being kicked out of two hospitals was that her presence at home would have drastically improved Juliette's attitude and behavior. But that hadn't happened. If anything, Juliette's apparent anxiety was even worse because Emma's illness made it difficult for her to meet her daughter's needs. As a result, Juliette was back to refusing to eat, was again voicing vague bodily complaints, and was displaying frequent temper tantrums.

Brian's worst fears were substantiated the moment he entered through the front door. Standing in the foyer and removing his shoes, he could hear both his wife and his daughter distantly sobbing and complaining, one from the kitchen and the other from the upstairs guest room. Flipping a mental coin of which situation took precedence, he first went into the kitchen. Juliette was sitting in the breakfast nook and Camila was at the sink washing a frying pan. For a brief moment Brian and Camila exchanged a glance and Camila rolled her eyes.

He slid into the banquette alongside Juliette. In front of her on a plate was a freshly made grilled cheese sandwich. "What's the matter, my sweet?" Brian asked. Juliette cried harder.

"She said she was hungry for a grilled cheese," Camila said. It was obvious her patience was being tested. "Now she won't eat it." Camila finished with the pan and then turned to face the room, leaning back against the sink arms akimbo.

"Why are you not eating?" he asked his daughter.

Choking on her tears, Juliette managed: "I don't feel good."

"I'm sorry, sweetheart," Brian said. He looked over at Camila, who was at her wits' end. "Why don't I spend a little time with her?"

"I'd appreciate that," Camila said, and immediately left the room.

"If you don't want to eat, what do you want to do?"

"I want to watch cartoons with Bunny." Bunny was propped up against her as per usual.

"Why don't you?" He pushed the TV remote in Juliette's direction.

"Camila said I couldn't until I finished my sandwich."

Brian guessed there had been a mini test of wills, which wasn't un-common or unusual considering both individuals' personalities. He took the remote and turned on the TV. "What do you mean when you say you don't feel good?" Brian was curious about Juliette's ongoing long list of mild complaints, which had started with Emma's seizure and hospitalization, and had only gotten worse since her homecoming.

Juliette rubbed her hand vaguely around her stomach, which is what she'd done previously when he had asked for specifics. "And my head hurts."

"I'm sorry you are not feeling well. Does Bunny have the same symptoms?"

Juliette nodded.

"The more I check out that grilled cheese sandwich, the better it looks," Brian said. "Do you mind if I have a bite?"

Juliette pushed the dish in his direction. Brian took a bite and chewed thoughtfully. "Not bad! Actually, really good! Maybe you should let Bunny give it a try."

After offering the sandwich to Bunny to take a bite, Juliette took one herself. Brian purposefully didn't comment. Instead, he was content to just sit with her and enjoy a portion of a *Curious George* episode. As they watched, Juliette toyed with her food without eating any more, until Camila eventually returned.

"I'm sorry," Camila said. "I don't know what came over me."

"Don't be silly," he said, waving her apology away. "I understand completely. We're all under stress."

"I think you'd better see if you can help Aimée and Hannah. They're having a difficult time with Emma."

"Right!" Brian slid out from the breakfast nook. The whole time he'd been in the kitchen, he'd occasionally heard distant sobbing and raised voices. With some apprehension about what he was going to face, he climbed the stairs. If both Aimée and Hannah were struggling, he thought the chances he could help were mighty slim.

The hospital bed was in the center of the room with the head pressed up against the wall between the two windows that looked out over the driveway and the neighboring house. The guest room bed, where Hannah had spent the night, had been pushed back against the common wall with the hallway. Aimée was on one side of the hospital bed and Hannah on the other, while Emma was lying in the bed with her upper body on a towel. Her face was streaked with tears, and a basin with soap and water was on a stool on Hannah's side. As Brian entered and approached the foot of the bed, Hannah draped a towel over Emma's midsection.

"She's refusing to let us bathe her," Hannah explained with irritation.

To Brian it was clear that everyone in the room was emotionally overwrought. The question was: What to do?

"I want to take a shower," Emma complained, her voice catching. "They won't let me!"

"It's too dangerous," Hannah lectured. "You are not walking right, and you might fall. Then you'd be worse off than you are now."

"It's true," Aimée added.

"How about a bath in the master bathroom?" Brian offered. It was clear Emma was feeling ganged up on, and the guest room bath only had a shower.

"That might work, but only if she lets us get her there and then back to bed," Hannah stated as the domineering mother she'd always been.

"How about you guys take a coffee break?" he suggested, trying to be diplomatic toward Aimée and Hannah. Since he was highly dependent on their help, the very last thing he wanted to do was offend them in any way. "I think I'd like to have a few moments with my wife."

Aimée and Hannah exchanged a questioning glance, then reluctantly agreed. They filed out without another word. Hannah, who was the last to leave, closed the door behind her.

"I don't want to be here," Emma said, surprising Brian. Over the last few days, she'd been suffering various stages of confusion. But now she sounded not only oriented, but lucid and almost like her old self. "I feel that I'm getting worse, not better. I need to be back in the hospital so I can be treated to get back to normal."

Brian nodded but struggled with what to say. After he had read that the vast majority of encephalitis survivors ended up with serious neurological deficits, he was reluctant to bring up the issue of what getting back to normal was going to mean. He also wasn't prepared to explain to her why it wouldn't be possible to get her back into MMH Inwood, even if that was what she preferred and even if it made the most sense medically. The whole situation was much too complicated and heartbreaking.

"Besides, I'm a big burden being here at home," Emma continued as new tears formed in the corner of her eyes.

"You are not a burden," Brian said, trying to protest but knowing in many ways that her presence was more difficult than he had expected. He gave her a hug and then gripped her hand. "And your mother and my mother are thrilled you are here. They see it as an opportunity, certainly not a burden. They're happy to help."

Taking advantage of her sudden lucidity, he broached the subject of Juliette. Brian could tell that she was horrified to learn that her actions since arriving home on Saturday had exacerbated Juliette's behavioral problems.

"I had no idea," Emma said regretfully. "I hardly remember anything since I've been here, which is scary."

"She's missed you terribly. If I had to guess, I think it's mostly from having witnessed your seizure in the car. That's frightening for anyone, especially a four-year-old who's as close to her mother as Juliette is to you."

"Oh, gosh! I'll have to make it up to her. It just makes me feel awful, the poor thing. She's been through a lot."

"It's certainly not your fault," Brian said. "But anything you do or say will undoubtedly help."

Without any warning, Emma pulled her hand away from his and slapped her palm to her head, gripping herself hard enough that her forehead wrinkled and knuckles blanched. At the same instant, her other hand noisily grasped one of the bed's metal guardrails. Shocked by the sudden motion and noise, Brian blinked and retreated a full step backward.

"What's going on? What happened? Are you okay?"

Emma withdrew her hand, blinked, and looked over at him. "Wow! That was strange. I guess I'm okay. I just had a sudden jolt, and now I have a headache."

"Do you want me to get you something? An ibuprofen?"

"No, I'm okay. I just feel a little odd, and the headache is already going away."

Brian moved back alongside the bed and gripped Emma's arm. "Are you sure?"

"Yes, I guess." She blinked several times. "What I'd like to do is get this ridiculous bath conundrum over with. As much as I hate to admit it, my mother is correct about it being dangerous to try to shower in my current state. I don't want to fall, nor do I want to burden them with giving me a bed bath like I'm a child."

"Okay, I'll run the bathwater," he said. "And then can I call the mothers back? They are desperate to help."

"I guess. Sure. Call them back! Meanwhile, put down one of the guardrails so I can sit here for a few minutes on the side of the bed to adjust to being upright. What will you be doing while I take a bath?"

"If you don't mind, I'll spend a little more time with Juliette."

"Good idea," Emma said, sounding like her old self. "Tell her that I look forward to seeing her after my bath."

"I'm sure she'll like to hear that," Brian said, giving his wife's arm a reassuring squeeze.

CHAPTER 13

August 31

A fter spending nearly a half hour with Juliette watching *Ask the StoryBots* and getting her to eat the rest of her grilled cheese sandwich, Brian was glad she seemed back to near normal. When she and Camila began coloring together, Brian had checked on Emma's situation before retreating to the home office. His plan was to try to get an idea of what they would be able to cover with their current depleted cash reserves if they were forced to endure the entire fall season with few or no security gigs, which was how it was beginning to appear. The reality was that by the New Year, they were going to be in bad shape even with Camila gracious enough to be willing to defer receiving her salary. The thought of losing her, especially under the current circumstances with Emma and Juliette, was painful.

While deep in his depressing thoughts, a sudden nerve-shattering, shrill scream reverberated around the room, sending a shot of adrenaline through Brian's body and propelling him out of his desk chair and into the hallway. Instantly he could tell the continued shouts were coming from above, although already there was an answering softer wail from the kitchen. Brian hit the stairs at a run and within a blink of an eye he'd reached the guest room. Inside he found both Aimée and Hannah frozen like statues with their hands clasped over their mouths and eyes thrown open to their limits.

Within the hospital bed Emma was in the throes of yet another full-blown seizure, with her back arched grotesquely and her arms and legs thrashing. Most disturbing of all, her head was repeatedly hitting against the bed's protective metal rails and making a horrific clamor. Without a second's hesitation Brian rushed to the bedside and pulled his convulsing wife more into the center of the bed to prevent any head trauma. With Brian's arrival, the mothers' screams trailed off.

"Thank God you came," Aimée wailed. She stepped closer to the bed. Hannah stayed away, her hand still clasped over her mouth.

"What happened?" Brian managed as he forcibly kept Emma away from the bedsides and struggled to roll her on her side, so she didn't choke. As muscular and athletic as Emma was, it took all of Brian's considerable strength.

"I don't know! Nothing particular. She'd had her bath, and we'd managed to get her back into the bed, which wasn't easy. It did make her really upset. Could that have caused this?"

"I can't imagine," Brian said, struggling to keep Emma centered in the bed and on her side. He noticed she was turning slightly blue from her breathing being suppressed.

"Should I find something to put in her mouth so she doesn't bite her tongue?"

"No, it's not necessary," Brian said. "That's an old wives' tale. It's enough to keep her on her side and keep her from injuring herself."

"Should one of us call an ambulance?" Hannah asked frantically.

She'd recovered to a degree but still hadn't moved from where she had backed up.

Brian didn't answer immediately because he didn't know what to do and keeping Emma centered was taking all his attention. He assumed the seizure would stop just as it did when she'd had a similar fit in the car on the way back from the Cape. But as the minutes ticked by, Brian got progressively frantic, especially since she was only getting bluer in the face.

"Hannah!" Brian yelled over his shoulder. "Go ahead and call an ambulance!"

Glad to have something to do, Hannah struggled to get her phone out of her pocket. She hit emergency and dialed 911, then put her phone to her ear.

"Tell the operator it could be a status epilepticus!" Brian shouted. "Tell them that an ALS ambulance is needed."

"What's an ALS ambulance?"

"Advanced life support!" Brian shouted back.

Since Emma's convulsions were still making considerable noise in the hospital bed, Hannah stepped out into the hallway. A moment later, with the phone still pressed against the side of her head, she returned and called out to Brian: "How long has the seizure been going on?"

"I don't know," Brian cried. "Say five minutes."

Hannah left again but was back quickly to stand next to Aimée. "Okay, an ALS ambulance is on its way."

Brian didn't answer. His concerns were quickly mounting as his wife was even more blue than she'd been just a few moments earlier. "Hurry, please!" he said under his breath.

"C'est très inquiétant!" Aimée said, catching Brian's words despite the noise Emma was making.

"Of course it's worrisome!" Brian responded irritably at what he thought was a foolish thing to say.

Suddenly a pitiful scream crying "Mommy!" penetrated the clatter Emma was making in the bed. All eyes turned to the doorway to see Juliette's form silhouetted against the backlight.

Aimée was the first to react, and she rushed to the doorway and guided Juliette away with soothing words. A moment later Camila appeared, taking in the commotion. "I'm so sorry," she blurted out. "I turned my back just for a second, and Juliette was out of the kitchen."

Brian didn't answer. As the seconds ticked by and Emma's lividity deepened, he was getting more and more concerned, since Emma's seizure was now at least twice as long as her first. "Someone should go down to the front door and let in the ambulance medics!" he shouted to no one in particular.

"I'll go," Camila said quickly, glad to do something to appease her guilt. She disappeared before anyone could respond.

"Will the medics be able to stop the seizure?" Hannah asked nervously. Though clearly still distraught, she'd recovered enough to come around the bed and was standing across from Brian.

"Who the hell knows!" Brian snapped insensitively. He was becoming so concerned himself that he wasn't thinking properly.

After what seemed like hours but had been only ten to fifteen minutes, undulating sirens could be heard. It was music to Brian's ears. From the sounds he could tell there was more than one vehicle, which surprised him. Quickly the sirens reached a crescendo, and then trailed off and stopped, indicating the vehicles were outside. A few minutes later four medics, one woman and three men, rushed into the guest room carrying a wide variety of equipment, including a stair chair used to get patients up and down flights of stairs. All of them were outfitted in full protective gear due to the pandemic.

The woman, clearly in charge and taking command, crowded Brian to the side. The noise from Emma's thrashing became louder. "I'm Alice, a paramedic, and this is George, my partner," she said quickly, motioning to the man who had gone to the other side of the bed. He was carrying an instrument case. "How long has the patient been convulsing?"

"I'm not sure," Brian admitted, but he knew it was important to give an answer. "Probably more than twenty minutes." Brian, along with Hannah, backed up into the doorway leading out into the hall.

"Okay!" Alice said, looking at George. "Break out the Arrow Intraosseous drill."

"What do you want for the injection?" George yelled as he opened the case and took out what looked like a normal carpenter's drill.

"Versed, five milligrams," Alice said. Then, looking at the two other medics, she added: "Tom, I need a glucose! And, Bill, set up an oximeter! She's looking way too cyanotic. And set up oxygen with a nasal cannula."

"I can't watch this," Hannah said, and fled to find Aimée, Juliette, and Camila.

Brian stayed riveted where he was. Although worried sick about Emma, he couldn't help but be impressed and reassured with the speed and confidence the medics were displaying. Most impressive was how much modern medics could do in the field. In olden times, meaning just a decade or so earlier, ambulance drivers were just that: drivers. They went out and brought victims to the hospital for care.

Nowadays it was totally different, with paramedics starting lifesaving treatment right at the scene just like they were doing here. He was hopeful that they'd be able to stop the seizure quickly.

To Brian's great relief, within only a minute or so after the intraosseous injection, Emma's agonizing full-body contractions slowed and then mercifully disappeared altogether. Quickly the medics took her vital signs. Alarmingly, Brian could see that Emma hadn't regained consciousness despite the seizure having stopped.

"Pulse is steady and blood pressure is low," Alice said, removing her stethoscope from her ears. "How about her oxygen level?"

"Not great," George said. "Below ninety but she seems to be breathing okay."

"Let's hook up an ECG and get her into the stair chair," Alice said. "Come on! Move it! We have to get this one to the ED now!"

Tom and Bill picked up the stair chair and brought it next to the hospital bed, which gave Brian an idea of the hierarchy with the medics. Alice and George were paramedics, manning the ALS ambulance, and Tom and Bill were EMTs probably manning a BLS ambulance, or basic life support. As Tom and Bill organized the safety straps in preparation for securing Emma in the carrier, Alice and George collapsed the hospital bed's rails in unison. The moment they did, almost as if in response, Emma exploded into another full-blown seizure.

"Draw up another ten milligrams of Versed!" Alice barked while she and George made sure Emma didn't convulse herself off the bed now that the side rails were lowered. A few seconds later Alice was handed the appropriately filled syringe, which she used to inject the drug into the cannula still positioned into Emma's marrow cavity. Emma's convulsions immediately began to slow and then stopped.

Alice was pleased until she tried to take Emma's blood pressure, at which point she realized that Emma had no blood pressure and no pulse, even though the ECG that George had attached was showing a slow but regular heartbeat. She wasn't breathing, either.

"Good lord!" Alice exclaimed. "We're looking at PEA. Start CPR stat!"

George climbed up onto the bed to start chest compressions. Alice took an ambu bag from Tom, attached the oxygen line to it, and then started respiring Emma.

Brian was horrified at this sudden turn of events, watching his thirty-four-year-old wife being given CPR and knowing she was at death's door. It was as if he was caught in a nightmare and couldn't wake up. Nor could he even move.

"How the hell could she have PEA?" George demanded between compressions.

"I don't know for sure, but I suspect loss of vascular resistance," Alice said. "Tom, draw up one milligram of epinephrine and give it stat."

"Circulatory collapse from anoxia?" George asked. He paused momentarily to allow Tom to connect a syringe to the tibial cannula.

"Yes," Alice said. "This is the kind of case where I wish to hell we had the capability for some kind of emergency electroencephalographic tracing to be one hundred percent, but that's my guess. Well, more than my guess. It's the only explanation."

Despite feeling like he wanted to run away and hide, Brian couldn't move. Knowing things had just gone from bad to worse, he was desperate to at least understand what was happening, so he managed to lean toward Bill, who for the moment was idle. "What's PEA?"

Obviously distracted, Bill still turned to Brian. "Pulseless electrical activity," he said. "The heart's trying to beat, but it can't. It usually means there's little or no blood coming into the heart because it's all pooled peripherally due to circulatory collapse."

Before Bill could explain more, Alice called out to him to run down on the double and bring up the Lucas CPR, a battery-driven cardiac compression device. As Bill headed out the door, he had to dodge Hannah, who was on her way in. Fearing what she was about to see, Brian intercepted her, blocking her view of the spectacle taking place.

"What's happening?" Hannah said, trying to peer around Brian's body. "How is Emma doing? Has the seizure stopped?"

"It's important for you and everyone else to stay out of the way," Brian cried out, purposefully evading Hannah's question. "Where is Aimée?"

"She's in the kitchen with the others. I just want to be sure Emma is okay."

"They are attending to her," Brian said evasively. "Really, it's better for you not to be here." To back up what he was saying, Brian herded Hannah out the door into the hallway. At that moment Bill was rushing up the stairs carrying the Lucas device, and he squeezed past into the guest room. "They'll be taking Emma to the hospital very shortly," Brian added. "You join the others. I'll go along with Emma if possible, and I'll call you guys just as soon as I can."

"All right," Hannah said reluctantly, and backed up a few steps. She then fled down the stairs.

When Brian returned to the guest room, he could hear from Alice's order that Tom was giving yet another dose of epinephrine, a major cardiovascular stimulant, meaning the first dose probably hadn't had any effect. Stepping over to the foot of the bed, Brian spoke to

Alice, who, with George, was rapidly setting up the Lucas. "I've had EMT training," Brian said. "Can you tell me what's happening here?"

"Sorry. We've got to get this patient out of here. I don't have time to explain."

Once they had the Lucas machine giving the chest compressions, they transferred Emma from the hospital bed to the stair chair. It was obvious to Brian that these people had prior experience working together since everyone knew their role without a lot of talk or direction. Then with Alice walking alongside and doing the breathing, Tom and Bill maneuvered the stair chair out of the guest room, down the stairs, and out the front door. George brought up the rear carrying the rest of the equipment. Brian followed, grabbing a face mask off of the foyer's console table and putting it on. Outside, a few of the neighbors who'd come out of their homes in response to the sirens silently watched as Emma was rapidly loaded into the ALS ambulance. For Brian there was a sense of unreality about the whole scene, especially with everyone wearing face masks. It was as if he were participating in a science-fiction horror movie. Alice leaped in the back to ride with Emma. George started for the cab, but Brian grabbed his arm.

"She's my wife," he rasped. "Can I ride in the ambulance?"

"Of course," George said. "Hop in!"

As Brian climbed into the front of the ambulance, he felt even more like he was caught in a nightmare that he couldn't escape. The fact that his wife was in the back, fighting for her life, seemed so far-fetched that it couldn't possibly be true.

CHAPTER 14

August 31

Riding in the ambulance with the siren wailing was a true déjà vu for Brian, reminding him of countless trips he'd made in one of the ESU heavy vehicles speeding out to handle some kind of disaster like an active shooter or a hostage incident. When you were a member of the NYPD ESU, most every call was a serious event, which required being prepared for the worst. The good and bad part of that was it was never boring like being a patrolman could be. As the ambulance drew closer to MMH Inwood, he found himself wishing he was back on the force and in an anonymous ESU transport, as it would mean Emma wasn't in the back struggling for her life.

George and Alice had used the radio to let the MMH Inwood Emergency Department know what they were facing, namely a patient in extremis and receiving CPR. Brian heard the back-and-forth exchanges with growing alarm. What tormented him was Alice's request for an emergency electroencephalogram with neurological consult. He knew that was out of the ordinary for someone with a run-of-the-mill cardiac arrest and receiving CPR.

At the ED receiving bay, a group of doctors, nurses, and orderlies, all in full personal protective gear and face shields, were waiting, including a rugged-looking, slim, white-haired man and the ranking emergency physician on the shift, Dr. Theodore Hard. By the time Brian had quickly climbed out of the ambulance's cab, Emma was already on her way inside with the Lucas apparatus pumping and Alice still respiring her with the ambu breathing bag. Brian had to run to catch up. He knew he probably wasn't supposed to follow, but he did anyway, and in the commotion, no one questioned his presence despite the fact that he was the only person without an impermeable protective gown and face shield.

The entire group raced into one of the Level 1 trauma rooms, where Emma was transferred from the ambulance gurney to the table. Brian stayed in the background while Dr. Hard yelled orders to set up an ECG, place an oximeter, and start an intravenous even though the tibial cannula was still in place. The oximeter gave a reading of 95 percent, suggesting that the CPR had been effective. The moment the electrocardiogram blip appeared, tracing across the monitor, everyone could see there was electrical activity, but it was obviously not normal. It was also quickly determined that when the Lucas was switched off, there was no pulse and no blood pressure. Instantly they reinstated CPR with manual compressions while Alice, who had not stopped using the ambu bag, quickly summarized for Dr. Hard what had happened in the victim's home and in the ambulance, listing the medications that had been given and the approximate duration of the initial seizure. She made a point of emphasizing how cyanotic the patient had been, and then described how surprised she was to be confronted with pulseless electrical activity after the second seizure and what she thought it meant.

"I think you are probably correct," Dr. Hard said. He'd been nodding as Alice had related what they'd done. After Alice finished her rapid synopsis, he took a small penlight from his pocket, bent over, and checked Emma's pupils. "Uh-oh! No reaction whatsoever," he stated as he straightened upright. "That's not encouraging, to say the least. It suggests no brain stem reflexes. Okay! Let's get the neuro guys down here and do an emergency electroencephalogram. Meanwhile, continue the CPR and draw blood for electrolytes, glucose, and troponin just to be sure."

As the only person in normal street clothes, Brian felt that he stood out like a sore thumb and was expecting to be asked to leave at any moment. Taking advantage of a new flurry of activity, enacting Dr. Hard's latest orders, Brian glanced around the trauma room, quickly spotting a long, white doctor's coat hanging on the back of a door. Trying not to garner attention, he walked over, lifted the coat from its hook, and slipped it on. It was unreasonably snug, but he couldn't be choosy. He was aware there was a name tag, but he couldn't make it out upside down. So attired, he felt considerably less out of place and only hoped no one asked him any difficult medical question, which would surely expose him as an outsider.

A few minutes later Alice and George informed Dr. Hard they had to call in their home base and be available for their next run. After they'd gathered their belongings and said goodbye to all, George recognized Brian despite the white coat and approached.

"Wait a minute, are you a doctor?" George asked, momentarily confused. He leaned forward and read the name tag on Brian's doctor's coat. "Dr. Janice Walton? I don't think so. I'm sorry, but you really shouldn't be in here."

Brian started to desperately explain that he needed to be with his wife.

"Sorry," George repeated. "I can only imagine how wrenching this must be for you, but you aren't allowed back here." He called out to one of the ED nurses named Tamara Reyes, who came over immediately. George explained that Brian was Mr. Murphy, the patient's husband.

"Good lord! Have you been watching all this?" Tamara said, eyeing him as he struggled out of the doctor's coat and returned it to its hook. "You poor, poor man. How did you get in here? Oh, never mind. Follow me! I'll take you out to the lobby. You should have gone out there to sign in your wife."

Resigned to having been discovered and mildly surprised he'd managed to stay undetected as long as he had, Brian followed Tamara. Out in the lobby there was a line of people waiting to check in, but Tamara ignored them and called out to one of the clerks. She introduced Brian as Mr. Murphy, the husband of the CPR victim, and told her to get all the info and a signed release pronto.

For the next fifteen minutes he gave all the usual information, including the Peerless policy number. As he did so, he wondered how Peerless might try to evade covering this emergency visit since Emma certainly hadn't walked in. He also wondered if the hospital computer would immediately spit out that he owed the institution almost two hundred thousand dollars when the clerk entered his name. If it had, the clerk didn't let on. After Brian signed what he needed to sign, he was free to find a place to sit. He chose a spot at the far end of the room, as far as possible from any other people.

Time dragged. Minutes seemed like hours. At one point he took out his phone to call home, more just to connect than anything else since he didn't have anything yet to report. As he held his phone, he noticed his hand was trembling. Try as he might, he couldn't stop it, and he realized it was because every muscle in his body was contracted. Changing his mind about calling anyone, he used his phone to check his email, but he did so with unseeing eyes. He couldn't concentrate. What he was really attempting to do was occupy his mind so as not to think about what was going on back in the trauma room, yet it was impossible. In his mind's eye he kept seeing the horrifying image of Emma being given CPR. From his EMT training and experience as a police officer, he knew all too well what that could mean if the patient didn't respond immediately.

In an attempt to avoid thinking the worst, Brian let his eyes wander around the ED waiting room. It was moderately busy as per usual. In contrast to him, no one seemed to be in an agitated state, which only made him feel worse. Then he suddenly saw Dr. Hard, who had just materialized from the depths of the Emergency Department. The doctor paused, and after a moment surveying the room, his eyes locked on to Brian's. He then immediately headed in his direction with a determined stride.

Assuming the man was coming to see him, Brian quickly rose to his feet. As the doctor approached, Brian's mind, which was trying desperately to divert his attention away from reality, decided that without his protective gown and with his lean and lanky body the man looked more like a cowboy hero in an old Western movie than a doctor in a New York City Emergency Department. Yet, unfortunately, he didn't appear as if he was coming to save the day. With his mask covering most of his face, Brian couldn't see the man's expression, but the way he was walking suggested a disturbing gravity. Fearing the worst, he tried to steel himself.

Dr. Hard stopped six feet away. "Are you Brian Murphy, husband of Emma Murphy?" he asked. He spoke with an aura of seriousness and empathy that cut to the chase.

"I am," Brian managed. His throat had gone bone dry.

"I'm afraid I have very bad news for you," Dr. Hard said. "Would you please come with me?"

BOOK 2

CHAPTER 15

August 31

Squinting his eyes, Brian walked out of the MMH Inwood Emergency Department into the glare of the late summer sun and then hesitated on the sidewalk. He was overwhelmed and had never felt so much in a daze in his whole life. Was he locked in a terrifying dream with no escape? If it was reality, was he depressed or furious? It was difficult to decide as his mind flipped back and forth from one extreme to the other.

Just an hour before, Dr. Hard had led him back into the depths of the Emergency Department, coming to a stop outside of the trauma room where the paramedics had taken Emma. After telling Brian he had very bad news for him, he'd not said anything until that moment. Brian had known what was coming and had tried to brace himself.

"We ran an emergency EEG, which is an electroencephalogram, on your wife, which is a recording of brain waves."

"I know what an EEG is," Brian had said irritably, not yet ready to hear what else the doctor had to say.

"Your wife had a flatline EEG, including no activity from the brain stem, which is responsible for basic life function. What we believe is that her status epilepticus had gone on too long, depriving her brain of oxygen for a protracted period."

Although Brian had suspected as much, Dr. Hard's words were like lightning bolts and suddenly the meaning was clear: Emma was dead. A seizure caused by brain inflammation from a disease carried by a mosquito had killed her. To him, the odds seemed impossible. Was human life really so fragile and tragic? The question kept reverberating in his mind, as did Emma's last wish to be readmitted to the hospital, where she could have been treated immediately for her third seizure and thereby might still be alive.

At that point Brian had been permitted to view Emma's body in the trauma room. Gazing down at the pale, lifeless form on the table with an endotracheal tube protruding from her mouth and an IV line going into her arm was an image straight from a nightmare. It was hard to believe that someone in her prime, with such vitality and strength, could be so easily brought down by an insect, which seemed so tiny and inconsequential in comparison.

After viewing Emma's body, Brian knew he had to make some decisions. In a kind of a trance he remembered the funeral home that had handled his father's funeral a year and a half prior. After a quick call, it was arranged, and he couldn't believe the finality of it all. Brian was told that after Emma was seen and cleared by a medical examiner investigator, her remains would be picked up by the Riverside Funeral Home. Then after signing some forms, he was told that he could go home.

The wail of a siren yanked Brian out of his momentary trance as he watched an ambulance race up the hospital driveway and then make a rapid three-point turn to back against the ED receiving bay. He watched the doors open as a patient was extracted, similar to the way Emma had been handled a few hours earlier. Had it really only been a few hours ago?

After taking a deep breath, Brian pulled out his phone. He'd been putting off calling home to report the news, but he knew he'd have to do it at some point. Of course, he could wait until he got back and do it in person, but he thought that was somehow unfair since he'd promised he'd keep everyone informed. Involuntarily he shuddered at the thought of having to tell Juliette that her mother was gone and never coming home. Considering how much she had suffered when Emma had been hospitalized, he knew this was going to be devastating.

Marshalling his courage, Brian opened his contacts and was about to tap on Aimée's number when he paused. Something arresting caught his attention. About a hundred feet away, a uniformed, mildly overweight driver carelessly flicked a cigarette butt onto the sidewalk. Equally attention-grabbing was the vehicle whose front passenger-side fender the chauffeur was leaning up against. It was a gleaming black Maybach parked in a clearly marked no-parking zone directly in front of the hospital's main entrance. Although Maybachs and other luxury cars were common in some areas of Manhattan, particularly Wall Street and Midtown, in Inwood they were scarcer than hen's teeth. Brian pocketed his phone and, desperate for a diversion from the paralyzing sadness, headed over to get a closer look. As he approached, the driver went through the ritual of lighting another cigarette, and after doing so, he proceeded to toss away the used match with the same disregard he'd exhibited with his cigarette butt. He then crossed his arms and assumed a posture of boredom and haughtiness that truly rubbed Brian the wrong way. The man had a face mask, but it dangled uselessly from an ear.

Without any particular plan in mind, Brian approached. The driver eyed him with a kind of colonial disdain as if Brian was a native of a distant, semi-civilized part of Manhattan. Feeling a tidal wave of anger at this individual's self-satisfied superiority as clearly a member of the capitalistic world that had also created Peerless Health and the MMH hospital chain, Brian tensed. From his experience as a police officer, he could see the man was wearing a shoulder holster from a characteristic bulge in his overly tight chauffeur's uniform. Even the fact that the man thought it necessary and appropriate to be armed for his visit to the "wilds" of Inwood struck him as offensive.

In fact, he was about to tell the man that he had to pick up his cigarette butt and used match, which he was certain the man would refuse, when a sudden realization popped into Brian's head. Up until that moment it hadn't occurred to him to question who the owner of the Maybach might be.

"Quite a nice set of wheels," Brian voiced, nodding toward the Maybach's imposing hulk.

The driver didn't respond but rather eyed him with hooded eyes that Brian could just make out through the man's aviator sunglasses. He was wearing a chauffeur's hat, but it was jauntily sitting back on his shaved head.

Purposefully being provocative while maintaining the required six-foot distance, Brian walked directly up to the Maybach's rear passenger-side door. With almost every muscle tensed in his six-foot-one, nearly two-hundred-pound frame, he quickly rapped on the window with his knuckle. As he expected, it made almost no sound, confirming his suspicion that the Maybach limo was armored.

The snobby chauffeur was caught off guard by Brian's actions. He straightened up, flicked away his half-smoked cigarette, and spoke in a strong Brooklyn accent: "Don't touch the car!" It wasn't a request but rather an order.

With his body taut like a high-note piano wire, Brian was fully ready to take the man down. But the driver did not follow up his threatening order with any gesture whatsoever. Instead, he added, "Please step away."

With some disappointment, Brian relaxed a degree and then said: "An armored Maybach! We don't get to see too many of these babies around here in Inwood."

"I'm surprised you haven't seen this one on occasion. It comes up here maybe two or three times a week." He then leaned back against the car's front fender and looked off into the distance as if Brian didn't deserve any more of his time.

Brian bent down and looked at the rear tire. "Wow! Run-flat tires, too." He stepped back from the vehicle so he could see both passenger-side tires at the same time. "Yup. Run-flat tires, front and back." He was now reasonably sure who the owner of the vehicle was, especially if this person visited the hospital two or three times a week and could afford an armored Maybach. It had to be the MMH Inwood CEO, Charles Kelley.

Turning his attention from the car, he looked over at the main entrance to the hospital. It seemed to him, particularly in his current state of mind, that fate might be providing him with a rare opportunity to address his pent-up anger at Emma's avoidable death. If she hadn't been discharged, she would have been under seizure watch and likely still alive. Suddenly there was little doubt in Brian's mind that Charles Kelley and Heather Williams bore significant responsibility not only for Emma's passing, but also for his future bankruptcy, the possible loss of his home, and the ruin of his life.

With a new sense of purpose, Brian turned his attention back to the snotty driver. "Tell me. Could this impressive armored vehicle belong to the one and only Charles Kelley?"

A slight but detectable smile briefly turned up the corners of the driver's lips as he turned to look condescendingly at him. "I'm not allowed to say exactly who it is I chauffeur."

To Brian the driver's response was the equivalent of admitting what Brian suspected, and the effect was immediate. As if propelled out of a cannon, he bolted for the hospital entrance, shocking the driver out of his staged indifference. "Hey!" the surprised driver shouted. "What the hell? Where are you going?"

Brian didn't slow or respond. He was a man on a mission. Having visited Roger Dalton's office so many times and even Kelley's office once, he knew exactly where he was going. Because the hospital had instituted visiting restrictions due to the pandemic, he was confronted the moment he navigated the revolving door by a woman with a clipboard who asked if she could help him. Besides her clipboard, she was holding a number of face masks for those who needed them.

Without slowing since he was already wearing a mask, Brian just called over his shoulder that he had an appointment in administration with Mr. Charles Kelley. That was sufficient for the greeter, who merely nodded and waited for the next arrival.

Although his decision to confront Kelley had been spur of the moment, now that he was on his way, he became progressively determined to follow through with his plan. He knew he'd undoubtedly be considered a persona non grata, but he was committed to saying his piece. As he pushed through the door separating the vast, marbled hospital lobby and the carpeted admin area, he made a beeline for Kelley's office after seeing that the conference room was clearly empty.

"Excuse me!" a receptionist-cum-secretary called out as Brian swept by, heading for the closed door. "Where do you think you are going? You can't go in there!" She was the same individual who had unceremoniously escorted Brian out of Kelley's office on his previous spur-of-the-moment visit. Swiftly she picked up her phone and frantically punched in a series of numbers.

Reaching Kelley's office door, he didn't bother to knock. Instead, he tried the knob, which was unlocked, and burst in. Inside Kelley was clearly having a meeting with five of his underlings, including Roger Dalton, all seated on the oversized leather couch or occupying assorted side chairs. Kelley was standing behind his massive desk, apparently in the middle of a PowerPoint presentation. There was a flat-screen wall-mounted TV displaying RAISING COLLECTIONS ON ACCOUNTS RECEIVABLE DURING THE COVID-19 CRISIS.

For a moment time stopped, allowing Brian to get a good look at Charles Kelley and to appreciate the skill of the painter who had done the man's portrait hanging over the faux fireplace. True to life, Kelley was a handsome man with high cheekbones, sharply defined features, carefully coiffed sandy-colored hair, and an expensive business suit. Unlike the portrait, he was darkly tanned, and his hair was streaked with golden blond as if he'd just returned from a Caribbean vacation despite the pandemic. To Brian he looked like a model in a top-of-the-line menswear advertisement. The only thing that surprised him was Charles's height, which Brian guesstimated to be somewhere in the six-foot-eight realm.

"Who the hell are you?" Charles demanded, having finally recovered from his momentary stunned silence at Brian's precipitous arrival. His tone was condescending, as was the facial expression he quickly assumed, reminding Brian of Heather Williams.

"I'm an aggrieved customer and a long-term resident of this community," Brian snapped as he strode toward Kelley, pointing his finger up at his face. "I need to talk to you about this hospital and its mission, and you need to hear me out."

Roger Dalton struggled to his feet from where he'd been sitting in the deep couch and leaped forward to intercept Brian. "He's Brian Murphy," Roger called out, positioning himself between Brian and Charles Kelley. "His account is seriously in arrears and has been turned over to collections."

Brian was briefly taken aback by the audacity of the rail-thin Roger Dalton. "Sit down, Roger!" he ordered, pointing back to where Roger had been. "You are not personally responsible for this travesty, unlike Mr. Kelley."

"Yes, sit down, Roger," Charles echoed. "Okay, Mr. Murphy. Exactly what do you think you can tell me that I don't already know and know invariably far better than you?"

"Fat chance you know it better than I!" Brian sniped, approaching closer to the desk while continuing to jab his index finger up into Charles Kelley's tanned face. "Do you have any conception whatsoever of what your profit-oriented leadership is doing to families like mine, struggling to get through this pandemic? My wife just died minutes ago from encephalitis after being discharged from this hospital while still ailing with EEE, all because I couldn't pay an outlandish and incomprehensible bill."

"I am sorry to hear about your wife's passing," Charles offered, casually crossing his arms. "But I can assure you that her discharge and her passing did not have anything whatsoever to do with your

ability to pay. At MMH all patients are treated with the same attention to clinical detail and are given the finest care possible."

"Bullshit," Brian countered. He could tell stock language when he
heard it and what Charles had just said certainly wasn't at all what he
and Emma had experienced. "Here are the facts: My wife needed to
be under seizure watch because she was still suffering brain inflammation, yet she was discharged even though neither of us wanted
that. If she had remained in the hospital, she wouldn't have died. It's
as simple as that."

At that moment two hospital security guards dressed in dark
suits came flying into Charles Kelley's office, clearly responding to
the distress call by the secretary. Without waiting to assess the degree of danger Brian represented, they made the mistake of rushing
at him.

Reacting by reflex and using his tested skills, Brian made quick
work of both security guards, throwing them ignominiously to the
floor and pulling their jackets up over their heads. As they struggled
to free themselves, Charles's demeanor changed dramatically as he
sensed real danger from Brian. Uncrossing his arms, he grabbed his
wheeled executive chair and stepped back from his desk. Brian, for
his part, had now moved up to the desk and was leaning on it with
both hands, glaring up into Charles's alarmed face.

"Here's what I think in a nutshell," Brian said with vehemence. "I
think you are running what amounts to fraud with your health insurance coconspirators by taking advantage of this country's laissez-
faire healthcare situation to maximize your profits. In the process,
you and your collections people are bankrupting me and hundreds
of others."

Before Charles could even respond to this denunciation, the limo driver doubling as a personal bodyguard came flying into the office in a manner similar to the hospital security people. Making the same mistake as they, he came at Brian at a run. On this occasion, not only did Brian throw him to the floor, pull his jacket over his head, and rip it in the process, but he also disarmed him.

By now the first two security people had managed to disentangle themselves from their jackets and had gotten to their feet. Thinking of trying their luck with him a second time, they took a step forward but then hesitated upon seeing that Brian was holding the limo driver's Glock pistol. But to their surprise and relief, Brian merely emptied the gun, tossing the shells into the corner of the room, where they clattered against the bare floor and hit up against the wall.

"I'm here to talk, not fight," he warned, looking both security men directly in the eye to make certain they got the message and were willing to stand down. "I need to get off my chest what needs to be said about what this hospital is doing to this community." With a particularly large clatter that made everyone in the room jump, he tossed the gun into a wastebasket beside the desk.

Intent on trying their luck again with Brian, both security guards took yet another step toward him, but now Charles held up his hand, intuitively sensing that Brian was more than capable of holding his own. "Stand down!" he ordered. "Let the deadbeat have his say."

"Thank you," Brian said insincerely, sensing that Charles was merely humoring him. "Until recently I had good health insurance, so I never concerned myself with hospital bills, like when my daughter was born prematurely. I now think that was a big mistake. Everyone, myself included, is guilty of giving you people free rein, and your greed and your secrecy has had no bounds. You are all new age robber barons."

Brian was just getting warmed up in giving this haughty, unprincipled businessman a dressing-down when he was again interrupted by the arrival of additional security. On this occasion it was an older uniformed patrolman who, like Brian had done years ago, was clearly earning some extra money covering the hospital on his day off. As he ran into the room, keeping the various police paraphernalia attached to his service belt from falling out, he pulled up short when he saw him. Almost simultaneously they recognized each other.

"Brian Murphy?" the officer questioned with shock. He'd been warned that a deranged individual had broken into the hospital CEO's office.

"Liam Byrne?" Brian questioned. He'd not seen Liam for almost two years, and the man had gone prematurely gray. Plus, the face mask made recognition more difficult.

Charles immediately pricked up his ears at this interaction between apparent old acquaintances. Speaking scornfully to Liam, he said: "Do you know this trespasser?"

"Yes. He's with the NYPD, like myself. In fact, he's a member of the elite Emergency Service Unit. And his father, rest his soul, was commander of my precinct."

"That's a shock," Charles said with a mixture of disgust and disbelief. "A policeman! It's hard to believe with the way he's carrying on. He should have known better. Well, you've saved him from himself, but get him the hell out before I have him arrested for trespassing and criminal intimidation."

"Yes, sir," Liam said. He stepped up to Brian and whispered, "I think it's best I walk you out of here with no arguments."

For a moment of indecision, Brian looked back and forth between Charles Kelley and Liam Byrne. He had a lot more that he wanted to say to Charles, but seeing a community friend, particularly one who'd known his father, shocked him back to a sense of reality. In his confused state of mind brought on by Emma's death, the last thing he should have done was rush into Charles Kelley's office and make accusations. He shuddered to think of what might have happened had the limo driver drawn his gun before coming into the room or if the other security people had been armed. Someone could have been killed, and there was a chance it could very well have been him.

Suddenly feeling embarrassed, he locked eyes with Liam and said: "Okay! You're right. Let's go."

Liam grasped Brian's upper arm, and the two of them walked out. The secretary didn't say anything as they passed her desk, but her expression suggested she was satisfied that her quick thinking had saved the day. They started down the hallway, but behind them they could hear Charles ranting and raging about how the hell such a miscreant had been able to saunter into his office.

Brian and Liam didn't say anything until they'd reached the hospital lobby, where they knew they could talk without being overheard.

"What on earth were you doing in there mouthing off to the hospital CEO?" Liam asked in a forced half whisper, sounding truly concerned. "He's a bad dude from what I know."

"My wife, Emma, died about an hour ago. I wasn't thinking," he said after letting out a deflating sigh.

"Mary, Mother of God, I'm so sorry. What was it, an accident? Or Covid?"

"No, neither." He struggled against tears and had to take a few breaths in an attempt to keep them at bay. Despite his best efforts his eyes brimmed and a few tears ran down his cheeks, which he wiped away with the back of his hand. "She died of a viral disease called eastern equine encephalitis," he added when he could.

"I've never heard of it," Liam said, putting an empathetic hand on Brian's shoulder.

"I hadn't heard of it, either," Brian admitted. He took a deep breath. "But apparently we are going to hear a lot more about it in the coming years thanks to climate change. It's transmitted by mosquitoes that used to live in the tropics, but because it's getting warm, they're now all the way up to Maine and beyond."

"Another virus we have to worry about besides coronavirus?"

"I'm afraid so," Brian said with another sigh.

"Were you really mouthing off to Charles Kelley about climate change?" Liam asked.

Despite his precarious mental state, Brian let out a brief laugh and shook his head. "Hardly," he said. "No, I wanted to make sure he knew that there was a chance my wife died after she had been discharged while she was still sick because I couldn't pay any of her nearly two-hundred-thousand-dollar insane hospital bill. At least that's what I'm afraid happened. I've been learning a lot of shady things about hospitals and health insurance companies the hard way. They're in this together, sucking money out of the system like there's no tomorrow."

"What about our great health benefits as members of the NYPD?" Liam said. "How did you end up owing so much money?"

Although he was tired of once again explaining, Brian went ahead and described how he and Emma had retired from the NYPD to form their own security company and ended up with Peerless Health Insurance, which he described as legalized fraud. "These short-term health policies collect your premiums but then figure out a way of avoiding paying for most everything. Of course, I didn't read the policy. I mean, nobody reads their health insurance policies."

"You got that right," Liam said.

"The hospital is already suing me," Brian went on to elaborate. "And as I understand, that kind of aggressive, sped-up approach is all Charles Kelley's doing. He even had the hospital form their own collections division."

"I've heard he's a mean son of a bitch," Liam agreed. "I steer clear. Do you remember Grady Quillen?"

"Yeah, I do," Brian said. "I'm surprised you brought him up, because he is the one who served me the papers for the hospital suit against me."

"That's why I mentioned him. I'd heard he worked as a process server after his retirement for the collections department here. I thought he might be someone for you to talk with for some advice."

"He gave me the name of a lawyer," he said. "He also told me how busy he is, meaning that MMH Inwood is suing a lot of people, so I'm not alone."

"I can second that. A neighbor of mine is also being sued."

"He said the same thing about one of his neighbors," Brian said. "MMH Inwood is a lot more predatory than I thought. Until this happened, I'd always considered it a valuable part of the community. Now I'm not so sure."

"How did you get here?"

"I came in an ambulance," Brian said.

"I could call the precinct and have a squad car come and drive you home," Liam offered.

"No need," he said. "It's a short walk. But thanks for offering."

After a final conversation about how much everyone at the precinct missed Deputy Inspector Conor Murphy, Brian said goodbye. He thanked Liam for coming to his rescue in Charles Kelley's office, admitting that he'd gone there in a fit of rage without giving it any thought.

As Brian emerged back out into the sunshine, he stopped for a moment to eye the gleaming black Maybach sedan again. Seeing as the luxury car was owned by someone involved with healthcare, it seemed immoral at best.

CHAPTER 16

August 31

In a kind of trance, Brian headed home totally unaware of his surroundings. The impulsive, histrionic display in Kelley's office was so contrary to his usual style of careful planning and goal-oriented behavior. He knew that there was no way the episode could help rectify the situation in which he now found himself trapped. To make matters worse, calling Charles Kelley a new age robber baron was probably kowtowing to the man's monumental ego.

Turning onto Park Terrace East and starting up the hill, Brian slowed his pace and then stopped. In the middle of his brooding, he realized what had really propelled him into Kelley's office: It had been a way to avoid facing Juliette, Aimée, and Hannah or even thinking about telling them the horrible news. In many ways he was unconsciously denying Emma's death, and the act of telling the others, including Camila, would shatter that tenuous denial.

"Maybe they already called the hospital," Brian wondered out loud, but he knew that was wishful thinking. The burden of the truth was most likely squarely on him. What he feared the most was telling Juliette. He couldn't even imagine what her reaction was going to be.

Taking a deep breath, Brian recommenced walking. He knew he

was not as adept in the psychological arena as he was in the action realm, so for the next few minutes he tried not to think at all.

From the moment Brian entered the house he could tell that the news had not preceded him. He could hear the songful cartoon soundtrack of *Pinkalicious & Peterrific* coming from the kitchen, and Aimée and Hannah were in the living room quietly talking. Both adults immediately appeared in the foyer's archway as Brian removed his mask and shoes.

"How is Emma?" Aimée asked warily. Hannah was standing next to her, but slightly behind, with a look of agonizing worry on her face.

Once again Brian choked up as he had with Liam Byrne. It took him a minute to pull himself together. By then both women knew what was coming. "Emma didn't make it," Brian finally managed with difficulty.

Hannah let out a high-pitched but thankfully short-lived wail as her face contorted into an expression of horror. In contrast, Aimée responded by putting her arms around Brian and hugging him tightly. "I can't imagine what you are feeling. I'm so, so sorry, mon fils."

"Thank you," Brian choked. While Aimée held on to him, with a halting voice he recounted the details of what had happened. It was difficult to repeat, but he thought they deserved to know.

Finally, Aimée let go of Brian and exchanged a quick glance with Hannah, who had quieted down. "We have to tell Juliette," Aimée said, keeping her emotions in check.

Hannah nodded several times, wiping tears from her face. "Yes, that's the first thing that needs to be done, no question, and it should be Brian who does it."

"Bien sûr," Aimée added. "I agree completely."

"And a wake has to be planned and notices sent out," Hannah said. "There is a lot to do."

"I don't want a wake," Brian blurted. He was shocked that such a suggestion was Hannah's first reaction, but he knew he shouldn't have been. He was well aware that Hannah's method of dealing with any crisis was to suppress emotion with activity and planning. Emma had pointed it out on multiple occasions.

"But there has to be a wake!" Hannah countered in a manner that brooked no argument. "It's expected!" She was equally shocked at Brian's response, which was a sharp break from recognized and revered Irish tradition.

"Not here," Brian pleaded. "Not around Juliette. And I have to think about what I can afford. Plus, these are not normal times." As he spoke Brian realized he had no idea what Emma would have wanted. Despite the dangers they'd confronted as NYPD ESU officers, they'd never spoken with each other about their deaths and what their preferences might be.

"Well, there has to be a wake and a funeral mass even if it is limited because of the pandemic. And we can help with the expenses."

"Not here," Brian repeated, but realized this spur-of-the-moment response might seem selfish to Hannah and her family. He and Emma, although they'd grown up with a strong Irish connection to the Catholic faith, had drifted away from it during college. Neither had made a complete apostasy, but both felt the church was too ritualistic and out of touch with the times. As a consequence, they had not kept up with all the obligations on a regular basis, like going to mass and attending confession.

"That's fine," Hannah said with resignation. To her credit, she recovered quickly. "We can have the wake at our house. I can also make all the arrangements for the funeral mass at the Church of the Good Shepherd. Meanwhile you two and Camila can concentrate on Juliette. Is there a funeral home involved yet?"

"I called Riverside on Broadway," Brian said.

"A good choice," Hannah said. "I've worked with them before. They are very professional."

"That was my experience, too," Aimée said. "They were particularly helpful with Conor's funeral."

"I remember," Hannah recalled. "All right, I'm off. Good luck with Juliette." Without waiting for a response, she bent down and slipped on her shoes. She then put on her mask. "Let's be in touch," she added before leaving.

"Wow," Brian let out as he closed the front door behind Hannah. "She's really motivated."

"Hannah has been like that for as long as I've known her," Aimée said. "It's her defense mechanism. And I'm not surprised. After all, it is an Irish tradition with a death to channel emotion as much as possible into celebration rather than pure mourning. It's a tradition I've come to appreciate, especially after your father's passing."

"Yes, I remember you saying as much."

"Now it is time for the difficult part," Aimée said. "Are you ready to face your daughter?"

"Hardly," Brian admitted, his heart squeezing in his chest. "Do you really think I can do this?"

"Absolutely," Aimée reassured him. "It has to be you. Do you want a suggestion? I don't want to interfere, but as your mother I do have some advice."

"Please," Brian said, desperate for any guidance.

"This would be a good time to take advantage of some of the consoling power of faith," Aimée advised. "For the last year I've been taking Juliette to mass with me, which I've appreciated you and Emma allowing. She's absorbed a lot. Although she mostly enjoys the dressing-up part, she has been responsive to discussions about beliefs, especially when we talked about heaven and Grandpa Conor. I think it is a way of making death seem not so final, particularly in a child's mind."

"Okay, I guess I can do that," Brian said, thankful for any suggestions.

"I know you can," Aimée said while giving Brian's shoulder a reassuring squeeze.

Together, Brian and Aimée went into the kitchen. Juliette looked up at them briefly but then went back to watching her PBS cartoon. Brian motioned for Camila to step out into the hallway, while Aimée sat down with Juliette and watched TV.

Once out of the room, Brian told Camila the news about Emma.

"No, no!" Camila muffled her voice as she made the sign of the cross. "I'm so sorry, Brian."

"Thank you. I'm still in a kind of denial about it all, but I have to tell Juliette, as hard as it will be. How has she been doing after seeing the seizure?"

"Not so good," Camila said. "At first, I couldn't get her to talk about it. Then, when she did, she didn't say much and instead started complaining again about not feeling well."

"How so?"

"First she says she's not hungry and feels sick to her stomach," Camila began. "She won't eat anything no matter what I suggest. And she's complaining again she has a headache. But it can't be much of a headache because all she wants to do is watch TV, so I don't know what it is. In general, she's very cranky, which I suppose is entirely understandable."

"Has she said anything at all about what she saw?"

"No, not a word," Camila said. "And I didn't know whether to bring it up. I mean, it upset me. It was so violent."

"It's very disturbing," Brian agreed. "Especially the second time. All right, thank you. Either way, I have to tell her that her mother is gone and hope we can handle her reaction."

Despite all the hostage-negotiating seminars and discussions he'd had during his ESU training, Brian now felt totally unequipped to deal with his own four-year-old daughter. Nonetheless, he walked back into the kitchen and sat at the breakfast nook table across from his mother and Juliette. Unsure how to begin, he first reached out, picked up the remote off the table, and turned off the TV.

Juliette reacted instantly and angrily, reaching for the remote, but Brian extended it beyond her reach. "I need to talk with you, Juliette," he told her. "After that we can turn the TV back on."

Juliette looked at her father with obvious anger as if she knew what was coming, yet Brian persisted, trying to think of the best way to take his mother's suggestion. "Mommy was very sick, as you know," he began, "and she wasn't feeling better, but now she has gone to heaven and all her pain is gone. She's with Grandpa Conor, and they are very happy being together."

For a few seconds Brian closed his eyes, feeling monumentally unsuited for this discussion, saying things he didn't quite believe himself. And for a brief moment he wondered if Heather Williams and Charles Kelley ever thought that their behavior led to horrible situations like these, ones that should never have to happen. When he opened his eyes, Juliette was still staring at him as if digesting what Brian had said. Taking a deep breath, he continued: "So, Mommy will not be coming home. But I want you to know that I am here for you, as are your grandmas and Camila. We are all here for you."

Suddenly Juliette let out a tortured wail somewhat akin to Hannah's, then scrambled out of her seat and leaped onto Brian's lap. With her arms around his neck and her legs around his midsection, she hugged him tightly and buried her face in his shirt. He could feel her sob. Brian hugged her back and exchanged a helpless glance with Aimée. He didn't know what to do or what else to say. But one thing he did know was that Juliette was his sole responsibility and his life's work from that moment on.

As suddenly as Juliette had begun crying, she stopped and disengaged herself from Brian's embrace. She regained her seat and spoke up for the first time: "When will Mommy come home from the hospital?"

"Honey, I told you she won't be coming home," Brian said. "She's with Jesus and Grandpa in heaven."

Instead of asking any more questions, Juliette lunged for the TV remote, and this time Brian let her have it. In the next instant the happy, melodious soundtrack of *Pinkalicious & Peterrific* filled the room, especially after Juliette raised the volume. Aimée stood up and tried to give Juliette a reassuring hug, but Juliette resisted, preferring to keep the TV in view.

"Your daddy is right." Aimée spoke loud enough to be heard over the TV. "We're all here for you, so you are safe even if your mommy had to go to heaven."

Camila then followed suit and got the same lack of response from Juliette. The three adults exchanged a glance and a shrug, communicating that there apparently wasn't anything else to do for the moment. Juliette had been told, even if she didn't want to believe it for the time being.

For several minutes Brian just stood there leaning against the sink, looking at his daughter and mother, and thinking about his mother-in-law's reaction while his mind flip-flopped between disjointed thoughts and emotions about Heather Williams, Charles Kelley, and Emma. Focusing on Emma, he found himself questioning if it could possibly be true that she was gone forever. Or equally as disturbing: Would she still be alive if he'd insisted somehow on her staying in the hospital? How responsible was he for having let it happen?

Brian felt a new wave of emotion well up inside of him, which he hardly thought would be appropriate to display in his daughter's presence. Pushing away from the kitchen counter in hopes of having a moment alone, he left the room and headed for the home office. For the time being he'd let Aimée and Camila bear the burden of comforting Juliette.

Seated at the large partner's desk positioned under a chandelier, Brian made it a point not to look across at Emma's empty seat. Instead, he woke up his sleeping monitor to go over finances in a vain attempt to rein in his emotions. With Emma gone, he'd need to seriously think about the viability of Personal Protection LLC and whether it would survive now without her input and partnership. Then, with surprise, he found himself wondering if he should investigate the possibility of trying to reverse his retirement and get his old NYPD ESU job back. Under his current circumstances the idea of a guaranteed salary, decent health benefits, and pension plan had enormous appeal.

In the middle of such thinking, the business landline started to ring. Hoping it meant someone was in need of security, Brian snatched up the phone. To his dismay it wasn't a prospective client, but rather a Premier Collections agent. With an irritatingly high-pitched voice, the individual launched into a rapid threatening tirade, saying that if Brian didn't immediately offer an acceptable plan for paying off his $189,375.86 debt, his credit rating was going to be trashed, making it impossible for him to get a credit card, any kind of loan, or a mortgage.

In his hyperemotional state, Brian lost control, telling the caller to go fuck himself. He then slammed the phone down with such force it caused a portion of the handset to pop off. For a split second Brian scanned the desk's surface for something else to destroy, but the urge quickly passed. Then the phone rang again. This time Brian didn't answer it. Knowing what he did about collection agencies, he was aware that he was destined to be pestered relentlessly. It was the name of the game.

Letting the phone ring, he pulled up his online banking account and looked at the balances. Things were hardly looking rosy, especially with the thought of an upcoming funeral. He really had no idea what kind of money would be involved, and he wondered selfishly how much his in-laws, the O'Briens, might be willing to shoulder following Hannah's offer. Unfortunately, he knew that he would soon be finding out answers to these questions. Finally, the phone stopped ringing, and except for the distant sounds of the PBS cartoon coming from the kitchen, the room returned to silence. The one thing the call did do was remind him that he was indeed being sued, meaning he needed to do something before his time limit to respond to the complaint ran out. The specter of losing the house loomed in the back of his mind. He could not let that happen for a number of reasons, chief of which was Juliette. Losing her mother was going to create a terrible insecurity, and losing her home on top and the familiarity of her room would just add immensely to the impact.

"All right, that's it," he said out loud. Pulling out his phone for a Google search, he typed in "Patrick McCarthy." He needed a lawyer, expense be damned, and with Grady recommending him, Patrick seemed like a good risk to take, especially with him being part of the community.

To his surprise, the lawyer answered on the second ring, making Brian wonder if that was a positive or a negative sign. He'd fully expected having to talk with either a secretary or leave a message. For a moment, Brian was caught off guard, but that changed as soon as he introduced himself.

"I know you," Patrick said. "Wasn't your father chief of police?"

"He was," Brian confirmed. "Commander of the 34th Precinct."

"I know your sister as well. We were in the same grade. What can I do for you?"

"Well, I'm being sued for almost two hundred thousand dollars by MMH Inwood," Brian said. He liked the sound of Patrick's voice, as it conveyed a sense of confidence.

"That, unfortunately, is a familiar story."

"Really?" Brian was still a bit surprised to hear that. "Have you handled many such cases?"

"Quite a few," Patrick said. "Especially lately with the pandemic. Have you been served?"

"Just this morning, by Grady Quillen."

"Then we have thirty days to respond," Patrick said. "When would you like to get together?"

"As soon as possible." Knowing himself as a man of action, Brian needed to be active to keep from being overwhelmed by Emma's passing and worry about losing the house.

"I could see you as early as tomorrow. Would that work for you?"

"Absolutely," Brian said. "The earlier the better."

"I could be here at the office at seven-thirty. Is that too early for you?"

"That would be fine," Brian said. He thought the chances he'd be able to sleep very much that night were slim.

"I'll see you then," Patrick confirmed. "Bring your service papers, of course. And also a mask. I require it in my office."

"No problem," Brian said. He liked hearing that Patrick was sticking to appropriate Covid-19 pandemic rules.

"My office is at 5030 Broadway," Patrick said. "I don't have a secretary, so when you get here in the morning, call me, and I'll come down and let you in."

"I look forward to meeting you," Brian said before disconnecting.

CHAPTER 17

September 1

As he had expected, Brian found sleep almost impossible that night. Even with the sleep medication, which he felt guilty taking since it had been prescribed for Emma, he spent most of the night wandering the house with his mind in turmoil. On multiple occasions he found himself looking in on Juliette. Each time he found her asleep, holding on to Bunny and looking peaceful. He was impressed the child seemed to have weathered the news with more equanimity than he had anticipated, which relieved him to a degree. He gave full credit to the grandmothers, both of whom had spent the rest of the day and evening with her. They'd even taken her out for a walk in her beloved Isham Park and then on to the Church of the Good Shepherd to light a devotional candle for Emma. When Aimée had told Brian of the plan, he'd rolled his eyes at the idea of resorting to ritual with a four-year-old, yet the episode seemed to have soothed Juliette considerably, making him wonder if he should rethink the role of religion in his and Juliette's life. There was absolutely no doubt in his mind that what was holding him together at the moment was his responsibility to his daughter to make sure she could navigate this emotional sea of losing her mother.

By seven A.M., with Juliette and Camila still sleeping, Brian prepared to leave the house. He wrote a note for Camila and texted Aimée to let her know where he was. He then collected the papers Grady had served him from the home office.

One of the many beauties of living in Inwood was how close everything was. Because the neighborhood was only a little more than a square mile, with a third of it forest-covered parkland, everything was within walking distance, in particular the commercial establishments along Broadway. Brian's route took him down the West 215th Street double stairway, a unique Inwood landmark that played a fond role in his childhood.

When he reached Patrick McCarthy's building, which was one of the few multistoried modern commercial structures in Inwood, he followed Patrick's directions and called to be let in. As he did so, he briefly questioned what it might mean if the lawyer wasn't successful enough to have a secretary, but he let the thought go when he saw Patrick get off the elevator and approach. He was impressive-looking and younger than Brian expected. He was tall, maybe even close to Charles Kelley's height.

"Welcome," Patrick said as he opened the door. His voice in person was more confident sounding than it had been on the phone.

As Brian passed by the man on his way inside, he did feel an immediate if minor bond. Like him, Patrick had dark, almost black hair with blue eyes.

"I appreciate you being willing to come in person despite the pandemic," Patrick said as they walked back to the elevator. "I think it is important for us to literally see eye to eye if we are going to work together. Besides, I need the papers you were served, which I see you have brought." Brian handed them over as they got into the elevator.

As they rode up to the fourth floor, Patrick leafed through the papers while Brian gave a capsule history of Emma's illness, hospitalization, and then death the day before. That news took Patrick by surprise. "I'm so sorry," he said with real empathy. "You are being sued for several hundred thousand dollars and you've lost your wife. What a terrible combination."

"I lost my wife and my business partner," he added.

"I'm in awe that you are able to function so soon after your loss."

"I suppose I'm still in denial, if I'm being honest," Brian said. "I'm also a very active person. It's always been difficult for me to sit around under any circumstances."

Inside Patrick's office, which was singularly spartan, Brian sat in one of two metal folding chairs while Patrick lowered himself into in an aged desk chair behind a metal desk. The only other furniture was a small bookcase and a file cabinet. The décor was hardly suggestive of a lucrative practice. The only hint of it being the twenty-first century was an iMac, keyboard, and mouse on the desk.

"Well, I will answer the complaint, and we will get a court date," Patrick offered as he aligned the court papers by tapping them on the desk before carefully laying them down in front of himself. Looking directly at Brian, he said, "I have to be up front with you. We've got an uphill battle here."

"When Grady served me, and, by the way, he gave you a good recommendation, he said you had tried to help his neighbor Nolan O'Reilly, but that things hadn't worked out."

"That's an understatement, but we tried our best."

"That's not a very good advertisement," Brian said, hoping for some reassurance that his situation would be different.

"I can understand why you might feel that way. As I said, it is an uphill battle, and I'll tell you why. Judges are, more often than not, forced to rule in the hospital's favor because services have been rendered and everyone had been forced under duress of the admission process to sign a form that they will be responsible for the bill. Plus, the hospitals can charge whatever they damn well please without telling the patient or the family anything beforehand."

"I can attest to that," Brian said with a short, mirthless laugh. "But I would like to know if my case is significantly different than the O'Reillys', since there'd been a summary judgment involved in theirs."

"I'm sorry, but because of attorney–client confidentiality rules, I can't discuss the details of other cases. I hope you understand."

"I suppose," Brian said. He didn't think merely confirming a summary judgment would be a violation, but he let it go. "Have you had a lot of experience with this kind of case?"

"Tons of experience, unfortunately. I've got more than twenty open cases right now."

"Similar to mine?"

"Strikingly so," Patrick confirmed. "MMH Inwood has been suing many families for outstanding hospital bills, particularly since the Covid-19 pandemic began."

"Have you had some cases where the outcome is a bit better than the O'Reillys'? Grady told me they even lost their house."

"Absolutely," Patrick said. "Rest assured, I've had many with a significantly better outcome."

"Okay, that's encouraging. To be honest, my biggest concern is losing my house."

"Understandable," Patrick said with sympathy. "Are you up to date with your mortgage payments?"

"No," he admitted, feeling a jolt of fear. "Does that make a differ-ence?"

"I'm afraid it does." Patrick raised his eyebrows. "With the New York State Homestead Act, a home is protected in a bankruptcy fil-ing, but not if the home is in arrears on the mortgage."

"Shit," Brian responded. "It's only been a couple of months' lapse because of the pandemic."

"If you can possibly manage it, I'd strongly recommend bringing it up to date as soon as you can."

"The bank is aware why I've not paid," Brian said. "I've certainly been in contact with them, and they actually encouraged it. My wife and I started a new security business at the worst possible time: the middle of December, just before the pandemic hit. We'd been trying to preserve our cash to hold the business together."

"I understand, but I'm sure the other side will try to exploit it. So, if you can, I'd bring it up to date."

They then spent a few minutes talking about Patrick's fees, which he agreed to put off after an initial, modest retainer of five hun-dred dollars. "Believe me, I can understand your situation," Patrick said. "We're all in it, thanks to this pandemic. You can pay me the balance when your company gets back to providing you with an income."

"That's very kind of you," Brian said, thankful and pleased. He felt strongly that such trust was yet another benefit of living in this community.

"Okay," Patrick said, placing both his hands flat on top of Brian's papers. "I'll take care of these with the court immediately. Mean-while, I'll need to get the hospital bill. Have you been given one?"

Brian let out a short, disgusted laugh. "With effort I got one, but it's useless. The damn thing is in code. I can't make sense of nine-tenths of it."

"That leads me to another question. Have you considered retaining a medical billing advocate?"

"It's interesting that you ask. My mother asked the same question. I'd never even heard of a medical billing advocate."

"It is a sign of the times," Patrick said. "Many hospitals have become so rapacious because they are being driven by private equity people to maximize profit, and one way to camouflage it is to make the billing process as incomprehensible as possible."

"How might a billing advocate help my case?"

"He or she would go over your bill with a fine-toothed comb. They understand the confusing language and invariably find all sorts of mistakes and overcharges. Sometimes they alone can reduce the bill by half or more."

"Who would have thought it would come to this?" Brian said, throwing up his hands in amazement. "It's so damn ironic. Hospitals are supposed to save people, not cheat them."

"As I said, it is a sign of the times. The US Congress has been asleep at the wheel, allowing medical costs to go through the roof. And it's across the board: hospital prices, drug prices, or device prices like artificial joints—it's all the same."

"So you recommend I find an advocate?"

"Very strongly recommend it," Patrick said. "Even if it is yet another expense for you."

"Do you have anyone specific you recommend?"

"I do. There's one right here in this building who is excellent in my experience. She's helped me on a number of cases. Her name is Megan Doyle, and she also went to PS 98 like we did."

"Megan Doyle," Brian repeated. "She's actually the one my mother mentioned. She said she'd helped a neighbor."

"I'm not surprised. Megan has helped a lot of people."

"Do you have her contacts by chance?"

"I can do better than that," Patrick said. "I could give her a shout right here and now. It's better to start the process ASAP because she'd need to get a complete copy of your hospital record, and hospitals are not cooperative with billing advocates to say the least. In fact, they make it as difficult as possible, creating all sorts of hoops and delays that have to be navigated."

"I already have a hospital bill, which I could provide her," Brian offered.

"She'll get a better, significantly more complete one," Patrick said. "Mark my words. The bills a hospital gives to patients are never broken down like she'll demand. Should I call her? She'll need to see you to start the process."

"Do you think she'd see me now while I'm here?"

"I believe she will. This wouldn't be the first time she's helped a client of mine."

"Fine, give her a try," Brian said.

Using the speaker on his phone, Patrick made the call. In contrast to him, Megan Doyle had a secretary who put Patrick through directly to her. The call was friendly, curt, and decisive. Megan would squeeze him in between appointments, and told him he should come down directly after seeing Patrick.

After a short conversation involving another shared client, Patrick disconnected the call, then looked over at Brian. "You'll like her," he said. "She's very personable but very professional, and she's good at what she does."

"Even if my bill is reduced to half, I'm going to be hard put to pay it off," Brian said warily. "But let me ask you something else. What about going after my supposed health insurance company called Peerless? They've turned down my claims, denying any fiscal responsibility despite all the premiums I paid. To me it's a fraud."

"I'll be happy to look into it, if you insist, but I can tell you up front that the chances it would be successful are minuscule. Short-term health insurance is a tolerated scam in my experience. They have spent millions in legal fees to protect themselves with their contracts. Did you read your policy?"

"No, I didn't," he admitted.

"That's what they count on," Patrick said. "They advertise themselves as being inexpensive, and they are. They love to take your premiums but are loath to pay out anything at all, and when they do, it is never even close to being adequate."

"Why is it tolerated?" Brian asked, genuinely confused.

"That's a question I can't answer," Patrick said with a shake of his head.

"I have one other issue that should be looked into. I think there's a chance my wife was discharged before it was safe and possibly because I wasn't paying the bill. I think that Charles Kelley, the hospital CEO, has created a very strongly profit-driven culture that's willing to put patients in danger."

Patrick's eyebrows raised. "Let me understand what you are implying. Do you think there might be negligence involved?"

"I do," Brian said. "If she had still been in the hospital under a seizure watch, she'd probably be alive today."

"Hmm. That could possibly put a different spin on the situation down the road," Patrick pondered. "At the same time, I wouldn't count on it influencing this current case. What I can do is run it by a malpractice attorney friend of mine, provided you give me the okay."

"Sure, if you think it is appropriate."

"I'll give it more thought," Patrick said. "Meanwhile, I'll start the process of getting you a court date." He stood up, and Brian did the same, interested to meet his very first medical billing advocate.

CHAPTER 18

September 1

Conveniently it took Brian mere minutes to go from Patrick McCarthy's office down to Megan Doyle's on the ground floor. But the change was substantial. In contrast to Patrick's space, there was a generous-sized waiting room and a receptionist, suggesting that Megan was doing significantly better financially than Patrick. Business for Megan was apparently brisk in spite of the pandemic, or maybe because of it.

To Brian, the elderly receptionist looked strikingly similar to the librarian of his middle school, and he was tempted to ask if she was related but couldn't remember the librarian's name. In keeping with the needs of the pandemic, a plexiglass shield had been added to the woman's desk. Combining that barrier with his mask, he had to speak up when he gave his name.

"Miss Doyle will see you as soon as she can between patients," the receptionist responded equally loudly. "Meanwhile, please fill out this form so we have all your contact information."

Armed with the form on a clipboard, Brian turned to look for the most appropriate spot to sit in the waiting area. Despite it being as early as it was, there were two people waiting who had chosen opposite corners of the room beneath the windows that looked out on Broadway. In keeping with social distancing requirements, Brian went to the other end of the room.

As he was filling out the form, he thought about the receptionist calling Megan's clients "patients." It struck him as mildly bizarre that Megan was considered an integral part of the medical community, suggesting that dealing with a ridiculous hospital bill was somehow akin to setting a broken bone.

As he finished with the form, a fourth person came into the waiting area. What caught Brian's attention was the woman's age. Although the man and the woman under the windows were somewhere near his mother's age of seventy, this newly arrived individual was closer to Brian's thirty-six. She was dressed in biking shorts and a bright pink jersey with white stripes. And similar to Brian, when she gave her name to the receptionist behind the plexiglass, she spoke up to make sure she was heard. Her name was Jeanne Juliette-Shaw. Then the receptionist told her the same thing she'd said to him, indicating she, too, was being squeezed in. The only difference was that she was not given a form to fill out, implying that she was an existing client.

Despite the circumstance of being in a medical billing advocate's office, his life in total disarray, and it being in the middle of a pandemic, Brian couldn't help but be intrigued with this stranger on three accounts. The first was the woman's youth, which suggested that similar to Brian, she shouldn't be struggling with a difficult hospital bill. Second was her obvious French accent. When she pronounced her given name, it was "jhân," not "jēēn," suggesting that she had grown up in France just like Aimée. And third was her family name: Juliette-Shaw, calling to mind his daughter's given name.

Jeanne retreated to the remaining corner of the room, relatively close to him although certainly more than the required six feet away. As she sat down, she nodded a greeting to Brian, who couldn't help but closely watch her despite recognizing he might be acting mildly impolite. She then took out her phone from a pocket on the back of her bike jersey and became engrossed.

"Excuse me," Brian said, unable to restrain himself. "I couldn't help but hear the first part of your hyphenated family name, Juliette. It's quite . . ." For a brief moment he didn't know what to say, as he had spoken impulsively and hadn't planned ahead. Finally, after an awkward pause, he added: "It's quite beautiful."

"Thank you," she said, but quickly reverted her attention back to her phone.

"It caught my attention because it's my four-year-old daughter's name," Brian added, in an attempt to initiate a conversation.

Jeanne looked up again. Because of her face mask, he couldn't be sure of her reaction, but there was a faint crinkle of the corners of her eyes at least suggesting a smile, but to his dismay she didn't speak, forcing Brian to stumble ahead: "The reason we chose the name is that it was my mother's maiden name. My mother grew up in France. She didn't come here to the United States until college age, actually to go to Barnard College, where she met my father, who was going to Columbia on a hockey scholarship and then had us kids."

Brian felt distinctly uncomfortable, which was why he'd carried on so long. Although social to a fault, he'd never been particularly comfortable talking with women he didn't know.

"Juliette is not that common as a surname," Jeanne said. "Even in France. Where in France did your mother come from?"

"Normandy," Brian said, relieved to be asked a question. "Near Bayeux."

"That's a very interesting part of France."

"Have you been there?"

"Of course. Everyone visits Bayeux because of the tapestries."

"I suppose you are right," he said. "Even I have seen the tapestries: several times, in fact. My mother took me and my brothers and sister to France every year to visit our French grandparents. To make it easier, she even got us all French passports so we could zip through immigration. My middle name is Yves, after my mother's dad." Brian didn't know why he felt pressured to keep speaking. Being a private person normally, it was unlike him to be so revealing about himself.

"You and your siblings were very lucky," Jeanne said.

"We were," Brian agreed. Then, in hopes of turning the conversation away from himself, he said: "You have a distinctive and charming accent. Are you French?"

"Yes and no," she said. "Like your mother, I grew up in France. I, too, came here to the USA to attend college but ended up staying and becoming a citizen. I consider myself American as well as French."

"As you should. Could you be related to my mother's family since, as you say, Juliette is not a common family name?"

"I doubt it," Jeanne said. "I grew up in a totally different area of France that's not that well known outside of the country. It's called the Camargue. It's way in the south, and all my relatives have lived there forever."

"You are right, I've never heard of the Camargue, but I'll ask my mother."

"She'll know of it; it's the Rhône River delta," Jeanne explained.

"It's marshy and agricultural with more birds, cattle, and horses than people."

"I'll check it out with Google," he said. "I should introduce myself. My name is Brian Murphy."

"Nice to meet you, Brian," she said. "I'm Jeanne Juliette-Shaw."

"It's a pleasure to meet you, too. If you don't mind, let me ask you a question about Megan Doyle. Is this your first visit, like it is mine?"

"No, she's been working with me for a number of months. I'm just here to sign some final paperwork."

"Has she been helpful?"

"She's been most definitely helpful," Jeanne confirmed. "I just wish I had come to her sooner. I wasn't even aware such people existed."

"Nor was I, not until a few days ago."

"One of the main things I miss about France is the healthcare system," she said. "It is so, so much better. Here it can be a disaster, and I am living proof."

"So, I assume you had a large hospital bill, too?"

"Énorme," Jeanne said. "Huge."

"Were you sued as well?"

"Oh, yeah! Yes, I was sued."

"A local hospital?" Brian asked.

"Yes again. MMH Inwood."

"Did you not have insurance?" Brian asked.

"We had insurance, but it was a short-term policy and ultimately worthless," Jeanne said. "They didn't pay anything."

"Could it have been Peerless Health Insurance, by any chance?"

"How did you guess?" she said, eyebrows raised.

"Merely by your saying they didn't pay anything," he said with a scoff. "We had the same insurance, and they haven't paid a dime. I've learned it's their modus operandi, thanks to their CEO, Heather Williams."

"I've heard of her," Jeanne said. "She's popular with Wall Street."

"What excuse did Peerless give for not paying any of your bill, if you don't mind me asking?"

"They claimed my husband's heart attack was due to a preexisting condition," Jeanne began. "Somehow they found out he had gone to a doctor several years ago with chest pain. Even though the doctor at the time found nothing except mildly elevated cholesterol and blood pressure, the insurance company claimed his heart attack was due to a preexisting condition. Unfortunately, it held up in court. We were duped. We didn't know that short-term health insurance could do such a thing."

"That is criminal. I mean, almost everything can to some extent be considered a preexisting condition."

"I couldn't agree more," she said. "It is criminal."

"Did your husband at least do okay medically?"

"I wish," Jeanne said. "He died after multiple procedures, waiting for a heart transplant. It didn't happen. With lousy health insurance, which wasn't going to cover anything, and without adequate personal resources for the half-million-dollar procedure, the hospital dragged its feet. It became clear to us that the chances of him getting a heart were not good. He lived for a while with what's called a ventricular assist device, but it wasn't much of a life."

"I'm so sorry to hear that," Brian said, feeling self-conscious he'd asked. And then he surprised himself by saying with a catch in his voice: "I can certainly sympathize. I lost my wife, too, just yesterday."

"Oh, no!" Jeanne exclaimed. "What happened?"

"It was a viral disease called eastern equine encephalitis, or EEE for short, that she got from a mosquito. I think she'd been bitten while we were having a beach barbecue a few weeks ago."

"Good lord! So tragic. I've never heard of EEE."

"I hadn't, either," Brian said. "But it's a developing problem that I'm afraid we are all going to hear more and more about. The Asian tiger mosquitoes that carry it have spread all the way up to Canada from the tropics."

"Between that and coronavirus, it seems that viral diseases are becoming an existential threat. And you say your wife died just yesterday?"

He nodded.

"You poor man. How can you be out and about? I couldn't even leave home for weeks after my husband died."

Brian took several deep breaths, started to speak, and then had to pause again. Finally, he managed: "I'm still in the denial and anger stage, I suppose. But I had to get out, especially with MMH Inwood suing me and threatening my house. That's why I'm here to see Megan Doyle and a lawyer upstairs, hoping they can help."

"I assume you mean Patrick McCarthy. Wow! You are on a similar trajectory as I. If it is any consolation, I can at least assure you that they work well together."

"That's good to hear. Thank you."

"This kind of situation would never happen in France," she said. "It's enough to make me think seriously of moving back even though there is a lot to love about this country." Then, wrinkling her forehead, she added: "You said you have a daughter. How is she taking this tragedy?"

"Not well, I'm afraid. She's always been a mommy's girl. She's had a lot of trouble since my wife was hospitalized two weeks ago. Telling her yesterday that her mother died was possibly the most difficult thing I've done in my life."

"It's an awful experience for a child to lose a parent, particularly a mother, no offense to you as a father."

"No offense taken. I get it."

"Your biggest challenge will be to convince her you will be there for her, that she is safe. Fear of abandonment will be her biggest concern, which you'll need to address head-on."

"It sounds to me like you know more about this kind of situation than I. Have you had some professional mental health training? Or are you a parent yourself?"

"No, I'm not a parent," Jeanne said. "But I did study psychology at Fordham University, where I met my husband, probably similar to the way your mother met your father. I also took a master's degree in school psychology and was an elementary school psychologist for a few years. While in that position, I had to deal with several students who had lost parents."

"Well, that explains it," Brian said, impressed by her experience.

"You'll have to be prepared for a potentially wide range of symptoms on your daughter's behalf," she explained. "She could get psychosomatic symptoms, like gastrointestinal complaints. In the mental arena, she could exhibit practically no change to outright regression."

"What do you mean by 'regression'?"

"Reverting to an earlier age. For instance, she could stop talking, forget her potty training, or demand a bottle and refuse to eat solid food. There's no way to predict. You'll have to be prepared for whatever comes."

At that moment the door to the inner office opened, and a white-haired man appeared on crutches. He was immediately followed by a woman Brian assumed was Megan Doyle. Despite the mask covering half her face, she looked younger than he expected, quite a bit younger than Patrick McCarthy, more like a college-aged woman than a professional with graduate training. She was dressed in a blue blazer over blue jeans with a white, open-necked blouse. Her medium-length light brown hair was a forest of curls. But what he liked immediately was that she projected a sense of assurance and almost cheerleader exuberance as she greeted the two older clients who were waiting by the windows, saying she'd be with them shortly.

After handing off some papers to the receptionist and taking the clipboard that contained the form Brian had filled out, she also greeted Jeanne before calling out his name and waving for him to follow her back into her office.

"Good luck," Jeanne said as Brian got to his feet.

"Thanks," he said, taking a deep breath. "I'm going to need it."

CHAPTER 19

September 1

Like Megan's outer office, the inner one was a polar opposite of Patrick McCarthy's shabby domain. It was hardly posh, but the furniture was relatively new, indeterminately modern, and constructed of a blond wood with a Scandinavian simplicity. Besides the obligatory desk and chairs, there was a good-sized bookcase that Brian could see was nearly filled with myriad hospital billing manuals and coding texts, underlining his ignorance of the entire field, one he never even knew existed.

"Please," Megan said, pointing to one of the chairs that was a bit more than six feet away from her desk. She sat behind her desk and quickly scanned the form that Brian had filled out.

"Okay," she began cheerfully. "This preliminary meeting won't take but a few minutes, and it is mainly to get you to sign a patient advocacy authorization form, so we can get the ball rolling to get a complete copy of your hospital bill. It will also give us an opportunity to talk about my fees. I see you are being sued by MMH Inwood for nearly one hundred and ninety thousand dollars."

"It's going to go up," he warned. "There will be an additional charge for an ED visit yesterday." Brian then gave her a quick history of Emma's illness and her death the day before.

"I'm so sorry to hear you have lost your wife," Megan said with genuine empathy. Her shoulders visibly sagged.

"It's the worst part," Brian said. "But the financial impact is a real issue I still have to deal with. Do you think you can help me?"

"Absolutely, without a shred of doubt," Megan said, regaining her fervor. "I've yet to have a client whose bill I haven't significantly reduced. I can assure you that MMH Inwood pads their bills and makes billing errors with as much or more regularity than the other hospitals in the city, especially for the uninsured or poorly insured. By poorly insured I mean those people whose health insurance companies haven't negotiated significant deductions in the hospital's charge master price."

"I apologize, but what is the hospital's 'charge master'? Is it like a list of prices for their services? I've never seen that."

"Nor will you see it, even if you ask," Megan said. "It's not meant for the public to see. It's a list of artificially high prices for goods and services that merely serves as a starting point for negotiating deductions for the more powerful, meaning large, health insurance companies. These prices have nothing to do with cost plus profit, which is how prices are usually determined in a real market and how Medicare tries to determine how much it will pay. And to make matters worse, hospitals keep raising their charge master prices, particularly when a hospital chain buys a failing community hospital. It's all a big game as hospitals and health insurance both benefit the more money is thrown at healthcare. Unfortunately, it is people like you who suffer the most because of this stupid and enormously expensive game.

You end up being charged the artificially high charge master price, which is much more than everyone else pays."

"Good grief. I knew none of this. I feel like a babe in the woods, for Christ's sake."

"Don't be hard on yourself. Most people have no idea of any of this unfortunate reality, and most people still labor under the delusion that all hospitals and health insurance companies exist to help them in their time of need."

"I'm afraid I fell into that group for sure."

"All right, enough of this grim reality," Megan said, regaining her enthusiasm. "As soon as you sign this patient privacy authorization form, I will start the uphill climb of getting a complete, fully itemized bill, which is never easy because they will try hard to keep it from me. But don't worry. I know all their tricks and all their delay tactics. Have you been dealing with anyone in particular in the hospital's billing office?"

"Yes," Brian said. "A Roger Dalton."

"Good. He's almost human." She laughed at her own joke. "And I assume you are working with Patrick McCarthy as well since he called me?"

"Yes, starting just today," Brian confirmed.

"Perfect!" Megan said. "We have a good working relationship. Do you have any questions for me?"

"I don't know enough to have any questions at the moment." He knew he'd probably have a dozen as soon as he walked out of the office.

"Let me give you a quick thumbnail sketch of what will most likely happen," she added. "Although I can't promise you anything, but by my past experience with MMH billing, I should be able to reduce your bill anywhere between twenty-five to ninety percent. I know that is an awfully large range, but that's been my experience. As soon as I get your completely itemized bill, I'll start to work. After this in-person meeting, we can work remotely for the most part. I assume you have a computer and internet."

"Yes, of course," he said. "Actually, I have thought of a question. You seem to be busy. Are there a lot of Inwood people in need of your services?"

"Too many. And the pandemic has made it worse with people losing their employment-based healthcare and either going it alone or resorting to short-term health policies like you did. It's another developing part of the Covid-19 American tragedy."

"What about your fees? How will I be paying you?"

"You can either pay by the hour or as a percentage of what I save you," Megan said. "It will be your choice, and you can decide at some later point. After I get a look at your hospital bill, I'll be able to give you a better idea of what my fees might be."

"Patrick offered to put off payment until after the pandemic eases up and my business picks up. Are you willing to offer that as well?"

"I am," Megan said. "I'm sorry to have to cut this short, but I need to get back to seeing my scheduled clients. But first, let's have you sign this patient privacy authorization form to get the ball rolling."

"Of course." He got to his feet and approached the corner of the desk where she had slid the papers that needed his signature.

With the papers signed and in hand, he followed Megan out into the waiting room. While she called one of the elderly clients, Brian went to the receptionist as he'd been instructed and handed over the signed form. As he was doing it and listening to her saying she would be in touch if anything more would be needed on his part, he was trying to work up the courage to re-engage Jeanne Juliette-Shaw. Luckily, he didn't have to improvise. To his relief, as soon as he was finished with the receptionist, Jeanne stood up and approached him. In her hand she was holding a business card.

"Excuse me, Brian," she began. "I am truly sorry about your wife, and I have been thinking more about your daughter. The experience I had as a school psychologist suggests it is not going to be easy for you or her. If I can be of help in some way, particularly if there are problems, I'd be happy to do so. I'm not working presently for a number of reasons, which I won't bore you with, so I would be available if you were so inclined. Of course, it would be entirely pro bono."

Brian was immediately overwhelmed by Jeanne's generosity and impressed with the force of her character. "That's incredibly kind of you," he stammered.

"I wanted to give you my number if you are interested," Jeanne said, extending the business card.

He took the card and tried to read it but with difficulty. His eyes had teared up at Jeanne's offer and her altruism threatened to dissolve the veil of denial he'd erected to keep his emotions in check. "I might very well call you," he stammered.

"I'm sorry if I'm upsetting you," Jeanne said. "But I would like to help if you think I could."

"You are not upsetting me," Brian struggled to say, even though he was lying. He focused on the business card to get himself under control. In bold letters it said: SHAW ALARMS followed by a Washington Heights address. Her title was vice president. There was an office telephone number, but it was crossed out, and below that was a mobile number.

"Whoa," Brian said, taking a deep breath to pull himself together. "All this time I didn't know I was speaking with a vice president!"

"Vice president of a bankrupt alarm company," Jeanne corrected with a laugh of dismissal. "Shaw Alarms was forced into bankruptcy after I tried to pay MMH Inwood what I owed, which was impossible, and then was sued by them."

"My God," he remarked as rising anger saved him from his mournful emotions. Jeanne's story was a stark reminder of how predatory MMH Inwood was and how perverse Peerless was to more people than just him. "MMH's suit caused your company to go under?"

"Yes, with a little help from the pandemic."

"Sounds like a perfect storm," Brian said. "A storm I'm caught in as well. My wife and I started a personal security company just as the pandemic was starting in Wuhan, China. There's been almost no work for us since it arrived here in the US."

"You'll notice on the card that the office landline phone number is crossed out," Jeanne remarked. "But the mobile number is still operative. So please call if you decide you'd like to get ahold of me for some professional advice regarding your daughter. Or yourself, for that matter. Having recently lost my spouse, I can imagine what you are going through."

"Do you live in Inwood?"

"I do. On Seaman Avenue. My unit overlooks Emerson Playground."

"That's one of my daughter's favorite spots," Brian said, managing a smile.

"I can understand why," Jeanne responded. "Where do you live?"

"West 217th Street."

"Nice! I'm familiar with the neighborhood. Do you by any chance live in one of those darling single-family homes?"

"I do, and I'd like to keep it from MMH Inwood's predatory hands," he said, his mood going dark and anxious again.

"Amen," Jeanne responded, giving him a sympathetic look.

CHAPTER 20

September 1

As Brian came in through the front door of his house, he had no idea what to expect. No one had texted him for the two-plus hours he'd been away. The first thing he noticed was the soundtrack from a PBS cartoon coming from the kitchen; it sounded like *Curious George*. Thankfully there was no arguing or crying. The second thing he heard was Aimée and Hannah talking in the living room. Aimée waved and beckoned him to come in.

"Did you have any luck?" she questioned.

"It depends on what you mean by luck," he said. "I did retain a lawyer. His name is Patrick McCarthy, he was in Erin's class in elementary school, and he seems competent enough although he looks younger than I expected."

"I'm sure he'll be good," Aimée reassured him. "It's a fine family. And his father is a lawyer, too."

"I also retained a medical billing advocate. It's Megan Doyle, the one you mentioned helped a neighbor. I have to say she seems very professional although she looks even younger than the lawyer. The important thing is that she's confident she can lower Emma's hospital bill significantly. It crossed my mind that she might even be a bit overconfident, but we'll see."

"I'm pleased to hear you've taken my advice. She certainly aided Alana Jenkins. But we want to warn you about Juliette. She's not doing so well."

"What's wrong?" After taking the sound of the cartoon coming from the kitchen as a modicum of promising news, this was not what he wanted to hear.

"She refuses to talk to either one of us."

Brian nodded while replaying in his mind Jeanne's warning about regression.

"And she won't eat," Aimée continued. "Camila has really risen to the task and bent over backward, even making her favorite breakfast of eggs, bacon, and toast strips with sugar. To give Camila a break, I sat with Juliette for a time, trying to get her to interact with me, but I had no luck. It's such a change from yesterday afternoon when we took her to the Church of the Good Shepherd, and she was acting herself. Now all she wants to do is watch cartoons, and she cries if anyone tries to interfere."

"That's not good," he said. "All right, I'll go in and see if I can turn things around."

"Before you do, how are you doing?" Aimée asked, catching Brian off guard.

As if his mindset were poised on a knife blade, as soon as Aimée asked her question, he felt a wave of emotion wash over him. She saw it and responded by standing up, coming over to him, and giving him a long hug. Brian didn't resist. When she finally let go, he wiped the corners of his eyes with the back of his hand. "Sorry," he managed.

"Nothing to be sorry about," Aimée insisted. She pulled him toward the couch where she'd been sitting. "Before you see to Juliette, join us for a moment. Hannah has some news she needs to share with you."

Lacking the strength to resist, Brian sat and sighed, sounding like a balloon losing its air. Hannah spoke up immediately. "I'm happy to say I've made a lot of progress," she began. She moved forward where she was sitting on the opposing couch. "I've been in touch with Riverside Funeral Home, and they have been most helpful. As soon as Emma is prepared, which I've been told will be in a few hours, they will bring her to our home for a proper wake, which will start this afternoon and continue overnight. Some family members and even neighbors have offered to help with food, drink, and other preparations like candles and flowers and arranging the house. How does all this sound to you?"

Hannah paused in her monologue and looked at him for some kind of response. Brian didn't know how he felt about all this traditional rigmarole but was unwilling to openly object even if he did. It was so apparent to him that Hannah was trying to come to terms with her daughter's death by attending to all the details. Once again, he wished he and Emma had discussed death in some form or fashion so he'd have some idea of what she would have wanted. If he had to guess, he thought she'd want her mother to decide if that could somehow be a help. With that in mind, all he did was nod.

"Okay," Hannah said, as if relieved by Brian's tacit agreement. "For tomorrow, I have arranged a funeral mass at the Church of the Good Shepherd, followed by interment at Woodlawn Cemetery. I hope you don't mind, but we have gone ahead and covered the expenses."

"That's very generous of you," he managed to say. He wasn't one who expected or generally accepted handouts, but this was an exceptional time, and he was grateful, considering the state of his finances.

"We're happy to help, knowing your security business is struggling," Hannah said, offering him a sympathetic look. "The one thing I'd like to ask you to do is to alert some of Emma's NYPD friends and colleagues about her passing even though attendance will be limited at both the wake and the funeral mass because of the pandemic."

"I can do that," Brian said. It also occurred to him that at the same time it might be an opportunity to at least float the idea of his returning to the NYPD with the ESU commander, Deputy Chief Michael Comstock. With Emma gone, he truly had no idea how much enthusiasm he still had about Personal Protection LLC, especially with the ongoing pandemic.

"Good!" Hannah voiced, slapping her knees with the palms of her hands before getting to her feet. "I'm sorry to have to leave you two to handle Juliette for the time being, but I have to get home to make sure everything goes smoothly. There's so much to do."

"We understand," Aimée said. "We'll see to Juliette, and thank you for bearing the burden of the wake and the funeral."

"It's the least I can do," Hannah said with a wave of dismissal. She turned around, hurried into the foyer for her shoes, and disappeared out the front door.

For a moment mother and son eyed each other.

"She's a whirlwind," he offered at last.

Aimée nodded. "She needs to be, and you are generous to allow it."

"I don't have the energy to interfere. Besides, I don't know what Emma would have wanted other than not wanting her mother to suffer."

"Je comprends," Aimée said. "Besides, your worry at the moment really has to be Juliette. My mothering instinct tells me she is going to need a lot of your attention. I'm more than willing to help, but I'm afraid the major burden will fall on you."

"My fathering instinct is giving me the same message," Brian agreed as he reached into his pants pocket and produced the card for the defunct business that Jeanne had given him. "To that end, I had an unexpected experience waiting to see Megan Doyle. Another of Ms. Doyle's clients came in, and I heard her give her name: Jeanne Juliette-Shaw." He handed the card to Aimée.

"Really?" she questioned. She looked at the business card and raised her eyebrows. "That's surprising. Juliette is not a common family name."

"That's exactly why I had the nerve to strike up a conversation," he said. "It turns out that she, like you, grew up in France and, also like you, came to the United States for college, Fordham University to be exact, and met her husband-to-be."

"Une telle coïncidence," Aimée said. She handed the business card back. "Mon Dieu! Did you ask where in France she's from?"

"I did. She's from the Camargue."

"Fascinating, but I surely don't know any Juliette families from the Camargue," Aimée said. "I'll have to ask my mother. It's a unique part of France, rather sparsely populated. I've never visited myself. What I do remember about it is that they have a special breed of horse called the Camargue, which has a unique light gray, almost white coat."

Suddenly the sound of the cartoon emanating from the kitchen stopped, yet there was no further sound from Juliette. Brian tensed, and he and Aimée exchanged a questioning glance as they listened for a moment.

"I wonder what that means?" he asked.

"I wonder the same. At least there's no complaint from Juliette, so it can't be all that bad."

"I guess," Brian said as he visibly relaxed. "Anyway, to get back to my story, I know it sounds odd under the circumstances for me to have had a conversation with a stranger while waiting to talk to a medical billing advocate, but our situations are surprisingly similar. Jeanne also recently lost a spouse and was sued by MMH Inwood. But most interesting of all is that we talked briefly about Juliette. She has a graduate degree in psychology, had been a school psychologist, and had experience with students who'd lost parents. She offered to give some advice, which is why she gave me the card with her mobile number. In fact, she even warned me that Juliette might regress and have psychosomatic symptoms."

"Sounds like she could really be useful," Aimée said. "Considering how Juliette has behaved this morning, I think some professional advice might be wise. Perhaps you should call her. My sense is that Juliette is going to need help, and your presence and attention are going to be crucial but might not be enough."

"You might be right," Brian said, getting to his feet and starting for the kitchen. Instead of following, Aimée headed toward the foyer. "Aren't you coming, too?" he asked.

"I think I should go and give Hannah a hand, and I think Juliette needs your undivided attention."

He nodded and continued into the kitchen. To his surprise Juliette wasn't there, just Camila rinsing the dishes and putting them in the dishwasher.

"Where's Juliette?" he asked.

"She's upstairs in her room," she said. "She suddenly said she wasn't feeling well and wanted to go to bed. To tell you the truth, although I wasn't happy to hear her say she wasn't feeling well, I was glad to hear her say something. It was the first time she has spoken since she woke up."

"That's not good," Brian said, recalling Jeanne's warning about regression.

"She did look a little flushed to me and I thought I saw her have a chill, so I took her temperature. It was 101."

"Uh-oh," Brian voiced. "Why would she have a fever? But wait! Is 101 a fever for a four-year-old?" He knew temperatures varied considerably during the day, even in adults but more so in children.

"Interesting you asked," Camila said. "I questioned it myself, so I googled it. I got the impression that anything over 100.4 could be considered a fever, but it's sort of borderline. But combined with her saying she doesn't feel well the last few days, it makes me nervous."

Remembering also that Jeanne mentioned Juliette might develop psychosomatic symptoms, he wondered if that could include a fever. He truly didn't know, and despite his EMT medical knowledge, he'd not had much pediatrics experience. Although he was mildly reluctant to call Jeanne the same day he'd met her for fear of taking advantage of her generosity, he thought the potential fever issue serious enough to overcome his hesitation. Sitting down on the banquette, he took out his phone and Jeanne's old business card. After giving Camila a brief description of Jeanne's professional qualifications, he placed the call, hoping Jeanne wouldn't think he was being too pushy by calling so soon. It had to ring a number of times, and just when he thought her voicemail message was about to start, she answered. He could tell she was out of breath. After he gave his name, he asked if he was calling at an inopportune moment and if she was still at Megan Doyle's.

"Heavens no, on both accounts. I'm glad to hear from you. I'm on my bike in Inwood Hill Park not too far from the Indian Caves. It just took me a minute to get my phone out of my back pocket."

"I'm sorry to interrupt what must be a fun ride," Brian said. "But I have a specific question, if you have a moment. You mentioned that my daughter might have psychosomatic symptoms in response to my wife's death. Can a fever be a psychosomatic symptom?"

"Good question! If I remember correctly, fever can definitely be a psychosomatic symptom. But I think it has only been seen in children considerably older than your daughter. You said she is four, correct?"

"Yes, she's four, but also like you suggested, just today she seems to be behaving as if she is much younger. She's stopped talking for the most part."

"Oh, dear," Jeanne said. "That doesn't sound so good. Listen, I can stop by if you would like and see if I can talk with her. I'm generally pretty good with kids. If you are concerned about Covid, I can also reassure you that I had a test just last week that was negative, and I abide by the pandemic rules to the letter."

"I would appreciate that very much," Brian said, and gave his house number. He then added that he'd had a relatively recent negative test as well, and as a family they'd been careful about following all the recommended precautions.

"Sounds good! We should be okay in that regard, and I'm on my way."

After he disconnected the call, he sat at the banquette for a few minutes, thinking how lucky he'd been by striking up a conversation with Jeanne. Even though he'd been fully engaged in the process of raising Juliette, Emma had been most definitely in the driver's seat. Now on his own, he felt like a fish out of water. "Well, that couldn't have gone any better," he said to Camila, who had sat down across from him. "She's coming over."

"I hope she can help," she said.

"I'm going to go up to Juliette's room and see if she'll talk. Do you want to come with me, or do you need a break?"

"I'll come. There's nothing for me to do in the office."

On the way up the back stairs, Brian gave Camila a thumbnail sketch of meeting Jeanne similar to what he'd told his mother.

"What a lucky encounter," she said as they headed along the upstairs hallway and entered Juliette's room. "She could be a big help."

Still in her pajamas, Juliette was lying on her side on the bed, facing away. As Brian came around the end of her bed, he could see that her eyes were open and unblinking, yet she didn't move. She was also sucking her thumb, which she hadn't done for years. It seemed to him further evidence that she was regressing. Her other hand was clutching Bunny to her chest.

"Hello, Pumpkin," Brian said, using one of his many endearing nicknames for her. She didn't respond or even move. "Camila said you weren't feeling well. Can you tell me what's wrong? Do you have a sore throat or is your stomach upset?" There was no response. "Camila said you had a chill, is that right?" Still no response.

Brian put his palm on Juliette's forehead, and she felt warm to him. "How about coming back to the kitchen and we'll watch something, whatever you want? We'll watch it together. What do you think? Is that a good idea?" Juliette didn't move or answer. He looked back at Camila, who shrugged her shoulders as if to say "I told you so." Redirecting his attention back to Juliette, Brian said: "I want to take your temperature again. Should we do it here or in the kitchen?"

"I want my mommy," Juliette whispered just loud enough for him to hear, and it melted his heart.

"I know you do, Pumpkin," Brian whispered back. "I miss her, too, but Mommy is in heaven. I'm here and someone else is coming who wants to meet you. Are you okay with that?"

When Juliette didn't respond or move, he gave her shoulder a squeeze just to make contact. "Okay, I'll get the thermometer, and I'll be right back."

CHAPTER 21

September 1

Jeanne, Camila, and Brian stepped out of Juliette's room, and all three hesitated at the top of the main staircase. Both Brian and Camila had been impressed with the creative way that Jeanne had managed to interact with Juliette and gotten her to talk. What she'd done was first engage Bunny as if Bunny was the one suffering, telling Bunny that as a little girl, she had a very similar rabbit friend who was so important to her that she'd brought her to America. Jeanne had then asked Juliette if she could hold Bunny, and to Brian's and Camila's surprise, Juliette had handed her the floppy stuffed rabbit.

"Oh, poor Bunny," she had said, stroking its head. "No wonder she's not feeling well. She's missing one of her eyes."

"But she can see fine," Juliette responded. With that little exchange Jeanne had started a conversation and had been able to switch the topic to Juliette's symptoms. Within a relatively short time she was able to get the child to admit to a sore throat, a headache, and an upset stomach.

"You certainly have a way with children," Camila observed.

"Thank you," she said. "I had a lot of practice being a school psychologist."

"So, what do you think?" Brian asked.

"I do think Juliette is experiencing psychosomatic symptoms, but I'm a little concerned she might also actually be sick," Jeanne said. "The fever issue is what bothers me. You say you confirmed her temperature is elevated?"

"I did," he said. "I took it again just before you got here. It's 100.8, which I guess is just over borderline. She has a fever, but not much of one."

"Whether it's a fever is beyond my expertise. I'm hardly a doctor, but tell me this: Is there any chance she might have been exposed to the coronavirus? I hate to say it, but there is a very slight chance she could have Covid."

"Not while I've been with her," Brian said. "And not here in the house." He looked at Camila questioningly.

"Certainly not here in the house," Camila said. "We haven't had any visitors, aside from the medical personnel yesterday, and they were in full protective gear. And I can't imagine when she could have been exposed on the few times she and I have gone out since Emma was hospitalized. On those occasions we only went to Emerson Playground or Isham Park, and she didn't socialize and wore her mask. But you know, thinking about how she has been acting makes me think she hasn't been feeling well for some time."

"I agree," Brian said. "Ever since my wife got sick, and Juliette saw her have a seizure, she hasn't been herself."

"Well, if we have learned anything over the last eight months, coronavirus spreads remarkably easily in certain situations," Jeanne remarked. "My advice is that she should at least be seen by her pediatrician. Does she have one?"

"Of course," he said. "Dr. Rajiv Bhatt on Broadway. Let's go down to the office, and I'll give him a call."

Brian led while the others followed. As they filed in, he turned on the light.

"A nice touch," Jeanne said as she glanced around. "I haven't been in too many offices with a crystal chandelier."

"It was a formal dining room that my wife and I turned into an office for our security business," Brian explained as he gestured for Jeanne to take one of several side chairs.

"I'm going to get some coffee and then check on Juliette to make sure she is still sleeping," Camila said. "Does anyone want anything from the kitchen?"

"I'm good," Brian called out as he searched his contacts for Dr. Bhatt's office number.

"Thank you, but I'm fine, too," Jeanne said with a wave.

As the call went through, he looked over at his visitor, who was still dressed in her biking clothes. "You look like you are an avid biker," he said. "My wife and I were, too."

"It was the one sport my husband and I did together."

Brian raised his hand to indicate his call had connected. He listened but didn't speak, then quickly disconnected and put the phone down. "Busy," he said.

"Camila seems very committed to your daughter," Jeanne said.

"She is. Unbelievably so. I am so lucky to have her. We hired her because of her business background, but she ended up moving in with us because of the pandemic. Since then she's become family in a very real way. I truly don't know what I'd do if she were to decide to leave."

"I hope you aren't offended by my asking," she said, "and you don't have to answer if you don't want to, but I'm intrigued by you saying that you and your wife had a security business. What's your background to have that kind of expertise?"

"We were both New York City policemen," Brian explained. "But more importantly we both were graduates of the Emergency Service Unit Academy and then served as ESU officers for a combined total of ten years, which is an extraordinary amount of law enforcement experience between the two of us."

"Excuse my ignorance, but I'm not familiar with ESU," Jeanne said.

"It stands for Emergency Service Unit. It's like special forces with the military. Whenever the NYPD are confronted with someone dangling off a skyscraper or a bridge, an active shooter, a hostage situation, a mass casualty event like 9/11, or even serving a high-risk warrant, we were the ones who were called to take care of it."

"You mean you were a member of a SWAT team?"

"Special Weapons and Tactics was just one small aspect of our role," he said. "ESU training was really extensive and intense. We were cross-trained in multiple disciplines and immersed in SCUBA, negotiation tactics, jumping out of helicopters, EMT requirements, you name it. My wife, Emma, was one of very few women who took the training. It was very physical to say the least."

"My word. It sounds to me like you are overtrained to do mere personal security."

"That was the idea. We thought we'd be in high demand with our backgrounds. It's just that the timing turned out to be problematic thanks to Covid-19." He raised his phone. "Let me try the pediatrician again."

Brian redialed and listened. He listened for longer than Jeanne expected without speaking and then let out a sigh of frustration before disconnecting. "Damn, he's on vacation!"

"Did the recording give the name and number of a covering doctor?"

"No," he said. "I'm not surprised. There aren't too many pediatricians in the immediate area. What's suggested in his outgoing message is for anything that can't wait until he gets back this coming Monday should be seen at the MMH Inwood Emergency Department. He's made arrangements that the MMH ED doctors have online access to his records if it's needed for the continuity of care."

"Might continuity of care be important in Juliette's case?" she asked.

"It could be," Brian said reluctantly. "I don't know for sure, but Juliette was a premature baby and spent her first couple of months in the Children's Hospital at Columbia-Presbyterian Hospital. That was where we originally met Dr. Bhatt."

"Okay, that solves it. Let's have her be seen at MMH Inwood. It might even be easier since they can go ahead and do a Covid-19 test straightaway."

"I don't know!" Brian said with a questioning expression. "In the middle of being in for nearly two hundred thousand dollars, the MMH Inwood ED might be the last place I want to take her. Hell, they might even refuse to see her for all I know."

"They aren't going to refuse to see her," Jeanne scoffed. "By law I don't think they can refuse."

"Maybe so, but they sure as hell might be less than accommodating or even rude to us."

"I can't imagine," Jeanne said. "The MMH Inwood might be predatory and overly profit centered, but I've come to understand there is a definite divide between their clinical side and their billing and collections shenanigans. Not once did I have the impression the doctors doing the day-to-day care had any idea of what was going on on the business side. Of course, whether they should have is an entirely different question."

"I disagree," he countered. "With my wife, it was the chief medical officer who saw fit to discharge her, and I've been worried it might have been because the hospital wasn't being paid."

"Hmmm," she voiced. "You might be right. Do you know that the position of chief medical officer is a relatively new position in hospitals?"

"I didn't," Brian said.

"During my lawsuit and because of my budding interest in business issues when I changed from being a school psychologist to running an alarm company, I've spent many hours researching modern-day hospital business practices. It's eye-opening, to say the least, or maybe horrifying is a better term. One of the things I came to understand was that the chief medical officer, or CMO in hospital jargon, is really an administrator hired by the hospital CEO. Although originally trained as a doctor, the CMO usually has some subsequent business background like an MBA, so their main interests revolve more around hospital costs than clinical outcomes. Although it sounds similar, the chief medical officer isn't the same as chief of surgery or chief of internal medicine, whose orientation is just the opposite."

"I had no idea," Brian said. "I thought the CMO might have been a combined position representing both surgery and internal medicine and still more attuned to what's best for the patient."

"No, it's definitely administrative and mostly geared toward keeping costs down to maximize profits," Jeanne said. "I hope I'm not boring you with all this economic minutia."

"Quite the contrary, but you are making me more concerned my wife was discharged prematurely. I feel so naïve about this current medical world."

"You and a lot of other people. Unfortunately, it's all about money. The sheer amount of money involved in healthcare attracted private equity because of the sky-high potential profits. It's the private equity investors who have forced hospitals to hire a bevy of compensation consultants."

"What the hell are compensation consultants?"

"They are highly trained businesspeople whose sole goal is to maximize revenue," Jeanne explained. "They don't care if the company is a hospital or trucking firm. Their shenanigans and advice have contributed significantly to a major uptick in hospital prices and thereby profit."

"I thought a lot of hospitals were now struggling financially," he said, realizing he'd been getting mixed information from Roger Dalton.

"That's true," she said. "But that's just since the coronavirus has forced them to cut back on lucrative elective surgery like joint replacements. Otherwise, hospitals, particularly chain hospitals, have been virtual gold mines thanks in large part to their teams of compensation consultants. It's the community hospitals and rural hospitals, which are still primarily oriented toward patient care and the neighborhoods they serve, that are hurting. They are either going out of business or being snapped up by hospital chains backed by private equity, which quickly turn them into money-making machines. And it's happening across the country, thanks to all their compensation consultants and CEOs like Charles Kelley. Welcome to the twenty-first century."

"It all infuriates me," Brian snapped. "With what you are saying, I'm even more convinced my wife was discharged because of economics. What a disaster!"

"It's possible," Jeanne said. "I give you that. But the point I want to make is that the MMH Inwood CMO and the compensation consultants have nothing to do clinically with what happens on a day-to-day basis in the Emergency Department. No one there will have any idea you owe the hospital money or that the hospital is suing you. And to get back to Juliette, I really think she should be seen and seen at MMH with her medical records available if needed and get a Covid test. Actually, what I think will be more of a problem is that she's going to refuse to go, but I'll be happy to help convince her if you would like."

"I'm sure you are right; she won't want to go. She can be very willful. It's very generous of you to offer help, which I sincerely appreciate, but *why* are you, if I might ask without sounding ungrateful?"

"To be entirely honest, it's mostly because I feel for you having just lost your wife yesterday," Jeanne said. "I have a visceral idea of what you are going through because of my own recent grief. I don't know how you are coping as well as you are."

"Like I said in Megan's office, it's with a lot of denial, but I'm also one of those people who needs to be doing something, and Juliette needs me to support her and hold together what I can of our life."

"I understand," she said, getting to her feet. "Let's see if we can get her to cooperate without too much difficulty."

At that moment his cell phone rang. He answered as he got to his feet, motioning to Jeanne to hold on for a moment. It was Aimée calling from the O'Briens'.

"Emma's wake is about to start," Aimée said. "Hannah asked me to call because she wants to know when you and Juliette are going to come over? I know you sounded reluctant earlier, but she thinks it is important for Juliette to say goodbye to her mother and maybe leave something for her in the casket."

"A problem has arisen," Brian began, wincing at the whole idea of the wake, particularly in relation to his daughter. He had forgotten all about it with his rising concerns about his daughter's health status. "Juliette seems to have a fever and doesn't feel great, making us worry she might have coronavirus."

"Oh, no!" Aimée exclaimed. "Mon Dieu! What are you going to do? Are you going to have her tested?"

"Yes, I think we must, as it could have dire consequences if she's positive. We're going to take her to the MMH Inwood ED."

"You and Camila?"

"No, with Jeanne Juliette-Shaw, the woman I mentioned earlier," Brian said. "I called her because Juliette hasn't been talking, and Jeanne came over and has been very helpful. She was able to get Juliette to open up. That's how we know Juliette's not feeling well, because up until then she wasn't talking. Luckily, she doesn't have any cough or breathing issues, but what can I say? We can't ignore it. I tried to call her pediatrician, but he's on vacation."

"Oh, goodness, mon fils," Aimée said empathetically. "I'll let Hannah know so she can perhaps hold things up. If Juliette is positive, we'll have to cancel the wake since we'll all have to quarantine. This could be a disaster on top of a disaster. Can you call me as soon as you know? Hannah's going to be really upset. All this planning activity is what's holding her together."

"Of course," Brian said, feeling a tinge guilty with his reservations about the wake, especially whether Juliette should be subjected to seeing her mother's body. He wasn't even sure how he felt about it himself.

As they headed for the stairs with Brian in the lead, Jeanne asked: "What was the name of the chief medical officer who encouraged your wife to be discharged before she probably should have been?"

"Dr. Kathrine Graham," he called over his shoulder.

"I thought so," she said irritably. "What a lousy ambassador for the medical profession! She was also the one I blame for MMH Inwood not being all that motivated to find a heart for my husband. Of course, the real fault really falls on Charles Kelley, who's responsible for the culture and hiring her. Doesn't it all irritate you to death when you think about it?"

Brian paused at the top of the stairs and waited for her. "It makes my blood boil," he admitted angrily as she gained the landing. "I even stormed into Kelley's office right after Emma died, and I would have done the same for Heather Williams's if it had been handy. But I can't think about this kind of stuff right now. I've got to concentrate on Juliette and finding a way out of this mess."

CHAPTER 22

September 1

Reaching into his pocket, Brian took out his phone and checked the time. "Shit," he whispered. "We've been here almost two hours." He was talking to Jeanne but didn't want Juliette to hear, which was unlikely because she had earbuds in and was watching cartoons on his laptop. The three of them were sitting relatively by themselves in the corner of the ED waiting room.

Getting Juliette to come to the hospital hadn't been easy. At first, she downright refused, but Jeanne used the same tactic she'd used to get Juliette to talk in the first place. She spoke extensively to Bunny, explaining to the toy why she had to go to the hospital for a Covid-19 test. Then when Bunny finally agreed, Juliette did the same. Camila drove them and also agreed to come and pick them up after Juliette had been seen.

"I'm starting to think they are definitely being passive-aggressive and making us wait," Brian said, still speaking softly. "I'm not as confident as you that there is the disconnect between the business side and the clinical side here in the ED. It doesn't seem that busy for us to have to wait almost two hours with a sick four-year-old."

"Let's avoid jumping to conclusions. They've been busy enough with the three ambulances that arrived since we got here. And the clerks and the triage nurse couldn't have been nicer. Plus, we have no idea what's going on back in the treatment rooms."

"I'm surprised that Juliette hasn't complained," Brian said, glancing over at his daughter.

"She's been an angel," Jeanne agreed. "Let's give the ED team the benefit of the doubt and hope she'll be seen shortly."

"I have another question for you as a school psychologist. When we were in my office, it was my mother who phoned. She was calling me to say that my wife's wake was about to begin and wanted to know when I would be bringing Juliette. I don't know how I feel about subjecting a four-year-old to her mother's wake. What's your opinion?"

"Probably like your mother, as an outsider of sorts I've developed a lot of respect for Irish funeral traditions, including wakes. There was a wake for my husband, and I was surprised by how many children showed up, including a nephew of ten and two nieces about Juliette's age."

"But it's her mother, not an aunt or uncle. I'm worried that forcing her to see the body will just add insult to injury. I mean, she already had to witness her having two seizures."

"My advice is to ask Juliette what she wants to do. Spell it out as an opportunity to say goodbye but remind her that her mother will not speak to her or even respond in any way at all. Just be totally up front and let her decide."

"Really?" he questioned skeptically. It seemed beyond him to turn such a decision over to a four-year-old.

"In my experience, children are capable of making a lot of decisions for themselves," Jeanne said. "More than a lot of people give them credit for. Anyway, that's my advice."

"Okay, thanks. I'll think about it."

"What about the viral illness your wife had? Is it at all contagious?"

"No, eastern equine encephalitis needs the mosquito vector," Brian said. "I've learned the mosquito has to bite an infected songbird, which is the normal host, and then bite a human or some other animal."

"Why is it called 'equine'?"

"It first showed up in horses."

"Thank God it at least doesn't spread like Covid-19," she said.

"You got that right," Brian said without a lot of enthusiasm. He had too many other things to worry about.

"It's terrifying to think you can get a fatal disease attending a summer barbecue. What's amazing to me is that I've never learned so much about viruses until this year."

"We healthy human beings have no real appreciation of how close we are to the precipice at any given time," he said. "It's especially disturbing when the institutions you count on to help when you need it, like hospitals and health insurance, can't be depended upon."

"It's a scary situation on so many levels."

"How much did MMH Inwood sue you for?" Brian said. "I hope you don't mind me asking."

"No, I don't mind at all," Jeanne reassured him. "It was a bit over four hundred thousand dollars."

"Yikes," Brian said. "How did your bill get that high?"

"It's easy," she said. "There were multiple admissions involved, several stays in the cardiac intensive care unit, and the surgery to implant the ventricular assist device. It adds up quickly, especially for people like you and me with lousy health insurance."

"That's what I've been learning," he said bitterly.

"The four hundred thousand–plus was before I got Megan Doyle involved. She's cut it down almost in half."

"That's encouraging."

"Yeah, but it's still about a quarter of a million dollars," Jeanne said. "That's enough to bankrupt most Americans except the top one percent. What excuse did Peerless give for not paying any of your hospital bill? It couldn't have been the preexisting excuse they used for us."

Brian gave a short, disgusted laugh. "No, they didn't claim Emma's problem was a preexisting condition. There were two parts to their strategy. The first part was the ED bill, which they said they weren't going to cover because Emma was ambulatory and should have gone to a GP who could have arranged admission. They said they were trying to rein in the overuse of hospital Emergency Department visits. It was just a bogus excuse, and they invited me to sue, the bastards. With the hospital bill it was a unique way of interpreting the deductible. I won't bore you with the details. But even if they were going to pay, it would have only been a thousand dollars a day, which, when my wife and I were in the market to get health insurance we could afford, we mistakenly thought was a significant contribution. We had no idea how pitifully inadequate it is."

"We were duped in the same way."

"How long ago did your husband pass away?" Brian asked. "If you'd rather not talk about it, I understand."

"It's all right. It was just a little over a year ago."

"Did MMH Inwood sue you right away like me?"

"No," Jeanne began. "Stupid me tried to pay them the original amount. There was some cash in the business, so I gave them sixty-five thousand up front and agreed to pay twenty thousand a month for two years. I'd made several monthly payments, but then the pandemic hit, and everything shut down, and the alarm business mostly dried up. That's when they sued me."

"Did they have something to do with your company's bankruptcy?"

"Of course," she said. "They also garnished any income I might have earned from the business if I'd tried to keep it going. But to tell you the truth, with my husband's passing, I wasn't all that interested in running the company even though I had learned a lot about alarm technology and business in the three years I'd spent involved. While he was alive it made sense because he was a techie, not a business-man, and he had been paying someone much too much to run the business side of the operation."

"I can understand. I'm already wondering if I have what it takes to try to make a go of Personal Protection LLC without my wife. I'm probably more like your husband, since Emma handled the business side along with Camila. I've already wondered if I should try to get my old position back with the NYPD ESU."

"I'm going to go back to school psychology as soon as the legal dust settles," Jeanne said. "The only reason I've held off is because I certainly don't want MMH Inwood garnishing my wages."

"I want to go home," Juliette said suddenly, taking out her ear-buds.

"I'm sure you do, sweetie," Brian agreed. "I do, too. I think I'll see what is holding things up." As he started to get up, Jeanne reached out and gripped his arm.

"For what it's worth, I don't think you'll get any satisfaction making a fuss," she said. "And you could make things worse. Just a suggestion."

He hesitated, looking over at the information desk, which was always a beehive of activity. When they'd first arrived two hours earlier, a triage nurse had listened to their story about Juliette's symptoms, noted she was a patient of Dr. Rajiv Bhatt, whose records were available if needed since she had been a preemie, checked Juliette's vital signs, and told them they'd be seen shortly. That was the last contact they'd had without any apology or explanation. At the same time, he knew Jeanne was correct and that raising a ruckus could very well be counterproductive.

"I'll be a perfect gentleman," Brian promised. "I just need to make sure we haven't been forgotten somehow."

CHAPTER 23

September 1

Juliette Murphy!" a nurse in gown and mask called out after emerging from the depths of the Emergency Department.

"God! It's about time," Brian mumbled as he got to his feet. It had been more than three hours that they had been waiting. Mercifully, Juliette had fallen asleep about a half hour earlier.

"It's been a long wait," Jeanne agreed. "But, again, try not to act angry, for Juliette's sake."

"It's going to be difficult for me not to point out that we've seen a number of people arrive, be seen, and leave while we've been sitting here with a sick four-year-old."

"I can't imagine you'll get any satisfaction if you act irritated," Jeanne said. "And try to remember that at least she's going to be seen, and you'll get the Covid-19 test out of the way."

"Okay, okay," he said, taking a deep breath to calm himself. "You are right. I'll try to be nice." He then reached down and picked Juliette up. "Come on, Pumpkin!" he urged. "We'll get you checked out and then get you home." She mumbled a brief complaint but fell back asleep almost immediately in Brian's arms with her head on his shoulder. While he reached for Bunny, he added to Jeanne: "No matter what you say, I'm convinced they've been keeping us waiting because of the outstanding bill I owe. I'm sorry, but it's the only explanation."

"You don't know that for sure," Jeanne said.

"I feel it."

"Feeling it and knowing it are two different things."

"Maybe," Brian said. "Can you get the rest of the stuff?"

"Leave it! I'll watch it. No worries."

"You're not coming with us?"

"I'm not family and with the pandemic rules, we're lucky they let me even in the waiting area. I'll be here when you're done. Good luck."

"You're probably right," he said. "Okay! We'll try to at least make this part quick."

With the sleeping Juliette in one arm and Bunny in the other, Brian walked the width of the waiting room and approached the nurse who'd called out Juliette's name. She was wearing a face shield as well as a mask.

"Well, well," the nurse said good-naturedly. "The sweetie seems to have fallen asleep. I think that is a good sign, maybe she's feeling better."

"We've been waiting more than three hours," he said, struggling to keep his voice neutral.

"Sorry about that. We've been busy as usual. My name is Olivia. Would you please follow me?"

Still carrying the sleeping Juliette and Bunny, Brian trailed the nurse back to a tiny ambulatory examination room with an exam table, a sink, two chairs, and a built-in desk with a monitor. Olivia patted the exam table, asked him to put Juliette down, and then washed her hands. At first Juliette resisted, but then became cooperative in the new surroundings when Olivia gave her a hemostat to hold. In a gentle and kind fashion, Olivia took Juliette's vital signs while keeping up a conversation about Bunny, which Juliette had taken from Brian.

"What's her temperature?" Brian asked.

"Ninety-eight point six," Olivia read off the number. "Nice and normal."

"Really?" he questioned. "Last time we took it at home it was almost 101. Are you sure of your reading?"

"I'll take it again," Olivia offered happily. She was using a thermal scanner. "Yup! Normal." Addressing Juliette, she asked: "And how do you feel now, love?"

"I want to go home," Juliette said.

"I'm sure you do," Olivia responded. She looked briefly at the tablet she was holding and then asked, "But what about your sore throat, and headache, and upset stomach?"

"I'm okay now," Juliette said.

"Are you sure?" Brian asked, butting in, shocked at the reversal of Juliette's complaints.

"Yes," Juliette insisted. "And Bunny feels better, too."

"I'm so glad," Olivia said. "Okay, Dr. Kramer will be in to see you, Miss Juliette, in just a few minutes. Is that okay?"

Juliette nodded, handing back the hemostat before Olivia left the room.

"Are you sure you don't have a sore throat any longer?" Brian asked, mystified.

Juliette nodded and then started to climb down from the exam table, but Brian stopped her and sat down next to her. Taking a cue from Jeanne, he talked more about her symptoms using Bunny as a go-between. She continued to be insistent that Bunny's throat, head, and stomach were fine.

It was almost twenty minutes before an extremely youthful Dr. Mercedes Kramer came swooping ebulliently into the tiny exam room along with Olivia. Now bored, Juliette answered all the doctor's rapid-fire questions with a curt no: no sore throat, no congestion, no headache, no coughing, no vomiting, and no generally feeling bad. Maintaining a happy chatter, Dr. Kramer quickly washed her hands and then rapidly but thoroughly examined the child, even allowing Juliette to listen to her own heart. When she was finished, she said: "Miss Juliette, I think you are in fine shape." She then gave Juliette a reassuring shoulder squeeze.

"Dr. Kramer, can I speak with you alone for a moment?" Brian said when the doctor turned to him, presumably to declare Juliette a picture of health.

"Of course," Dr. Kramer said, motioning for him to step out into the corridor.

"I thought it best to tell you that my daughter is under a lot of stress," Brian said, struggling to stay in control of his emotions, now heightened by the long wait to be seen and Juliette's disappearing symptoms. "Her mother died yesterday from EEE and my daughter happened to witness her suffering two grand mal convulsions, including the one yesterday that resulted in her death."

"Oh, what a terrible story," Dr. Kramer voiced with sympathy. "I'm so sorry for your loss. Was your wife seen here in our ED?"

"Yes," Brian said. "Yesterday. She was brought in by ALS ambulance."

"Oh, yes. I heard about that case. Such a tragedy for an otherwise healthy young woman. EEE is a bad disease, but it seems that your daughter is weathering your wife's passing rather well."

"Actually, she hasn't," he argued. "During the two weeks that my wife had been sick, my daughter had been struggling emotionally and behaviorally. Then it all came to a head yesterday when she was told her mother had died. She stopped communicating, and then today she had a chill, and when her temperature was taken, it was 101."

"She's afebrile now," Dr. Kramer stated.

"But her fever was real," Brian insisted. "I took it myself. It wasn't quite 101 but very close. I'm worried that she might be coming down with something, like Covid."

"Has she been exposed to someone with Covid?" Dr. Kramer asked. "Or has she been to any large functions or gatherings?"

"No, not at all."

"Have any of her friends or anyone in the family tested positive?"

"No, no one. And even when she was occasionally out, she didn't socialize, and she has been very good about wearing a mask. Or at least that is what I was told. But, still, her symptoms made us worry she might have the virus."

"She likely doesn't have Covid-19," Dr. Kramer said. "And she has plenty of reason to have significant psychosomatic symptoms, including a slight elevation in body temperature. If someone has contracted Covid-19 and has begun to have symptoms, even mild symptoms, they don't just spontaneously recover in a matter of hours. Trust me!"

"How can you be sure about my daughter?" he questioned. "I'd like her to at least have a Covid-19 test and maybe some blood work just to be on the safe side."

"Mr. Murphy, your daughter is afebrile, currently has no symptoms, and has a completely negative physical exam. She doesn't need blood work or a Covid-19 test. Besides, we currently are swamped with Covid-19 tests for people with real indications and for those being admitted as inpatients."

"We've waited for more than three hours to be seen," Brian snapped. "The least you could do is indulge me."

"I'm sorry to hear you've had to wait," Dr. Kramer said, trying to remain calm. "We make an effort to see everyone in a timely fashion according to their need."

"I've heard that before, but it's not been that busy. Three hours is a long time to wait with a sick child."

"We try to triage as best as we can," Dr. Kramer said with growing irritation. "We need to give priority to the sickest patients."

"You're not hearing me. We've witnessed a number of people who walked in after us who didn't look or act sick, were seen, and walked out while we were ignored. I'll tell you what it makes me think. I think we have been forced to wait because I owe the hospital a ton of money for my wife's treatment. And now, also because of that, you are refusing to really look into my daughter's symptoms. You don't want to do any lab tests because you worry you won't get paid."

Clearly taking offense, Dr. Kramer said: "Mr. Murphy, we here in the ED have no idea of any patient's financial status vis-à-vis the hospital. We don't discriminate at all for any reason whatsoever except the degree of emergency involved. With an ambulatory patient, once they are signed in, we diagnose and we treat just as soon as we can. We order tests when we think they are called for. That's the long and short of it."

At that moment, Olivia stuck her head out from the examination room. "Sorry to interrupt, but Miss Juliette and Bunny very much want to go home."

"Mr. Murphy, I strongly recommend you listen to your daughter and go home. You both are under a lot of stress. I'm sorry for your loss." With that, Dr. Kramer turned on her heels and walked away.

Feeling newly annoyed at now being patronized, Brian stared after her, resisting going after her to get in the last word. Instead, he turned around and went into the examination room.

"Let's go, Pumpkin!" he said, reaching to pick Juliette and Bunny up into his arms.

CHAPTER 24

September 1

By the time Brian got out to Jeanne in the waiting area, he'd calmed down to a degree. What had helped was seeing that Juliette had been entertained while he was having words with Dr. Kramer. Once again Olivia had given her the hemostat to play with, and now Juliette was telling him she wanted to be a surgeon when she grew up.

"Well, what was found?" Jeanne asked, pocketing her phone. She stood up and picked up his laptop.

"Absolutely nothing," Brian answered, his frustration clearly showing. "They gave her a clean bill of health, and they refused to do any blood work or give her a Covid-19 test. We waited for three hours for nothing."

"What about her fever?"

"It was gone," Brian said. He sat Juliette down so he could get out his phone to call Camila. "I couldn't believe it. They took her temperature twice with a thermal scanner. Both times 98.6. I'm not sure they believed that it had been 101 earlier."

"Are you okay?"

"A little stressed," he admitted. "I was hoping that they would have been willing to be a bit more aggressive diagnostically."

As Brian made the call to arrange for them to be picked up, Jeanne asked Bunny how she felt about the examination. Juliette responded by talking about playing with the hemostat and explained how it functioned. As soon as he finished contacting Camila, all three walked out into the warm afternoon sunshine to stand at the turnout in front of the hospital. While they waited, Jeanne asked why the doctor didn't do a Covid-19 test at the very least.

"She didn't think it was necessary, especially with no history of exposure or symptoms," Brian explained irritably. "She told me that their testing was currently swamped with people with definite symptoms and those who were about to be admitted as inpatients."

"Isn't a temperature elevation, a sore throat, and a headache enough to qualify?"

"By the time Juliette was seen she didn't have any symptoms and had no fever," Brian said with obvious frustration. "I still tried to force the issue, but the doctor was adamant, saying that Covid-19 symptoms don't resolve over the course of a few hours, and for what it's worth, I'm sure she is right. As for Juliette's symptoms, the doctor attributed them to being psychosomatic."

"Even the fever?"

"Yeah, even the fever."

"Well, at least Juliette seemed to have enjoyed herself and now wants to be a surgeon," Jeanne said, trying to look on the bright side.

"I wish I could say the same for myself," Brian said. "The doctor's attitude irked me, and I'm afraid I kind of provoked her by accusing the ED of purposefully making us wait."

"Uh-oh, I was afraid of that."

"I couldn't help myself," he confessed.

"Well, at least we know Juliette is okay," Jeanne offered. "Now I think you should call your mother and let her know so the wake can get underway."

"Oh, shit!" Brian whispered, gritting his teeth. "I was trying not to think about that. I still don't know how I feel about the whole wake idea. I'm not sure I can face it or want to subject Juliette to it."

"I know exactly what you mean. I felt the same reservation going to my husband's, Riley's, wake a year ago. But you know what? Ultimately, I was glad I was forced to participate, and it gave me an appreciation for the Irish funeral traditions as a celebration of a life rather than purely a mourning for a loss. On top of that, I actually became closer to my in-laws because of it."

"So you really changed your mind about your husband's wake after going?"

"Yes, I did," Jeanne said. "It definitely helped me deal with the whole situation. I truly was glad I was pressured to attend."

"All right, I'll take your word for it, but what about you-know-who?" He nodded down at Juliette, who was holding on to Brian's hand. "Do you really think I should ask her if she wants to go?"

"As I said, Riley had a young nephew and two young nieces, all of whom came to his wake. Two of them I think were four, same as your daughter. At the time, I was somewhat fearful of the effects on their young psyches, but they weathered it well and seemed to have been appreciative of being included. As I said, my advice is to ask her. Kids that age have some intuitive idea of what death means."

"Oh, boy," he muttered. He looked down at Juliette, who had let go of his hand to retrieve Bunny from the sidewalk. As she was wiping off the stuffed rabbit, Brian said, "Juliette, I have a question I need to ask you."

"You are going to do it here?" Jeanne asked with alarm. "Do you think this is the right place?"

"Why not? Suddenly I have the courage and need to get it out. Do you think asking her here is a mistake?"

"No, I guess not."

"Juliette, love," Brian continued while retaking her hand. "Yesterday we lost Mommy. She died and went to heaven, and today Grandma and Grandpa O'Brien are having a celebration of Mommy's life called a wake. Mommy's body will be there for people to see for the last time to say goodbye before she is buried."

"How can Mommy's body be at Grandma's if she went to heaven?" Juliette asked, looking up at him.

"Her spirit or soul went to heaven," Brian explained, exchanging a rapid glance with Jeanne for reassurance. She nodded encouragement. "Her empty body is still here with us. But there is no life. She won't talk or move."

"Will she look icky?" Juliette asked, making a face.

"No, she will probably look beautiful just like always," Brian reassured her, struggling with his own emotions. "You can bring something to leave with Mommy's body if you would like to keep her company."

"Can I bring Bunny?"

"Of course you can bring Bunny," he said, taking a deep breath to keep himself under a semblance of equanimity. He glanced again at Jeanne and could tell she was having the same control issues. "I'm sure that Mommy's spirit will be very happy if you bring Bunny."

"I want to go and bring Bunny," Juliette insisted.

"Okay, perfect. You, Bunny, and I will all go together." He again looked over at Jeanne, who gave him a thumbs-up.

"I want you to come, too," Juliette said, looking up at Jeanne.

"Thank you, sweetheart," Jeanne said. She was touched and exchanged a quick, teary glance with Brian. "But I don't think that would be appropriate. The wake is for family, especially during the pandemic when the number of visitors will likely be limited. But if you'd like I'll come and visit you tomorrow, and you can tell me all about it."

"Okay," Juliette said agreeably as the Murphys' Subaru appeared, coming up the driveway onto the hospital grounds.

CHAPTER 25

September 1

The ride from MMH Inwood to the house took only a few minutes, but it was long enough for Brian to call Aimée and report that Juliette had been given a clean bill of health, providing a green light for Emma's wake. Aimée had been pleased on both accounts and promised to let Hannah know immediately. She then asked when Brian and Juliette would be arriving, and he said they'd come over within the hour.

Camila turned into the Murphy driveway and stopped alongside the house. After everyone got out, Camila and Juliette headed for the back door, which led directly into the kitchen. Jeanne held up, saying she'd get her bike from where she'd placed it back by the garage and head home. "I hope all goes well at the wake," she added. "And I hope it has the same effect on you my husband's had on me."

"I hope so, too. And I want to thank you sincerely for your help and generosity. You've been amazing with Juliette. Really! I can't thank you enough."

"It's been my pleasure," Jeanne said. "She's a darling little girl. And dealing with her has reminded me of what I missed about being a school psychologist. It's so much more rewarding than running a business. So, if you need more help with her, say, after the wake and funeral, I'm certainly available, and you have my number."

"As I said and I say again, I appreciate your generosity."

After Jeanne retrieved her bike Brian walked with her back out to the street.

"I'm sorry about the pavement around here," he said. "Be careful. They ground down the street in preparation to repave it, but when it's going to get done is anybody's guess. With all the utilities sticking up, it's treacherous."

"I'll be careful," Jeanne promised. "I'll walk the bike, until I think it's safe."

"Good idea. Thanks again for everything. Truly."

"You are welcome," Jeanne said, waving over her shoulder as she walked her bike down toward Park Terrace West. Brian watched her until she turned the corner.

Using the front door, he entered the house. He found Camila and Juliette upstairs in Juliette's room, trying to decide which of her many church dresses that Grandma Aimée had bought for her that she wanted to wear. While that was in process, Brian went into his closet, got out the only dark suit he owned, and put it on. He couldn't remember the last time he'd worn it. He then pushed around his unruly, relatively short hair with a hairbrush. Returning to Juliette's room, he saw that she had made up her mind about her outfit and was now almost ready. She looked precious in a pink dress with her golden hair braided and tied with a matching ribbon. On her feet were black patent-leather shoes. Whether such clothes were appropriate for a wake, he had no idea, but he didn't care. If that was what Juliette wanted to wear, it was fine with him. She was holding Bunny tightly, clutched against her chest.

As he was admiring his daughter, he felt his phone vibrate, indicating he'd gotten a text message. Taking it out, he saw it was from Roger Dalton, and opening the message, he read that Roger wanted him to call as soon as possible. Brian couldn't help but wonder what it might be about, knowing it couldn't be anything good. But then he thought that perhaps it had something to do with Patrick McCarthy or Megan Doyle and their need to obtain a full printout of the hospital record. But whatever it was, he decided to put it off until after the wake. He was already under enough stress despite everything that Jeanne had said and still had reservations about going, both for himself and Juliette. He also decided at some appropriate time in the future to let it be known that when his own time came, he'd prefer not to have his body go through all such rituals.

"How about you, Camila?" he said when Juliette was completely ready. "I apologize for not asking earlier whether you'd like to come with us, but you are welcome."

"No, thank you. I think a wake is for immediate family," Camila said, echoing Jeanne.

"You feel like family to me," Brian observed.

"Thank you for that, but others might not feel the same. I prefer to stay here." She then pulled Brian to the side and said in a lowered voice, "With Jeanne gone, Juliette seems to be reverting back to her silent mode. She's hardly talking again."

"Oh, no," he said. "Good grief! That's not encouraging. What's your opinion? Should I rethink taking her to the wake?"

"No, I'm convinced she wants to go," Camila said. "She wouldn't have been so involved in picking out a dress and her hairstyle if she didn't. Just keep it in mind that the whole situation is extremely stressful for her."

"That's understandable," Brian said, thinking of his own ambivalence. "All right, let's get it over with."

As they exited the house, he complimented Juliette on how lovely she looked but got no response. Nor did she speak as they descended the steps in the front yard when he asked how she felt about going to the wake now that they were on their way. The only response he got was when he asked her if she had enjoyed meeting Jeanne. The answer was a simple *yes* without any elaboration.

The trip only took a few minutes, and the only minor problem was Juliette navigating the roughly striated street in her patent-leather shoes when they needed to cross to the other side. As they got closer to the O'Briens', which was also one of the very few single-family homes in Inwood, they could see about a dozen people standing in the small front yard and a few more on the front porch, all engaged in small group conversations and mostly maintaining a reasonable amount of social distancing. All were wearing masks, including the handful of children who were present. Many of the adults were holding cut-crystal glassware, which Brian assumed contained Jameson whiskey. Despite the masks, he recognized most people although there were a few he couldn't place. Over the years he'd met almost all of Emma's many relatives at various holiday gatherings. Emma had three older brothers with families, and Emma's mother and father had a total of five siblings altogether. Brian also recognized a few of his relatives on his father's side, including an uncle who was a retired NYPD officer. He didn't see any of his siblings, but assumed they'd merely not yet arrived. None of them were currently living in Inwood.

After coming through the front gate of the proverbial white picket fence and heading for the steps up to the front porch, Brian nodded to a number of people and he also thanked those who were close enough to voice their condolences, but he didn't stop. As he and Juliette gained the porch, Hannah appeared from within the house as if she had been watching for them.

"Welcome, you two," Hannah said with a kind of nervous energy. Then, taking Juliette's hand, she added: "Come, Juliette. Come and say a proper goodbye to your beautiful mother." She then scooped Juliette up in her arms and headed indoors. Brian was mildly taken aback by her fervor, but realized it made sense given that Emma had been the beloved baby as well as the only girl with three older brothers.

Suddenly bereft of his daughter, he was besieged by well-wishers. Brian thanked all and touched elbows with a number of others, all the while wondering what was happening with Juliette inside the house. As soon as he could, he excused himself and went inside.

In the foyer Brian noticed the mirror above the console table had been turned around. It was a tradition he'd seen before at Irish wakes he'd attended. Pausing, he glanced around the interior of the O'Briens' large house. In the background he could hear Celtic music playing softly, and a dozen-plus people were standing in small groups in the living and dining rooms conversing quietly.

In the dining room the table was heaped with food, mostly sandwiches. Brian's father-in-law, Ryan O'Brien, a large and considerably overweight man in his early sixties, was in the living room manning a makeshift bar on a bureau. To the right in a leaded-glass windowed alcove was the bier with a large, expensive-looking open coffin and a cascade of white flowers, mostly roses, which were emitting a pleasant aroma. From where he was standing he could see Emma's body outfitted in a white dress with her head and striking red hair resting against a white satin pillow. The image gave Brian a physical and emotional jolt, but he was distracted by the sight of Hannah standing next to the coffin, holding Juliette in her arms. It was obvious Hannah was talking but because of the distance compounded by the background music, he couldn't hear what was being said. Regardless, Juliette appeared frozen, staring at her mother with one hand around Hannah's neck and the other still clutching Bunny.

Moving closer in hopes of hearing what Hannah was saying, Brian's effort was thwarted by laughter coming from several male relatives grouped around Ryan. Just as he was getting close enough to hear, someone behind him called out his name. Turning, he saw his mother coming in his direction. She'd emerged from the kitchen, carrying a tray of additional sandwiches even though the dining table was already heaped with them.

Momentarily torn between his daughter and his mother, he turned toward his mother as she rapidly approached.

"Great to see you two," Aimée said. "How are you holding up, mon chéri?"

"Reasonably well," Brian answered. "I'm just concerned about Juliette."

"Have either of you eaten anything? We've got lots of food, with more coming."

"I'm not hungry," he said. The last thing he wanted to do was eat or drink.

"I'm glad you brought Juliette. I sensed you were reluctant. What changed your mind?"

"Jeanne Juliette-Shaw," Brian said. "The woman I told you about from Megan Doyle's office. She suggested I ask Juliette if she wanted to come, which I did, and Juliette agreed. It surprised me but maybe it shouldn't. Jeanne seems to really understand children."

"Well, I know how pleased Hannah is," Aimée said. "She's been beside herself waiting for you and Juliette to arrive."

At that moment Brian and Aimée watched as Hannah leaned forward, allowing Juliette to tuck Bunny in alongside Emma's right side at chest level. Then Juliette tentatively reached out with an extended index finger and touched Emma's firm and lifeless cheek. Almost immediately Juliette pulled her hand back as if she'd touched something scorchingly hot and let out a whimper loud enough for both Brian and Aimée to hear.

His heart skipped a beat, and he stepped forward just as Hannah turned around and faced into the room. Seeing her father, Juliette reached out with both hands. Feeling instantly protective, Brian gladly took hold of his daughter, who quickly buried her head in the crook of his neck and wrapped her arms tightly around his head.

"Juliette was very good and said goodbye to her mother," Hannah said. "And she gave her Bunny to keep her company. I'm very proud of her."

Feeling Juliette holding on to him with surprising force, Brian was immediately concerned that the experience hadn't been without some psychological pain, making him wonder if he'd made the wrong decision to bring her. It was yet another reminder that his life's work had totally devolved to her needs.

"Your cousins will be here shortly," Hannah told Juliette as she reached out and patted the child on the back. "Are you hungry? We have cake coming out soon."

Juliette didn't answer but rather gripped his neck with more intensity.

"I think I'll take her home," Brian decided on the spot. "My sense is that it has been a bit difficult for her."

"You should stay and have something to eat!" Hannah offered quickly. "We have a lot of food, including the cake I mentioned."

"I'm really not hungry. Thank you for all your efforts on Emma's behalf."

"You are welcome," Hannah said. "Will you be back? I'm sure there are lots of people who would like to offer you their condolences."

"Possibly," Brian answered, although he knew he didn't mean it. He'd had enough as well. His consuming love of his wife was for her essence or soul, certainly not for her eviscerated, empty body. He could appreciate that such funeral rituals were helpful for some people and served a social function, but not for him and maybe not for Juliette as well. Recalling the phrase "dust to dust" and its meaning from his catechism instruction as a child, he was developing a new regard for the benefits of cremation.

"Okay," Hannah said tensely. "Tomorrow the mass will be at ten at the Church of the Good Shepherd followed by the funeral. If you'd like to walk with us, you are more than welcome. We could come by and pick you up."

"Thank you," Brian said, not knowing how he felt about it. "I'll let you know."

Without putting Juliette down, he headed for the door. As he went, a number of people gestured toward him with their drinks as if making some kind of toast. He nodded in acknowledgment but didn't stop. Outside, as he crossed the porch, descended the front steps, and then walked the length of the walkway, other people did the same, but thankfully no one tried to stop him. It wasn't until they were on the street that Juliette indicated she wanted to be put down. After he had, he took her proffered hand, and they walked on in silence. At the halfway mark, he asked her if she was all right and if she was glad she'd said goodbye to her mother. When she didn't respond, he worried anew whether it had been a mistake to bring her to the wake, although at least he was glad he'd given her the opportunity to decide and hadn't forced her to go.

Sensing Juliette might have trouble coming to terms with the experience, Brian was glad that Jeanne had offered to help. He also found himself again wondering if the likes of Charles Kelley and Heather Williams had any conception of the real pain and consequences their selfish policies engendered in real families. It was enough to make him furious all over again.

CHAPTER 26

September 1

When Brian and Juliette came in through the front door, they were met by a concerned Camila.

"How did it go?" Camila asked. "You're back much earlier than I expected."

"Do you want to tell her?" Brian asked Juliette as they both took off their shoes and face masks. When she stayed silent, he added: "Juliette touched Mommy, and it upset her. Isn't that right, Pumpkin?"

Juliette made a beeline for the stairs, apparently retreating to the sanctuary of her room.

Brian and Camila watched her go. "In retrospect, I don't think her going to the wake was that great an idea," he said when the child was out of hearing range. "It wasn't a disaster, or at least I hope not, and it appeared she was doing reasonably well in her grandmother's arms until she touched Emma's face. I don't know if it was her decision to do it or if Hannah encouraged her, or even if it is important. One way or the other, it freaked her out. I'm not surprised. I wouldn't have wanted to do it myself. At any rate, I thought it best to bring her home right away."

"Oh, dear," Camila exclaimed, looking up the stairs. "I'll go up and help her out of her fancy dress and get her into something more comfortable. Then I'll see if she is hungry."

"Thank you," Brian said with a relieved sigh.

"What about you?" she questioned. "How are you holding up?"

"So-so," Brian said, holding his hand out and tilting it from side to side. "I'm finding the funeral rituals hard to get through. I didn't like them when my father died, and I like them even less in relation to Emma. For me, the grieving should be personal, not public."

"Are you going to go back to the wake?" Camila asked. "If you are, I'll keep Juliette occupied."

"I don't think so. I've also had enough public mourning for one day. I'll be in the office. I need to make a call."

Sitting at his desk, he found himself staring at Emma's empty work station. The sudden acknowledgment that she was gone for good swept over him, bringing an overwhelming sense of loss along with it. Luckily the emotions abated almost as quickly as they had emerged when he thought of Juliette suffering upstairs in her room. Her immediate needs trumped any thoughts of indulging his own emotions, and he had to concentrate on helping her come to terms with losing her mother at the tender age of four.

Yet looking at Emma's empty chair also reminded him of the thoughts he'd had yesterday about Personal Protection LLC and whether he wanted to continue building the company in such a difficult time. With that issue in mind, Brian put off calling Roger Dalton, which was who he'd intended to call, and instead rang Deputy Chief Michael Comstock, the commanding officer of the NYPD ESU. Fully expecting to have to leave his name and number and get a call back, Brian was pleasantly surprised when he found himself talking with his former commanding officer. Although the deputy chief had not been happy losing two very popular and talented officers when he and Emma had retired, he now sounded very happy to hear from Brian.

"How are you and Emma and how is your security company navigating the pandemic?" Michael asked.

"I'm afraid I have bad news on both fronts," he said. "The company is doing very poorly at the moment. It might have been the worst possible time to start a security firm because of the pandemic. There's been almost no work. But worse still, Emma passed away just yesterday from a virus."

"Oh, no!" Michael said. "Oh, I'm so very sorry. That's terrible news. Was it Covid-19?"

"No, it wasn't," Brian said with a catch in his voice. "It was eastern equine encephalitis."

"Is that something like West Nile virus?"

"It's similar," Brian said. "It's a different virus, but it is also spread by mosquitoes. We think she got it when we had a beach barbecue on Cape Cod."

"Such a tragedy, such a loss! She was an exceptional woman. When are the services scheduled, so we can send a delegation, myself included?"

"Services and funeral are tomorrow. Thank you for your offer to attend, but due to the pandemic, it's only going to involve immediate family."

"Understood," Michael said regretfully. "Well, you have my most sincere condolences to you and your whole family."

"Thank you, sir. There is something else I want to discuss with you. With my wife gone, I'm questioning my interest in continuing with our struggling company, especially with the pandemic and no end in sight. What I wanted to inquire is whether you might look kindly on me reversing my retirement and rejoining the ESU." Brian found himself superstitiously crossing his fingers, hoping for an affirmative reply even though he'd not yet completely given up on Personal Protection LLC.

"It depends on your level of commitment," Michael began. "With your indirect question, it sounds to me as if you haven't quite made up your mind, which is understandable since it's so soon after your wife's passing. Let me say this: With all your training, the city has a significant investment in you, and that's definitely to your advantage. But to give you a second chance here at the ESU, I'd want to be convinced you are one-hundred-percent committed to returning before I give the green light. To be perfectly honest, both your and your wife's sudden resignation had a negative effect on morale for a time since both of you were highly respected around here."

"I'm sorry," Brian said. "That certainly wasn't our intention."

"Here's what I recommend. When you are up to it, come out here to headquarters and meet with me and then spend some quality time participating in some of our activities. Because of the pandemic, there wasn't a new class of cadets this spring. Instead we've ramped up refresher and recertification activities for the entire ESU force, particularly in the TAC House and SCUBA unit. Does that sound appealing to you?"

"Very appealing," he agreed. "I'd love it and the sooner the better as far as I am concerned."

"Well, I'll leave that up to you and your family. I'm sure you need some time to adjust and mourn your wife."

"On the contrary," Brian said. "I need to keep busy. I would like nothing better than to get back into fighting shape and run recertification drills. It would actually help me cope."

"Okay, then," Michael said. "Without a new class of cadets, currently my calendar is flexible although all that will soon change. Next month there will be a new, small class despite the pandemic."

"Would as soon as tomorrow afternoon be possible for me to stop by and see you, say around three?" Brian asked. "I'd even like to participate in any drills if possible." The idea of experiencing simulated assaults in the TAC House had enormous appeal, as did any type of special weapons exercise. He had not practiced once with any firearm since December, not even with his omnipresent P365 Sig Sauer automatic, which he could currently feel pressing against the small of his back.

"I'm sure I can find the time. I'll also spread the word with the instructor team. It's good timing. I know there is going to be a sizable group in the TAC House tomorrow, including some officers from the A team. You can at least observe initially. I'm sure everyone will be delighted to see you."

"Likewise," Brian said. When he had been an ESU member back before his retirement, he'd often spend his days off at the ESU Academy at Floyd Bennett Field helping the instructors with the cadets and even participating, as it helped to hone his skills and maintain his recertification requirements.

"And if you change your mind tomorrow after the funeral I'll understand," Michael said. "Just let me know, and I can let the others know."

"Of course."

After appropriate goodbyes, Brian disconnected the call and

stared ahead for a moment with unseeing eyes. The idea of intense physical activity gave him a modicum of relief from the emotional devastation of Emma's passing as well as his ongoing concern about Juliette's adjustment to losing her mother. Unfortunately, it didn't last, since the memory of needing to call Roger Dalton intervened.

With his phone still in his hand, he placed the call. As it went through, he again wondered if it was going to have something to do with Patrick McCarthy and Megan Doyle needing a full printout of the hospital bill. From what Megan had said, he expected the hospital to attempt to drag its feet.

"I thought you should know that the value of the suit brought against you by Premier Collections might soon be raised by $26,399.46," Roger stated as soon as he came on the call. "Unless, of course, something miraculous happens."

With some difficulty Brian held himself in check. He was offended by Roger's derisive attitude, and had he been there in his office, he might have been hard put not to intimidate the skinny bastard in some physical way. In Brian's mind he'd been fully exposed as the irritating front man for the profit-crazy Charles Kelley.

"Did you hear me?" Roger demanded when Brian didn't respond.

"I did, but I was waiting for you to tell me what this additional twenty-six-some-odd-thousand represents?"

"It's the latest ED charges for Emma Murphy," Roger said. "As if you couldn't guess."

"Is this for yesterday?" he asked with surprise, even disbelief, at the speed involved in the billing.

"Yes, it is for yesterday," Roger said. "Since you are already significantly delinquent, the hospital doesn't have high hopes for payment. What people like you don't understand is that our considerable expenses mount second by second, day by day, and we don't have the luxury of avoiding paying them as soon as they are due."

"Go ahead and submit the bill to Peerless," Brian ordered as he was about to discontinue the call. He was growing to seriously dislike the man. It was as if the bureaucrat was deriving sadistic pleasure out of pushing the knife MMH Inwood had sticking in him a little bit deeper.

"I already submitted it," Roger spat. "You and your health insurance deserve each other. They got back to me within the hour to inform me that once again they would not be covering."

"Wait just a second!" Brian exploded. "How could that possibly be? This was an emergency of the highest order. My wife didn't walk in on this occasion. She was carried in while being given CPR!"

"Peerless was given all the records including statements from the paramedics who responded to your 911 call," Roger said. "Why they have refused the claim, I have no idea, but you better look into it quickly and get their decision reversed or the amount of money involved in your lawsuit by Premier Collections will be amended upward."

"I will certainly find out." Brian felt a renewed burst of anger toward Peerless and Heather Williams's schemes, a resentment that was now equal to his hate of Charles Kelley and Roger Dalton. At the same time, the amount of money involved for a few hours in the emergency room seemed beyond the pale and equally as infuriating. Although he knew complaining about prices to Dalton was an exercise in futility, he couldn't help himself. "I'll certainly talk with Peerless, but how the hell could a couple of hours in your ED cost more than twenty-six thousand dollars? That's highway robbery, especially considering the outcome."

"I resent that," Roger snapped. "As I've said, over and over, running a trauma 1 ED twenty-four-seven is hugely expensive. Your wife used the facility and the high-tech equipment. She also required an entire team of highly trained people and equipment to carry on the CPR and do an emergency neurological assessment. Furthermore..."

Unable to listen to another word, Brian cut Roger off by disconnecting the call. He felt like a volcano ready to explode. Getting up from his desk, he quickly went down into the basement, where he and Emma had set up a small workout room with a stationary bike, a rack of free weights, and a flat-screen TV. Needing an outlet for his anger and frustration, he picked up two forty-five-pound hand weights and did a series of curls until he couldn't do any more. With a loud clank, he dropped them back into the rack.

Feeling a bit less out of control, he reclimbed the stairs and returned to the office. After sitting down and taking a deep breath, he placed a call to Ebony Wilson, which, as he anticipated, took some time to connect. The process required him to suffer again through several long, agonizing bouts of Muzak.

"Hello, this is Ebony Wilson, claims adjustment supervisor," she said with her honeyed voice when she finally came on the line. "And with whom do I have the pleasure of speaking?"

After Brian identified himself, he asked if she remembered him, resulting in a short laugh: "Of course I remember you! How could I not? You became the talk of the company the way you waltzed in here despite all the security our CEO demands. I have to say, you were extremely lucky you weren't arrested or even seriously hurt."

"I'm not sure that would have been the outcome had the situation escalated," Brian countered, indulging in a bit of law enforcement patois. "But luckily that's water over the dam. What I need to talk to you about is yet another claim denial involving my wife, and I demand an explanation."

"I'm sure there is one. I'll be happy to look into it. Can you give me your policy number again, so I can bring it up on my screen?"

After Brian did as he was told and after he had to suffer through yet another bout of Muzak, Ebony eventually returned on the line. "Okay, sorry for the wait. I have the adjuster's report in front of me. I see the claim again involved another ED visit for your wife, Emma Murphy. I also see she is no longer with us. My sincerest condolences."

"Thank you," he said, rolling his eyes at the irony of someone from Peerless expressing condolences. "Last time Peerless saw fit not to cover an ED visit was because my wife had walked in during the afternoon. The explanation was that she didn't need the resources of a Trauma 1 ED just to be admitted to the hospital. On this occasion, as I'm sure you can plainly see, she was literally carried in while undergoing CPR."

"Yes, I see that," Ebony agreed. "But I also see that the CPR wasn't necessary."

"Come again?" Brian asked with astonishment.

"It appears that our adjusters went over this claim rather carefully from their extensive write-up," she said. "What they gathered from the paramedics' report was that the patient was already brain dead in the paramedics' judgment prior to even being put in the ambulance. In New York State, paramedics legally can determine death, meaning treatment efforts from then on were superfluous and Peerless is not fiscally responsible for them."

"That's crazy," Brian blurted. "The paramedics started the CPR in our home and continued it all the way to the hospital."

"That might have been the case, but they clearly thought the patient had suffered brain death from extended hypoxia. At least that's what was in the report. I can understand you might not like this decision, and the same recourses are open to you if you feel our adjusters are in error. You can request a review and/or you can seek legal advice. It's your right."

Unable to take any more of such self-serving malarkey, Brian disconnected the call. Feeling equally as upset as he did after speaking with Roger Dalton, he was about to return to the basement workout room for another bout with the barbells when Camila came in.

"I'm sorry to bother you," she said, unaware of Brian's state of mind, "but there's a new problem with Juliette."

Caught between two polar emotions of rage and solicitude, he let his head fall into his hands and for a moment he forcibly massaged his scalp while his brain tried to reboot itself.

"Are you okay?"

After gritting his teeth and then running his fingernails through his thick hair several times almost to the point of pain, he looked up at Camila. The whites of his eyes were bright red. "What's the problem?"

"She's crying and seems inconsolable. She wants Bunny back."

"Good God," Brian managed, unable to think of an easy solution.

"She's upstairs in her room and is really upset, and I don't know what to say to her."

"I'll handle it," Brian said. He stood up and headed for the stairs. Despite all his training both at the Police Academy and particularly at the ESU Academy about how to deal with psychological crises associated with hostage taking, suicide prevention, and talking down armed and desperate criminals, the thought of facing his bereaved daughter about her beloved stuffed rabbit seemed an impossible task.

As he entered her room and looked down on her coiled up in a fetal position on her bed and sobbing, he felt totally inadequate. The rage he'd felt only moments before evaporated and was replaced completely by concern for his daughter.

Sitting on the edge of her bed, Brian stroked Juliette's back. "Camila says you miss Bunny and want her back. Is that right?"

If anything, she seemed to respond by crying with more intensity.

"We can get her back if that's what you want," he said. "Or we can pick out a new Bunny."

When there was still no response, Brian looked up at Camila standing in the doorway. She shrugged her shoulders, indicating she was at a loss.

"Okay," Brian said. "Let's see if we can find any wonderful rabbit toys to get for you so Mommy can have the company of Bunny like you wanted." He reached for Juliette's tablet and searched online for stuffed rabbits. He wasn't certain there would be any, but he was pleasantly surprised. There was page after page of all sorts of stuffed rabbits, some that looked like Bunny and some that were significantly more attractive, especially given Bunny's worse-for-wear condition. "Look at this," he continued. "There's lots and lots of options."

If anything, Juliette's tears only increased, and when Brian tried to put the tablet in her line of vision, she roughly pushed it away. It was clear she wasn't going to have anything to do with searching for a new Bunny, but Brian was mildly encouraged. She'd at least responded.

"Do you want to go back to Grandma's house and get Bunny?" he asked. He put down the tablet.

She shook her head no, which encouraged Brian even more. "If you stop crying and talk to me, we can figure this out," he said. "Do you want me to go back to Grandma's by myself?"

He waited for a few minutes and even repeated the question about him going back to the wake on his own and retrieving the rabbit. But Juliette didn't respond although the tears lessened. Continuing with the back stroking, Brian remained sitting on the edge of the bed for several more minutes before getting to his feet and approaching Camila.

"I'm as lost as you are," he said in a lowered voice. "I have no idea what to do. Do you think I should just go back to the wake and get the damn rabbit?"

"I'm not even sure that would have much of an effect. What about calling Jeanne? She's amazing with Juliette. Maybe she might have a suggestion?"

"Actually, that's probably the best idea."

Taking out his phone, he stepped out into the hallway and made the call, hoping for the best. It felt a little embarrassing calling a woman whom he'd just met for advice for the second time in one day. But he was desperate. He was relieved when she answered in a friendly fashion using his name, meaning she'd at least probably added his name and number to her contacts.

"I hope I'm not catching you back in Inwood Hill Park," he said, trying to be lighthearted despite the circumstances.

Jeanne laughed. "No, I'm home, but I must confess that I did go back and finish my ride when I left you. How did it go at the wake for you and your daughter?"

"It was a big stress for both of us," Brian said. "And indirectly that is why I am calling. You encouraged me to call if I needed help. Well, Juliette put Bunny in the casket to keep my wife's body company."

"Bless her soul," she said.

"Unfortunately, she has had a change of heart. At the moment she is crying her eyes out, wanting Bunny back. To make matters worse, she's not talking again. I'm at a loss. Do you have any suggestions? I've offered to go back to the wake and get the damn thing, which I'm not excited about doing, but she won't acknowledge that will make her feel better."

"Oh, dear!" Jeanne voiced. Brian could hear her sigh. "Off the top of my head, I think your inclination is correct. I don't think you should go back and get the toy. She misses her mother and now misses Bunny, probably conflating the two. She might be somehow thinking that if she gets the rabbit back, she'll also get her mother back."

"I suppose that is possible. I'm also concerned that if she did get Bunny back, it would always remind her of seeing and touching her dead mother."

"Did Juliette touch her mother's body?"

"She touched her face. I don't know if she was encouraged or did it on her own. I was across the room when it happened, and her grandmother was holding her, letting her reach over into the coffin with the toy. I think it spooked her."

"I can well imagine. Would it be okay if I came over and tried to talk with her? I have an idea that might help."

"Oh, please do," Brian said gratefully. "Both Camila and I are at a complete loss of how to handle this. It's heartrending to see her suffer."

"I'll be over as soon as I can."

CHAPTER 27

September 1

It was just over forty minutes later that Brian heard the doorbell chime. He had been waiting impatiently, alternately sitting with Juliette and pacing in the living room.

"You are like the proverbial cavalry arriving at the last minute to save the day," he said, trying to make light of the situation as he welcomed Jeanne back. No longer in bike clothes, she was dressed in a white summer blouse and black shorts and carrying a shopping bag.

"I'm sorry if it took too long. I had to shower and get out of my bike gear."

"Not a problem now that you are here," Brian said. "But I have to admit, we've been eagerly awaiting your arrival. We're really at a loss." As she took off her mask, he noticed something he'd not noticed before. In contrast to his pale complexion, hers was almost as olive as Camila's. When he mentioned it as she removed her shoes, she explained that there was a bit of Algerian in her heritage and maybe even a bit of Moroccan even farther back.

"How is Miss Juliette doing?" Jeanne asked as they mounted the stairs.

"Not much change," Brian answered. "She stopped crying when

we told her you were coming over to see her, but she's still not speaking. Camila and I have alternately stayed with her since you and I spoke on the phone."

"Sometimes that's all you can do in a situation like this," she said. "Patience is a virtue with children. Insecurity is going to be a challenge for her for a while, maybe for life."

As they entered Juliette's room, Camila stood up from the bed where she'd been sitting. She'd been reading to Juliette even though Juliette had remained unresponsive and curled up on her side. As Camila and Jeanne exchanged a verbal greeting, Juliette surprised everyone by rolling over on her back. She stared up at Jeanne.

"Hello, ma Juliette," she said, trying to sound upbeat while sitting down in the spot that Camila had just vacated. "I've heard that your visit to your grandma's was upsetting. Is that right?"

Juliette nodded.

"Seeing your mommy like that must have been scary," Jeanne said. "But at least you got to say goodbye."

Juliette nodded again.

"Did it feel strange when you touched her?" Jeanne asked.

With an added expression of distaste, Juliette said, "It was icky."

"I'm sure it was. You were brave. I understand that you did something very nice: You gave your mommy Bunny to keep her company."

"I want Bunny back," Juliette demanded with a defiant expression.

"I'm sure you want both your mother and Bunny back. But I have an idea of what might help, and it is here in this shopping bag." She raised the bag so Juliette could see it plainly. "Are you interested to see what it is?"

Juliette's expression softened. "Yes," she said.

Jeanne opened the bag, reached in, and pulled out another stuffed rabbit. It was about the same size as Bunny but a light gray instead of a light brown and less floppy except for the ears, which were longer. It was also in far better condition and had both of its eyes.

"This is Jeannot Lapin," Jeanne said, pronouncing the name in a distinctly French fashion. "I told you about her earlier. She's been my friend since I was about your age, but she would like to live with you if you will have her and treat her well."

To Brian's surprise and joy, Juliette reached for the stuffed toy, and when she had it in her hands, she examined it closely. When it apparently passed muster, she tried hugging it. She then looked up at Jeanne and once again nodded.

"She is a beautiful rabbit," Brian said to his daughter. "I think she is fantastic. Do you like her as much as I do?" When Juliette indicated she did, he asked: "What will her name be: Jeannot Lapin or Bunny 2?"

"Jeannot Lapin," Juliette declared, impressing everyone by imitating Jeanne's French pronunciation perfectly.

"Jeannot Lapin it is," Brian said with relief. "What about Bunny: Can she stay with Mommy?"

"Yes," Juliette answered without hesitation.

He exchanged a grateful glance with Jeanne, once again feeling thankful he'd had the serendipitous pleasure of meeting her in Megan Doyle's office. Even if Megan Doyle's efforts were to come to naught, Brian was certain he'd feel indebted just for the opportunity of meeting Jeanne and the help she was bringing to Juliette.

Camila, who had been watching from the doorway, now came into the room and added her appreciation. After giving the stuffed rabbit a long list of praises, she asked the rabbit if she was hungry. Juliette answered for her, saying that she was hungry for eggs and bacon.

"Then let's take her down to the kitchen and see that she gets fed," Camila said. "I'm hungry, too."

As Juliette and Camila filed out of the room, Brian turned to Jeanne. "Bravo," he said. "Once again, I can't thank you enough. You really are a child whisperer. Thank you so much for all your help and for parting with such a personal possession. Can I at least pay you something for it?"

With true mirth, she laughed. "I've gotten more than adequate compensation from that toy. I couldn't have imagined a better fate for it now. It was my mother who insisted I bring it here to the USA. I'm lucky I was able to find it after we talked. When I moved into my current, smaller apartment, I had to pack away a lot of my belongings."

"Regardless, giving it to Juliette is enormously generous. Frankly, had you suggested it on the phone, I probably wouldn't have thought it would work. I tried to get her excited about looking at stuffed rabbits online, and she was totally uninterested. Again, it's obvious you have a way with children."

"Thank you for the compliment," Jeanne said. "Maybe it's the child in me, but I do love interacting with young people. Obviously, that was why I ended up in school psychology, at least for a time. And I find Juliette darling. You are lucky to have her. I truly regret that Riley and I didn't have children. We shouldn't have put it off for the sake of the damn business."

"I can understand your feeling. In many ways Juliette is holding me together."

"I can see how committed you are," she agreed.

"I've had some more bad news about Peerless and MMH Inwood," Brian said. "It never stops. Can I bend your ear? I feel like complaining to someone."

"Of course."

"Let's go down to the living room and at least be comfortable."

As they descended the stairs, Jeanne said, "I think you are doing a marvelous job trying to deal with Juliette's grief, but what about yours? You've lost a wife and a life partner, after all."

"You are right. As I've said, it's mostly denial. It's also true that I haven't had time to really let it sink in."

"If it is anything like my experience, it's going to be tectonic when it hits."

"I can imagine. I guess I should be thankful for Juliette."

"That's my point exactly," Jeanne said. "But beware, it might be paralyzing."

In the living room they sat on opposing couches beneath the large, multipaned window looking out onto West 217th Street. Brian related the calls he'd had, first with Roger Dalton at MMH Inwood and then with Ebony Wilson.

"I can't believe Peerless," Jeanne exclaimed when he finished his rant. "They certainly have perfected the art of disclaiming responsibility, but they can't have just singled us out. They must do it to all their policy holders."

"I'm sure they do," Brian said. "It's no wonder they have the money to pay their CEO millions. It's a type of legalized fraud. Like last time, I was told I could request a review, which is guaranteed to be an exercise in futility, or I can sue. Proceeding with a lawsuit is probably equally as pointless as asking for a review. With their in-house attorneys, they have undoubtedly prepared for any and every eventuality. On top of that, suing is expensive, with no guarantees."

"Having grown up in France where this type of tolerated robbery involving healthcare would never happen, I have to wonder how has it come to be here in the United States that hospitals and health insurance companies operate with such impunity?"

"I think it has been a kind of accident of history," Brian said. "It certainly wasn't planned that healthcare got associated with employment here in the USA way back during World War II. And from my own experience, having relatively good health insurance from being a member of the NYPD made me indifferent to cost. I never cared or questioned. I guess it's a kind of moral hazard, and the consequences have been dramatic over the years. Can you ever imagine that a few hours in the emergency room for my wife would cost almost twenty-seven thousand dollars, only for her to end up dead? Beyond the emotional costs, that's akin to being forced to buy something like a car without knowing the price and being given a nonfunctioning wreck with no recourse."

"In France the government has tried to hold down costs, but it's not easy with what's going on here in the USA."

"France and the entire rest of the industrialized world as far as I know have tried to rein in healthcare costs," Brian said. "It's a uniquely American disaster, although what's happening here is putting pressure on prices elsewhere I'm afraid."

"I agree with you. It's American capitalism run amok with no moral balance in an industry that's supposed to be altruistic. Private equity shouldn't be allowed to interfere in healthcare."

"You're so right," he agreed with a shake of his head. "Talk about irony: It's a tragedy of personal greed trumping altruism."

"Exactly, and the final result is to cause suffering for people like us," Jeanne said. "It's infuriating, and Charles Kelley and Heather Williams are poster children for the whole damn situation."

"It's a wonder they can sleep at night."

"They must make it a point to avoid thinking about the lives they turn upside down. Unfortunately, I'm a prime example. Not only did I lose my husband, but in the course of my lawsuit and bankruptcy, I lost my business, most of my savings until Patrick and Megan put a stop to it, and then even my house."

"Don't tell me that," he pleaded. "You lost your house?"

"I'm afraid so," Jeanne confirmed. "It was partially my fault. While trying to pay off the hospital, I got behind on the mortgage, which exposed it to Kelley's pit bull lawyers."

"Yikes," Brian said. "At the moment that's my biggest worry, especially if it aggravates Juliette's sense of security. I'm behind on my mortgage payments as well."

"From my experience, I'd advise you to change that if you can."

"I know. Patrick McCarthy recommended the same thing. The trouble is, I need some income. As I said when we were in the hospital waiting for Juliette to be seen, I've been thinking of trying to get my old NYPD job back. I even called my commanding officer a little while ago and made plans to go out to the ESU Headquarters tomorrow after the funeral to talk to him about it."

"That sounds like a prudent plan to me, as this pandemic is not going away tomorrow."

"I have to do something," Brian said. "He suggested for me to join in on some of the training opportunities they've set up in lieu of having a new class of cadets. I'd like nothing better than to immerse myself in some simulation exercises, whether I end up back on the force or not. The mere physicality of it would be therapeutic. I haven't gotten any real exercise since I came back from Cape Cod, and I need to find a way to take my mind off of things."

"I think it's a wonderful idea," Jeanne said. "And to encourage it, I'd be happy to come over tomorrow and help with Juliette, provided you wouldn't mind."

"Mind?" Brian questioned with an exaggerated expression of surprise. "I'd love it. It would be a great relief. Leaving Camila to carry the burden of Juliette, especially if the funeral upsets her as much as the wake, was the only reservation I had. One thing I can say without exaggeration is that my daughter seems to truly adore you."

"Likewise," she said. "It will be a pleasure to spend time with her. But to get back to what we were talking about earlier, I find myself wondering if you and I are outliers, or if there are other people in this community who have suffered like we have at the hands of Charles Kelley and Heather Williams."

"That's a good question. If I had to guess, I'd say we're not alone by a long shot. Grady Quillen, the retired cop who served me, said he's been a busy bee for Premier Collections, especially of late. And Megan Doyle seems pretty booked, too."

"The more I think about it, the more curious I am," Jeanne pondered. "If there is a huge number, why hasn't it been the subject of some kind of exposé in the media so that Kelley and Williams could get the comeuppance they deserve?"

"That's maybe even a better question. Personally, I'd hate that kind of notoriety myself with my sad story in the tabloids, but you are right: It seems like perfect fodder for the likes of the *Post* or *Daily News*. Tearjerker stories about powerful elite ogres who are being paid millions to exploit the masses have a strong appeal for obvious reasons. Maybe it has something to do with patient–client privilege that makes the media hesitant."

"But they wouldn't have to use real names," Jeanne said. "I think it's curious. At least I'm curious. I'd like to find out how many people right here in Inwood have suffered like we have and learn their individual horror stories. The local hospital is supposed to help people and the community, not bankrupt everybody."

"It wouldn't be difficult to get a good idea of the numbers regarding MMH and Charles Kelley in terms of lawsuits," Brian said. "It would be more difficult to dig up much of anything about Peerless Health and Heather Williams."

"How so?"

"That kind of general information about lawsuits is available on the New York Civil Court's and the New York Supreme Court's websites. All you'd have to do is run a search using Premier Collections as the plaintiff."

"I didn't know such information was available. How about giving it a try?"

"Come on into the office! We'll use my computer."

A few minutes later, with Jeanne looking over his shoulder, he brought up the New York City Supreme Court website and typed in his search parameters. A millisecond later they were taken aback. Just since 2014 there had been many hundreds if not thousands of cases in Manhattan involving MMH Inwood and the significantly larger MMH Midtown. Scrolling forward, they also could see that there had been a significant uptick in activity since the beginning of the Covid-19 pandemic.

"My God!" Brian murmured. "Who would have guessed? And these are only cases involving more than twenty-five thousand dollars. If we look at the Civil Court for under twenty-five thousand there will probably be a lot more. It seems as if MMH and Premier Collections have sued a sizable portion of the entire metropolitan New York population."

"Let's look at the Civil Court website," Jeanne said.

A number of clicks later, they were again shocked by the numbers. "This is certainly eye-opening," Brian said. "The trouble is we can't use this resource to tease out the cases here in Inwood like you wanted. At least I can't do it. Maybe Patrick McCarthy might be able to. As a litigator, he has more options available to him for online data on these websites. What would also be interesting to know is how many of the cases are pending like mine and how many are closed."

"This is a bigger problem than I could have imagined." As if weighed down by this new information, Jeanne collapsed into one of the side chairs with her legs splayed out in front of her, her arms limp at her sides. "And to think the hospital prevails in most all the cases because the 'services have been rendered.' Those are the words Patrick McCarthy used to explain to me why I lost my case. People don't realize what they are signing when they go into the hospital."

"You've got that right," he said. "Especially when it involves an emergency situation. They're told 'sign here' to get their loved one treated, and they sign without reading anything. I did, too."

"People also count on their health insurance to take care of things and not only think about their profits."

"The whole situation is outrageous. It's also frustrating during these lawsuits that the court can't rule on the prices the hospital charge, no matter how ridiculous they are. It's got to be discouraging to be a judge."

"Plus, most hospitals won't tell you their charge master prices, which they've spent the last fifty years raising beyond any reason."

"Oh, yeah," Brian said with renewed disgust. "I forgot about the infamous charge master prices. How do you know about that?"

"I told you that when I got sued, I spent quite a lot of effort researching USA hospital business practices. What do you know about it?"

"Only what Megan Doyle happened to tell me during our brief meeting."

"It's a major part of the hospital scam," Jeanne said. "The only time patients can find out what things cost is after the services have been rendered, and they get the bill, and even then, they have to hire someone like Megan Doyle to figure it all out. It's absurd."

"I know how we could get at least a partial list of Inwood residents that MMH Inwood has sued or is in the process of suing," he said. "We could ask Grady Quillen, who served me. He wouldn't be restricted by any patient–client confidentiality issues as far as I know."

"Do you think he would give you that information?"

Brian shrugged. "I don't see why not. We've been acquaintances for years, and my father was his commanding officer. We could assure him we wouldn't give out our source, so his employer wouldn't find out. He already gave me one name: Nolan O'Reilly, whose story rivals ours, as he lost his son and his house in the process."

"If we could put together even a couple of dozen or so stories combined with the sheer number of court cases, we might be able to get either the *Post* or the *Daily News* interested enough to run an exposé." Abruptly she sat up straighter in her chair, her amber eyes sparkling. "And do you know what else we could do?"

"No, not really," he said, raising his eyebrows in curiosity.

"We could go to our city council member for the 10th District," Jeanne said excitedly. "I'm sure we could get him interested and involved. The more I think about all of this, the stranger it seems that it has been allowed to go on for so long."

"It's definitely an unconscionable problem," Brian agreed, but without the enthusiasm she was exhibiting. He was much too emotionally caught up in his own precarious situation, with his wife's funeral scheduled for the following day and Juliette's problematic behavior, to think about some kind of social movement, no matter how appropriate.

"Suddenly I feel a little like an Erin Brockovich," Jeanne said zealously. "Did you see that film with Julia Roberts?"

"I think so," he said, struggling to reboot his brain. "Yes, I saw it."

Suddenly Camila appeared in the archway leading out into the front hall. "I'm sorry to interrupt, but Juliette just threw up and now says she's feeling sick again."

"Oh, God! Where is she?" Brian asked nervously, getting to his feet.

"She's upstairs in her room," Camila said. "I think you'd better go and check on her."

CHAPTER 28

September 1

Disturbingly similar to a few hours earlier, Juliette was lying on her side, immobile, facing the wall with her legs drawn up. The only difference was now she was clutching Jeannot Lapin against her chest in a firm embrace.

"Camila says you're feeling bad again, Sweet Pea," Brian said as he sat down on the edge of the bed and stroked her back as he'd done earlier. Jeanne moved to stand at the foot of the bed. "Can you tell me what's wrong?"

Juliette didn't respond or move and Brian could see she had her eyes closed. He also noticed she wasn't sucking her thumb, which he thought was mildly encouraging.

"What about Jeannot Lapin?" he asked, imitating Jeanne's earlier way of getting Juliette to talk by addressing the rabbit. "She looks like she's not feeling so good, either."

"She is hot," Juliette said, turning her head and looking up at her father. "She's cold and then she's hot."

Brian reached out and pretended to feel the rabbit's forehead and then did the same with Juliette's. "You are right," he agreed. "Jeannot feels a little warm to me. Maybe we should take her temperature."

"Her name is Jeannot Lapin," Juliette corrected before rolling over onto her back.

"You're right," Brian said. "I stand corrected." He turned, looked up at Camila, and asked her if she'd bring the thermometer.

"Of course," Camila said and disappeared.

"Does Jeannot Lapin have a sore throat?" he asked, redirecting his attention to his daughter and continuing with the indirect questioning.

Juliette shook her head.

"How about a cough, or does she just feel sick? Does she think she might throw up again?"

Juliette shook her head for the second time.

"How about a headache?" Jeanne asked.

"Yes, she has a headache," Juliette said.

Brian and Jeanne exchanged a glance. Each shrugged their shoulders, not knowing what else to ask. Camila returned with the thermometer. Juliette allowed her to put it under her tongue before Camila stepped back out of Brian and Jeanne's way.

"How long after eating did Juliette throw up?" Brian asked Camila.

"It was while she was eating. By the time I had made the bacon and eggs, she didn't seem very hungry and ate very slowly. Then she threw up sitting at the table. It was all very sudden."

He nodded. "Maybe there was something wrong with the eggs."

"I don't think so," Camila said. "I had some myself and had no problem."

After waiting for the usual three minutes, Brian took the thermometer out of Juliette's mouth and then twirled it in his fingers, looking for the column of mercury. "100.8 again," he said when it flashed into view. "No wonder Jeannot Lapin feels hot."

Standing up, he motioned for Jeanne to step out of the room with him. Once in the hall he said: "It's certainly not a particularly worrisome fever, but I think it is a fever, nonetheless. What should we do? God! I wish that Dr. Bhatt wasn't on vacation. The last thing I want to do is go back to the MMH Inwood ED, not with the way we were treated earlier."

"I'm with you there," Jeanne said. "I don't think it will be necessary, but I do wish they had at least done a Covid test."

"The doctor was adamant it wasn't indicated, but who knows. I'm still irritated. I also wish they had done basic blood work just to be sure she wasn't coming down with something."

"I have to use the bathroom fast," Juliette said urgently to Camila from inside the room yet loud enough for Brian and Jeanne to hear. As they ducked back inside, they saw Juliette and Camila disappear into the bathroom and the door slam behind them.

"Uh-oh," Brian said. "Sounds like more stomach issues."

While they waited, he picked up Jeannot Lapin as a nervous gesture and gave it a close inspection. "This little rabbit has been a godsend. I've never been into stuffed animals, but this one is damn cute. Did you really have it since you were Juliette's age?"

"Just about," Jeanne said. "Maybe a year older."

"How did it stay so pristine?" Brian asked. "In comparison, Bunny looks like she'd been through a war."

"I don't know, to be truthful. I guess I've always been on the meticulous side."

Five minutes later Juliette and Camila emerged from the bathroom. Juliette made a beeline for Brian and rescued Jeannot Lapin. Then she climbed back up on the bed and rolled over on her side, assuming the same position she'd been in when Brian and Jeanne had arrived.

"A bit of diarrhea," Camila reported. "And some cramps, but I think she feels better now."

"Thank goodness," he said. He placed his palm on her forehead. "She seems to be about the same temperature as before." Juliette pushed his hand away.

"She said she wanted to sleep," Camila said.

"I think that's a great idea," Brian said. "Is that right, Pumpkin? You want to take a nap?"

Juliette nodded, and he could see she had her eyes closed. "Okay," he said. "Hopefully you'll feel back to normal when you wake up. We'll be downstairs if you need us, okay?" He straightened up and herded the others out of Juliette's room.

As they were descending the stairs, Jeanne asked if Brian might be willing to give Grady Quillen a call to see if he was comfortable giving the names of the Inwood families he'd served over the last year.

"I suppose, but to be honest, I'm not sure I have the stamina at the moment to pursue the kind of Erin Brockovich investigation you have in mind."

"Of course you don't," Jeanne reassured him. "As I said, I don't know how you are functioning as well as you are. But I have both the time and the inclination. If you can get me the names, I'll start the process and you can participate as much or as little as you'd like."

"All right," Brian said. It was the least he could do in the face of all the help and support Jeanne was so generously providing.

CHAPTER 29

September 2

As dawn's light slowly crept into the master bedroom preluding sunrise, Brian's eyes popped open. Other than his eyelids, he purposefully didn't move a muscle lest he disturb Juliette, who was sleeping on her side with her head on a pillow facing him. She was in Emma's place in the bed, and Jeannot Lapin was on its back between them with Juliette's arm thrown over the stuffed rabbit's midsection.

As far as sleep was concerned, the first part of Brian's night had not gone well. He'd had trouble going to sleep even though he was clearly exhausted from having slept so poorly the night before. He'd even dozed off in the kitchen while having something to eat with both Camila and Jeanne. They'd encouraged him to go to bed, which he did, but by the time he got upstairs, out of his clothes, and brushed his teeth, he no longer felt tired.

Finally, after ten o'clock, he'd broken down and tried one of Emma's Ambien tablets, which provided a few hours of sleep before he was awakened by the sound of his bedroom door creaking open. By reflex from his martial arts training, he'd tensed, ready to spring up and face any potential intruder, but it wasn't necessary. With the help of the half-light in the room coming in through the white, gauzy curtains from the streetlight outside the window, he recognized Juliette in her nightgown holding Jeannot Lapin. Brian had sat up and asked her if she was okay, and she'd answered by asking him if she could sleep with him.

"Absolutely, Sweet Pea," Brian had said immediately, throwing back the edge of the sheet. Juliette responded by jumping up onto the bed, scrunching down under the covers, and placing Jeannot Lapin between them. A moment later she'd melted his heart by saying: "I miss Mommy."

With some difficulty, Brian had told her that he understood and that he missed Mommy, too. With those few words spoken, Juliette had fallen asleep and eventually he had dozed off while hoping he could at least partially fill the void that Emma's passing had created.

As the intensity of the daylight gradually increased, Brian got a progressively better view of his angelic daughter's features, and he marveled at the sheer mystery and mind-boggling implausibility of the reproductive process. How could it have been possible for him and Emma to create such a perfect human being? But then in the middle of his appreciation, he noticed something disturbing. Juliette's forehead was covered with tiny, iridescent droplets of perspiration, and the discovery brought a pang of fear down his spine. With the pandemic threatening a fall surge, a prolonged fever was certainly not a welcome sign.

Being careful not to wake his daughter, Brian slipped out of the bed. As carefully as he could, he folded down the light cotton blanket, leaving only the sheet to cover her. He then turned down the air-conditioning a few degrees before he went to retrieve the thermometer in her bedroom. Although he hated to do it because she was sleeping soundly, when he got back he woke her by gently shaking her shoulder.

Juliette's response at being disturbed was to cry and then complain that she didn't feel well. He could see that the whites of her eyes were mildly suffused red.

"What's bothering you?" he asked. "Is your throat sore?"

Juliette nodded. "And I have a headache," she said, putting her hand momentarily on her forehead.

"I think you might have a fever." He felt her forehead with his hand, admitting to himself that she did feel warm. "We need to take your temperature."

Although she initially complained that she didn't want her temperature taken, she eventually succumbed to Brian's persistent urging. As they waited for the requisite three minutes, he stroked her head, marveling at the color of her hair and wondering where it had come from in either his or Emma's genealogy. Juliette kept her eyes closed the entire time.

When the time was up, Brian took out the thermometer. When he read it he caught his breath. It was 102.3! Making an effort to camouflage his concern, he said: "Yes, you do have a fever. Do you feel warm?"

"No, I feel cold," she said, and ostensibly shivered.

Quickly, he replaced the blanket that he had earlier turned down. After he told her to stay in bed, he slipped on his robe and walked down the hall. When he reached Camila's room, he knocked softly. From inside he heard a muffled: "Just a minute." A moment later the door opened, and a sleepy Camila stood in the door frame, clutching her robe closed.

"Juliette has awakened with a temperature of over 102," Brian told her. "Sorry to wake you, but we need your help. As much as I hate doing it, I think she's got to be seen again at the ED, and I need you to drive us so I don't have to worry about parking."

"Oh, no! I'm sorry to hear," Camila said, now looking more alert. "She seemed fine yesterday after her upset stomach. Are there any other symptoms?"

"Yes, she again has a sore throat and headache. On the positive side, I don't think she has any digestive complaints, but I didn't specifically ask her."

"Do you want to go right away?"

"I do," Brian said. "I'd like to get in and out of the ED as quickly as possible. We're both expected to show up for Emma's funeral mass at ten and the sooner we get there the sooner we'll be seen."

"Let me throw on some clothes."

"Of course," he said. "I'll dress also and get Juliette's robe. At the moment she's in my room. She came in in the middle of the night feeling lonely and ended up staying with me."

"The poor dear. Okay, I'll be quick."

After returning to his room with Juliette's robe in hand, Brian approached the bed. Juliette appeared to have fallen back asleep, but her eyes opened the moment he sat down. "I was just talking with Camila," he said. "She's going to drive us back to the hospital so the doctors can take a look at you again."

"I don't want to go to the hospital."

"I'm afraid we have to go," Brian said, suppressing the urge to say he didn't want to go, either. He sat her up and helped her get her arms into her bathrobe. "We have to find out what's making you have a fever, so we can get you some medicine to make you and Jeannot Lapin feel better. I imagine she's not feeling so well, either."

While he ducked into the master bedroom's walk-in closet to dress, he found himself suddenly transfixed by the sight of the clothes hanging on Emma's side. At this moment, with no warning whatsoever, his glass house of denial spontaneously shattered, forcing him to acknowledge that his wife had died, that she was gone, that she wasn't coming back, and he was never again going to hear her crystalline voice or her infectious laughter or feel her touch or experience one of those marvelous episodes when they shared the very same thought at the same time. "Shit," he hissed through clenched teeth, quiet enough so Juliette couldn't hear. The existential question of why this terrible loss had happened to him leaped into the forefront of his mind, but he had no answer. All he knew was that this totally unexpected, unforeseen tragedy had happened because of a tiny mosquito.

Feeling suddenly drained of strength, Brian was forced to reach up and grab the hanger rod to keep himself upright. At the same time, he felt a rush of tears, and he let himself cry. But after a few quiet sobs, he regained his equilibrium. Remembering Juliette out in the room, he yanked himself back to reality. "Pull yourself together!" he commanded in a forced whisper, recognizing that Juliette's needs trumped feeling sorry for himself. She needed him to buck up, and with the kind of determination that had characterized his life to date, he rapidly put on the same dark suit he'd worn for his brief appearance at the wake. Not knowing how long he'd be in the emergency department, and certainly hoping it wouldn't be as long as the previous day, he wanted to be ready for the funeral mass at ten.

By the time they were in the Subaru heading for the hospital, it was going on eight o'clock. Hoping for the best but wanting to be ready for the worst, he again had his laptop with an attached DVD player and a selection of Juliette's particularly favorite movies in a backpack. He also knew there was internet in the ED, so they'd also be able to stream PBS cartoons or other movies if Juliette preferred. Also, at Camila's suggestion, he had some snacks if needed. All in all, he felt reasonably prepared provided they were treated fairly and didn't have to wait for three hours. As he had anticipated, Juliette was obviously not feeling well and had resisted going, but now that they were in the car, she acted resigned and silent.

"If you can give me a little warning, I can be back here, so you don't have to wait," Camila said as Brian and Juliette got out at the hospital. He gave a thumbs-up as he and Juliette donned their masks and headed for the door.

The ED waiting room was sparsely populated, which encouraged Brian. At the information desk there was no line, and Brian was able to check in straightaway with one of the clerks who recognized them from having been there the day before. The clerk then passed on the information to a triage nurse who seemed distracted as she read aloud the symptoms of a 102.2 fever, sore throat, and headache with an episode of vomiting and diarrhea the previous day. She then wordlessly took Juliette's temperature with a thermal scanner. Luckily Juliette was tolerant and silent through it all.

"What's the temperature?" he asked.

"100.8," the nurse replied.

"It was much higher less than an hour ago," Brian said. He was relieved to hear it had come down yet worried it might put them in a less urgent section on the patient list. "Maybe you could take it again, please, just to be sure."

Without comment, but with subtle signs of annoyance that were not lost on Brian, the nurse took the temperature again. "100.8," she voiced with a roll of her eyes as if retaking the temperature had been an imposition.

"Excuse me," he said. "Did my asking to retake my daughter's temperature provoke you in some way?"

"I've been here since eleven o'clock last night," the nurse responded, ignoring Brian's question. "We'll be with you as soon as we can." She then walked off.

"Good grief," Brian let out under his breath. Already his interaction with the ED staff was only marginally acceptable in his opinion, making him worried whether the current visit might end up rivaling yesterday's fiasco.

Retreating to a relatively deserted corner of the waiting room, he and Juliette made themselves as comfortable as possible. Juliette wanted to lie down, and Brian allowed her to do so on a blanket he'd brought with them from the car. When he asked her if she wanted to watch something on the laptop, she said she wanted to sleep. As she settled in, he noticed that the perspiration that he'd seen earlier on her forehead had disappeared, making him more confident that the thermal scanner temperature the nurse had taken had been correct. It also made Brian wonder why, like yesterday, Juliette's symptoms had suddenly disappeared.

"What about your headache and a sore throat?" he asked her, but she chose not to answer and already had her eyes closed. Thankful she was being cooperative, he didn't press her. Instead he made himself as comfortable as he could, wondering how long they would have to wait. In the distance he heard the undulating sound of an approaching ambulance. As the siren progressively increased, he couldn't help but selfishly hope it wasn't some major trauma that would engulf the ED and extend the wait.

Trying to avoid revisiting the momentarily paralyzing episode he'd had in the closet, Brian kept his mind busy by mulling over the conversation he'd had the day before with Jeanne about how many other people in the community out of its sixty thousand residents had experienced the kind of tragedy that he and Jeanne had suffered. Although at the time he had thought that he didn't have the time or the fortitude to participate in any intensive investigation in the near term, Jeanne had asked him to call Grady Quillen and ask if he would provide a list of all the neighborhood people he'd served in the last year or so.

As Brian had expected, Grady had been more than happy to provide the information, especially after Brian had assured him that his being the source would never be revealed to anyone, especially Premier Collections. Grady had promised he'd print out a list and get it to Brian, and also mentioned something particularly disturbing. Nolan O'Reilly, the friend who'd lost his son and house, had just died by suicide. If nothing else, that terrible news was enough to galvanize him to join Jeanne's commitment to look into the problem as a neighborhood disaster.

The ambulance he had heard approaching arrived, and it was obvious that it involved a major problem as various ED personnel started scurrying about. For a second Brian wondered if Emma's arrival two days ago had caused the same stir, but he quickly pushed the thought out of his mind lest it lead to another emotional storm.

Over the next thirty to forty minutes, more ambulatory patients began arriving, forming a line with six-foot separations at the information desk. There were also several more ambulances. It was disturbingly obvious to Brian that the ED was becoming busier.

After an hour of waiting and with Juliette asleep, he got up when there happened to be no one in line for the information desk. Trying to keep himself calm but feeling progressively irritated that he and Juliette were being forced to wait as long as they had, especially since the time of Emma's funeral mass was rapidly approaching, Brian headed over to the clerk who had initially checked them in.

After taking a quick glance back at Juliette to make sure she was still asleep, Brian got the clerk's attention. "Excuse me," he said, trying to keep the frustration out of his voice. "My daughter and I have been waiting more than an hour for her to be seen. What's the holdup?"

A free triage nurse who'd overheard his question stepped closer and intervened. "What's the name?" she asked in a neutral tone.

Brian gave Juliette's full name, and the nurse consulted her tablet. "Okay, yes, I see your daughter's name," she said. "She's definitely in the queue. You'll just have to be patient. We have to deal with real emergencies first."

For several beats, he debated whether to respond to the implication that Juliette's fever of 102.2 with flu-like symptoms was not an emergency or whether to raise the issue about his seeing other patients come and go into the ED, but for the moment he held himself in check. He could hear Jeanne's words from yesterday warning him that raising a ruckus could make things worse. Biting his tongue, Brian headed back to his seat next to Juliette's sleeping form.

Thinking about Jeanne, he took out his cell phone and called her in an effort to keep himself under control. As the call went through, he worried again he was taking advantage of her and hoped she wouldn't mind hearing from him so soon. To his relief, any concerns were instantly dispelled by the alacrity with which she answered.

"Good morning!" she said brightly. "I'm so glad to hear from you. I've been wanting to call you but was worried it might be too early. Have you gotten the defendant list from Grady Quillen?"

"Wow! I'm impressed. You really are motivated about this."

"I suppose I am," Jeanne said. "Have you heard from him? Is that why you are calling?"

"I'm afraid I haven't gotten the list yet," he said. "No, that's not why I am calling. Unfortunately, I'm back in the ED. Juliette woke up this morning with a 102.2 fever."

"Oh, no!" Jeanne cried. "That's not what I wanted to hear. Does she have other symptoms or just a fever?"

"She has a sore throat and headache again," Brian said. "I was hoping that by getting here as early as we did, we'd be seen quickly. It didn't happen. We've been here for more than an hour already, and we haven't been called."

"Oh, God! How frustrating!" Jeanne said. "I'm sorry. How is Juliette behaving?"

"She's being an angel," Brian said. "She's sleeping. I'm the one who might misbehave. I'm feeling paranoid again that we're being purposefully and passive-aggressively ignored."

"Is the ED particularly crowded?" Jeanne asked.

"It wasn't when we arrived," he said. "At least it didn't appear to be out here in the waiting room. Of course, I can't see when ambulances arrive, and I know at least one did. What bugs me is that just like yesterday people have walked in after we did and already have been seen, and it's getting more crowded now."

"Would you like me to come over and keep you company?"

"That's nice of you to offer," Brian responded. "But I'm hoping we'll be called soon, and I'm already feeling guilty about counting on you to come over later this afternoon to spend time with Juliette while I go out to the ESU Academy."

Before Jeanne could respond, Brian's phone vibrated in his hand, indicating he had a call coming in. It was Aimée. "I've got to go. My mother is trying to get through, and I'm sure it's about the funeral."

"No problem," Jeanne said. "I'm available if you need me."

He switched lines and greeted his mother.

"Why don't we all go to the funeral mass and burial together like Hannah suggested?" Aimée said with no preamble. "We could pick you and Juliette up on our way to the Church of the Good Shepherd. And tell Juliette that Grandma would love to see her in that new blue dress that—"

"There's a problem," Brian said, interrupting. "Juliette woke up with a high fever, and we are again back at the Emergency Department waiting to be seen."

"Mon Dieu! I'm sorry to hear," Aimée said. "How is she feeling now?"

"At the moment she's asleep," Brian answered. "Even that's not normal behavior for her." He didn't mention that the temperature was significantly lower now.

"Goodness gracious! This is not good news. What do you think; will you be able to make the church service?"

"It's totally dependent on when Juliette will be seen and then how she feels," he said. "I'm hoping she'll at least be seen soon, since we've already been here more than an hour."

"I certainly hope you and Juliette make it," Aimée said. "You'll be sorely missed, and I know Hannah will be beside herself if you don't. But will you come even if Juliette isn't up to it?"

"I'll try my best," Brian said, feeling a bit guilty that he wasn't being entirely up front. Not knowing how he felt about any of the funeral rites or how his wife might have felt, he wasn't as disappointed as he guessed his mother and Hannah would be if he and Juliette couldn't make the funeral mass or, perhaps, even the interment at the cemetery. Although he certainly wanted to honor his wife's memory and not offend anyone, so far the funeral rituals seemed to be more of a challenge to his emotional stability than a help. At the same time, he recognized the mass and the burial might be consoling on some level as a kind of closure and certainly not as upsetting as the wake. Brian desperately wanted himself and Juliette to remember Emma with the vitality that she embodied rather than as a cold, unresponsive shell staged with makeup to look as if she were merely sleeping.

"Well, I hope Juliette is seen soon," Aimée said.

Suddenly Juliette woke up as if from a bad dream and began crying.

"Uh-oh," he said. "I have to go. Juliette's awake and not happy."

"Okay, try to keep me informed, my dear," Aimée said and rang off.

"What's the matter, Pumpkin?" Brian asked soothingly as he pocketed his phone. Juliette was looking around, seemingly orienting herself.

"I'm hungry and I want to go home," she managed to say, choking back more tears.

"I'm glad you are hungry," Brian said as he got out the graham crackers and mentally thanked Camila for suggesting them. "But we have to stay until the doctor sees you and tells us why you have a fever. What about watching something fun?"

"I want to go home," Juliette repeated, obviously becoming more cranky.

"I do, too," he said. He got out the collection of DVDs he'd brought. Thankfully Juliette started pawing through them while munching on a cracker until she came across a *Pink Panther* DVD. Without saying anything, she handed it to Brian and with a sense of relief that she had found something, he set her up watching it.

With Juliette occupied, he sat back and tried to be patient, but as time passed, he found himself getting progressively irritated. Finally, after a total of two hours, at which point he knew the funeral mass was probably beginning, he couldn't sit still any longer. After making sure that Juliette had significant time remaining on her current DVD, he walked back to the information desk.

On this occasion, Brian had to stand in line before getting to talk with one of the clerks, and it wasn't the woman whom he'd spoken to earlier. It was a youthful man with hair down to his shoulders.

"My daughter, Juliette Murphy, and I have been here for more than two hours," Brian snapped, tired of forcing himself to be polite. "I'm beginning to think we are being purposefully ignored. I want to be reassured that is not the case and find out when we will be seen."

The clerk treated him to an overtly questioning expression that was obvious even with his mask. After telling Brian to wait a minute, he got up and stepped over to speak with one of the free triage nurses. Brian watched them converse and had the impression the clerk was new to his job. After checking her tablet, it was the triage nurse who came back to speak with Brian.

"We're sorry you've had to wait, Mr. Murphy," she said consolingly and with respect. "We try our best to see everyone as quickly as we can, but with the Covid-19 pandemic, we've been stressed, as I'm sure you have heard."

"That I understand," Brian said, struggling to keep the anger out of his voice but not succeeding. He told her he'd seen people arrive after them and already be seen, and voiced concern that he was being treated differently because he had outstanding hospital bills.

"Oh, heavens, no!" she said. "I can assure you that we have no idea of your financial situation with the hospital. We see the sickest patients first. Some of those people you've seen most likely came in for something very easy to solve, like a prescription refill. We will get to your daughter as soon as we can."

Feeling frustrated and questioning that people might come into the ED just to get prescriptions refilled, he went back to Juliette and tried to rein in his growing anger. Despite what the triage nurse had said about the ED not being influenced by financial considerations, he still had his doubts. With Charles Kelley so focused on profits, such an orientation and culture had to trickle down into all corners of the hospital. He was sure of it.

It wasn't until three-quarters of an hour later that Juliette was called, and by then Brian was fit to be tied. To him, as angry as he was and for having been forced to miss his wife's funeral mass, there seemed to be no explanation other than that they were being overtly discriminated against.

To Juliette's chagrin the nurse who greeted them wasn't Olivia, but she quickly established herself as being equally as good with children. After leading them back to the same exam room they'd visited the day before, Nurse Jane pretended to take Jeannot Lapin's vital signs as she took Juliette's. And when Juliette asked for a hemostat to play with, Jane happily complied. She also acted impressed when Juliette demonstrated how well she could use the instrument by attaching it and releasing it at various locations on Jeannot Lapin.

"What's the temperature?" Brian asked after the nurse took it. He made a distinct effort to keep his voice from reflecting his irritation.

"98.2," Jane said happily. "Same with the rabbit."

With this surprising news and despite his annoyance, it was time for Brian to roll his eyes, feeling mildly embarrassed as well as exasperated that the main reason for coming to the ED had vanished just as it had the day before. Of course, he was pleased the fever was gone, but he was also perplexed. Had she really had a fever or could the thermometer at home be malfunctioning? But then he reminded himself of the perspiration on Juliette's forehead. That had been real, meaning something must have been wrong. Particularly because of his EMT training, he knew more than most people about symptoms and signs of disease, and a disappearing fever of 102.2 made no sense to him, nor did it make sense that Juliette's sore throat had vanished when Jane asked her about it. The only symptom that remained was the headache. When Jane asked Juliette where she felt the pain and whether it was localized, Juliette motioned all over her head.

With the vital signs retaken, Jane said that the doctor would be in to see Juliette in a few minutes and left. Yet it was more than a few minutes; it was twenty minutes, long enough for Juliette to start crying, saying she wanted to go home, and long enough to allow his befuddlement to morph back to anger. In his mind, having been forced to wait three hours, two days in a row, couldn't have been by chance. It had to be punitively deliberate, not to mention inconsiderate and unethical.

Suddenly there was a loud knock on the door and before Brian could respond, in walked an ebullient Dr. Robert Arnsdorf along with Jane. He was an athletic-looking physician, who Brian guessed was in his fifties, comparable in height with Brian but slenderer and with a bit of white hair protruding from beneath his surgical cap. A stethoscope was casually slung around his neck. Brian was relieved it wasn't Dr. Kramer.

"Ah, I see Miss Murphy is a little unhappy," Dr. Arnsdorf said friskily, seemingly for Juliette's benefit. "What's the problem today, my chickadee?" Without waiting for an answer, he looked down at his tablet and began reading.

In his agitated state Brian found the doctor's breezy attitude and seeming unpreparedness galling rather than playful and certainly not endearing. Juliette didn't buy it, either, and continued crying until Jane got her reinterested in playing with the hemostat.

"The problem is we've been waiting for over three hours," Brian blurted out.

"Sorry about that," Dr. Arnsdorf said simply. "Let me finish Dr. Kramer's note." After a moment he put the tablet down on the desk. "Okay, seems that we've had a repeat from yesterday: A phantom fever and sore throat along with a single episode of vomiting and diarrhea yesterday afternoon. Interesting."

"I hardly think 'interesting' is an appropriate description," Brian said.

"First, let me extend my sincere condolences about your wife," Dr. Arnsdorf said, continuing to ignore Brian's displeasure. "It's entirely understandable that there have been psychosomatic symptoms, including a fever. But, to be on the safe side, let's take a look." He nodded as if agreeing with himself. Then after a brief wash of his hands, he quickly examined Juliette, starting by first looking into her mouth, throat, nose, and ears. He then listened to her chest and let her listen to his. Finally, he palpated her abdomen while she was lying on her back, managing to get her relaxed enough to elicit a little laugh. Brian watched the rapid exam and stayed quiet throughout although he already was concerned that the doctor had a low index of suspicion.

"You are in perfect health," Dr. Arnsdorf declared to Juliette while playfully touching her on the tip of the nose with his index finger. He then turned to Brian. "I think she is fine, very healthy in fact. And I'm impressed with her size, having been a preemie. My guess is she's out there on the positive side of the bell curve development-wise for her age."

"What does her having been a preemie have to do with anything?" Brian asked. In his hypersensitive state, it seemed like a statement out of the blue, like trying to change the subject.

"Nothing, really," Dr. Arnsdorf said. "The doctor's note from yesterday noted Juliette was a tiny baby when she was born. We've seen a handful of Dr. Bhatt's patients over the last couple of days. He's a fine pediatrician. Did you meet him when he was a resident at Columbia-Presbyterian Children's Hospital?"

"Yes," Brian said. He relaxed a twinge, realizing he shouldn't fault doctors for being thorough even though Juliette's current situation had nothing to do with her spending the first month of her life in a NICU at Columbia. She'd been transferred there from MMH Inwood right after delivery.

"My advice if these phantom symptoms continue is to consider having her talk to a pediatric social worker," Dr. Arnsdorf said, picking up his tablet as if he was about to leave. "Also, perhaps you should make an appointment to see Dr. Bhatt when he comes back after his vacation."

"Wait a second," Brian began. "I'm not comfortable assuming her symptoms are psychosomatic. She hasn't been acting herself even before my wife's passing, and this morning she woke up with a real fever. She had perspiration covering her forehead. Especially with this pandemic still going on and a second wave expected, I at least want her to have a Covid test. I'd also like to see if her blood count is normal."

"I disagree," Dr. Arnsdorf countered. "I agree with Dr. Kramer. Your daughter also complained of a sore throat, but her throat looks perfectly normal. Likewise, her ears. And her temperature at the moment is actually low, not high."

"I want her to have some blood work," Brian demanded, losing patience. "And a Covid test at a minimum."

"The hospital is backed way up on its Covid testing," Dr. Arnsdorf said with exasperation. He'd been making an effort to placate Brian but was beginning to resent his insistence.

"There's something not right with my daughter. This is the second time in two days we've been here."

"Calm down, Mr. Murphy," Dr. Arnsdorf said, forcing himself to be calm as well. "We've been asked by our lab on a temporary basis only to do testing on patients with a strong indication, who have sustained symptoms, or have been exposed to someone with Covid-19, or are being admitted to the hospital. Your daughter doesn't fit in any of these categories. Covid-19 symptoms vary from patient to patient, but they don't come and go over a few hours in the same patient, not in our experience. As for doing a blood count or any other blood work, I don't see any rationale whatsoever. Subjecting a child to a phlebotomy, which can be a traumatic experience, shouldn't be done unless there is a strong indication."

"Does your reluctance to do the little I'm asking have anything to do with this hospital suing me for the bill to treat my late wife's EEE? Are you people all so damn worried I won't pay whatever outrageous price you've put on these tests?"

For a second Dr. Arnsdorf stared at Brian in shocked surprise. "Absolutely not!" he said, finding his voice. "That's an insult. You are one paranoid individual, Mr. Murphy."

"Of course I'm paranoid," he retorted. "It's hard not to be paranoid in this day and age dealing with healthcare. Don't tell me you aren't fully aware that your CEO is one hell-bent profit-motivated individual intent on keeping prices high and costs low to justify his multimillion-dollar salary."

"I'm a doctor!" Dr. Arnsdorf retorted. "I take care of people, not business."

"That's a cop-out if I ever heard one," Brian snapped. "Yes, you are a doctor, and MMH Inwood is a hospital, which is supposed to be your house and not Charles Kelley's gravy train."

"I've had enough of this conversation." Dr. Arnsdorf turned back to the sink and rewashed his hands before swiftly leaving the exam room.

Equally fed up and sensing he was getting nowhere, Brian turned to Juliette and scooped her up in his arms. He ignored Jane as she said goodbye to Juliette. On their way to the waiting room, Brian struggled to get out his phone, and while walking and carrying Juliette, he used Siri to call Camila.

"My, you have been there a long time," Camila said immediately as she came on the line.

"Don't remind me," Brian said. "Can you come and get us?"

"Of course! I'll be there shortly. How is Juliette doing?"

"She's doing fine," he said. "I'm the one who's struggling."

CHAPTER 30

September 2

Once Brian and Juliette were in the car, Camila briefly tried to get both to talk to find out what had happened, but it quickly became clear to her that neither was so inclined. With Juliette it was because she was busy getting the laptop out of the backpack to return to the DVD she'd been watching earlier. With Brian it was apparent from the outset that he was seriously irritated. In Camila's experience, he rarely got upset, but when he did, she'd learned it was best to let him mull over whatever was bothering him, which usually didn't take long. And true to form, by the time they drove out of the hospital grounds, he let out a protracted sigh and said with a shake of his head: "Well, that was another exercise in futility."

"I'm sorry to hear," Camila said. "What happened? What did they find?"

"Nothing," Brian answered with disgust. "But in their defense, by the time we were seen after another three-hour wait, once again her fever had vanished along with most of her symptoms. I think she still has a headache, but that's it, and apparently even the headache is better. It clearly hasn't hindered her from watching videos." He glanced over his shoulder to see if Juliette was back to watching, and she was. "The doctors are convinced it's all psychosomatic, fever included."

"I suppose that's possible," Camila said. "Did they do any tests this time to make certain?"

"None," Brian said. "That's what irked me. I tried to get them to do even a routine blood test, but no go with the excuse they're backed up with their Covid testing. It's all very suspicious to me. I'm worried that they didn't do any tests because they're afraid they are not going to get paid since I already owe them so damn much money."

"Do you really think that is a possibility?" Camila asked.

"I do," Brian said. "Having to wait to be seen more than three hours two days in a row and then refusing to do anything I asked speaks volumes. And this morning when we first arrived, the triage nurse acted put out when I asked her to repeat Juliette's temperature."

"Next week Dr. Bhatt will be back."

"Hallelujah," he said. "I can't wait."

"By the way, a Grady Quillen stopped by and left you a large manila envelope. He said that you would know what it was about. It's on your desk."

"I do," Brian said. "It's a list of people like me and Jeanne who he's served."

When they pulled into the driveway and stopped, Juliette said she was hungry.

"How about you, Brian?" Camila asked as they all got out of the car. "Want to join us?"

"You guys go ahead. I've got to call my mom. I'm afraid Juliette and I have missed at least the funeral mass."

"Oh, my goodness," Camila said. "That's right. I'll hurry with Juliette."

"Don't rush!" he said. "Let Juliette enjoy her belated breakfast. I'm delighted she's hungry, and to be truthful, I'm not sure what I want to do at this point."

Once in the house, Brian went to the office. He knew he had to contact his mother, but he hesitated. It was now 12:20 P.M., and he imagined the interment was in progress, meaning even if he tried to rush out to Woodlawn Cemetery, he had probably missed the ceremony. He felt fairly guilty and worried that he'd let Hannah down, yet Juliette's well-being was far more important to him than his sense of responsibility to his in-laws. Besides, he had to admit that he felt relieved not to have witnessed the stark reality of putting Emma's body in the ground.

Instead of making a mad dash to the cemetery or even calling Aimée, he sat down at his desk and used a letter opener to get at the contents of the manila folder Grady had brought over. After he and Jeanne had seen on the internet the huge number of people the Manhattan Memorial Hospital had sued or was suing in the metropolitan area, he wasn't totally surprised the list comprised hundreds of Inwood residents whom Grady had served. Having spent his entire life in the neighborhood, Brian fully expected there would be a number of people he knew personally. Sure enough, just with a random glance, he found Donavan Bligh's name with an address on Indian Road, a ten-minute walk from where Brian was sitting. He knew the family because they had a son who'd been in his sister Erin's class at P.S. 98 like Patrick McCarthy.

Although Brian was now more interested to help Jeanne learn the gory details of a number of the cases to hopefully motivate the media and maybe even the local politicians to do something, he slipped Grady's list back into its envelope, and put it aside. He then got his phone out with the intention of calling Aimée, but still he hesitated. Instead of initiating the call, he put the phone down on the desk and stared at it. Not only did he feel guilty about missing the burial, but he also now worried about the possibility of his call coming at just the wrong time if the interment was still in progress. If that happened, he'd only be adding insult to injury. With that concern in mind, he wondered if he should wait just a little longer, or send her a text instead. He knew Aimée was expecting him to be in contact.

While Brian sat paralyzed by indecision, the phone suddenly rang with its raucous "old phone" ringtone, making him jump. In a kind of panic, he snapped it up to see who was calling. To his great irritation it was Roger Dalton. Recalling the anger the man's phone call had incited the previous day, he debated whether to answer. He was already in a foul mood, and Roger Dalton, as the embodiment of MMH Inwood's business tactics as well as Kelley's sidekick, was fast becoming for him a persona non grata. Yet rationality intervened, making Brian again question whether he might be calling concerning Megan Doyle's or Patrick McCarthy's need to get a complete printout of Emma's hospital bill. With that possibility in mind, he answered but quickly wished he hadn't.

"This is rapidly becoming a farce," Roger said without even identifying himself. "I don't know why I'm making the effort to call you other than feeling some sympathy for what's happening to your life. Another charge for which you are responsible was brought to my attention. Of course, I immediately sent it to Peerless Health, and in their usual rapid but disappointing way, they have refused any coverage. Ergo, if you don't get them to reverse yet another denial, it will be added to your growing delinquency. Can I expect you to look into this quickly and get back to me?"

For a moment Brian struggled to control an almost overwhelming vexation and didn't answer immediately, partially because Roger Dalton had at least expressed an ounce of empathy. "Is this new charge for my daughter's Emergency Department visit?"

"It is indeed," Roger said.

"You are not talking about today, are you?"

"No, yesterday," Roger said. "Did you return to the ED today?"

"Yes, I just got home. I was there all morning."

"Oh, dear," Roger said. "Well, that makes it more important to get in touch with your insurance company. Because your account is flagged, I'll be hearing about a new charge probably this afternoon. Both these charges will be added to your default unless you would like to take care of these ED bills yourself. Is that a possibility?"

"How much is the charge?" he asked hesitantly. Since nothing had been done in the way of laboratory tests or imaging, he thought there was a possibility he could show some good faith, but it depended on the amount.

"Yesterday's charge is $1,776.55," Roger said. "We'd be happy to accept a check or credit card."

"Wait a second!" Brian blurted. "That's almost two thousand dollars! There must be some mistake. We had to wait for so long that my daughter's symptoms disappeared, so nothing was done: no tests, no nothing. That's impossible."

"Quite the contrary," Roger said. "The facility was used and the facility charge is a good portion of the bill. On top of that, your daughter was seen by a doctor, so there was a charge for that."

"I have never even heard of a facility charge," Brian said. "What the hell does that mean?"

"It means that everyone who is seen in the ED has to pay some costs involved in constructing and maintaining the whole facility and all its necessary equipment, including all the X-ray machines, MRIs, you name it."

"How much was the facility fee?" he asked.

"Let me check," Roger said. There was a brief pause before he added: "Eleven hundred dollars."

"Good God! I'm being charged eleven hundred dollars for merely walking into the ED."

"No, you are being charged eleven hundred dollars for your daughter to be seen, examined, and treated in a Trauma 1 facility."

Brian tried to rein in his outrage. Instead he harkened back to the lecture Megan had given him about hospital-inflated charge master prices used to negotiate with the larger health insurance companies, but which Medicare didn't pay. "If my daughter was on Medicare, how much would the facility fee be then?"

"That's proprietary information," Roger answered.

"Oh, come on, Roger," Brian said. "I'm sure I could call Medicare and they would tell me. You expressed some sympathy for what I'm going through. Help me out here, so I can begin to understand what I'm up against. How much would Medicare pay? I won't tell anyone you told me." Brian rolled his eyes at his own falsity.

"It is true Medicare could tell you," Roger admitted.

"There you go," he said. "Save me the effort."

"Somewhere in the three- to four-hundred-dollar range," Roger said. "It depends on what part of the ED was actually used."

"That's quite a difference," Brian responded, keeping his real thoughts to himself. "When we first met, you gave a lot of credit to Charles Kelley. Has he been involved with this facility charge situation?"

"Of course," Roger said. "It's a key element in his turning the hospital around financially."

"Interesting," Brian managed. Struggling to contain himself, he changed the subject. He knew it was a hopeless cause arguing about prices with the likes of Roger Dalton or finding fault with his CEO and hero. "Did Peerless give you any reason for denying the claim for my daughter's ED visit?"

"No," Roger said. "They rarely do. That's for you to find out and try to rectify. What about this most recent ED bill? Do you want to use a credit card? I could take direct payment over the phone. It's your choice."

"I'll call Peerless," Brian said.

"Fine," Roger said with irritation. "You do that."

Without another word being spoken, he found that the call had been disconnected. Yesterday he'd hung up on Roger Dalton; today Roger Dalton had hung up on him.

With his own anger and resentment mounting, Brian subjected himself once again to the frustration of calling Ebony Wilson. As he waited through the required hold music, he tried to imagine what reason Peerless was going to give for denying Juliette's ED visit. He also marveled at what a nightmare American healthcare had become for himself, his family, and apparently for too many of his neighbors and friends. After this whole ordeal, he'd be happy to never have to speak with another healthcare representative again.

After more than a half hour, Ebony Wilson came on the line using her signature pleasant voice with its mildly southern accent.

"It's Brian Murphy again," he said in response to her initial scripted introduction. He then immediately rattled off his policy number without being asked and said he was again calling about a claim denial and wanted yet another explanation.

"Let me check for you," she said cheerfully. If she'd been offended by his abrupt disconnect the day before or his current supercilious attitude, she didn't let on. Brian assumed that she probably had to deal with a lot of angry people in her role as a claims adjustment supervisor of a company that made it a point to deny claims.

After less than five minutes of additional Muzak punishment she came back. "I see the latest claim was for Juliette Murphy at the MMH Inwood ED. Is this the claim you are inquiring about?"

"Yes," he said. "Why was this one rejected, or are all claims automatically rejected?"

"Our adjusters are experienced, hardworking, and very qualified professionals," Ebony said by rote, seemingly immune to Brian's brashness. She then went on to say: "This claim was denied for two reasons. The first was because of a preexisting condition, which your policy does not cover."

"What kind of preexisting condition?" he interjected with surprise.

"Serious prematurity," she said. "The attending physician had noted that the child had been born at thirty weeks, weighing only two-and-a-half pounds, which required more than a month in the neonatal intensive care unit."

"But that was four years ago," Brian sputtered. "After the first year she caught up size-wise, and she's been fine ever since."

"Prematurity has lots of potential complications down the road, or so I've been told," Ebony said. "Do you want to hear the second reason?"

"I'm not so sure . . ."

"The visit was in the middle of the day at a Trauma 1 Emergency Department," she continued. "Your daughter should have been seen by her pediatrician or an urgent-care center."

"I called the pediatrician's office and was advised to take my daughter to the MMH Inwood ED," Brian argued. "I was following doctor's orders."

"We here at Peerless take our responsibility of reducing healthcare costs very seriously," Ebony said. "That means encouraging people to use lower-cost alternatives."

"I've heard this argument from you already," he snapped. He could feel his pulse pounding in his ears.

"Again, if you don't like our adjusters' decisions you have the right to resubmit the claim and request a review or . . ."

"Or I can sue," Brian said, filling in the rest.

"That is correct, and thank you for being a Peerless Health Insurance customer," Ebony finished, again by rote.

Without another word and infuriated by the call, he disconnected and, like yesterday, immediately charged down the cellar steps and hurried into the small basement workout room. Using the same forty-five-pound weights, he quickly exhausted himself. Brian had always been a physical and mildly self-righteous person whose first instinct when attacked or wronged was to strike out. With his size, strength, and agility, he'd had to learn to suppress such urges, using sports as a release. When competitive athletics wasn't available, barbells or strenuous cardio activity would suffice.

Ten minutes later and feeling moderately under control, he returned upstairs and sat back down at his desk. Looking at the phone lying on the blotter, he again debated getting in touch with Aimée. He knew he should, but when he picked up the phone, he still didn't call his mother. Instead, he called Jeanne, more for moral support than anything else, although he planned on using the Grady material as an excuse.

Again the phone rang more times than he would have liked, and he felt guilty about calling her so much. As he was thinking about what voice message to leave and whether to leave any, she answered. It was clear she was out of breath.

"Am I catching you out on your bike again?" he asked, hearing what he thought was the sound of wind in the background.

"You are," Jeanne admitted. "Sorry. I had to get the phone out, this time from my backpack."

"No reason to apologize," Brian said. "I should be the one apologizing for interrupting your ride again. Are you back in the park?"

"I am, but now I'm riding along the Hudson River, and it's beautiful. I wanted to get out and get some exercise. What about Juliette? How is she? What did the doctor find this morning?"

"Once again they found nothing, and she's remarkably improved despite the 102.2 fever and multiple complaints when she woke up. And once again, they did absolutely nothing despite us again waiting more than three hours. I can't help but feel it was a deliberate slight, same as I did yesterday. Anyway, by the time she was seen, her fever was gone, same with her sore throat. I don't know about the headache. They said she was fine, thought her complaints were all psychosomatic, and recommended a social worker should her symptoms come back."

"Did they run any tests this time to be sure?"

"None, even though I made a big stink," Brian said. "No matter what I said, the doctor refused. I know you might think I'm being paranoid, but I really do think it is all about the money. I'm sorry, but having to wait more than three hours two days in a row and refusing to do any tests, even a simple blood test, has to be deliberate. It can't be a coincidence."

"There's no way to know," Jeanne said.

"True, but it's my gut feeling," Brian insisted. "The doctor tried to tell me some bull about him not knowing anything about the business side of the hospital, but he has to know. They all have to know. I wouldn't be surprised if the chief medical officer was on their backs all the time with the way that my hospital account manager carries on about the cost of running the Emergency Department. My guess is that Kelley is watching every penny they spend in the ED to make sure it's a money-making venture."

"You're probably right."

"Speaking of my hospital account manager, I had to have yet another phone conversation with him a little while ago that was as maddening as ever," Brian said. "Then of course I had to talk again to the Peerless claims adjustment supervisor, which was equally as infuriating. It never ends, but I'll tell you the gory details later."

"Oh, my," Jeanne said with sympathy. "What a day you are having."

"Well, at least Juliette's feeling better than when she awoke," Brian said. "She even said she was hungry when we got home."

"That's good to hear," she said. "I hate to ask, but what about the funeral services for your wife? Were they postponed?"

"I wish," he responded. "I'm afraid Juliette and I missed both the mass and the burial. We went to the hospital early enough that I thought we'd be back in plenty of time. It's unfortunate that didn't happen thanks to the damn ED, but what could I do? Juliette's fever of over 102 had to take precedence even though it spontaneously resolved. I know my mother will understand, and I just hope Emma's mother does, too."

"I'm so sorry," Jeanne said. "You poor man. You have so much on your plate."

"There is a bit of good news," Brian interjected to change the subject. "Grady delivered, as I was confident he would. I have his service list, and it's going to make our investigation easy now that we have hundreds of Inwood names and addresses."

"Terrific," Jeanne exclaimed. "I'm excited to get on with that. The more I think about it, the more important I believe exposing all of this is. Someone has to do it."

"Are you still planning on coming over this afternoon to spend time with Juliette?"

"Absolutely! I'm looking forward to it," she said. "That's why I wanted to get some exercise in this morning. What about you? Are you still planning on visiting the ESU Academy?"

"I am," Brian admitted. "With all this extra stress, I'm looking forward to it even more. I'll be leaving soon for a three o'clock meeting, and hope I, too, can get in some exercise while I'm there. It would do wonders for my psyche."

"I have a confession to make," Jeanne said. "Last night I googled NYPD ESU, and I have to say, I was really impressed. Kudos to you and your wife. The training you guys went through is intense. I had no idea. You put your life on the line, literally. Have you really rappelled down skyscrapers and out of helicopters?"

"That and more," Brian answered with a bit of pride, although he was usually more self-effacing.

"I'm truly impressed," Jeanne said. "In French we say 'très impressionné.'"

He laughed in spite of himself. "Je me rappelle the expression."

"I'm not sure I'll see you before you leave," she said. "I've got to bike home and shower. But I'll see you when you get back. Try to enjoy yourself!"

"Merci beaucoup," Brian said. He then disconnected before bringing up Aimée's number.

CHAPTER 31

September 2

The mere act of driving out onto the Floyd Bennett Field in the southeastern part of Brooklyn was therapeutic for Brian. He'd not been there for almost a year and had forgotten the effect of the huge expanse of 1,300 acres of mostly grassland, pristine salt marshes, and five enormous, decaying runways all within the confines of New York City. He knew something of the history of the place, as did all ESU officers who spent eight months training at the school. It had been a commercial airport in its early life but then was taken over by the federal government in World War II to be used mostly as a Naval Air station and a Coast Guard facility. It was now primarily administered by the National Park Service. The NYPD had used a small portion of the eastern part of the field as far back as 1934 for an aviation unit, which was still the case. The Emergency Service Unit's headquarters and academy were also positioned there a bit later in four recycled Coast Guard buildings immediately adjacent to the aviation facility.

As he pulled up in front of the ramshackle admin and classroom building that served as the heart of the ESU complex, he had to smile at its appearance. When he'd been part of the unit, he'd been there so often that he never appreciated how decrepit the old buildings were. Perhaps when they had been built by the Coast Guard more than a half century earlier as hangars and barracks, they hadn't looked too bad, but they clearly had never been architectural exemplars. When compared to the new, multistory NYPD Academy in Queens, the ESU Academy looked like a forgotten afterthought despite its enormously important mission.

After opening the car's door, Brian hesitated as another part of his brain interrupted the pleasurable reveries he'd experienced driving onto the field. Like a sudden thunderstorm plunging a beautiful summer day into gloom, thoughts of Emma came back in a rush. It was here at the academy and in this very building that he'd first met her when she was a recruit and just starting her training. Brian could well remember the day because it had been one of his days off, and he had debated whether to go out to the academy to lend a hand with the new class of cadets. Little did he know that the day would change his life. He could vividly recall as if it were yesterday and from their first interaction how impressed he'd been with the way Emma stood out from her classmates. Her enthusiasm was palpable and sheer athleticism was obvious, especially as one of the very few females willing not only to take the physical punishment the training entailed but somehow enjoy it. It had been the same way he had reacted to the training when he'd been a recruit.

In an effort to regroup from a sudden paralyzing stab of grief, Brian reclosed the car door, shut his eyes, leaned his head against the steering wheel, and took a few deep breaths. It seemed so utterly impossible that Emma was gone. Despite the understanding both he and Emma shared as ESU officers that they were putting themselves at risk of death on a daily basis, they hadn't given the possibility much thought. With their youth and health, it seemed a theoretical problem that had been easy to ignore.

Before leaving home to head out to Floyd Bennett Field, he had finally forced himself to call his mother. During the call he'd learned that the burial had indeed taken place. He'd also learned that he and Juliette had been sorely missed at the interment, but everyone understood the reasons for his absence. Aimée told him that at the conclusion of the ceremonies, Hannah had suffered a major emotional breakdown now that all the funeral planning she'd busied herself with was over.

"God damn it!" Brian shouted in the confines of the car as he pounded the steering wheel with his fist to the point of pain. Luckily both withstood the abuse. For a fleeting moment he thought about dashing into the makeshift weight room set up in the larger, hangar-type building to his left to let off some steam. But the urge quickly passed when he diverted his thoughts to Juliette, his new raison d'être. In a minor panic, he struggled to get his phone out of his pocket to put in a call to Camila. He felt a sudden urge to make sure everything was okay even though he'd only been gone an hour. Juliette's fever of 102.2 that morning still plagued him despite its rapid resolution, especially since earlier he'd googled "psychosomatic fever" to learn that it was considered rare in children Juliette's age, especially as high as 102.

Camila answered on the first ring and relieved him by immediately reporting that Juliette had eaten a healthy meal and that Jeanne had arrived. She added that they were all busy playing an old board game that Juliette enjoyed called Dinosaur.

"I just arrived at the academy," Brian said. "I haven't yet gone inside but I'm about to. I just wanted to check in before I get involved in a training exercise."

"All is well here," Camila assured him. "Juliette is acting completely normal and seems happy, so relax and enjoy yourself. Everything is under control. By the way, a call came in about a possible security gig. I said that you would call them back. Are you up for that?"

"Of course," Brian said, trying to be positive, although if pressed he wasn't entirely sure he could handle a difficult job under the circumstances. "Was there a rush on the callback?"

"Heavens, no," Camila said. "It's a possible wedding, but it's not until December, and it didn't strike me as a definite. Do you want to speak with Jeanne?"

"Tell her I'll speak with her later," he said, checking the time. "I'm on the brink of being late for my meeting."

After a quick goodbye, Brian disconnected, turned the ringer off, and pocketed the phone. He then took a few more deep breaths. Hearing that Juliette was acting normal was reassuring, and he was confident Jeanne could help if need be. The sudden, paralyzing rush of grief reminded him he had a long way to go to deal with Emma's loss, but at the moment it was important for him to hold his own emotions in check as much as possible. Translated into the near term, that meant he needed some income and benefit security and rejoining the ESU, if they would have him, would accomplish both. With that in mind, he reopened the car door and got out.

As he walked toward the admin building door, he noted how quiet the entire, relatively large compound was. All he could hear were some seagulls in the distance. In normal non-pandemic times, the place would be hopping with thirty to fifty recruits in training, dispersed into smaller groups. Beyond the large hangar building and to the right of the huge ESU garage he could see the group of cars used for practicing with the "jaws of life" to rescue people after car wrecks. Beyond the car wrecks was an NYC subway car, which looked like a huge fish out of water in the middle of an old airport. It was used for tactical and rescue training, seeing as it was the ESU who was called to get people—or what was left of them—out from under subway trains when they jumped or were pushed. Brian could well remember training for all sorts of rescues, whether from the tops of bridges, the sides of skyscrapers, or underwater, and most all of it happened here at the ESU Headquarters.

The interior of the admin building reflected the exterior in all its ramshackle glory. The first person Brian encountered was Helen Gurly, a very capable African American woman who'd served the last four ESU commanding officers. When an ESU officer had an administration problem, they all knew Helen was the first person to go to.

"Well, well, what a sight for sore eyes," Helen said with her usual candor and humor. "The boss man is waiting on you, so go right on in!"

He thanked her and said that seeing her made him feel like coming home. She responded with a wave of dismissal, accompanied by a smile that he could detect despite her face mask.

Although the usual uniform for ESU personnel was dark blue for normal activities or black for tactical situations, Deputy Chief Michael Comstock always wore a bracingly white, impeccably ironed shirt with epaulettes and scalloped breast pocket flaps. He was a big man with a completely shaved head, hazel eyes, and a full rounded face with a ruddy complexion. Although certainly part of the brass, with his rank of deputy chief, he could compete physically with the rest of the ESU team and was respected for it. He was, in short, what a leader should be. His office and its furniture, like the entire building, looked worse for wear, but the ensemble had a homey touch with lots of family pictures alongside the compulsory head shots of the mayor and police commissioner.

As soon as Brian walked in, Michael put down his pen and stood up. With a smile he extended his elbow over his desk, so he and Brian could do the pandemic-inspired elbow-touch greeting. Michael laughed while he did it as a kind of acknowledgment that everybody was caught in the Covid-19 nightmare and had to make the best of it. He then pointed to a seat a good six feet in front of his desk.

"Let me again express my sincere condolences for your loss," Michael began. "It's a loss for all of us. Everyone I've told is heartbroken. She was, like yourself, well liked and respected around here."

"Thank you, sir," Brian said. "It's been a shock, as you can imagine. It might have been the very last thing I could have expected happening." He braced himself against tears, which he could feel coming on. He hadn't wanted to talk about Emma but knew it was inevitable.

"We and the rest of the staff are sorry we couldn't attend the burial today to pay our proper respects," Michael said.

"I appreciate that." Brian purposefully avoided saying he'd not been there, either, hoping to move the subject away from that day's events.

"After your call yesterday, I talked to a number of the staff," Michael continued. "I particularly made it a point to talk with your A team commander, Captain Deshawn Williams. I also talked with Sal

Benfatti, our TAC House sergeant. I'm happy to report that the response was uniformly positive. Everyone would be thrilled to have you back on the force, Deshawn in particular. So, if you were at all concerned about how you would be received, I can tell you there would be no problem whatsoever."

"That's reassuring to hear," Brian said. He had hoped there wouldn't be any resentment, and it was reassuring to have it confirmed.

"But I have to emphasize again that your rejoining has to be a true commitment," Michael warned. "I don't want to put through the paperwork if there is going to be any waffling. You have to be sure. Are we clear on this?"

"Perfectly clear," Brian said. "My plan is to spend a week or two re-immersing myself here, running recertification drills and just getting back into physical shape. After that, I'm certain I'll be able to make an absolute commitment. I'd also like to spend some time at one of the shooting ranges. I didn't realize how much I'd miss the opportunity to practice and stay current. This has been the first year in the past decade I didn't attend the spring Sig Sauer course up in New Hampshire."

"I can appreciate what you are saying," Michael said, "which is why the ESU puts so much emphasis on retraining and recertification. No worries! I can arrange for you to have access to one of the shooting ranges. Do you have your NYPD ID?"

"Of course," Brian responded. He'd never been without his ID since joining the force more than a decade ago, even after his retirement.

"Where would you prefer? Camp Smith or Rodman's Neck in the Bronx?"

"Rodman's Neck," Brian answered without hesitation. "It's closer. I've got a four-year-old daughter who is having a difficult time with my wife's passing, and I'd like to stay closer to home, at least in the short run." Brian knew Rodman's Neck was less than a half-hour drive from Inwood.

"I understand," Michael said. "I'm sure she is suffering, the poor child. I'd forgotten about your daughter although I do remember the anguish you had when she was born and spent so long in the hospital. I trust that she's been healthy since."

"Very healthy, thank you," Brian said, reluctant to mention the recent health concerns.

"The reason I even suggested Camp Smith is that it has a considerably longer range, if that is something that interests you."

"Rodman's Neck has a three-hundred-yard rifle range," Brian said. "That's long enough for my purposes. Actually, at least initially, I'll probably only use the pistol range."

"I had an ulterior motive mentioning Camp Smith's longer range," Michael said. "I don't know if you've heard, but we are in the process of possibly replacing our Remington 700 sniper rifle, the old standby, with the newer Remington MSR. Since I recall you were quite extraordinary with the sniper rifle, I'm wondering if you would mind giving the new one a try and give us your impression. We're trying to figure out if the benefits justify the cost. The MSR is considerably more expensive."

"I'd be happy to give my opinion," Brian said eagerly. Playing a bit of an advisory role in the face of everything else that was going on had a lot of appeal. "Would you like me to check the rifle out sooner rather than later?"

"The sooner the better," Michael answered. "Today, in fact, if it is possible. I'm tasked to submit a report on it, and to that end, I've had a few people try it, and the response has been mixed. Of course, some people have trouble with change of any kind and are accordingly biased. I've tried it, but I was never that good with a sniper rifle. Your opinion would be helpful, having been one of our crack shots."

"I'll enjoy putting it through its paces at three hundred yards," Brian said. "And today will be fine. Will they have one out at Rodman's Neck for me to use?"

"I imagine they do, but I can do better than that. I'll sign one out to you, and you can take it with you to the range. Having it in your possession will give you a chance to make the customizing adjustments beforehand. I'll call Rodman's Neck while you are over at the TAC House. I assume that the TAC House was your plan for this afternoon?"

"It is," Brian responded. "Other than speaking with you, sir."

"Perfect," Michael said. "I'll sign you out a Remington MSR and call Rodman's Neck and make the arrangements. How many rounds of ammo would you like?"

"A couple of boxes should be enough. Can you also give me a couple of boxes of nine-millimeter for my Sig Sauer, so I can use one of the pistol ranges as well?"

"Not a problem," Michael answered. "But I'll give you three boxes for the MSR just to be sure. You can bring back what you don't use. Is there anything else you wanted to do here this afternoon besides the TAC House?"

"Yes, I'd like to meet up with Detective Jose Garcia. I assume he's still the SCUBA instructor."

"Oh, yes!" Michael confirmed. "He's not going anywhere. He's here for life."

Jose Garcia had been one of his favorite instructors. Jose had managed to turn the required SCUBA training Brian had to undergo from a dreaded experience into a joy. Although he was still certified, he hadn't made a refresher SCUBA dive in well over a year. Prior to his ESU training, Brian had never been that comfortable in the water. He'd always joked that it had taken life millions of years to get out of the water, and he didn't see any reason to reverse the trend. Now he loved it.

"Could you let him know I'll be stopping by after my session at the TAC House? I'd like him to pick me out some equipment so that I can do a recertification dive in the next couple of days."

"You got it," Michael said. "And when you are done with your rounds, stop back here. I'll have one of the Remington MSRs and the ammo available."

"Thank you, sir," he said. "I really appreciate your help and support." Being back at his former stomping grounds and with his former colleagues, he was already feeling more secure about the future.

CHAPTER 32

September 2

J ust to the north of the ESU admin building was another sizable, nondescript commercial structure that looked equally as aged and dilapidated as the others. This building contained the TAC House, or Training Ammunition Combat edifice. As Brian approached, he again had to smile. On this occasion it wasn't because of its run-down appearance. It was because from the outside there was no hint whatsoever of what was inside.

Brian pushed through a battered outside door and stepped into a simulated night scene. What confronted him in the expansive, darkened, several-story interior was a worse-for-wear modular structure the size of a modest one-story house. It had no ceiling and could be configured in various ways to represent an entire apartment with an outer door, a kitchen, living room, bathrooms, and bedrooms, an office, or any indoor structure. It was used for adaptive urban, nonballistic assault exercises in various lighting conditions and with various numbers of targets played by instructors positioned inside, sometimes armed with non-lethal weaponry. Several catwalks above were used by the instructors to watch the simulated assaults so they could comment and make recommendations.

In addition to the TAC House structure, Brian was also confronted in the half-light by a group of seven ESU officers heavily
armed and outfitted in the usual ESU tactical gear with midnight-
black uniforms and bulletproof vests with multiple pockets for gear
and ammunition. In addition, they were wearing helmets, gloves, eye
protection, and balaclava face masks in anticipation of taking part in
the next drill. Although Brian had no chance of identifying anyone
in face masks and dim light, most of the officers recognized him and
immediately crowded around to say hello and extend their sympa-
thies about Emma's passing. One officer, Carlos Morales, who was a
member of the A team and who Brian knew well, said he'd heard a
rumor that Brian might be rejoining the ESU. All of them cheered as
a group when Brian told them he was giving it serious thought.

"Do it, do it, do it!" rang out as a spontaneous chant from the
group. Brian laughed, unsure of how to respond. Finding his voice,
he admitted he was leaning toward rejoining but wanted to make
sure it was the right decision for his daughter and career.

For Brian this was even more of a homecoming than seeing Helen
Gurly in the admin building, and it soothed his soul. It made him
remember how much he valued being a member of a group with a
common interest, extending all the way back to grammar school
when he first began participating in organized sports. Through high
school and college, it had been the same, and it had been one of the
reasons he'd gravitated toward law enforcement as a career. In many
ways he'd not been entirely aware of how much he missed this type
of camaraderie since his retirement.

Suddenly the animated conversation was interrupted by someone
within the TAC House yelling "Police! Police!" followed by a series of
non-lethal rounds being fired, indicating that the simulation drill

that was in progress when Brian arrived had terminated in gunplay. The blanks were particularly loud in the confined spaces.

"That's it, guys," Carlos called out to the group. "We're on deck, front and center!" He then picked up a ballistic shield that he had leaning against his leg. He was going to be the lead man on the next assault simulation. Another officer picked up a Blackhawk Halligan bar used to breach the outer door. Every member of the assault group had a specific, planned role to play to maximize safety, which was key if it were a real-life situation.

"Where's the tactic sergeant?" Brian asked Carlos.

"He's up on the catwalk," Carlos said, pointing to the wooden stairs to Brian's right.

"Good luck," Brian said, making a halfhearted salute gesture. He then walked to the stairs and started up. At the top Brian could see down into the illuminated mock living room/kitchen below, which was empty for the moment. Raising his eyes, he searched the maze-like elevated walkways that created an opportunity for the instructors to closely follow the activity below during a simulated assault. Brian could make out Sergeant Sal Benfatti with two of his instructors at the far end over the bedroom area. The tactic sergeant was leaning over the railing while talking down to the assault team below. Brian assumed he was giving a mixture of both praise and criticism regarding the simulation.

By the time Brian made it over to where the group was standing, Sal had finished his analysis with the group below and was conferring with the two instructors by his side. Below, Brian could see the team that had just completed the drill along with several instructors who had been acting as the bad guys. Brian had the sense the drill had been a mock-up hostage situation.

"Ah, Brian Murphy," Sal said welcomingly, seeing Brian approach. They knew each other well, not only from Brian's cadet days, but also because Brian had frequently helped out and participated in TAC House activities. Sal introduced Brian to his two instructors, who'd come on board since Brian's retirement.

As expected, Brian initially had to weather a brief conversation with Sal about Emma, but they soon turned to discussing why Brian was there; namely, to participate in a number of assault simulations. "I hope you weren't counting on starting today," Sal said. "This next drill is our last."

"That's fine," Brian said. "With your permission, I'd like to come back in the next couple of days."

"Terrific! We'll look forward to it. We'd love to have you. Do you want to stay and watch the next drill with us?"

"Absolutely," Brian answered.

The group moved from over the bedroom area to over the living room/kitchen. On this occasion there were to be two armed suspects, one in the kitchen area behind an island and the other in the living room sitting on the couch. When all was ready, Sal initiated the assault with a remote device. In the next second the front door was quickly breached with the Halligan bar, and Carlos swooped into the room with his ballistic shield followed closely by his team, all yelling "Police! Police!" at the top of their lungs while executing a predetermined set of movements.

On this occasion, with the two suspects in the front area of the sham apartment, there was an immediate shootout. Since the two officers directly behind Carlos precisely followed their preordained ballet with one concentrating on the kitchen and the other on the living room area, they bested the suspects. Within seconds the drill was over to well-deserved acclaim.

Twenty minutes later Brian walked out of the TAC House building, feeling particularly good about the visit. Having watched the drill and having experienced the palpable esprit de corps of the people involved made him progressively confident that rejoining the ESU was the proper decision for him, especially when he compared it with some of the security gigs he'd done. A number of those jobs involved squiring around and kowtowing to the demands of entitled wealthy narcissists and their spoiled offspring. In many ways Brian was coming more and more to identify himself as a blue-collar kind of guy who liked to get his hands dirty. It almost seemed as if the NYPD ESU, with its constant action, was tailor-made for him.

Rounding the northern end of the admin building, Brian walked into the middle of a dozen ESU officers who'd just finished a recertification SCUBA dive and were busy rinsing their equipment. In a repeat of what had happened when Brian first entered the TAC House, there was a warm interaction with condolences about Emma and encouragement for Brian to rejoin the ranks.

Entering the largest of the four buildings that formed the ESU complex, Brian walked into the SCUBA section. Passing through the storage and maintenance area, he entered Detective Jose Garcia's cramped and rather messy office. The detective was at his desk with the guts of a regulator exposed, as he did most of the upkeep and repair work himself. Similar to Michael Comstock, Jose was a big, thickset man, and except for a significant difference in complexion, they could have been brothers, down to the shaved heads. The main difference was that Jose had an impressive number of tattoos covering his forearms from a stint in the US Navy directly out of high school.

Although Brian would have preferred not to talk again about Emma's passing, he knew he didn't have a choice. Emma was extraordinarily well liked both at the academy and in the unit, probably more than Brian because of his mild but recognized self-righteous streak on certain subjects, including extremists on both sides of the political divide. One of Emma's admirable qualities had been her acceptance of others.

"So, Michael says you are interested in doing a recertification dive with us," Jose said.

"I am," Brian confirmed. "It's not critical since I'm still certified, but I would enjoy it. It's your fault. You turned me from a committed terrestrial into an amphibian."

Jose laughed with true mirth. "You were a tough cookie to crack, but I was optimistic."

They then spent a few minutes reminiscing about some of the dives they'd done together, particularly one to retrieve the body of a suicide jumper in the East River, where the currents can be notorious.

"Well, then," Jose said when there was a pause in their reminiscing. He slapped his desk with the palms of both hands and stood up. "Let's get you ready for a dive by setting you up with a locker, a wet suit, whatever else you might want, including one of our newest regulators. You are going to love it."

Fifteen minutes later, with all the dive equipment set aside in a locker, Brian left the SCUBA area and walked the length of the large hangar-like building. He emerged back out in the sunshine on its west side, and from there it was a short route back to the admin building. As he neared it, he felt really good about his visit as well as progressively convinced that in the not-too-distant future he would be back to being an ESU officer.

"Deputy Chief Comstock had to leave for an impromptu meeting downtown with the police commissioner," Helen Gurly explained when Brian approached her desk. "But no worries. He had me make the arrangements with Rodman's Neck and all you have to do is show your ID at the gate and then meet up with Captain Ted Miller, one of the firearms and tactics instructors, at the gunsmith. He'll be expecting you, provided you get there before six. There's also a surprise for you waiting on the deputy chief's desk that I'm told you already know about."

"You are talking about the Remington?" Brian asked.

"None other. Have a good day, I'm outta here." With that, Helen grabbed her bag, said that it was a joy to see him again, and pushed past on her way out into the corridor.

Entering Michael's office, Brian saw a camouflaged rifle bag with a shoulder strap on the desk along with five boxes of ammunition: three in 7.62mm NATO caliber for the rifle and two in 9mm for his pistol. Unzipping the bag, he found himself admiring a particularly lethal-looking, light tan sniper rifle with a folding stock and a suppressor. What impressed him immediately was the amount of customizing adjustments available, and how intuitive they were to utilize. Within minutes he adapted the length between the stock and the trigger to his needs, as well as the height and position of the cheek piece and the position of the scope. As for the finer adjustments of the telescopic sight for parallax and minute of angle, he'd do that at the shooting range when he'd be able to experience how well engineered the firearm actually was in comparison with the older Remington 700. After refolding the stock, Brian returned the weapon to its bag and slung it over his shoulder. Picking up the boxes of ammunition, he headed back out to his Subaru.

As he climbed into the car, he felt pleased with his visit to ESU Headquarters and more inclined to believe that rejoining the NYPD would be a wise move for many reasons. What especially encouraged him was that Michael Comstock, the commanding officer, had ostensibly recovered from his pique about his and Emma's retirement and wanted him back on board.

CHAPTER 33

September 2

Ten minutes later Brian was heading north on the Belt Parkway with Jamaica Bay off to his right and sparkling in the summer sunlight. The traffic was moderate, but being late afternoon and rush hour, he knew that would significantly change despite the pandemic. As far as the timing was concerned, he thought it was a good time to visit the Rodman's Neck shooting range. As an active NYPD officer, he'd been there more times than he could count for various firearms classes and recertification exercises, which usually had been in the mornings when it was always crowded. There were seven shooting ranges, of which six were for pistols and one for rifles, and the complex was used by not only the NYPD, but also the FBI, NYC Correction, New York Fire Marshals, and even ICE.

As he drove, his thoughts drifted back to Juliette and how the day had begun, including the aggravating visit to the ED. After the disturbing call with Roger Dalton earlier and finding out the cost of yesterday's visit, he wondered what the charges were going to be for today. Reluctantly, he assumed it would be equally as outrageous considering what he now knew about hospital business practices.

Facing at least an hour of downtime before arrival at Rodman's

Neck, Brian thought it a good opportunity to check in with Camila to give her an idea of when he'd be arriving home. He also considered broaching the idea that he was thinking of rejoining the NYPD, as such a move would impact her life, though he realized it wasn't the best time. As for Juliette, he was relatively confident she was doing okay following the positive news about her behavior he'd gotten earlier. Surely if anything significant had changed, Camila or Jeanne would have called or texted. For that reason, it was shocking when Camila started the conversation by saying that Juliette's fever had returned.

"Good grief!" Brian responded with alarm. He sat up straighter, gripping the steering wheel. This was not what he wanted to hear. "How high?"

"Not high," Camila responded. "Nothing like this morning. It was 100.5."

"What made you decide to take her temperature?" he asked. He relaxed slightly, settling back into his seat. He wasn't happy about the fever returning, and it brought back with a rush his frustration that he'd been unable to get the ED doctors to do any kind of testing, even a simple blood count. Although he was the first one to admit he wasn't a doctor or a psychologist, his daughter's on-again-off-again symptoms bothered him, and he had a reluctance to ascribe them to being psychosomatic at this point.

"She suddenly had a visible chill," Camila said. "Both Jeanne and I saw it. When we asked her about it, she said she wasn't feeling good and wanted to go up to her room. It came as a surprise because she'd eaten well and was clearly having fun playing Dinosaur."

"What about her headache?" Brian said. The headache seemed to be the one constant symptom.

"Yes, she still says she has a headache," Camila said, "but that's it: no other complaints like sore throat or upset stomach. I asked her specifically. As for the headache, I thought it had improved given the way she was interacting with us. She seemed to be her old self."

In the back of his mind, he wondered what should be done if a high fever returned, vowing that there was no way he'd take her back to MMH Inwood. Briefly he considered taking her to one of the neighborhood urgent-care centers, but he nixed the idea because they wouldn't be able to do a Covid test and have the results right away. Instead, if need be, he decided he'd drive her down to Columbia-Presbyterian in Washington Heights, thinking that was probably what he should have done originally. "I've finished my meeting at the ESU Headquarters," Brian said after a pause. "I'm on my way to the NYPD shooting range for an hour or so. But I could cancel and come directly back home if you think I should."

"Not for Juliette's sake, if that's your thought. While I was taking her temperature, she got very sleepy. She's up in her room resting. I've just checked on her. I think we should let her sleep."

"Okay, fair enough." Preoccupied with this surprise news about Juliette, Brian decided against bringing up the issue of his possible return to the police department. "Call or text if there is a change in her status, and I'll come back straightaway. What about Jeanne? Is she still there?"

"No, when Juliette went to sleep about a half hour ago, Jeanne left. She did take the papers that your friend Grady Quillen dropped off. I hope that was okay."

"That's fine," he assured her.

After ringing off with Camila, Brian considered contacting Jeanne to get her take on Juliette, but he held off, thinking it might be best to first check on Juliette himself when he got home. He worried he was taking too much advantage of her generosity by contacting her so often; plus, if this was a medical problem and not a psychological issue, he wasn't sure she could add much.

As he expected, traffic did slow up considerably approaching the Whitestone Bridge to cross the East River, but then it sped up again once he was on the other side. All in all, he turned in to Rodman's Neck peninsula just about an hour later. For the next quarter of a mile, after passing a broad field containing a baseball diamond and a number of warning signs about unauthorized entry, he drove through virginal forested land that was almost as unexpected within New York City as was the wide-open expanse of Floyd Bennett Field.

Ahead appeared a guard gate similar to those on military installations. He pulled to a stop. Lifting his mask up over his nose and mouth, he rolled down the window and presented his NYPD ID to the friendly uniformed NYPD officer. There was no problem thanks to Helen Gurly's efforts, and Brian was permitted to drive into the shooting range. Reminiscent of Floyd Bennett Field, it was composed of a motley group of buildings, some in better shape than others and some reflective of their military origins. Like Floyd Bennett Field, Rodman's Neck had a history that included use by the armed forces, this time both the army and navy, although the facility eventually had been given over to the NYPD. Besides the shooting ranges there were also outdoor TAC facilities and even a biohazard safety level 4 lab, and at the far end of the peninsula there was an isolated pit for detonating bombs and other explosive devices like confiscated fireworks.

As he expected, the expansive parking area was nearly empty this late in the afternoon, allowing him to park directly in front of the

admin building. Although he'd been mildly concerned about finding Captain Ted Miller of the Firearms and Tactics Unit, it turned
out to be extremely easy, as the man was expecting Brian and was
waiting for him just inside the entrance door.

"You just made it under the wire," Ted said. He was a mildly overweight man with a salt-and-pepper crewcut whom Brian recognized
from having dealt with him in the past. "There's been no one using
the rifle range for more than an hour and Mark Bellows, the range
master, has been eager to close up shop, so we best head there first
and then use the pistol range after. Is that okay with you?"

"Fine with me," Brian answered, thankful for the man's assistance.

Once he had been supplied with the required eye and ear protective gear, they used Ted's vehicle to drive the mile or so out to the
rifle range. It was hardly an impressive physical setup and the immediate area looked more like a partially deserted dump thanks to a
handful of abandoned vehicles and storage containers sprinkled
about. Brian had used the range in the past, so he wasn't surprised.
The row of connected shooting positions was constructed of rough-
hewn, unfinished lumber that had grayed over the years and, taken
together, looked a little like the starting gate at a horse racetrack.
Ahead stretched a grassy field of more than three hundred yards facing a dunelike hill.

Sergeant Mark Bellows was a beefy firearms and tactics officer
who looked somewhat long in the tooth and ready for retirement. He
was friendly enough but clearly eager to leave for the day. "What
distance are you looking to use?" he asked in a tired voice.

"I'd like to use all three," Brian said. He knew the range was set
up for one hundred, two hundred, and three hundred yards, so he
wouldn't have to use a range finder.

"Okay," Mark said resignedly. "Pick any firing position that suits your fancy and let's do it. I've refreshed all the targets, so you are good to go. Just let me know when you are ready."

Brian didn't care which position he used and just picked one at random as Ted and Mark stood back and chatted together. After getting the rifle out of its bag, he unfolded the stock and placed the gun on its bipods, using the rifle bag under the stock for added stability. Once again, he appreciated the mere appearance of the gun as a stunningly formidable weapon, particularly with its perforated handguard and suppressor. The fact that he knew it was reportedly deadly accurate close to a mile added to his sense of awe.

Quickly Brian used the cloudless sky as a backdrop to adjust the ocular so that the crosshairs visible within the scope were clear. Then he adjusted the focus on the side of the scope for the target at one hundred yards, opened a box of ammunition, filled the rifle's magazine with ten cartridges, and inserted the magazine into the underside of the rifle.

"I'm ready," he called over his shoulder.

"Okay," Mark responded immediately. "Commence firing."

Using the bolt handle on the rifle, Brian loaded the first round into the barrel chamber. The ease and the feel of this action impressed him. There was no doubt in his mind that he was using a precision instrument. Totally relaxed, he sighted through the scope and saw the target clearly. Using a very steady pull on the trigger, Brian shot a round and immediately saw the hole appear in the target slightly lower than he anticipated. After a minor elevation adjustment of minute of angle, he shot another round, and on this occasion the hole appeared exactly where he intended: dead center. The sound and the feel of the weapon were outstanding, far better than what he remembered with the Remington 700. Then in rapid succession he fired eight more times, emptying the weapon.

After quickly refilling the magazine with ten more cartridges, he moved to the target positioned at two hundred yards. Repeating the process, he found he didn't have to change the minute of angle to achieve equivalent and impressive accuracy. Moving then out to the three-hundred-yard targets, he again repeated the process, shooting ten more rounds and finding that he did have to make a very slight adjustment as he'd done initially.

Knowing that the range master was impatient to leave and concerned about getting home himself after hearing about Juliette's latest fever, Brian checked the gun's breech to be absolutely sure it was empty, removed the magazine, and called over his shoulder that he was done.

"Cease fire," Mark called out as if there were other people firing besides him. Then he added: "Wow, that was quick. Are you sure you are finished?"

"I am." Brian stood up and started to repack the Remington MSR back into its shoulder bag. Under normal circumstances he would have enjoyed continuing to put the gun through its paces, but he felt guilty about not getting home earlier. And he felt that with the thirty rounds he did fire, he could give Deputy Chief Comstock a definite thumbs-up about the weapon. In his estimation it was clearly better than the older model, but whether it was worth the increased cost was another question entirely, especially since he didn't know the details.

"Would you like to go downrange and retrieve your targets?" Mark asked.

"No, thanks," Brian said. "I could see what I needed to see through the scope."

From the rifle range, Ted dropped Brian off at the pistol range, telling him that the range master was expecting him.

At the range, he wasn't alone despite the lateness of the afternoon, sharing the facility with a half dozen other NYPD officers. As a consequence, he couldn't be quite so efficient timewise, as safety protocols had to be scrupulously followed. Still, Brian managed to go through a full box of fifty cartridges in relatively rapid order. After forty minutes, he was already on his way back to his car, having left the protective equipment with the range master. Climbing in after putting the Remington in the back of the Subaru, he forwent the opportunity to have either gun serviced at the gunsmith, which he'd usually done in the past. Instead, to save time, he planned on cleaning the pistol himself later in his basement, and as for the rifle, it had been used so little he doubted it needed any attention whatsoever.

As soon as Brian could, he put in a call to Camila. Although he hadn't gotten any call or text from her, he was still uneasy about Juliette. He was relieved when Camila reported that all was quiet.

"Is she still sleeping?" he asked.

"Last time I looked, about a half hour ago," Camila said. "I have a feeling she's down for the night as soundly as she is sleeping."

"I'm on my way now," Brian said. "I'll be home in twenty minutes, tops."

"There's no need to hurry."

"Okay, good," he said, feeling some relief. "In that case, how about I pick up some Mexican takeout from Tijuana Restaurant on my way home?"

"That's a good idea."

"Why don't you call and order for the three of us in case Juliette wakes up?"

"Okay," Camila said agreeably. "What should I order for you?"

"I don't care," Brian said. He actually wasn't particularly hungry although Mexican food sounded good. "Just double up whatever you want."

"When you called earlier, I forgot to tell you that your mother and your brothers and sister stopped by after the funeral," Camila said. "I told them where you were. I hope that was okay."

"Of course," he said through gritted teeth. Hearing that his family had come by fanned his guilty feelings about missing the funeral formalities. "They're probably at my mother's. I'll call them when I get back."

"There was also another request about a possible security gig," Camila said. "It's for another potential December wedding. The info is on your desk with the other one."

"Okay, thank you," Brian said. He thought it mildly ironic that just when he was seriously thinking about going back to the NYPD, there'd been two requests for security work after it had been so quiet. He couldn't help but superstitiously wonder if such a coincidence was a kind of subliminal message that he shouldn't be so quick to abandon Personal Protection LLC.

Traffic was heavy and the driving slow, even stop-and-go in places. Still mystified by Juliette's recurrent fever, he changed his mind and decided to call Jeanne after all. Although earlier he'd worried about calling her too much and planned on waiting until he was able to check on Juliette himself, he still felt comfortable enough to get her opinion and perhaps ameliorate some of his anxiety that was mounting the longer it took to get home.

"How was your visit to the ESU?" she asked the moment they were connected, dispensing with any traditional hellos. She sounded happy to be hearing from him, which relieved him of his concerns of calling her too frequently.

"The visit couldn't have gone better," he said. "The best part is that it made me feel even more inclined to go back to being a cop. At the same time, ironically enough, there've been a couple inquiries about security gigs this very afternoon to muddy the waters."

"Serious inquiries?" she asked.

"That I don't know until I call them back," Brian said. "Both involve possible December weddings."

"I'm not sure if you should count on December weddings," Jeanne said. "Especially with the coronavirus spike that's expected."

"You're probably right," he agreed.

"More to the point, it sounds as if your visit to the ESU was a good idea."

"It was a great idea," Brian agreed. "I even got a chance to visit the shooting range, which I enjoyed just as much. I hadn't been able to do that for almost a year."

"Good for you," Jeanne said.

"Now to a more important topic: Juliette. I was distressed, to say the least, when Camila told me that her fever had returned, and I wanted to get your take."

"I'm not completely convinced it was a fever even though she had an obvious chill," Jeanne said. "It was only a tad over a hundred: certainly nothing like the 102 you saw this morning. But I'll tell you what surprised me more than the possible fever was how quickly her mood changed. One minute she was enjoying herself immensely, even giggling because she was doing so well with the board game the three of us were playing. But then it was like a shadow came over her face, and she seemed miserable. She didn't want to finish the game even though she was clearly about to win fair and square."

"That is strange," Brian agreed. "It's not like her at all. She's a competitive little thing." He audibly sighed. "I can't help it, but I think she's fighting something off. Whether it's a cold or flu or what, I don't know. Luckily it's unlikely to be Covid, with the way the symptoms come and go, at least according to the MMH ED docs. But I wish they weren't so quick to label them psychosomatic. It irks me to death that they refuse to do any testing, even a simple blood test, much less a Covid test."

"Well, in their defense, she certainly has reasons to have a psychosomatic reaction," Jeanne said. "How is she doing now?"

"Camila just told me she's still sleeping soundly. I'm actually not home yet. I'm stuck in traffic, but I'll be home shortly, and I'll let you know what I think if you'd like."

"Please do," Jeanne said. "On another note, I've had a chance to look at the list that your friend Grady supplied. Although we suspected as much, I'm shocked at the number of Inwood residents MMH has sued. It's unconscionable. It's like they want to suck every last penny out of this neighborhood. I'm looking forward to hearing some of the actual stories and putting together a real exposé. This can't go on."

"I agree," Brian said, but he wasn't interested in getting into a protracted discussion about MMH at the moment, as caught up as he was with Juliette's ongoing problems. And then as traffic began to speed up and require more of his attention, he told Jeanne he'd call her back after he'd had an opportunity to check on her.

Unfortunately, after loosening up, the traffic again quickly bogged back down, with some of the worst congestion in Marble Hill, just across the Harlem River from Inwood. By the time he pulled up in front of the Tijuana Restaurant, the trip from Rodman's Neck had taken over an hour rather than the twenty minutes he'd expected. Less than ten minutes later, with their takeout dinner in hand, he pulled into his driveway.

"Is Juliette still sleeping?" Brian asked as he entered the kitchen and put the sizable bag on the table. Camila had come into the kitchen when she heard his car arrive and was getting out the dishes and flatware.

"To be truthful, I haven't checked since you and I talked on the phone," Camila said. "I've been in the office again looking at our books." She grimaced. "I do hope one of these inquiries materializes into a gig. It's not a pretty picture if they don't."

"Tell me about it," Brian said sardonically. "And the books are going to look even worse when I catch up with the house mortgage, which I should have done today. The longer I wait, the more chance the house will be at risk with the MMH Inwood lawsuit."

"Both callback numbers are on your desk."

"Duly noted," Brian said without a lot of enthusiasm. After his conversation with Jeanne, he wasn't optimistic that either wedding would take place. Although he was beginning to feel guilty he'd not mentioned to Camila the possibility of his rejoining the NYPD, he was loath to bring up the issue before he was more certain of what he thought was best for him to do.

With Camila busy unpacking the food, he climbed the stairs to look in on Juliette. Soundlessly he pushed open the door. With the blackout curtains closed, the room was filled with a dim half-light, just adequate enough to see the outline of her sleeping form but no details. Moving closer, he silently bent over for a better view. Now he could make out that she was on her back with her slender arms out of the covers and her right hand clutching Jeannot Lapin to her chest. As his eyes adjusted to the near darkness, he could appreciate the cherubic features of her face. To Brian she looked like the most beautiful child in the world, suddenly reminding him of Emma's verbatim adoration of her that fateful afternoon in Wellfleet, Massachusetts.

The sudden remembrance of his wife's words caused him to catch his breath. It had been just over two weeks since their fateful barbecue, but it seemed like a lifetime with all that had happened. Pulling himself together with some difficulty, Brian went back to observing Juliette, noticing with relief that her breathing was gentle and rhythmic.

Just to be sure and being careful not to disturb her, he gently placed the palm of his hand against her forehead to feel if it was overly warm or moist with perspiration. To his relief, neither was the case. Removing his hand yet still bending over her, he felt almost intoxicated by parental love and so very thankful that he and Emma had had a child so soon in their relationship. Although Juliette was without a doubt her own person, Brian felt she embodied an essence of Emma that would live on.

Straightening up, Brian tiptoed out of the room, carefully closing the door behind him. Confident her temperature was normal and that she was sleeping soundly, he felt a definite sense of relief. As the foundation on which he intended to rebuild his life, her well-being was by far his primary concern. As long as she was okay, he felt empowered to face the current challenges of dealing with the impending

MMH lawsuit, deciding between continuing with Personal Protection or rejoining the NYPD, and otherwise surviving the ongoing coronavirus pandemic. On top of all that, he even felt that by combining efforts with Jeanne, the two of them could possibly do something about the toxic healthcare system that was responsible for her woes, his and Juliette's suffering, and probably Emma's death.

CHAPTER 34

September 3

Brian awakened from a vivid dream he was having about effortlessly running through a landscape sprinkled with abandoned vehicles that was visually reminiscent of Rodman's Neck shooting range. As he opened his eyes, he noticed the streetlight sifting through the white gauzy curtains. As he held his breath to figure out what might have roused him from his deep slumber, he heard a car's tires complain against the striated pavement. Glancing around the darkened room, he also noticed the curtains were rustling from a soft breeze, but he couldn't imagine that could have disturbed his sleep.

Turning over, he glanced at the bedside clock, noting that it was 3:25 A.M. Rolling back, he stared up at the ceiling and again listened as the sound of the car out in the street faded, wondering if another mosquito could have gotten inside. He strained his ears for the characteristic whine, but heard nothing. But then he became aware of a rhythmic, distant thumping that he seemed to feel rather than hear. For several minutes his mind tried to place the disturbance, wondering if something could be amiss with the refrigerator or the washing machine way down in the basement, thinking perhaps Camila couldn't sleep and decided to do a load of laundry.

Unable to come up with an explanation, Brian turned over onto his stomach, putting the pillow over his head in an attempt to go back to sleep before his mind latched on to one of the many problems that had been making sleep impossible lately. Yet despite the pillow, he could still feel the thumping even though it was nearly subliminal. Angrily throwing off the pillow, he sat up and as he became progressively more and more awake, the thumping sound suddenly sounded all too familiar.

"No!" Brian gasped as he leaped to his feet. Clad only in his Calvin Klein pajama bottoms, he rushed from the bedroom, and dashed down the hallway into Juliette's room. Snapping on the light, he was confronted by his worst nightmare. Juliette was in the throes of a seizure, her back arching and her head rhythmically banging against the headboard. The image was all too familiar.

Screaming Camila's name, he rushed to the bedside and pulled Juliette's convulsing body away from the head of the bed. Her face was scrunched into a grimace, but most worrisome of all, her lips were startlingly blue. Quickly he rolled her onto her side, and saliva spilled out onto the sheets from between her clenched teeth.

Camila appeared in the doorway in her pajamas. As she caught sight of Juliette, her face metamorphosed into an expression of horror. "Should I call 911?" she shouted through the hand covering her mouth.

"There's no time," Brian shouted back, understanding too well that by the color of her lips, she'd been seizing much too long. "You'll have to drive us to MMH Inwood."

As he tried to scoop up Juliette, which he found extraordinarily difficult with the strength of her contractions, Camila disappeared. When Brian finally got the child into his arms, he found it equally as hard to carry her through the doorway and particularly down the stairs. Running along the main hallway on the ground floor and into the kitchen, he was relieved to see that Camila had left the door ajar for him. Outside, she had also opened the rear door of the car, and she was now in the driver's seat with the engine running.

Ducking headfirst into the car while clutching Juliette against his chest, he managed to climb in and collapse back against the seat. Holding the bucking child as best he could, he reached out and pulled the door closed.

"Go, go!" he shouted, making sure Juliette's head couldn't hit any surfaces as Camila rapidly backed out of the driveway and accelerated up West 217th Street. Again, when Camila turned left onto Park Terrace East and then right onto West 218th Street, Brian had to use all his strength to keep himself upright and Juliette's head safe.

Although the ride was just minutes, with Camila merely slowing at red lights instead of stopping, the eight-minute journey seemed to take a lifetime as he held his seizing daughter against his body. "Please stop, please stop," Brian murmured over and over again until Camila pulled up to the emergency entrance with squealing tires.

Leaping out of the driver's seat, Camila ran around the car to help open the door for him. It again took all of his strength to exit the car with Juliette in his arms. He then ran for the entrance, impatiently waiting for the automatic sliding door to open enough to run inside.

Despite the hour, there were more than a dozen people in the waiting room. Without the slightest hesitation, Brian ran directly up to the counter. Immediately one of the triage nurses, upon seeing Juliette's convulsions, waved for him to follow her back into the treatment area. Within seconds she guided Brian at a run into one of the Trauma 1 rooms.

"Put her here on the table!" the nurse ordered, patting the location with a gloved hand.

Brian laid Juliette down on the sheet-covered exam table, holding on to her lest her convulsions caused her to fall off onto the floor. To his relief word must have spread quickly because other medical personnel flooded into the room and pressed in around the table. All were dressed in scrub clothing. One youthful woman quickly asked Brian how long Juliette had been seizing.

"I don't know," Brian cried. "I heard a kind of thumping from my bed for maybe five or ten minutes and couldn't figure out what it was. How long it had been going on before it woke me up, I have no idea. Then it took about ten minutes to get here. I'm afraid it's probably been going on at least thirty minutes, though probably more."

"Okay!" the woman said quickly, redirecting her attention to the medical people in the room. "We need an IV immediately or intraosseous access. Start oxygen and an oximeter! We'll need an ECG and glucose and let's get a body temperature, BP, and intubation setup. Draw up four milligrams of midazolam. Let's go!"

As a flurry of activity erupted around his daughter, a nurse pulled him back and away from the table. Brian resisted, not wanting to leave Juliette. "I've had EMT training," Brian said in his defense.

"That doesn't matter," the nurse said. She handed him a face mask. "You need to leave! And you have to check in properly and provide the patient's name."

"She's been seen here several times," Brian sputtered while putting on the face mask. "In fact, she was seen here less than twenty-four hours ago. Her name is Juliette Murphy. Just look it up on your tablet."

"You have to check in at the front desk today as well," the nurse said evenly, trying to calm him down.

"But why?" Brian demanded. He knew he was beside himself and not thinking clearly. "I'm telling you, she was just seen yesterday by Dr. Arnsdorf, and Dr. Kramer the day before. Really, look it up! You can get all you need to know and then some." As he spoke, he was trying to keep his eye on Juliette over the nurse's shoulder. There was a lot of frantic activity, which encouraged him and terrified him in equal measure.

"What was found on those two occasions?" the nurse asked.

"Nothing," Brian snapped. "Nothing was found and nothing was done. Both times we were here for more than three hours, and they wouldn't even do a damn blood test. They insisted her symptoms were psychosomatic. Obviously, they weren't!" He noticed more medical personnel arriving, enhancing the sense of a developing crisis and magnifying his fears. More urgent orders were called out, including a call for anesthesia and neurology consults.

"Do I have to call security?" the nurse asked calmly but decisively. Gently she urged Brian to move toward the hallway.

Finally, sensing the inevitable, Brian allowed himself to be led from the trauma room and then out into the waiting area. His last image of Juliette was a gaggle of medical staff hovering over her convulsing body. A few minutes later he found himself waiting to talk to one of the intake clerks. As he was waiting, the nurse who had urged him out of the trauma room returned with a set of scrub pants, shirt, and slippers. Despite his state of anxiety and irritation, he thanked her and immediately put the outfit on over his pajama pants.

When he finally got to talk to a clerk, he felt stupid even bothering to list Peerless Health as his health insurance carrier, but he did anyway. With that out of the way, he found a seat and tried to calm himself. As he waited, time dragged. Each minute was emotionally exhausting, and he tried not to think about what was happening back in the treatment room.

A short time later he was shocked to see Camila walk into the waiting area and search for him. He stood up and waved. Once she saw him, she came over, carrying a shopping bag.

"How is she?" she asked when she got close, her face creased with worry.

"I haven't heard anything yet but hoping I will soon," Brian said. "I'm surprised to see you. I didn't expect for you to come back until I called."

"I didn't expect to come back, either," Camila said. "But when I got back to the house, I remembered that you were in your pajama bottoms. So I got a pair of jeans, a shirt, socks, and shoes out of your room." She held up the shopping bag. "But I see they have supplied you with some hospital clothes, so maybe you don't want them. I can take them back."

"You're so kind," he said, moved by her thoughtfulness. "Thank you, but these scrubs will do, and I don't want to go through the angst of finding a place to change."

"Understandable," Camila said. Then, reaching into her pocket she added: "Oh, also, I brought your phone from your bedside table. I know I'd feel naked without mine."

"That I can use," Brian said. He took the phone and turned it on. "Again, thank you for your kindness. I don't know what Juliette and I would do without you. Truly." Despite the fear of not knowing what was currently happening with his daughter, he marveled at the luck of having teamed up with Camila. He truly felt she'd become like family given the way she clicked with Juliette, especially with all the crises they had gone through lately.

"It's been a mutual win-win," Camila said. "Do you need me to stay and keep you company? If so, there's a problem with the car. It's right out front in a no-parking zone."

"No, I'm okay," he said. "I'll call you when we are ready to come home."

"Do you expect Juliette will have to stay in the hospital?"

"I have no clue," Brian answered. He was trying not to think about the immediate future. "But given how serious it looked, I imagine so."

"It's probably best. I'll be waiting for your call."

Brian watched Camila as she walked back to the exit, wondering if he should have encouraged her to stay, given how unhinged he felt. As she waited for the sliding glass door to open, she turned and waved to him. Camila's question of whether Juliette would need to stay in the hospital was unsettling, to say the least. Since Juliette had never had a seizure and since Emma's EEE started with a seizure, the implications were now suddenly obvious to him. He had thought it was just a flu, but Juliette could have contracted the same horrible illness at the same fateful barbecue two weeks earlier.

With shaking fingers, he used his phone to pull up the Wikipedia article he'd found about eastern equine encephalitis back when Emma had been diagnosed. Scrolling to find out about the length of the incubation period, he felt his stomach sink when he learned that it could take between four and ten days for symptoms to appear, which is a rather large variation. From his EMT training, he knew that such an interval was based on statistics, meaning for some cases it could take less and in others more.

Still holding his phone but now staring straight ahead with unseeing eyes, Brian suddenly reluctantly acknowledged there was a very good chance that Juliette had been suffering from EEE the whole time, especially when he thought back to her multiple flu-like complaints over the previous ten days or so. Emma's illness had had a faster trajectory, but started out like the flu.

"God damn it," he murmured through clenched teeth. This sudden very real possibility not only terrified him, but it also made him wonder why it hadn't been considered by the doctors who had seen Juliette, especially since they knew Emma had died of EEE right here in their hospital.

Going back to his phone, Brian quickly searched to find out whether there was a blood test for EEE. Finding out there was only fanned the growing antipathy he had for MMH Inwood. Not only had the powers that be made him and Juliette wait more than three hours on each of their two visits, but they had refused to do any testing even though it could have been key to properly diagnosing and treating her.

Forcing himself to go back to the EEE Wikipedia article, Brian reluctantly reread with growing horror that a large portion of those patients suffering encephalitis as evidenced by a seizure or other serious neurological symptoms ended up with severe intellectual impairment, personality disorders, significant paralysis, and cranial nerve disfunction.

Suddenly he stood up with the urge to run back to the treatment room where Juliette was to shout out that she could very well have EEE. But he held up, realizing that making the diagnosis at that moment was secondary to getting her seizure under control. Not only could the interruption do more harm than good, it might get him thrown out of the ED, and he needed to be there for Juliette when things settled down. As difficult as it was, Brian held himself in check. He also faulted himself for not thinking about EEE when Juliette first complained she wasn't feeling well and for not specifically demanding the test. Had he insisted, it would have been more difficult for the two doctors to fall back on assuming all of Juliette's complaints were psychosomatic.

Instead of running back to the treatment room, he nervously paced back and forth. Sitting still and waiting was driving him crazy. A few people eyed him warily, but he didn't care.

The siren of an approaching ambulance caught his attention as it got louder and louder before trailing off upon arrival outside. A few minutes later there was evidence of a flurry of activity back in the ED's treatment area, but it soon passed.

Twenty minutes later and unable to stand the wait any longer, Brian hurried back to the information desk. Forced by security to wait his turn, he demanded to know how his daughter was doing and if the seizure had been controlled.

"What's the name?" a bleary-eyed clerk who was nearing the end of his shift asked in a tired voice.

"Juliette Murphy," Brian practically shouted angrily.

The clerk rolled his eyes at his tone before spending what seemed like an excessive amount of time on his monitor. Just before Brian was about to boil over, the clerk said, "There doesn't seem to be any information yet, but I'm sure the doctors will be out to talk with you soon. Next!" He tilted his head to the side to get the attention of the person behind Brian.

Hardly satisfied, Brian returned to his seat, beside himself with anxiety. Out of desperation, he took out his phone. He needed to talk to someone and for a few moments debated whom to call. It wasn't an easy decision, since it was now five in the morning. He thought first of Camila since she'd been already disturbed by the situation, but he hesitated, thinking she might have gone back to sleep and that she'd already helped enormously. He thought about his mother but was afraid she might make things worse by being more anxious than he. He thought about some of his ESU buddies, particularly those who worked the graveyard shift, but he nixed the idea, as he'd not spoken to them in months and they might be in the middle of a call. He then thought about Jeanne, whom he knew would probably be the best choice considering her background with children, yet he wavered.

Despite all his reservations about taking advantage of her and as a sign of his desperation, he impulsively called, especially because she was the only one who could truly sympathize with his problems from her own experience. While the connection went through, he winced at disturbing her sleep, and he struggled to think of what to say. After the fourth ring, he seriously considered disconnecting, but then she answered.

"Uh-oh," she said sleepily, the moment she answered. "This can't be good news."

"I'm sorry to disturb you—" Brian began.

"Don't be silly," Jeanne interrupted, already sounding more awake. "What's up? Did Juliette's fever spike again?"

"Worse than that," he admitted. "She's had a seizure in her sleep, a bad one. I don't even know how long she'd been seizing when the noise woke me up, but it might have been for a while."

"Mon Dieu! Where are you?"

"I'm afraid I'm back at the MMH Inwood ED," Brian said. "My least favorite place."

"How is she?"

"I haven't heard," Brian said, running a hand nervously through his hair. "We've been here about an hour. They haven't told me anything. They haven't even told me they've stopped the seizure. Nothing!"

"You poor man," Jeanne said with true empathy in her voice. "Would you like me to come and join you to keep you company?"

"Thank you for offering," he said. "That's a lot to ask, and besides, I imagine I'll be hearing shortly that she'll be admitted. I just needed to talk to someone. I'm sorry I woke you."

"Don't be silly," Jeanne chided. "I'm glad you called. And I'm going to come join you whether you want me to or not. Case closed."

"Are you sure?" Brian asked. He wasn't the kind of person who normally asked for favors, and he considered self-sufficiency a virtue, but even he recognized he was particularly vulnerable at the moment. Besides, he didn't have the mental strength to talk her out of it.

"I'll be there in fifteen to twenty minutes," Jeanne said definitively.

With a bit of surprise, Brian found that she had hung up on him. Slowly he pocketed his phone, then bent over and cradled his head in his hands. He'd never felt quite so weak in his life, and as a consequence found himself praying, not in the way he'd learned as a child, but more as an attempt to bargain with a God he wasn't sure he believed in. He promised that he could learn to accept losing his wife and soul mate, but only if his daughter made it out of this unscathed.

Sudden yelling interrupted his thoughts, and he straightened up. The disturbance was coming from an obviously inebriated individual who'd stumbled into emergency with his business attire askew. Uniformed hospital security personnel responded immediately by emerging from their windowed enclave overlooking the ED entrance and the waiting room. The man was efficiently corralled and escorted to a separate section of the ED. After that, an expectant peace returned.

Brian tried to go back to his bargaining, but he found he couldn't after the drunken disruption. His growing worry about Juliette's condition was crowding out the possibility of any other thoughts. Twenty minutes later, Jeanne dashed into the waiting area, searching for Brian. He stood up and waved. The moment she spotted him, she hurried over. Despite the social distancing protocols and their short friendship, they embraced, holding on to each other to the point that Brian began to feel self-conscious.

"Sorry," he managed as he released her.

"No need to apologize," Jeanne said as they both sat down. "Have you heard anything?"

"Nothing at all," he responded. "I don't know why they're keeping me in the dark like this. It's torture. They could have at least come out and told me the seizure's been controlled but that they want to do X, Y, and Z. Hell, I'd understand. I'm all for testing. For all I know, they're doing an MRI or some other test that takes a long time. I just wish they'd let me know."

"We should hear soon," Jeanne said, trying to be encouraging.

"With her having a seizure like this, I'm concerned she got infected with EEE just like Emma, even on that same night. I read someplace that mosquitoes prefer female hosts."

"You're joking," Jeanne said.

"No, I'm serious. It's true. Female mosquitoes, which are the ones that bite, prefer human female type O blood. If Juliette does have EEE, it would explain all the complaints she's had over the last week or so, including the fever. What irks me to death is that when we brought her in here, not once, but twice, they never thought of testing her for it."

"That does seem surprising in retrospect," Jeanne admitted.

"It's more than surprising," Brian said. "To me it smacks of malpractice, especially when there's a good chance they didn't do any testing because I owe them so damn much money and they were afraid they'd not get paid. And that's on top of treating us like second-class citizens, making us wait for so long."

"Maybe it's best if we talk about something else while we wait," Jeanne said, seeing Brian's face flush and sensing his anxiety.

"As if I can think of anything else."

"How about talking about our upcoming investigation," Jeanne said. "I spent some time looking at your friend Grady's list. I counted the cases and there are almost five hundred Inwood families that have been sued or are being sued. Can you imagine?"

"Now I can. I used to think we as a community were lucky to have MMH here, but not any longer."

"It should be an asset," Jeanne said, "and it could be again."

"Maybe if . . ." he started. He wasn't so sure, not with Kelley and company in charge, but he didn't finish his thought. At that moment, both he and Jeanne saw two doctors emerge from back in the treatment area and head in their direction. They were both dressed in scrubs, although the male doctor was wearing a long white coat. As they got closer, Brian recognized the woman despite her mask. She was the one who'd called out orders back in the Trauma 1 room. Both had grave looks on their faces.

A new burst of worry propelled him to his feet, and Jeanne followed suit as the two physicians halted about six feet away from them. The male doctor, with a name tag that said DR. ANISH SINGH, CHIEF OF EMERGENCY MEDICINE, spoke with a lilting subcontinent-Asian accent. He identified himself and asked if Brian was the father of Juliette Murphy.

"I am," Brian managed as his pulse raced. He could feel Jeanne clutch his arm.

Dr. Singh cleared his throat, obviously uncomfortable. "I'm very sorry to have to report that despite our efforts, your daughter didn't make it. We tried—"

With lightning speed and before the doctor could finish his sentence, Brian lunged forward, grabbed a handful of Dr. Singh's scrub shirt and coat from the front of his chest, and practically lifted the slightly built doctor off his feet. He yanked the man's masked face within inches of his own, all the while yelling over and over: "No! No! No!"

Jeanne tried to pull Brian's arm away without success. She was shocked by the suddenness of the assault and overwhelmed by his strength. Several security guards burst out of their windowed alcove and came running over. Everyone in the waiting room, clerks and patients alike, stopped whatever they were doing and stared at the sudden ruckus like a freeze frame in a movie.

"You people let her die!" Brian snarled through clenched teeth behind his face mask. "You could have made the diagnosis yesterday, but no, you didn't, you wouldn't! All because of money."

The two security men arrived, and they, too, tried to break Brian's iron grip on Dr. Singh's clothing, but it wasn't until he let go that they succeeded. "Easy now!" one of the guards said.

While Dr. Singh calmly rearranged his shirt and jacket, he told the security guards that he was fine and that they should back off. Reluctantly, they let go of Brian, who was continuing to eye Dr. Singh with barely controlled fury. Jeanne regrasped his arm, although she, too, was aghast at the news and had trouble finding her voice.

"We tried very hard to save your daughter," Dr. Singh said. "I don't know what you are implying about money, but I can assure you that concerns about cost do not influence one iota of what we do with patients here in the Emergency Department, and they certainly didn't in regard to your daughter. We pulled out all the stops."

"I don't believe you," Brian snapped, causing the two guards to step forward once more.

Dr. Singh motioned for the guards to stand down. "You don't believe in the last hour we tried everything possible for your daughter? Is that what you are saying?"

"She was seen here yesterday and the day before," Brian blurted. "No diagnostics were done. Nothing, and it was probably because the hospital believes I owe hundreds of thousands of dollars. It should have been determined that she possibly had EEE like her mother, who died from it days before right here in this Emergency Department. And if that had happened like it should have, we would have known there was a risk for seizures. But no! Charles Kelley and his profit culture reigns supreme and no testing was done on either occasion."

"We have no idea of who owes the hospital money," Dr. Singh said. "I can assure you of that. We take all comers and treat them equivalently. As for a missed diagnosis, that concerns me, and I have already planned to look into it. Meanwhile I have to ask . . . do you want to view your daughter's body?"

Brian felt the strength suddenly drain out of his body. The instantaneous rage that had overwhelmed him moments earlier was replaced by a paralyzing sense of loss. There was no way that the daughter who'd become the bedrock of his life and lifeline of his emotions with Emma's passing could be taken from him, too.

"What do you think?" Jeanne asked softly. "Do you want to see her?"

"I don't know," he said weakly. "I don't know if I can take it, but I suppose I should."

"Do you want me to come with you?"

It took Brian a moment to decide. "Yes," he said at last. "I would appreciate it. Thank you."

With Jeanne holding on to his limp arm, they followed the doctor back into the treatment area and finally into the trauma room. A clean white sheet had been draped over the treatment table, covering Juliette's small body.

Dr. Singh stepped up to the table and grasped the edge of the sheet. He then looked over at Brian and Jeanne. "I want to warn you that by medical examiner rules, we don't remove various equipment like endotracheal tubes and intravenous devices until the body has been cleared by an authorized medical examiner investigator."

Neither Brian nor Jeanne responded audibly, but both nodded that they understood.

Respectfully, Dr. Singh slowly pulled down the sheet, progressively exposing Juliette's pale, fragile body down to the navel. As the doctor had warned, an endotracheal tube distorted her mouth. Intravenous lines ran into both arms, and ECG leads were still attached to her chest. For both Brian and Jeanne, it was a jarring, horrifying sight.

"Did she have EEE like my wife?" Brian asked, averting his eyes.

"The neurology consult believes she did," Dr. Singh said with regret. "To be sure we'll have to wait for the blood test to confirm it."

"Why bother?" he responded bitterly. "Isn't it a bit too late?"

"Yes, I believe it is too late," Dr. Singh said as he bowed his head. "I will leave you two. No rush. Stay as long as you would like." He turned around and walked out into the corridor.

Brian and Jeanne looked at each other, standing alone among all the high-tech equipment of the Trauma 1 room. His eyes brimmed with tears he'd been fighting. "I don't know why I didn't think of EEE, either," he managed between gasps. "I should have." He picked up the edge of the sheet and pulled it back over Juliette's body, unable to grasp how he had also been so mentally blind.

With tears running down her own face, Jeanne enveloped Brian with both arms and for several minutes they hugged in silence. "It's not your fault. You're not the doctor."

"I suppose," he said listlessly.

"You were correct about what you said to the doctor," Jeanne insisted. "Ultimately it is Charles Kelley's fault."

"Charles Kelley and Heather Williams," Brian added. "I'd be hard put to say who was more responsible."

Still holding on to each other for mutual support, they headed for the door leading out into the hallway, wondering where they could possibly go from here.

BOOK 3

CHAPTER 35

September 3

What are you going to do with her things?" Jeanne asked. She and Brian were standing at the open door of Juliette's bedroom, looking in at the disheveled bed. Jeannot Lapin was in a heap on the floor after apparently being batted off the bed during Juliette's seizure. Jeanne had been surprised when Brian suggested they make the visit the moment they had entered the house.

Without answering, Brian stepped into the room, picked up the stuffed rabbit, and then returned out into the hallway. As he did so, he closed the door behind him. "I'm not going to do anything with her things," he said. "At least not now. Maybe sometime in the future."

"Are you sure that is wise?" Jeanne said. "I could at least pack everything for you to get it out of sight. I'm afraid it is going to be painful keeping them around."

"That's generous of you," Brian said. "There's no need. I'm just going to leave the door closed, but I wanted to return Jeannot Lapin. I know it means something to you, otherwise you wouldn't still have had it." He held out the plush toy.

Jeanne took the rabbit and hesitated before responding. The day had been extremely painful for her, and she could only imagine how traumatic it had been for Brian. She'd grown fond of Juliette in the few days that she had known her, and realized it was perhaps that Juliette represented the daughter she'd wanted but never had. And now Jeannot Lapin would always be associated in her mind as Juliette's friend and not hers. "I appreciate the gesture," she said at length. "I hope you understand, but I'd prefer to let Jeannot Lapin remain with Juliette." She reached out and grasped the doorknob to Juliette's room, looking up at Brian but not yet opening the door. "Do you mind?"

"Of course not."

Leaving the door ajar for moment, Jeanne went into Juliette's room. After straightening the covers, she carefully placed Jeannot Lapin on the bed. Once back in the hall, she closed the door behind her.

"I'm sorry to have caught you up in all this," Brian said as they descended the stairs.

"Don't be. The best way to stop feeling sorry for oneself is to start feeling sorry for someone else. Losing a spouse is a terrible experience, I can attest to that. But losing a child is far worse. Would you like me to leave or do you want to talk or maybe sit in silence?"

"I'm not sure," Brian admitted. "But I don't want you to leave. That's for certain. I think I'd like to talk."

"Where should we sit?"

Brian shrugged. He was taking everything moment by moment. "I guess in the office."

As they entered, Jeanne noticed the bulky, strange-looking shoulder bag on Emma's desk. She couldn't make out what it was, partially because of the dimness in the room. The only windows of the former dining room were high and made of leaded glass. Most of the light was coming in through the archway leading into the living room. Preferring semidarkness, Brian had not switched on the chandelier.

"It's a rifle bag," Brian said as he noticed Jeanne peering at it. He threw himself heavily into his desk chair and groaned. On the day Emma died, he thought he had experienced the worst moment of his life, but the pain he was experiencing with Juliette gone was unparalleled.

"It looks odd," Jeanne said, bending over and looking at it closer. One end came to a protruding cylinder about the size and shape of the business end of a duster. "It doesn't look long enough to hold a rifle."

"It's a special rifle," Brian said. "It's a sniper weapon, meaning it is very, very accurate. In order to make it easier to transport, the stock folds against the barrel."

"My goodness," Jeanne exclaimed. "What they won't think of next." She sat in one of the several side chairs and, like Brian, groaned as she settled in.

Both Brian and Jeanne were physically and emotionally exhausted. Starting at 3:25 A.M. for Brian and 4:45 A.M. for Jeanne, it had been a long day—what felt like the longest day of his life.

The most emotionally difficult part had been in the ED waiting to get the required paperwork done right after they had viewed the body. All at once, there had been a flood of emergency cases arriving by ambulance, including several early morning automobile accidents that had taken the attention of most of the doctors, nurses, and even clerks. To complicate the situation, just before ten o'clock Aimée and Hannah had arrived, both in a panic. From a call to Camila, Aimée had learned Juliette had had a bad seizure during the night and was in the ED. Aimée in turn had called Hannah and both had come directly to the hospital without phoning ahead. When they arrived, it fell to Brian to tell them that Juliette had passed, which put them both into a hysterical condition. As a result, Brian had to spend considerable effort to calm both of them, rather than come to terms with his own deeply broken state.

Luckily for Brian, Hannah eventually took control. Although she had been depressed since Emma's burial, this new tragedy caused her to regain composure, and she again accepted the burden of planning the next few days. At first Brian expressed some reluctance to go along with the full funeral procedure again after the experience of Emma's passing, but his reservations were immediately dismissed by Hannah and Aimée. Ultimately, he yielded to their wishes both because objecting would have taken too much energy, which he didn't have, and because he thought it would be selfish to deny them fulfilling what they thought was their responsibility. It was painfully obvious to Brian that they both were hurting and it was also apparent to him that the planning process was helping them deal with the horror of losing a beloved granddaughter.

Once the paperwork and other formalities had been done at the ED and the body was released, it was off to Riverside Funeral Home. Both Brian and Jeanne followed along but didn't say much nor were their opinions actively sought. In some regards it had surprised them that neither Aimée nor Hannah objected to or even questioned Jeanne's presence, since neither had met her before now.

From the funeral home it was on to the O'Briens', so Brian could tell Emma's father that one of his granddaughters had passed away and that there was to be another wake in their home. Why it had to be him rather than Hannah, Brian didn't question, but since Ryan was going to be paying, as Hannah had offered and as he'd done for Emma, Brian felt obligated to deliver the horrible news. It was only after that visit that Brian and Jeanne were able to excuse themselves and walk home to Brian's house. It felt like the calm after a wildly destructive storm.

"What would you like to talk about?" Jeanne asked after a few minutes of silence.

"I don't know," Brian admitted. "It's hard to concentrate. My mind and emotions are going a mile a minute."

"I'll tell you what I'd like to talk about," Jeanne declared. "I want to talk about feeling pissed that MMH Inwood and Peerless Health have essentially killed both our spouses and your beautiful child. Just sitting with you in the ED brought back the entire saga of my husband's torture and death like it was yesterday. There were more times than I'd like to count that we were forced to wait in that same waiting room while he suffered and ultimately died."

"We have a right to be enraged," Brian agreed. "In fact, I've never felt this deeply furious before. Well, that's not really true. I felt this way the day Emma died, but it's worse today. There was an ounce of doubt about whether the hospital was responsible for Emma's death, but there's none in respect to what happened today. They should have diagnosed Juliette and the fact that they didn't or wouldn't infuriates me. Psychosomatic? Please!" Brian's eyes darted around the room as if he was looking for something to destroy. "I want to break something. Anything."

"I know how you must be feeling," Jeanne agreed. "I can remember when Riley died, I had the same inclinations, and I'm embarrassed to say I did break some dishes. But it certainly didn't solve anything. Let's funnel this rage we're feeling into exposing this disaster by using the list your friend has provided us. The fact that there are almost five hundred cases possibly just like ours in Inwood shocks me. What does that mean for the entire city, or the entire country for that matter? This surely can't be an isolated phenomenon."

Listening to Jeanne had Brian trying to focus his anger. What she was saying was undoubtedly true, and the details of the one case that Grady Quillen had mentioned to him involving Nolan O'Reilly sounded as heartrending as his own.

"I think this could be a true media event," Jeanne continued passionately. "Especially if they question how the hell it has come to this in the richest country in the world. There's no doubt in my mind that the finger will ultimately point at the profit motive of private equity."

"And Charles Kelley and Heather Williams are certainly poster children for that culture," Brian added.

"What shocks me is that none of the politicians are focusing on this," Jeanne said. "There's lots of talk about healthcare in general, but not specifics about what the situation is doing to individual people like us and how Kelley and Williams and people like them can get away with what they are doing."

"My guess is that it's all about money, appropriately enough," Brian said. "I've heard in the past that the healthcare industry, mostly hospitals, health insurance, and drug companies, spend millions on lobbying to maintain the status quo. They like their profits and don't want change. It means giving big bucks to politicians on both sides of the aisle."

"Like how much? I'm sure that doesn't happen in France."

"Let's check it out," Brian said, eager to do something, anything. He turned on his monitor. After typing into Google, "how much per year does the healthcare industry spend on lobbying," he hit enter. In a millisecond the results flashed onto the screen. "Here it is! My God! Five hundred and ninety-four million dollars in 2019! That's more than one and a half million dollars a day. That's absurd."

"It's more than absurd," Jeanne said. "It's crazy. As I said, that would never happen in France, or anyplace in Europe for that matter. No wonder it's come to this point. Why is this bribing allowed? I mean, they maybe call it lobbying but surely in this instance it's pure bribery."

"As I recall, it has something to do with 'free speech,' which I personally think is ludicrous," Brian said. "It got turned into a constitutional issue. Whether we uncover five hundred stories as sad and tragic as ours, I can't imagine it would be enough to change this entrenched system, mostly because of the wildly extravagant lobbying but also because of the news cycle. It could be a big story and most likely would be, but then twenty-four hours later, it would be on to something else."

"Maybe we could dribble the stories out over time," Jeanne suggested.

"I don't think that would work, either," Brian said with some discouragement. "A handful of sad stories might get on page one the first day, but then subsequent ones would quickly get relegated to less prominent positions. It's the way the media works. A scoop on day one is often yesterday's lunch on day two."

"Does that mean you are giving up on the cases Grady Quillen gave us?" Jeanne asked, sensing Brian's pessimism.

"Not necessarily. But what we have to do is think up a way to give the story staying power, so that it evolves over time and maintains public interest."

For several minutes neither Brian nor Jeanne spoke as they pondered. The news cycle was short, particularly in this day and age with the internet supplying instantaneous information 24/7. They stared at each other expectantly, hoping the other would come up with an idea, something to assuage their anger and sadness yet have enough staying power to effect change. But neither spoke until after a kind of visual pas de deux that involved their eyes drifting in tandem over to the bag on Emma's desk before coming back to stare at each other. Later they would question whose eyes strayed first, but they couldn't decide. It was as if the idea germinated in both of them simultaneously.

"You said the sniper rifle is very, very accurate," Jeanne said, breaking the silence. "What does that mean in terms of distance?"

"More than a half mile for most of them," Briand found himself responding.

"How about this one?" Jeanne said, nodding toward the rifle bag. "Does it have a specific name?"

"It's called a Remington MSR. And it is particularly accurate out to nearly a mile."

"Hmm," Jeanne thought out loud. "Call me crazy and desperate, but I'm starting to think of a story that would have real staying power and one that the media would devour as rightful revenge. Everyone loves a good revenge story, after all."

"If you are thinking what I think you might be thinking, I have to confess it crossed my mind, too. Especially when I was using the rifle yesterday at the shooting range."

"How easy would it be, if I may ask? I assume you have some idea, as a security expert."

"Very easy, would be my guess," Brian said. "And that's even with them wasting significant money on personal protection. I've seen Kelley's and Williams's day security people, and none of them impressed me. As kind of a joke, I even offered my services to Heather Williams."

Emotionally wrought, Jeanne and Brian stared at each other with unblinking eyes. "I can't believe myself, yet there is something utterly satisfying about the idea," Jeanne said after a few moments of silence.

"I know precisely what you mean," Brian said. "It's crazy on one hand but gratifying on another. It brings to mind the moment I learned about the Hammurabi code, or 'an eye for an eye,' back when I was in the fourth grade. It made sense to me then, even more than what I was learning in catechism on Sundays about turning the other cheek. And it certainly makes sense to me now."

"Is this something we could do together?" Jeanne asked with a gleam in her eye.

Brian looked at Jeanne askance, trying to gauge her mindset. "Are you offering?" he asked after a pause.

"I suppose I am," Jeanne said. "I mean, if you went ahead and did something on your own, by our even discussing it as we're apparently doing, I'm technically already a coconspirator."

"Well, I suppose we could do it together," Brian said, warming to the idea. There was no doubt that while dealing with his anger after Emma had died, he'd thought about getting rid of both Charles Kelley and Heather Williams, yet he'd dismissed the idea as a passing retribution fantasy even though he'd spent considerable time mulling it over. And now with Juliette's death, it had resurfaced but had been relegated to the back of his mind as repressed anger, waiting to be brought forward as Jeanne's comments were now doing. "There's no doubt it would be far easier as a team approach, especially if it involved dealing with an alarm system, since I trust you are up on all the latest technology." One of his fantasies had involved breaking into the executives' homes and confronting them directly.

"Unless something earth-shaking has appeared over the last year, I'm up to speed," Jeanne said. "Since it's obvious you've thought about this, what would hypothetically be the most efficient way to accomplish it?"

"Through very careful planning and preparation," Brian said firmly. "Both killings would have to happen the same evening or night, one after the other, for it to work. If there was a delay on the second one, even of only a day or so, that individual's security people might be on guard, making it more difficult. That's number one. Number two: We'd have to keep from being detained. Otherwise, we wouldn't be able to feed the media, and the search for us would be a big part of the ongoing story. That's what will keep it on page one for as long as we are at large. And three: We'd have to present a manifesto to various outlets of exactly why the assassinations were done to raise the story above and beyond the pure eye-for-an-eye, tooth-for-a-tooth revenge aspect. I'd like every hospital and health insurance CEO to live in fear that they could be next unless there is significant change to the system."

"How would we avoid being arrested?" Jeanne asked. "Surely your NYPD colleagues would figure out the whodunit rather quickly, particularly with a manifesto, and be after us, especially if we were continuing to try to feed the media."

"We'd avoid arrest by not being found," Brian said simply. "That's why our planning will have to include a sanctuary: someplace where it will be hard for them to find us, and when they do, their hands are tied."

"Like what kind of sanctuary? I don't understand."

"The same night that the killings are done or at least by the next morning, we'd have to leave the country. Probably the best place to go would be Cuba. It's close, easy to get there, and there are quite a few US fugitives living on the island whom the Cuban government refuses to extradite. Cuba loves giving the middle finger to the US government. Hell, we might even be considered heroes since we'd be able to give them the ability to prove that their healthcare system is a lot more equitable than ours, which it is, by the way."

"Wow, you have been thinking a lot about this," Jeanne said, clearly impressed by Brian's thoroughness.

"I confess I've spent many sleepless, angry hours pondering the idea," Brian admitted. "Just not all that seriously, I suppose. But I can tell you that with Juliette's passing and in my current state of mind, it doesn't sound so preposterous anymore. They ruined my life for their own personal gain, and they should suffer. I know that is not very Christian, but that's how I feel."

"Let me ask you this," Jeanne said. "If and when you have one of these lowlifes in your sights, could you actually pull the trigger? As much as I would ultimately like them to be gone, I'm not sure I could do it."

"That's a good question," Brian answered. "But I don't think I'd hesitate. In the line of duty, regrettably enough, I've had to make that decision in milliseconds when confronted by bad guys. I didn't hesitate then and each of those perps was responsible for one or two deaths. I'm certain that Charles Kelley and Heather Williams are in another league in causing deaths above and beyond our spouses and my child. On top of that, they've ruined the lives of countless others. So no, I don't imagine I would hesitate for a moment, especially if it might serve to expose and change the whole hideous system."

"Do you know anybody in Cuba?" Jeanne asked. She felt her pulse quicken. In her mind the discussion had definitely moved from the purely hypothetical to the possible.

"Not personally," Brian said. "But I know Camila has some extended family in Cuba who I imagine would be willing to help us if she were to ask. Obviously, I wouldn't even broach the issue with her until we were there. No one can know what we are planning, and I mean no one. Not even family."

"This is beginning to sound serious," Jeanne said. "Am I right or are you still fantasizing out loud? Be honest."

"I'm not sure," Brian admitted. "But the more I think about it, the more serious I become."

"Which means you would be willing to give up your life here in the United States?"

"I've already lost what I valued most, my wife and my child."

"What about this house?"

"I'll deed it to Camila," Brian said. "If I hang around here, there's a good chance the hospital would get to repossess it through the courts. Without Emma and Juliette, it doesn't mean anything to me, and Camila deserves it. If she owns it, the hospital can't touch it."

Jeanne took a deep breath to organize her thoughts. The extent of Brian's planning had left her mind in disarray. She'd had her own fantasies about revenge, but over the year since Riley's passing, they'd faded. Suddenly, with Juliette's death, they were back with a vengeance. Just like Brian, she felt strongly that Charles Kelley and Heather Williams had ruined her life as she knew it, taking away her spouse, her savings, and her most recent livelihood all because of their insatiable personal greed. But when she thought about everything Brian had just said, her only hesitations were about Cuba. She'd been to the Caribbean with her husband on several occasions, and it had been pleasant enough for a week, but ultimately boring. The idea of spending the rest of her life there was daunting.

"I have another idea about a sanctuary," Jeanne said suddenly. "Are you open to hearing it or are you set on Cuba?"

"Of course I'm open to hear," Brian said. "Fire away."

"When we first met, I believe you told me your mother had gotten you a French passport when you were a child. Do I remember correctly, or have I dreamed that up?"

Instead of answering, Brian leaned over and opened the middle drawer of his desk. Reaching in and rustling through the contents, he extracted a burgundy-colored pamphlet and plopped it on the desktop. The front of the passport was embossed with gold lettering and an impressive seal. "Voilà," he said.

"Parfait! That means you are a French citizen."

"So?" Brian questioned. "You're not thinking we can sanctuary in France, are you?"

"Yes, I am," Jeanne insisted. "I assume you recall the saga about the film director Roman Polanski."

"Vaguely," Brian said. "I'm not much of a film buff, and I don't think I could name any of the films he directed. Why do you ask?"

"Do you recall that he's a fugitive from US criminal justice?"

"Now that you mention it, I do. What's the point?"

"The point is that France doesn't extradite its citizens to the US," Jeanne continued. "And Roman Polanski is living proof. He fled the US awaiting sentencing on five criminal charges, including rape."

"Interesting," Brian admitted. He immediately warmed to the idea of finding sanctuary in France. It would be immeasurably more rewarding on just about every conceivable level than being restricted to Cuba, especially a Cuban prison, which wasn't out of the question.

"I'm not a lawyer," Jeanne continued, "and we could still eventually be subject to arrest and prosecution, but it would be in France, not here in the US. In France I'm certain public opinion would be far more kindly in our favor. French people will be outraged at our stories. I certainly would have been."

"We'd still need to hide out, at least in the short run and maybe for a month," Brian countered. "How would that work?"

"We could hide out in Camargue," Jeanne suggested. "It's really off the beaten path, and my family has several isolated, deserted farmhouses that were acquired with large tracts of grazing land. One of them I remember isn't that far from one of the towns, called Saintes-Maries-de-la-Mer, which is close to the sea. It's actually very beautiful in its own fashion. Do you like to ride horses?"

Brian laughed in spite of himself. It suddenly seemed vaguely humorous under the circumstances to be asked if he liked to ride horses as part of a plan to off two healthcare executives. "That's something I haven't done much of," he admitted. "But I suppose I could learn to like it."

"My family has a lot of horses," Jeanne said. "It's the main way to get around in Camargue. I started riding when I was five or six. Re-

gardless, I think France is our best bet. When the authorities investigate, it's going to lead to you, not me, for multiple reasons. First,
your disappearance is going to ring all sorts of alarm bells, especially
given that you've just lost a wife and a child. And you have the skills
and means. My medical horror story is old and won't draw any more
attention than any of the other almost five hundred cases. And right
now, since I'm not working and have lost my business, I could leave
tomorrow, and no one would notice or care, except maybe for a few
friends and Riley's family. But that will be easy to take care of, as I
can just say that I've had enough of America, and I'm returning to
my home country, case closed.

"So here's what I propose. On the evening or night in question we
make separate air arrangements, so we're not associated, and we fly
separate routes to some major European city, like Frankfurt or Ma-
drid or Rome, just not France. I rent a car and pick you up, which ends
your tracking, meaning Interpol won't have much to go on. And then
we drive to Camargue. Until they find you, which isn't likely as long
as we're discreet, I doubt I'll even be a suspected accomplice."

For a moment Brian was dumbfounded as he went over the details of what Jeanne had proposed. It was brilliant, and he couldn't
help but be impressed. He'd been mulling over hypothetical thoughts
like this for days, namely, how to keep the media enthralled enough
to have a major impact on the healthcare system. But Jeanne had
come up with a terrific plan of escape and sanctuary in minutes.
"That's a great idea," he admitted once he found his voice. "It's perfect. Let's start planning and see how we feel. I imagine the planning
process alone will be therapeutic for me."

"For me, too," Jeanne agreed, sitting back in her chair. "Where do
we start?"

CHAPTER 36

September 3

Turning left off Broadway, Brian drove up the long driveway leading to MMH Inwood. He and Jeanne were in the Subaru. He had merely told Camila he was going out for a drive, which she had accepted without question. In many respects she was as devastated as Brian over Juliette's death and had been trying to help Aimée and Hannah with the plans for the wake.

"You know what a Maybach looks like, don't you?" Brian asked as they crested the small hill and the whole hospital and the modest, outside parking area came into view. When she had asked him how they would start, he'd told her that they had to find out where each target lived by following them home. They had flipped a coin to see who would be first, and Charles Kelley had won.

"I suppose," Jeanne said, but in truth she wasn't certain. She wasn't a car person. For her they generally all looked the same except that some were larger than others.

"Nope, it's not here," Brian said. To find Kelley's Maybach, he had assumed they'd have to drive to the East Side, where MMH Midtown was located. Yet on the slight chance the CEO might have been on one of his relatively infrequent visits to Inwood, Brian thought the ten minutes it would take to check was worth it. Discovering he wasn't there didn't faze Brian, and he used the hospital turnaround to head back down to Broadway.

"How long do you estimate the planning stage will take?" Jeanne asked as they headed south on the Henry Hudson Parkway running alongside the Hudson River. "Now that we have officially started, I'm eager to get this done."

"It all depends on what we find," Brian said. "I'm relatively confident they live in the ritzy metropolitan areas of either Long Island, New Jersey, or southern Connecticut. And, frankly, the ritzier the better, where homes are widely separated from each other with expansive lawns and private outdoor sports facilities, like swimming pools and tennis courts. That's what I'm counting on. It would also be nice if their homes weren't too far apart to make logistics easier, especially since we're obligated to do both in the same night. But we'll have to take what we get."

"At least we have the rifle," Jeanne said. "That's the key piece of equipment, but I suppose you could always get one."

"It would not be hard," Brian agreed. "Whatever we do need, I'm sure I can get now that I've got access to ESU Headquarters. For instance, if we end up having to break and enter, they've certainly got all the assault tools we'd need. I'll feel guilty about taking advantage of Deputy Chief Comstock's hospitality, but this is important. Honestly, giving up the camaraderie of the ESU might be the only thing besides my family that I will miss after all this is said and done."

"What do you think the chances are that we'll have to do a home invasion?" she asked.

"No way to guess. As I said, it will depend on what their living arrangements are. But if we do, that's where your role will be key. Tell me this: If we do have to go into one or both homes, do you have the equipment you might need or will you have to obtain it?"

"I won't need much," Jeanne reassured him. "I already have a powerful eight-watt handheld radio that should do just fine."

"Really?" Brian questioned. "That's all? These people are pulling down multimillion-dollar salaries. They've surely been talked into expensive, elaborate alarm systems."

"No doubt, but expense aside, they all use the same technology, transmitting wirelessly to their base station or receiver. All I'd have to do is figure out the frequency and then swamp it."

"I don't understand, but I'm going to trust that you do," Brian said.

"I do," Jeanne affirmed.

Within just a few minutes they were able to cross Central Park, and ten minutes later had reached Manhattan Memorial Hospital on Park Avenue. To Brian's relief, it was obvious that Charles Kelley was still on-site, which he admitted had been a minor concern. His Maybach was parked in a no-parking zone right in front of the hospital's main entrance where patients were either dropped off or picked up, the same way it had been at MMH Inwood the day Emma had died. As an added confirmation, the same overweight chauffeur-cum-bodyguard was leaning up against the vehicle's passenger-side fender. As Brian cruised by, he could see that the man was smoking just like he'd been doing on their first interaction, looking as cocky as ever.

"That's encouraging." He pointed out the car. "There's Kelley's Maybach."

"Where?" Jeanne asked, turning around to look behind. There were cars all over the place, most double-parked with their hazard lights on.

"It's the limo right smack-dab in front of the hospital where there's supposed to be no waiting," Brian said. "You didn't see it? It's the only Maybach."

"The cars all look the same to me," she said as she continued scanning the area. "Oh, now I see it. The one with the chauffeur."

"Yes, that's it." He continued up Park Avenue for several blocks before making a U-turn. After passing the hospital again while heading in the opposite direction, he made yet another U-turn. A block away from the Maybach, he pulled over to the curb at a fire hydrant and turned off the Subaru's motor. "Now we wait."

Jeanne used her phone to check the time. "It's perfect timing," she pointed out. "It's after five, when executives begin to head home to their mansions."

He nodded. "Have you ever seen Charles Kelley?" he asked.

"Not that I know of," Jeanne said.

"He's got some height," Brian recalled, the man's image seared in his memory. "Sandy-colored hair and very tall. He'll stand out when he appears."

"I suppose this is a good car to follow someone without them knowing," she said.

"It's perfect," Brian agreed. "Completely nondescript."

"Do you think they'll figure out they are being followed?"

"It depends on the level of professionalism of the driver," he said. "Kelley's chauffeur, who is probably doubling as a bodyguard, didn't impress me, which will lessen his index of suspicion. A true professional has to think that at every minute the worst can happen. I imagine for us, if there is to be a problem, it will be when we get off the main roads, especially if Kelley lives in a particularly isolated area. The key thing is always to have a few cars between you and your mark if possible."

"That makes sense."

Timing turned out to be near perfect, and they didn't have long to wait for Kelley to appear. The chauffeur, whom they could see over the roofs of the intervening cars, suddenly stiffened, adjusted his hat—which had been tilted back on his head—and threw away his cigarette. In the next instant they got a very brief view of the tall, sandy-haired Kelley as he emerged from the hospital and in a blink of an eye disappeared from view, presumably ducking down into his limo. Brian responded by starting the car, saying, "Here we go."

He pulled out into the traffic but slowed as he neared MMH Midtown, to the chagrin of the yellow cab behind him. In a fit of displeasure and horn blowing, the cab pulled out from behind Brian and passed him, briefly slowing down as he came abreast to give Brian the finger before speeding off. The reason Brian was slowing was to make sure Kelley's car pulled away from the curb before the Subaru arrived at the hospital entrance.

"We've got to stay close until we're relatively sure where Kelley is heading," Brian said.

"I understand." Jeanne nodded her head.

Once the Maybach was clearly traveling north, Brian picked up speed to catch up. After going four or five blocks he added: "I guess we can eliminate South Jersey because they would have gone in the opposite direction toward the Lincoln Tunnel."

Jeanne didn't answer. She was holding on as best she could. To stay close to Kelley's car, Brian was driving aggressively.

It wasn't until they crossed over the Robert F. Kennedy Bridge and connected with the Long Island Expressway that he was reasonably sure where they were going. At each major freeway intersection, Brian had rapidly closed the gap between the Subaru and Kelley's

Maybach to a single car, but then had dropped back again when it was apparent Kelley was not turning.

"So, we're heading to Long Island," Brian announced, ostensibly relaxing and allowing as many as four cars between them. Jeanne eased up on the death grip she had on the passenger handle on the Subaru's dash.

Forty minutes later they turned off the Long Island Express-way onto Community Drive. It was an area he was familiar with to an extent, having assisted the Great Neck Police Department on occasion.

"Now I have a more specific idea of where we are going," Brian said. "I'd guess Kings Point. It's certainly appropriately ritzy. Now it gets touchy. We're going to have to close the gap."

Luckily there was still considerable traffic, but it dwindled the farther out on the peninsula they drove. By the time they got to Shore Drive in Kings Point, the Subaru and the Maybach were alone. Since the road was relatively straight, Brian let a considerable distance intervene, and slowed when he saw the Maybach's brake lights go on before it turned off the road into a gated driveway. By the time Brian and Jeanne arrived, the wrought-iron gate was closing. He slowed to a crawl and stopped briefly. Looking through the gate, they could see a massive, relatively new, faux-Mediterranean home.

"It looks like an impregnable oasis," she commented.

Around the property was a reinforced concrete wall at least eight feet high whose top was embedded with shards of glass. Above the wall were coils of razor wire. "Appropriately enough, it looks more like a prison from out here than a home," Brian scoffed. "But I doubt it is as impregnable as it looks. The name of the road is encouraging."

"How so?" Jeanne asked.

"I'll show you in a second," he said. "Now that we have the address, let's check it out with Google Maps' satellite view."

After driving ahead for a hundred yards, they pulled over to the side of the road. Most of the homes were hidden behind high walls, fences, or vegetation. Brian got out his phone and used Google Maps to bring up the area on his screen. Jeanne leaned over so she could see as well.

"As I remembered, Shore Drive is literally a road along the shore, bordering Long Island Sound," he said while he zoomed in on the image of Kings Point, New York. He then pointed off to the right out of the car window. "All these houses along this side of the road are shorefront."

"Got it."

Returning his attention to the phone, Brian zoomed in more and used his finger to point. "And here's Kelley's house. Do you see it?"

"In all its glory. Rather large, I'd say."

"It is, and quite impressive. It's also encouraging for our purposes. It's got a swimming pool, a guest-house-cum-garage, and a tennis court with what appears to be a basketball hoop. Obviously, Mr. Kelley thinks of himself as quite an athlete. And look at the size of the pier with a cabana at the end. Pretty fancy."

"But the wall?" Jeanne questioned. "Isn't that a major problem if we're thinking of using a sniper rifle?"

"That might be true if we were looking to shoot from the landside of the property," Brian said. "But from the waterside you can see it's a different story, which is why I'm pleased that Kelley's property is waterfront. See how the wall ends at the water's edge? It's typical for security-minded people to spend lots of effort on the landside but nothing from the seaside. They don't want to block their view, which is entirely understandable. It's why they paid such a premium for the lot."

While they were concentrating on Brian's phone, they weren't aware of the car pulling up behind them until the police cruiser's emergency light penetrated into the Subaru's interior.

"Oh, shit," Brian murmured, glancing in the side mirror.

She turned to look out the back window at the police car. "What's the matter?" she asked nervously. "Is this going to be a problem?"

"Not in the short run," he reassured her. "But if it gets recorded, it's got me situated near the MMH CEO's house."

"Do you care?"

"Not necessarily, I'd just prefer it didn't happen." Brian got out the car's registration, his driver's license, and his NYPD ID in anticipation of the officer's arrival.

A few minutes ticked by. "What do you think he's doing?" Jeanne asked, continuing to peer out the back window.

"I'm sure he's calling his dispatcher," he said. "The Kings Point PD is a modest organization. I'm sure he's solo, and you're supposed to let dispatch know what you're up to."

A few minutes later the uniformed police officer got out of his cruiser, put on his peaked cap, adjusted his gear belt, then walked up to the Subaru. Brian lowered the window as he came closer.

"Afternoon," the policeman said. He was an older gentleman with white hair and fleshy jowls. "May I see your license and registration, please?"

"Of course," Brian replied pleasantly. He handed them out the window, being sure to keep the NYPD ID on top, which the policeman immediately noticed.

"Hmm," he said. "Retired NYPD?"

"Yup," Brian affirmed. "Retired from the ESU not quite ten months ago to start a private security firm."

"Interesting," the policeman said. "Excuse me, but I'll be right back."

"What's he doing now?" Jeanne fretted as she watched the policeman climb back into his vehicle.

"Just checking if it all matches up," Brian said knowingly. "He's being appropriately careful."

A few minutes later the policeman got out of his car and returned to the Subaru. He handed back Brian's license, registration, and ID. "Sorry to bother you people," he said. "But the homeowners out here are sensitive about strange cars, particularly strange parked cars. They call us all the time. Are you lost? Do you need any directions?"

"We're fine," Brian reassured him. "Thank you, Officer. Just making our way home."

"Okay. Have a nice evening," the policeman said.

Brian returned the documents to their proper locations, pocketed his phone, and put the Subaru in gear. "I didn't see that coming, but it is a good lesson. You have to expect the unexpected in what we are doing. Regardless, I'd say we've made significant progress. Next up is finding out where Heather Williams lives. Once we have that, we can get down to business."

"How about we do it tomorrow?" she said.

"I'm with you," he said. "I need this. It will keep me from the reality of what happened this morning."

CHAPTER 37

September 11

As there was no place to pull over at the bed-and-breakfast Jeanne had found on Seaman Avenue just down the street from her former apartment, Brian had to double-park. In Inwood, as in the rest of Manhattan, double- and even sometimes triple-parking was a way of life. With his hazard lights on, he used his phone to text her that he was outside waiting.

It had been just a little more than a week since he and Jeanne had followed Charles Kelley's Maybach out to his fancy estate in Kings Point, and it had been an enormously busy time for both. They had continued their extensive and meticulous planning with progressive zeal and, in the process, became only more committed to exacting revenge on both Charles Kelley and Heather Williams. From a practical standpoint he attributed their efforts as the chief reason he'd been able to get through the immediate aftermath of Juliette's death. Had it not been for the considerable concentration that the planning involved, he doubted he would have been able to emotionally weather the wake, the funeral, and the interment. Even so, it hadn't been easy by any stretch of the imagination. During his appearance at the wake, he tried his best not to look at Juliette's body, which he was mostly successful at doing, and at the burial he kept his eyes closed during the ceremony and spent the time going over in his mind all the contingencies he could imagine for the plan.

After Brian had left the wake at around two P.M., he'd gotten in his car and picked up Jeanne from her apartment on Seaman Avenue. She had not attended the wake since they had decided it best if they were no longer seen together by his family and Camila, so she'd be less likely to be implicated when all hell broke loose. By three they had been parked by a fire hydrant on Sixth Avenue in view of the building where Peerless Health had its home office. As a reward for their patience, they'd seen Heather Williams emerge at four P.M. sharp with her entourage and climb into a waiting Mercedes.

As they'd started the following process, mimicking what they'd done with Kelley, they'd made a wager on where they might be going, with Brian favoring Greenwich, Connecticut, because of Heather Williams's apparent love of horses, and Jeanne favoring the fancy areas of New Jersey for the same reason. Both had turned out to be wrong. When they found themselves again heading out to Long Island, they started to entertain the hope that the two like-minded executives lived in the same very wealthy town, which would make things a lot easier. But that had not turned out to be the case, as they'd sped past both turnoffs from the Long Island Expressway that led out to Kings Point.

Instead, the Mercedes had left the expressway and then headed north on the way out to the second north-facing Long Island peninsula. It had turned out that Heather Williams lived in Sands Point, essentially across the Manhasset Bay from Charles Kelley's house, reminding Brian of the fictitious East Egg and West Egg of F. Scott Fitzgerald's novel *The Great Gatsby*. As such, it was just as convenient as if they lived in the same town and maybe more so because Heather Williams's house was also waterfront property. The difference was that Heather's mansion was on a significantly larger plot of land that included a stable and a fenced-in paddock, which they had been able to discover by looking at satellite maps. Neither could be seen from the road. Like Kelley's house, the property had a wireless controlled gate, a surrounding wall, a swimming pool, and a lengthy pier.

Brian's phone chimed, indicating he'd gotten a text message. When he checked it, he saw that Jeanne was on her way down. Accordingly, he got out of the car and opened up the back. The rear seats were down to provide more storage space, and a blanket covered what was there. Brian pulled the blanket aside for Jeanne's things. Already present was his luggage, the rifle bag with the Remington MSR, assault tools he'd borrowed from the ESU Academy, night-vision goggles, a ketamine dart pistol, rope, a window anchor for rapid escape, his P365 Sig Sauer fitted with a different barrel and a suppressor, and a few other sundries he thought he might need. In his luggage was his French passport and as much cash as he could amass without causing undue alarm. For clothes he was wearing his black ESU tactical uniform but stripped of any markings.

As he waited, Brian called on all his extensive experience as an ESU officer about to initiate a dangerous mission to keep his emotions in check. He knew all too well how important it was to maintain a clear mind so as not to make inadvertent, silly mistakes. Part of it was to control his breathing and even heart rate, but most important was to keep his attention homed in on the details of the plan.

Jeanne appeared at the heavy glass art nouveau door to the six-story apartment building that housed the bed-and-breakfast she had booked when she moved out of her rented apartment, having given away what furniture and household equipment she had. Seeing she was struggling with a large shoulder bag, a roll-on suitcase, and another sizable valise, he rushed to help. As he had requested, she, too, was dressed in dark clothing.

"Let me help," Brian offered after pulling the glass entrance door completely open. He took the valise, which was a good deal heavier than he anticipated. "What's in this?" he questioned with a quizzical chuckle.

"Books I can't live without," she answered with a laugh of her own, though he could tell by her movements that she was on edge more than he.

They got Jeanne's things into the back of the car, and Brian replaced the blanket that served as a tarp. They were planning on leaving the car for a number of hours and didn't want to invite a break-in. Luckily it would be in a safe, supervised place.

A few minutes later they were heading north on Broadway en route to City Island, New York, part of the Bronx. Six days earlier they'd rented a black inflatable Zodiac boat with a forty-horsepower outboard motor, a mooring slip, and fishing gear from Butler Marine.

"I can't believe we're really doing this," Jeanne admitted, trying to get herself to relax now that they were underway. "Is this really happening after all this planning and preparation?"

"I hope so," he said, also coming to terms with the fact that his life as he knew it was about to be over.

"Are you as angry now as you were the day Juliette died?"

"Even more so," Brian said. "The more we learned about the lifestyle of these extortionists, the more outraged I've become. I've lost everything I love and cherish while they wallow around in their swimming pools. And to add insult to injury, MMH is still dragging its feet after all that has happened just to provide Megan Doyle with a full copy of the hospital bill."

"I feel the same way," Jeanne agreed.

"Of course, things can still go awry despite our planning," Brian cautioned. "There could be unexpected glitches, but everything is looking good, including the weather. Luckily both Kelley and Williams are such creatures of habit, which makes it possible for everything to fall into place."

The first thing that they had done after discovering where the two executives lived was to rent the Zodiac boat on City Island, a mere two miles across the Long Island Sound from both locations. They'd then spent the next four days supposedly fishing in and around Manhasset Bay armed with a pair of powerful binoculars. Since they weren't using any bait, they didn't have to deal with actually catching any fish. Instead, they were able to study both mansions, noting, as Brian had suspected, that there were no walls or fences on the waterside of either property. Despite constantly moving from place to place to avoid being at all suspicious, they'd quickly learned that both executives adhered to predictable workday schedules upon their arrivals at home.

Although Heather Williams lived a bit farther from Manhattan than Charles Kelley, she was the first to arrive home, at five o'clock. When she got there, the first evidence was several dark-suited men who walked the grounds, even checking inside the substantial sailing yacht tied to the long, massive pier. A few minutes after they left the scene, she appeared in a riding outfit along with several beagles. With the dogs frolicking along beside her, she walked across the paddock to her nearby stable, where she was greeted by a stable hand. A half hour or so later she reappeared mounted on a horse. For the next hour, she exercised the horse in the paddock at varying speeds, even doing a few jumps. An hour later she was in the pool, swimming laps. Having watched this program over a few days, they understood it as her daily warm-weather routine while in residence in her Sands Point mansion. Online, Jeanne had learned that she spent July and August at her house in the Hamptons with her horses, often playing polo at the Meadowbrook Polo Club. All in all, from Brian's perspective, he was encouraged that both the riding and the swimming would offer multiple opportunities for a sniper shot.

Charles Kelley's routine was somewhat similar, although on arrival he did a cursory property check himself, accompanied by his liveried driver. A half hour later they both re-emerged onto the terrace, one from within the house and the other from around the side, both dressed in T-shirts, shorts, and high-top sneakers. Since the driver didn't come from inside the house, Brian assumed he lived on the premises but in the guest house. He recognized that the driver's presence would need to be taken into consideration if a home invasion became necessary.

After reappearing in athletic gear, both Charles and his driver proceeded to the tennis court. They didn't play tennis but rather played one-on-one basketball, during which Charles invariably prevailed by a wide margin. In contrast to Heather Williams's solitary riding routine and its favorability for a sniper shot, Charles Kelley's basketball playing was not ideal, not only because he wasn't alone, but because the court was surrounded by a metal chain-link fence. As Brian explained to Jeanne, trying to target through the fence could be a problem, since there was a substantial probability that a bullet would be deflected, potentially wounding the target instead of killing him.

The most disappointing aspect of Charles Kelley's routine, as they observed on the first day, was that after his basketball triumph, he didn't swim solitary laps like Heather Williams in his Olympic-sized pool as they had hoped. But it was a good thing they had been patient and stayed while the sun set because Charles had eventually reappeared. To their surprise he suddenly emerged out of a Moorish arched door onto a second-floor balcony, and what surprised them even more was that he was naked save for a towel casually thrown over his shoulder. Later, thanks to the floor plans they had obtained online from the Kings Point Building and Assessor's Office, they learned that the door led out from a master bedroom/bath complex. While they watched him on that first occasion and on subsequent evenings, Charles Kelley always took lengthy outdoor showers. Thanks to his significantly above-average height, he was visible from mid-thorax to the crown of his head the entire time—a perfect setup for a sniper shot.

"I hope you remembered your French passport," Jeanne said half in jest and half to break the tense silence as they turned onto the Cross County Parkway, heading east. In contrast to his practiced calmness, she was a ball of nerves.

"I remembered mine," Brian said. "I hope you brought yours, too."

"No problem for me. I'm bringing everything I still own. You are the one leaving an entire house full of furniture, an extended family, all your personal stuff, and a lifetime behind."

It was true. The last few days had been hectic for him, trying to get everything done, including signing the new deed to transfer the house to Camila and sign over the car as well. Luckily Patrick McCarthy had been willing to help, since he wrongly assumed it was merely a private deal that Brian had arranged with Camila to keep the house from the hands of MMH Inwood via their subsidiary Premier Collections.

With the major assets out of the way, Brian then tried to decide what to bring with him as souvenirs of his past life. Ultimately, he settled on just taking some clothes and nothing else. The mere process of trying to decide on more personal things had evoked too much pain and even more anger in him. The only thing he was going to miss was his family and some of his NYPD buddies, though he was confident he'd be seeing them sometime in the future.

The plan that they had settled on, provided things went as they envisioned that day, was for him to take Jeanne directly to JFK Airport, where she was scheduled to take one of the last flights of the night heading to Europe. It was a Turkish Airlines flight to London. From there she was scheduled to go on to Frankfurt, Germany, where she would pick up a rental car. Brian was to go from dropping Jeanne off at JFK to Floyd Bennett Field in order to return the Remington plus the equipment he'd borrowed from the ESU Academy. He was then to drive out to Newark Airport where he was scheduled to take a morning Delta flight to London. From there he was to also connect to Frankfurt, where he and Jeanne would meet up and drive to the South of France.

Ten minutes later they were heading south on the Hutchinson River Parkway, and Jeanne again broke the silence. "What do you think are the chances we'll need to break into one or both houses?"

"I'm counting on the chances being relatively small," Brian said. "Both Kelley and Williams strike me as mildly obsessive-compulsive creatures of habit, as we've observed. If there is to be a break-in, it will be at Charles Kelley's and only if he fails to follow his normal outdoor shower routine. You've remembered your handheld two-way radio, right?"

"Of course." She patted the shoulder bag on her lap. "And one for you, too, so that we can communicate if need be."

"Good idea," he said.

One of the first things they'd done after determining where each executive lived was to go by the homes the following morning so that Jeanne could figure out the frequencies of their respective wireless security systems. She'd done it with her laptop when the outer gates had opened and closed for a delivery. She had explained that by dialing in the frequency on her radio, she would be able to swamp the respective systems, making it possible if need be for her and Brian to walk in their front doors without being detected and deal with any indoor motion detectors. She reminded him that the key thing that she'd have to remember was to let her radio stop transmitting for a second or two every so often to keep the central alarm system from recognizing it was being artificially overwhelmed. Brian wasn't sure he understood, but was confident that she knew what she was doing.

"I know it sounds silly considering what we are planning to do," Jeanne said, speaking up yet again after a few more miles of silence. Although he was pensive under the circumstances, as accustomed as he was to anticipating action and controlling his emotions, she had a nervous urge to talk. "But I'm glad we learned that both of them had been recently divorced."

"I know what you mean," Brian agreed.

During their intense, weeklong investigation of Heather Williams's and Charles Kelley's habits, they had learned a number of unexpected things, some of which were encouraging for what they were planning to do. They discovered that prior to the coronavirus pandemic both executives had undergone messy and rather public divorces, during which custody of the involved children had been awarded to the respective former spouses, none of which surprised them. This information bolstered the impression Brian and Jeanne had that Heather and Charles were grossly egotistical, greedy, unempathetic, narcissistic people, and accordingly bad parents.

A few minutes later they drove across City Island Bridge and turned onto City Island Avenue, a straight-shot street that ran due south the entire length of City Island. It was now slow going because of traffic, both vehicular and pedestrian, made worse by numerous double-parked cars and a series of traffic lights.

"I like this neighborhood," Jeanne commented as they passed numerous hole-in-the-wall restaurants, all of which had expanded their outdoor dining onto the sidewalk and into the street due to the pandemic restricting their indoor seating. "It feels authentic and reminds me of parts of the Jersey Shore, with a kind of run-down but charming honky-tonk feel." The architecture ran from ramshackle modern to bastardized Victorian.

Brian was preoccupied and didn't answer. At this point of the journey, it was taking longer than he'd planned, as they had never driven the length of City Island Avenue in the afternoon. It was now almost four-thirty, and he wanted to be in position at least by five, when Heather Williams would arrive home. The plan was to wait until after the security people had done their daily sweep of the grounds before he would take up his intended position within a group of dark green Adirondack chairs grouped at the end of Heather Williams's pier. His intention was to shoot supine, using the chairs as cover. Jeanne was to remain in the Zodiac beneath the pier alongside the sailing yacht to be prepared for a fast getaway if it was necessary. A similar strategy was to be used at Charles Kelley's, only there Brian was going to take advantage of being able to shoot from within the cabana, which offered significantly more cover.

"Jesus Christ!" Brian complained, losing a bit of his composure as they were forced to wait behind a pickup truck double-parked outside of the Original Crab Shanty. There was no break in the line of cars coming from the opposite direction.

"Are you getting nervous?" Jeanne asked, glancing in his direction.

"Only time-wise," Brian admitted. "I hope we haven't planned this too tightly."

Finally, there was a break in the incessant oncoming traffic, allowing Brian to skirt the truck blocking the road. He quickly accelerated but then immediately had to stop for a traffic light that inconveniently turned red.

"I think we are good," she reassured him. "We're almost there."

Jeanne was correct, and they were able to pull into Butler Marine just a few minutes later. It was on the opposite, east side of the street such that the marina faced out toward Hart Island. Traversing the parking lot, he drove as close as he could to the base of the dock, which was home to the slip where their Zodiac slowly bobbed. Once there he quickly did a three-point turn and backed up as close as he could.

"Okay," Brian said, jumping out of the car. "Let's get her loaded up quickly. No turning back now." They gave each other a look of agreement.

Along with some of the fishing gear and several canoe paddles, Brian gingerly picked up the bag containing the Remington MSR

and slung it over his shoulder. Jeanne gathered up the rest of the fishing gear, and the two of them walked out to the boat without attract-
ing any undue attention from the half dozen or so people attending
to their boats farther out on the dock. While Jeanne climbed on
board to stow everything and make ready, he went back to the car to
get the equipment he'd borrowed from the ESU if a home invasion
became necessary, including the ketamine dart pistol. The dart gun
was in case they had to deal with Charles Kelley's two pit bulls, which
they had learned about during their extensive reconnaissance.

With everything shipshape in the Zodiac and the outboard idling,
Brian went back to the Subaru, pulled the blanket back over their
luggage, and moved the car to park as close as possible to the marina's office. He thought that would be the safest place in the lot because the office was open until eleven P.M. with people coming and
going. At that point of the venture, a theft of their luggage would be
an unqualified disaster.

"Are you happy time-wise now?" Jeanne questioned nervously
once they were underway and heading out through the marina's
rather elaborate dock system. Following the rules, he had the boat
going at a very slow speed to avoid any wake.

"We're good," Brian said, knowing that the distance between the
marina and Heather Williams's pier was just a little more than two
miles. Since there was little wind and no waves or chop, crossing the
Sound into Manhasset Bay would only take five to ten minutes.

Once out in the open water, Brian pushed the boat's throttle forward and let the forty-horsepower engine do its thing. With the resultant noise and stiff breeze, conversation was near impossible. Instead
of trying to converse, they both mused privately about what the next
few hours would bring. At the same time, they couldn't help but ap-

preciate the near-perfect late summer day and the salty smell of the sea. And once they cleared the southern tip of City Island and were in open water, they could admire the impressively jagged skyline of Manhattan along the horizon off to their right. Had the circumstances been different, they might have even enjoyed themselves.

Entering the mouth of Manhasset Bay, he cut back on the throttle, and the boat rapidly slowed and settled into the water. There were a few fishermen in view, and the last thing that Brian wanted to do was draw attention to themselves by potentially irritating anyone. Several hundred yards out from the tip of Heather Williams's pier, Brian turned off the engine completely. He handed one of the fishing rods to Jeanne and picked one up himself. They both dropped their weighted lines into the water on opposite sides of the boat and pretended to be fishing.

Thanks to the prevailing westerly breeze, they were drifting directly toward their ultimate target. About a hundred yards away from the pier, he tossed out the anchor and the boat's westward drift slowed dramatically. It was now five o'clock. Pretty much on schedule, the security people appeared, meaning Heather had arrived at home, and Brian and Jeanne watched as they followed their established routine of inspecting the grounds, the pool house, and the sailboat. As he watched one of them board the vessel, he wondered if there'd been a problem in the past with the yacht, perhaps a homeless person taking up residence or something of that nature to explain its invariable inclusion in their rounds.

Most important, they never gave any heed to Brian and Jeanne while doing their security check. If they were at all concerned about a couple of people fishing a hundred yards or so off the end of the pier, they didn't let on. Brian was mildly surprised but gave them the benefit of the doubt since they weren't the only fishermen in the area. Once the security men were on their way off the pier, essentially finishing their inspection, he quickly pulled the anchor. In response, the boat's westward drift recommenced.

By the time Heather appeared from inside the house decked out in her riding gear, which comprised a tattersall vest, a black velveteen riding helmet, and a pair of white, form-fitting riding breeches, Brian and Jeanne were close enough to the pier for the deck to restrict their view. Depending on the tide, the pier could be as much as seven feet off the surface of the water, but at the moment it was about six. Although they couldn't see the beagles, they could hear them in their excitement as Heather followed her normal routine, heading for the stable.

As close as they were to the pier and wanting to avoid being seen by neighbors, Brian and Jeanne snatched up the paddles and quickly moved the Zodiac under the pier's expanded T-shaped end. Shaded from the sun, it was like entering a forest of pressure-treated pilings with the deck above serving as the forest's canopy. Speaking curtly in hushed tones and using mostly gestures, Brian directed Jeanne to help turn the Zodiac around and then hold it in position facing out into the bay in case a fast escape was necessary. As they had earlier decided, Jeanne would be staying in the boat.

With care, he then removed the Remington from its protective cover. Before he'd left home, he'd readjusted its telescopic sight from its three-hundred-yard setting back to the hundred-yard setting, which was the distance Brian estimated from the end of the pier to the waterside edge of the paddock. All he had to do to the gun was unfold the stock and secure it since he'd already made all the other adjustments prior to his visit to Rodman's Neck. He then handed the readied rifle to Jeanne while he climbed out of the boat and moved around to the outside of the ladder. When he was in position, she handed him the rifle.

"Bonne chance," she whispered, giving his arm a squeeze.

After flashing Jeanne a thumbs-up, Brian carefully made his way up the perfectly vertical ladder. While holding the rifle in his left hand, it was a difficult process and would have been far easier if the gun had a shoulder strap. It required hugging the ladder with his body and sliding his right hand up its side between each step.

Finally gaining the deck, he immediately crouched down among the gaggle of Adirondack chairs while he slowly and silently rearranged them to form an outward-facing U. He made sure there was ample space for him to lie supine in the middle. After being in the relative darkness beneath the deck, he now had to squint against the bright, late afternoon sunlight. Once he was happy with the chair placement, he lay down, facing in toward land. Carefully he advanced the barrel of the rifle beneath the chair that formed the base of the U and set it on its bipod. After making himself comfortable, he leaned against the cheek-rest and sighted through the telescopic sight. Using the bolt action, he loaded a shell into the firing chamber.

Since Heather Williams had yet to appear from inside the stable, Brian used the time to scan around the swimming pool with the aid of the telescopic sight. If a paddock shot proved unacceptable for some unexpected reason, he wanted to have a plan for the pool. While he was so occupied, he saw Heather appear out of his left eye already mounted and coming toward him. Quickly he moved the gun to bring her image into the telescopic field. As was her normal routine, she started out at a walk coming toward him and moving clockwise around the paddock. Later she would trot, and canter, and even gallop. Since this walking entailed the least up-and-down movement, Brian was eager to make the shot quickly. As for the velveteen riding helmet, he was mildly concerned about what it might do to the bullet. Instead of taking any risk for a deflection, he decided to target just below the helmet from the rear, aiming for the brainstem. As he waited, she reached the curve and began turning to her right. The dogs at this point were considerably out in front of her in their eagerness.

With some difficulty but benefitting from experience, he maintained his breathing at a calm pace although he was conscious his pulse had quickened. All of their planning came down to mere moments. Without moving any other muscle in his relaxed body, he slipped his right index finger within the trigger guard and gently connected with the trigger. Through the telescopic sight, he followed Heather Williams's progress on the turn as well as her methodical up-and-down movement. Soon he was observing her profile, and then as she began to turn away, he increased the pressure on the trigger while lining up the crosshairs on the base of the woman's skull. At just the right moment, he made the shot. With the suppressor there was just a thumping hiss with the recoil. By reflex he used the bolt to rapidly eject the used cartridge and reload. But a second shot wasn't necessary. Heather Williams fell off the horse with such suddenness the horse didn't interrupt its walking even though it was now riderless.

A quick check of Heather's body with the telescopic sight confirmed no movement whatsoever. Knowing he had no time to lose, Brian pulled the rifle back from beneath the Adirondack chair and pocketed the empty casing. He quickly scampered over to the ladder and in a repeat of how he'd climbed up, he descended. A moment later he handed off the rifle to Jeanne.

"How did it go?" she asked in a forceful whisper.

He flashed another thumbs-up as he boarded the Zodiac. Quickly he started the outboard engine, put the boat in gear, and steered out from under the deck. After going some fifty feet, both he and Jeanne looked back. The horse and the dogs could be seen at the far end of the paddock, where the horse had stopped to eat the grass. Heather Williams in her tattersall vest and white breeches was still in the exact position she'd been when she'd tumbled to the ground.

It was Jeanne's turn to give Brian a thumbs-up as he increased the speed to a no-wake fast walk. It wasn't until they were a good three or four hundred yards away that Brian slowed even more so they could talk without shouting. Several boats passed them, heading into Manhasset Bay from the Long Island Sound, one with a water skier.

"It went perfectly, without a hitch," he assured her. He looked back yet again to the Williams mansion, this time using binoculars. The scene hadn't changed. The horse and dogs were still at the far end of the paddock, and Heather Williams's body was at the near end. It still had not been discovered, although it was only a matter of time. "I've never done anything like that. It was so quick, and so different from the messy shootings I've been involved with in the line of duty. I don't know how to feel, except relieved that one nasty, greedy narcissist is gone."

"Which is a tribute to the love you had for your wife and child," Jeanne said. "I exhaled, too, when I heard the gun, which, by the way, I barely heard."

"That's thanks to the suppressor," Brian said. "It definitely bought us some needed time."

"I suppose I shouldn't be saying this," Jeanne said. "But it's rewarding that so far everything is going so well. The world is already a better place without her."

"It's thanks to our careful planning. One down and one to go. Let's hope the Charles Kelley portion goes as smoothly. I'd really like to avoid having to do a break-in. With the sniper rifle there are infinitely fewer chances of complications and collateral damage."

Following her suggestion, they went back to using the fishing rods by putting them in holders mounted in the stern, pretending they were trolling as they slowly motored across Manhasset Bay on their way to Charles Kelley's. They were not in a hurry now that they were at least a half mile away from Heather Williams's and with a significant number of other boaters in the area, taking advantage of the beautiful weather. They also preferred not to arrive at Kelley's mansion too soon, as he wouldn't appear on his outdoor shower balcony until it was near sunset or soon thereafter. At that moment it was just a little after six and almost a full hour before they needed to be in position.

"Are your parents excited about your homecoming?" Brian asked, eager for conversation to avoid any nerves setting in. He knew that Jeanne had only recently informed her parents, in case a glitch in the planning process made it necessary to put off the operation.

"You have no idea," she said. "They're ecstatic, figuring I was a lost cause. They are already busy setting up that farmhouse I mentioned."

"When will you tell them about me?" Brian asked. He'd spent his life constantly and comfortably ensconced in various groups like athletic teams, which was part of the reason he'd joined the NYPD originally right out of college. It was going to take time to adjust to feeling both rootless, solitary, and totally dependent on others.

"As the saying goes, 'we'll cross that bridge when we come to it,'" Jeanne answered. "I'm not at all concerned."

When they were a hundred yards or so off of Charles Kelley's pier, Brian cut the outboard engine and again tossed out the anchor. This side of the bay was shallower, and the anchor immediately took hold. With fishing poles in hand again, they passed the binoculars back and forth.

"It's encouraging to see he's humiliating his driver/bodyguard again," Jeanne commented when it was her turn to survey the scene.

"I agree. It means he's following his normal routine. Fingers crossed that he keeps it up, especially by taking his nightly outdoor shower."

"I'm not worried," she said.

"Lucky you," Brian responded teasingly.

At a little after seven, they made their move. Following the successful playbook they'd used at Heather Williams's, they paddled in under the end of Charles Kelley's pier, positioned the Zodiac for a fast exit if necessary, and Brian used the ladder to get up to the deck. He then entered the cabana, which afforded considerably more concealment than the group of Adirondack chairs on Heather's pier. Conveniently the cabana had a window-like opening facing inland with louvered shutters and a table that Brian turned lengthwise to serve as a perfect placement for the Remington on its bipod. Cracking open one of the shutters while sitting in a chair, he sighted through the telescopic sight. The waterside view of the Spanish-themed house was par excellence, even better than he'd had at Heather Williams's, which had proven to be so efficacious.

The problem, however, was that after waiting some time, there was no Charles Kelley in sight. Although he and his driver/body-guard had long since stopped their basketball, Kelley had not appeared, even after the sun set. Just when Brian was beginning to despair and had begun reluctantly thinking about the timing of a break-in, which he assumed would have to be after full darkness, the light in the master bedroom flicked on.

Trying to be optimistic, Brian leaned his head against the cheek-rest and sighted through the scope. His view of the second-story outdoor shower couldn't have been better, and he estimated that the distance was very similar to what it had been when he shot Heather Williams, namely a hundred yards or so. Using the bolt action, he put a shell into the firing chamber and slipped his index finger inside the trigger guard, hoping for the best.

Slowly the minutes ticked by, but still no Charles Kelley. Normally steady under stress, Brian could feel the trickle of perspiration on his forehead as well as his pulse significantly quicken. Still, with self-control, he kept his breathing slow and steady.

Then suddenly the Moorish arched door swung open, and Charles Kelley appeared towel in hand rather than over his shoulder. Even from a hundred-plus yards and sitting inside the cabana, Brian could hear the intermittent strains of some rock music emanating from within the house, causing Charles to bob and weave to the beat. With such erratic movement, Brian bided his time, watching through the scope as Charles turned on the shower and adjusted the temperature. Finally, when all was to his liking, Charles stepped into the enclosure, shut the door, and put his head directly under the torrent.

Since he was visible from mid-thorax up and facing away, it was a perfect setup for another brainstem shot. With careful precision, Brian placed the crosshairs directly at the base of the man's skull, and hesitated for a moment, thinking of Emma and Juliette. The subsequent wave of emotions urged him to press against the trigger.

The rifle made the same thumping whoosh as it had when he'd shot Heather Williams. By force of habit and reflex, Brian used the bolt to eject the empty shell and load another bullet. But again, a second shot was not necessary. As with Heather, Charles instantly fell, disappearing from view behind the shower door. Brian could clearly see a large circular bloodstain centering on a sizable crater in the tiled wall. There was little doubt that the armor-piercing bullet had completely traversed Charles's head to exit out the forehead.

He pocketed the rifle's magazine and removed the bullet from the firing chamber. He took a deep breath before standing up and retracing his steps to the ladder. A moment later he started down.

"Well, how did it go?" Jeanne questioned in a whisper, yet loud enough to be heard over the lapping of the water against the pier's piling. She took the rifle so he could climb aboard the Zodiac.

"Again, it couldn't have been better," Brian managed. "They're gone. It's over. Emma, Juliette, and Riley and countless others have been avenged and maybe, just maybe, we've started the ball rolling to change a sick healthcare system."

"That's the hope," Jeanne said. "Now I think we'd better get out of here."

"Right you are," Brian managed, starting the motor.

Five minutes later he gave the Zodiac's engine full throttle and brought it up to planing speed as they rounded the tip of Kings Point and headed due west. A mile and a half ahead they could see the twinkling lights of City Island. Although the sun had long since set, the sky was still a light silver-gray, and Brian turned on the boat's running lights even though they'd be back at Butler Marine well before total darkness.

With the sound of the outboard, speech was near impossible. Both Brian and Jeanne were isolated in their thoughts, but he didn't mind, as it gave him time to recover. With the stiff sea breeze in his face, he felt a strong sense of peace despite having little idea what the next chapter of his life was to be.

EPILOGUE

October 18

similar to what he had been doing for more than a month, Brian tried to imitate the ease with which Jeanne mounted her horse. As per usual, it didn't quite work, as the horse moved just as he was throwing his leg over the animal's back. Getting himself up off the ground and readying himself for another try, he was prepared to blame the horse if Jeanne said anything derogatory, but she didn't. Although he didn't fall on his next attempt, it was hardly an impressive mounting, and he could hear her giggle as he settled into the saddle.

Prepared on their white Camargue horses, they started off just after four P.M. on a lazy Sunday afternoon. Their goal was the Mediterranean coast, which lay about nine miles due south. This was to be their first visit to the beach since their arrival in Camargue five weeks earlier. It had been Jeanne's idea to go for a seaside picnic as a change of scene. She'd been eager to show the coastline to him, as it had been one of her favorite destinations when she was a teenager.

The Camargue had turned out to be as interesting for Brian as Jeanne had suggested it would be. He had no idea such a wild, mostly uninhabited place existed in France where there were many more horses, cattle, and sheep than human beings. Those parts of north-ern France where he'd visited as a boy along with his siblings had every square inch taken up by old stone walls, carefully planted hedges, paved roads, planted fields, and venerable buildings, all evi-dence that the area had been occupied and altered by humans for untold centuries. In sharp contrast, Camargue was more than three hundred square miles of open space with a flat horizon that seemed to go on forever. One-third of it was lakes, brine lagoons, and marsh-land. Often the only signs of human interference in the natural order were some cultivated agricultural fields in the northern part, a num-ber of man-made canals that were straighter than natural waterways, and a lot of dikes to keep certain areas dry in times of rising waters. The rare homes were simple, quaint, white stucco structures with picturesque water-reed roofs, exactly like the one that Jeanne and Brian had been occupying since their arrival.

The night of the shooting had gone exceptionally smoothly, which they had attributed to a combination of their extensive planning and the rigid schedules of both Charles Kelley and Heather Williams. On top of that was good luck—a lot of good luck. By the time they'd returned to Butler Marine that night, gotten their deposit back for the Zodiac and fishing gear, and picked up the Subaru, it still wasn't quite seven-thirty. With such efficiency, they had time to spare, giving them an opportunity to stop for food on City Island, which they ate while driving out to Floyd Bennett Field in Brooklyn to return all the borrowed ESU equipment. The original plan was for Brian to make the visit himself after dropping Jeanne off at JFK Airport, but with so much time on their hands, she had preferred to stay with him to limit how long she'd have to cool her heels in the terminal.

Even returning the equipment took less time than planned. Probably because of the pandemic, there were only two duty officers at the ESU Academy, neither of whom Brian knew. Usually there were always a number of ESU officers hanging out instead of cruising the city awaiting action. What took the most time was Brian's decision to write a thank-you note to Deputy Chief Comstock for offering him the chance to rejoin the ESU. In the note he explained that Juliette's sudden and unexpected death had caused him to change his plans, and he wouldn't be rejoining. As a postscript, Brian said that he thought the Remington MSR was a superb piece of engineering and that it should be considered as part of the NYPD's armory, the cost notwithstanding. He left the rifle on Michael's desk with the note on top.

Then after dropping Jeanne off at JFK, Brian had so much free time that he decided to drive home to leave the car in the driveway, blow off some steam for a few hours in the workout room, and then use a ride-share to get out to Newark around 6:30 A.M. Originally, he had planned to leave the car at the airport and call Camila to retrieve it.

"Come on, slowpoke," she teased as she interrupted his reverie by suddenly turning her horse off the dirt trail to begin galloping across a wet, marshy field and putting a huge flock of greater flamingoes to flight in the process. Another thing he had learned about the Camargue was that it's the home to more waterbirds than he'd seen anywhere else in his life.

Brian urged his horse to follow, but the animal wasn't so eager to pick up the pace, and he wasn't sure how to make him change his mind. Finally, he was able to get the horse to canter but not gallop. Ahead, Jeanne had pulled up to wait for him. For several weeks both of them had been riding with the *gardians*, otherwise known as the Camargue cowboys. The *gardians* had begun a roundup of the semi-feral cattle that lived on Jeanne's parents' land. As a consequence, he was learning to ride, and he was also recalling his French.

All in all, Brian was slowly becoming comfortable with his new life, had begun to relax to a degree, and felt extraordinarily lucky that he'd met Jeanne. Otherwise, he might have ended up in Cuba for whatever that might have meant. When the two of them had first arrived in Arles, the major French city just north of the Camargue, after their drive from Frankfurt, Brian had no idea of what the near future would bring. Although he'd worried about his acceptance by her parents, it turned out to not be a problem. They had driven north to Arles to pick up Jeanne when she returned the rental car. If they had been surprised by his presence or the fact that Jeanne had driven all the way from Frankfurt rather than flying into France itself, they didn't let on. She had explained that they were so surprised and pleased by her unexpected return to live in France that they weren't about to question any of the details, including what the relationship was between her and Brian, at least in the near term.

"You have to move your body more forward if you want your horse to gallop," Jeanne reminded Brian as he reached her. "And don't be afraid to use your legs, that's the key."

"You make it look so easy," he complained.

On the opposite side of the expansive marshy field, they picked up another trail heading south, lined on both sides by tamarisk and white poplar trees. Jeanne explained that it was a more direct route to the sea, which she'd forgotten about.

As they walked southward, Brian went back to his musings. So far, the fallout from Heather Williams's and Charles Kelley's deaths had exceeded expectations. The following day it was front-page news, with wild speculations regarding the perpetrators. Some journalists, particularly those on Fox News, indulged in creative conspiracy theories involving homegrown far-left terrorists, citing the victims' wealth and standing in the financial world. On the second day the killings had moved to a back section, but on the third day, thanks to the manifesto Brian and Jeanne had sent to the *New York Times* about the two executives and the role that private equity and the profit motive were playing in healthcare, along with the complete list of the residents of Inwood that the Manhattan Memorial Hospital was suing for extravagant bills, the story moved back to the front page. Healthcare, its costs and payment arrangements, plus the fact that US legislators had been asleep at the wheel while the system got out of hand, were becoming a progressively bigger story, to which the killings of Charles Kelley and Heather Williams were adding a real immediacy.

Although the media response so far was better than he'd hoped, there was one issue that confounded Brian: how long it was taking for him to become more than a person of interest. His only explanation was that the detectives of the NYPD weren't approaching the case with their usual gusto, perhaps because of his many friends, particularly in the ESU. What he did know was that his sudden disappearance combined with his enormous debt to MMH had raised appropriate suspicions and that he'd been tracked to Frankfurt and Interpol was supposedly looking for him. But that was it. According to the papers, his parents and siblings had all been interviewed, but Brian had made sure that they knew absolutely nothing. He imagined they must have felt confused and devastated by his sudden disappearance, but he knew it was for the best.

And now Brian was actually looking forward to being exposed. He wanted the story of Emma's and Juliette's avoidable deaths to be

revealed, as it would put a shockingly human touch to the general-
izations put forth in the manifesto. His current pleasant interlude in
Camargue was just a precursor of what was to come when he'd be
formally charged, and his extradition requested. Only then would
the whole US healthcare mess become an international story of
shame about capitalism run amuck with real victims.

"Well, what do you think?" Jeanne asked when they finally arrived at the seacoast. They had pulled to a stop at the edge of a vast,
totally empty, sandy beach that stretched out in both directions.
Huge cumulus clouds were arranged along the horizon with the late-
afternoon sun tinting them gold, and a mild onshore breeze caressed
their faces.

"It's gorgeous," Brian observed. Despite there being only small
dunes at the beach's edge, the scene and time of day reminded him
of the fateful afternoon two months earlier on Cape Cod. With some
effort he pushed the recollection out of his mind, as he didn't want to
think of the disastrous consequences set in motion on that August
day. "Where are all the people?" he asked, to stay in the present.

Jeanne laughed instead of answering, and with a toss of her head,
she gave free rein to her horse, which was eager to gallop in the wash
of the waves. Brian attempted to follow by rising up in his stirrups,
leaning forward, and using his legs as she had explained to him earlier. To his surprise and glee, the horse obeyed on this occasion. A
moment later he was racing behind Jeanne, holding on for dear life
while scrunching his eyes against the salt spray that her horse was
kicking up.

The sense of freedom was exhilarating and for a few minutes he
reveled in the ability to think of absolutely nothing. Unfortunately, it
came to an abrupt end when Jeanne pulled back on her reins and

Brian followed suit. For a few minutes they walked the horses, allowing the animals to catch their breaths.

"Let's stop here," she said, pointing to a copse of gnarled tamarisk trees at the back of the beach. They dismounted and let the horses forage for what they could find in the beachgrass and wild alfalfa behind the narrow dunes.

Surprising Brian, Jeanne pulled a blanket out of her backpack along with some local cheese, bread, and a split of white wine. "Surprise," she exclaimed with an impish smile. "A little treat for us."

He spread the blanket while Jeanne opened the wine. A moment later they were sitting down, savoring the seascape and the wine. But their cheer and good spirits didn't last. Within minutes Brian realized they weren't alone. Over the sound of the breaking waves and despite the onshore breeze, he heard the characteristic whine of mosquitoes, and a second later several landed on his bare arms intent on a blood meal. With a sense of panic he recognized the characteristic markings: black bodies with white polka dots and white ringlets on their legs. There was no doubt in his mind—they were the dreaded Asian tiger mosquitoes.

"Oh, my God!" Brian shouted. He leaped to his feet while feverishly fanning away the cloud of insects now circling his head. "We're being attacked."

Taken aback, Jeanne said: "It's just mosquitoes. Camargue is known for them."

"These aren't 'just' mosquitoes," Brian cried. "They're Asian tiger mosquitoes. We have to get the hell out of here!"

Sensing his desperation and urgency, she rapidly gathered the food, the wine, and the glasses. Brian snatched up the blanket. They then ran back through the dunes to fetch the horses.

A short time later as they were cantering back along the water's edge to the spot where they'd arrived at the beach, Jeanne called over to Brian, who was riding abreast: "It just occurred to me why you are so upset. The day we met you told me about Asian tiger mosquitoes and your barbecue."

He nodded before yelling back: "The bastards carry the virus that killed Emma and Juliette as well as a bunch of other deadly diseases. I didn't know they were in France, too."

"I didn't know, either," Jeanne said with worry. "But we don't have eastern equine encephalitis here. At least I've never heard of it."

"You can't be sure in this day and age," Brian countered. "Just two months ago, I didn't know we had EEE in the United States. And now with climate change and the way the world is interconnected, it could be anywhere, just like the Asian tiger mosquitoes. As the Covid-19 pandemic has shown, we're in an existential war with viruses, and I'm afraid we're at a distinct disadvantage."

"What are you talking about?" she questioned. "What kind of disadvantage?"

"Viruses have been around adapting and evolving for more than a billion years before we humans ever appeared on the scene. Biologically speaking, that is one hell of a head start, so only God knows who is going to prevail."

"You're scaring me," Jeanne said, casting a troubled look in Brian's direction.

"We all should be scared. A competitive viral challenge is one we humans have to face."

ACKNOWLEDGMENTS

Viral could not have been written without the support and help of several family members and friends willing to read early drafts and offer helpful comments and suggestions. Thank you! However, there are two people I want to specifically acknowledge, as they were instrumental in acquainting me with the highly selective New York City Police Department's ESU, or Emergency Service Unit, and with the impressive amount of training required to become a member. Although these two individuals bear no responsibility for any descriptive mistakes I may have made in the novel, their input was critical, particularly by allowing me to visit and observe the ESU Academy in action. In alphabetical order . . .

Tom Janow, retired NYPD Detective First Grade and now a Critical Care Paramedic

David Reilly, NYPD Emergency Service Unit Lieutenant

ANNOTATED BIBLIOGRAPHY

The goal of the novel *Viral* is to entertain and utilize the fact that most people are riveted by dramas and movies of "justified" revenge despite the moral dictum that "two wrongs do not make a right." But the larger goal is an attempt to use fiction as a method to awaken the general public's indignation about the sorry state of American healthcare, which is all too often not providing the help and support expected, and even destroying some people's lives in the process. The reason is simple: American healthcare has mushroomed into an economic behemoth, where clever financial types can enjoy ever-increasing profits for themselves and for the funds they manage. *Viral* might be the first novel to specifically address this issue, but there have been a number of terrific nonfiction treatises that have sought the same objective. For those readers who would like to look into the problem in greater depth, I recommend the following books, all of which are wonderfully readable and disturbingly enlightening:

Brill, Steven. *America's Bitter Pill: Money, Politics, Backroom Deals, and the Fight to Fix Our Broken Healthcare System.* New York: Random House, 2015.

Makary, Marty, MD. *The Price We Pay: What Broke American Health Care—and How to Fix It*. New York: Bloomsbury Publishing, 2019.

Rosenthal, Elisabeth. *An American Sickness: How Healthcare Became Big Business and How You Can Take It Back*. New York: Penguin Press, 2017.